image comics presents

CHEW

created by John Layman & Rob Guillory

"Just Desserts"

written & lettered by
John Layman

drawn & coloured by
Rob Guillory

color assists by
Steven Struble

IMAGE COMICS, INC.

Robert Kirkman - chief operating officer
Erik Larsen - chief financial officer
Todd McFarlane - president
Marc Silvestri - chief executive officer
Jim Valentino - vice-president

Eric Stephenson - publisher
Todd Martinez - sales & licensing coordinator
Betsy Gomez - pr & marketing coordinator
Branwyn Bigglestone - accounts manager
Sarah deLaine - administrative assistant
Tyler Shainline - production manager
Drew Gill - art director
Jonathan Chan - production artist
Monica Howard - production artist
Vincent Kukua - production artist
Kevin Yuan - production artist

www.imagecomics.com

International Rights Representative: Christine Meyer - christine@gfloystudio.com   ISBN: 978-1-60706-335-3

Dedications:

JOHN: To Fredric Brown and Dave Sim. Imagination and inspiration.

ROB: To my unborn child (who we are calling Aiden for now), who will be born about a month after this gets printed. Maybe you'll read this one day and realize how friggin' cool your old man was.

Thanks:

Steven Struble, for the color assists.
Tom B. Long, for the logo.
Comicbookfonts.com, for the fonts.

And More Thanks:

Brandon Jerwa, Robert Kirkman, Charlie Adlard, Charlie Chu, Lance Curran, Jonathan Daniel Brown, Chris Fenoglio, Kody Chamberlain, Kim Peterson and April Hanks.

Plus the always-amazing Image crew of ericstephenson, Tyler Shainline, Drew Gill, Jonathan Chan, Branwyn Bigglestone, Todd Martinez and Betsy Gomez.

Olive's wardrobe provided by Threadless.com
Designed by Keith Kuniyuki

Chew 13 covers inspired by the movies of Quentin Tarantino.

Chapter 1

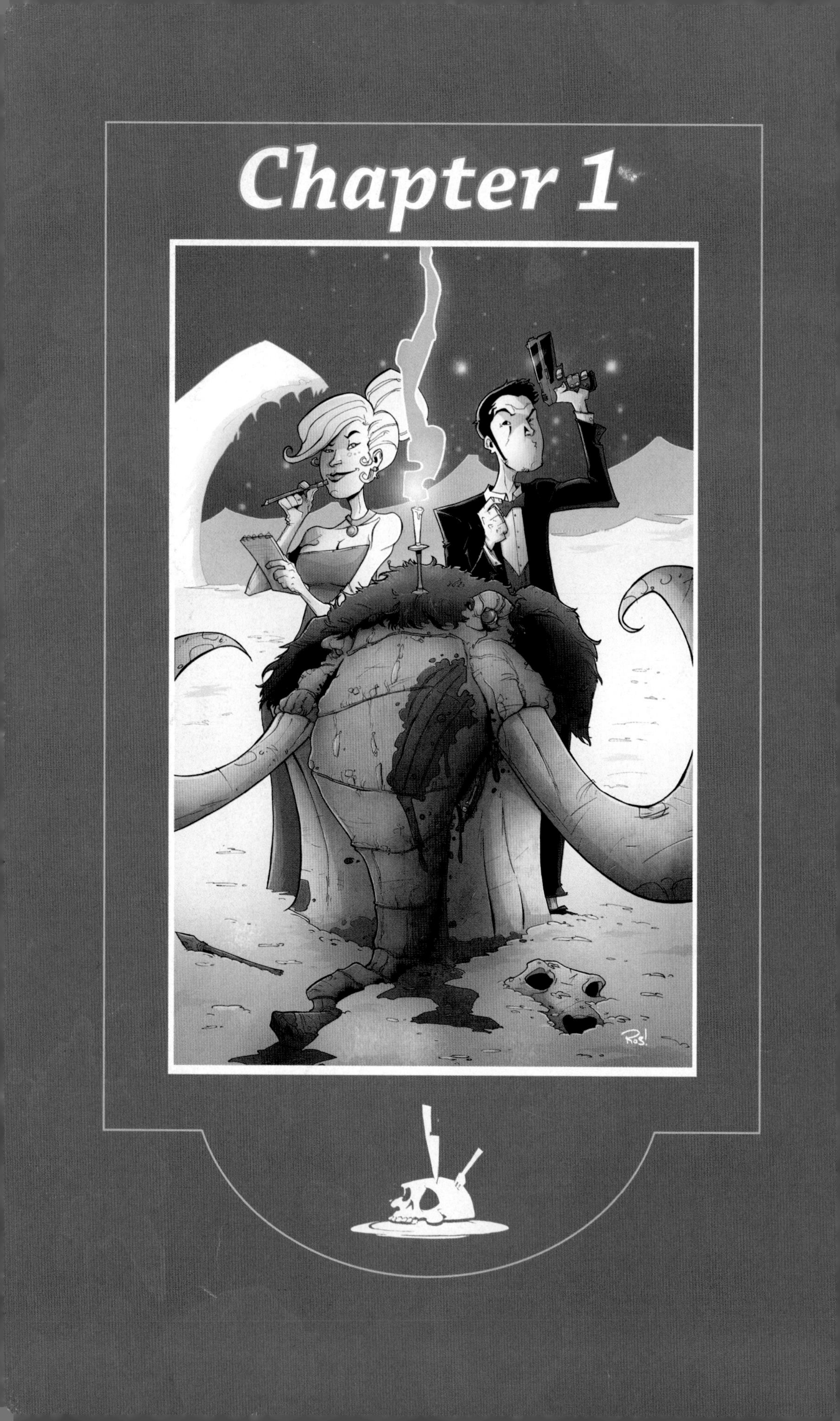
ROS!

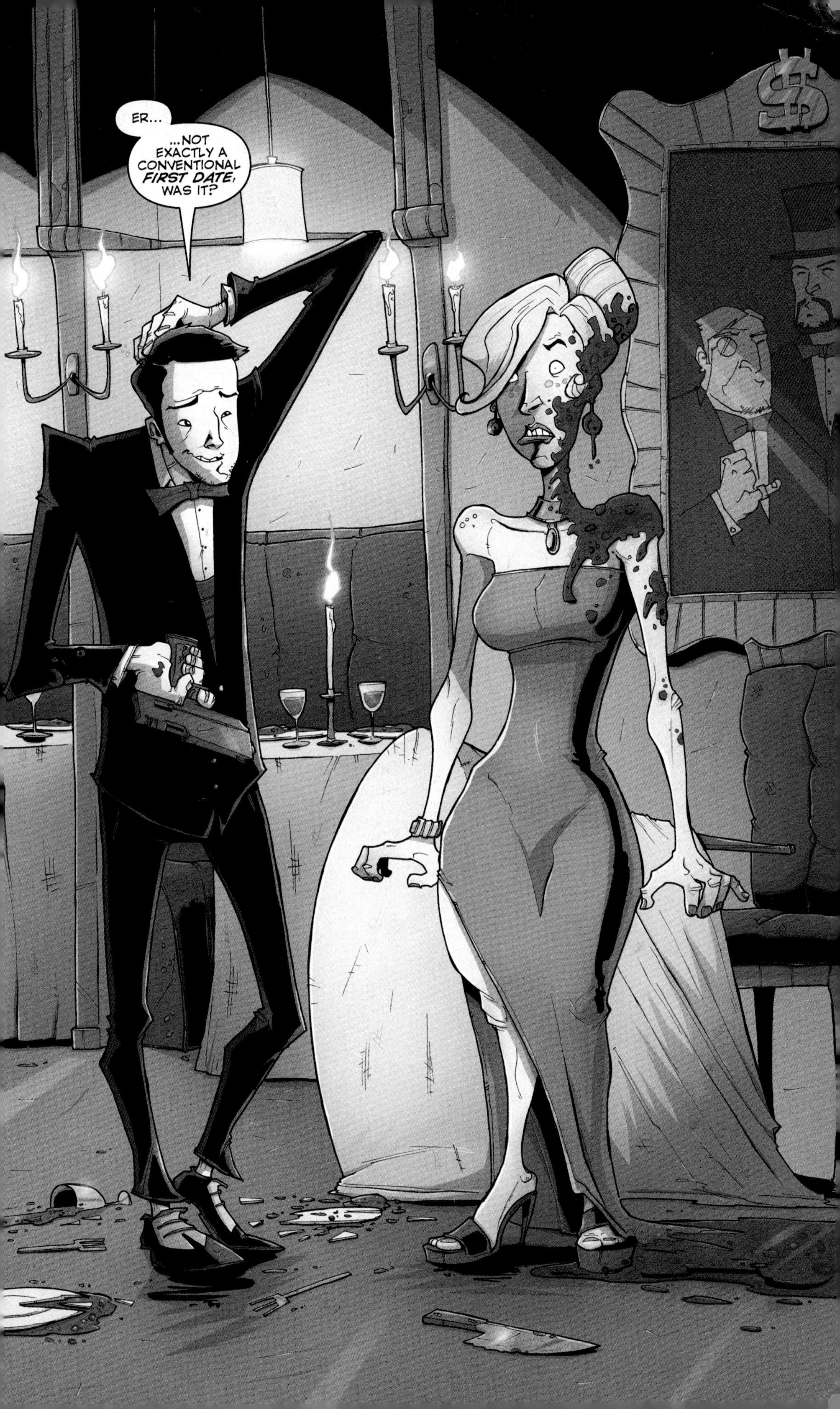
ER...
...NOT EXACTLY A CONVENTIONAL FIRST DATE, WAS IT?

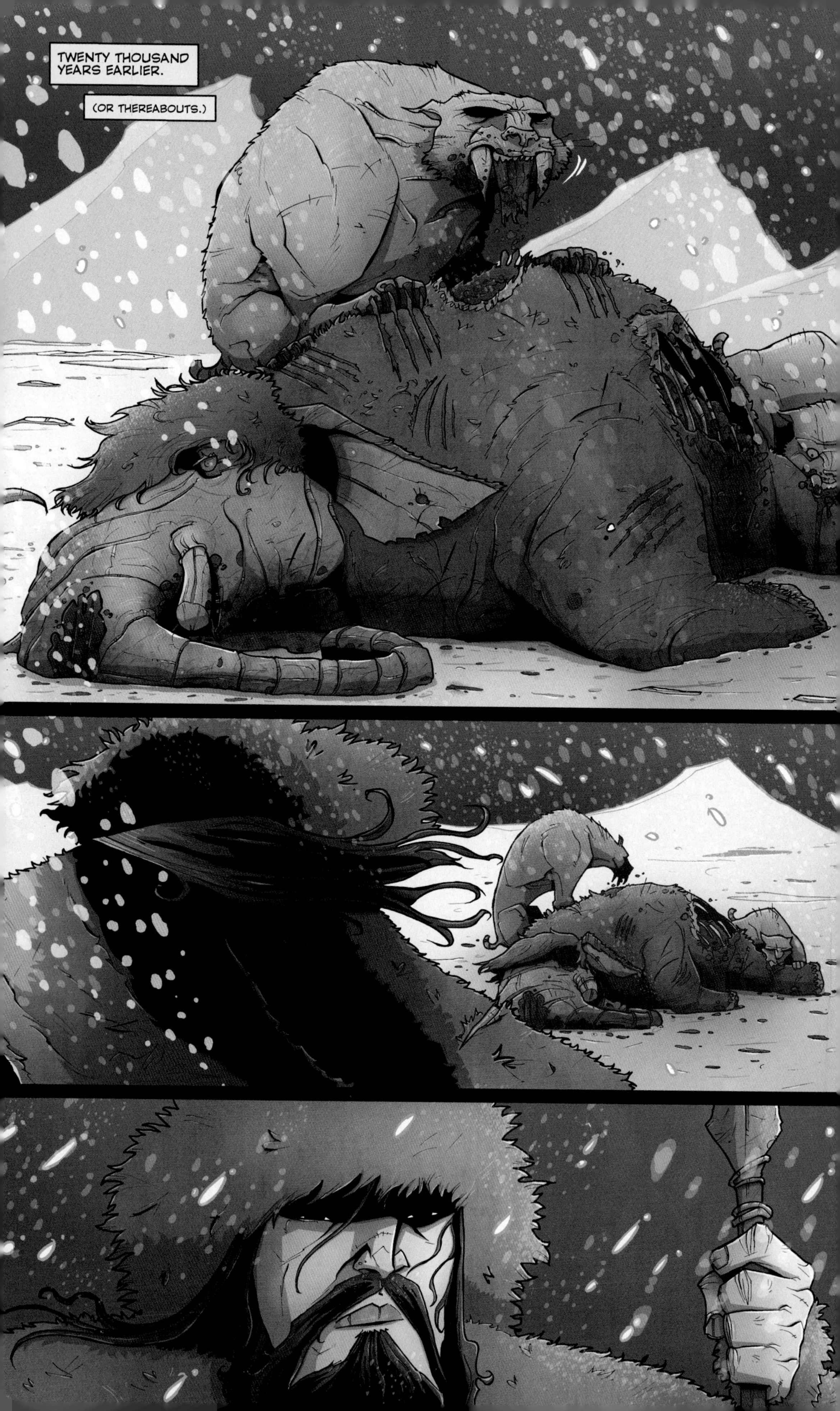
TWENTY THOUSAND YEARS EARLIER.
(OR THEREABOUTS.)

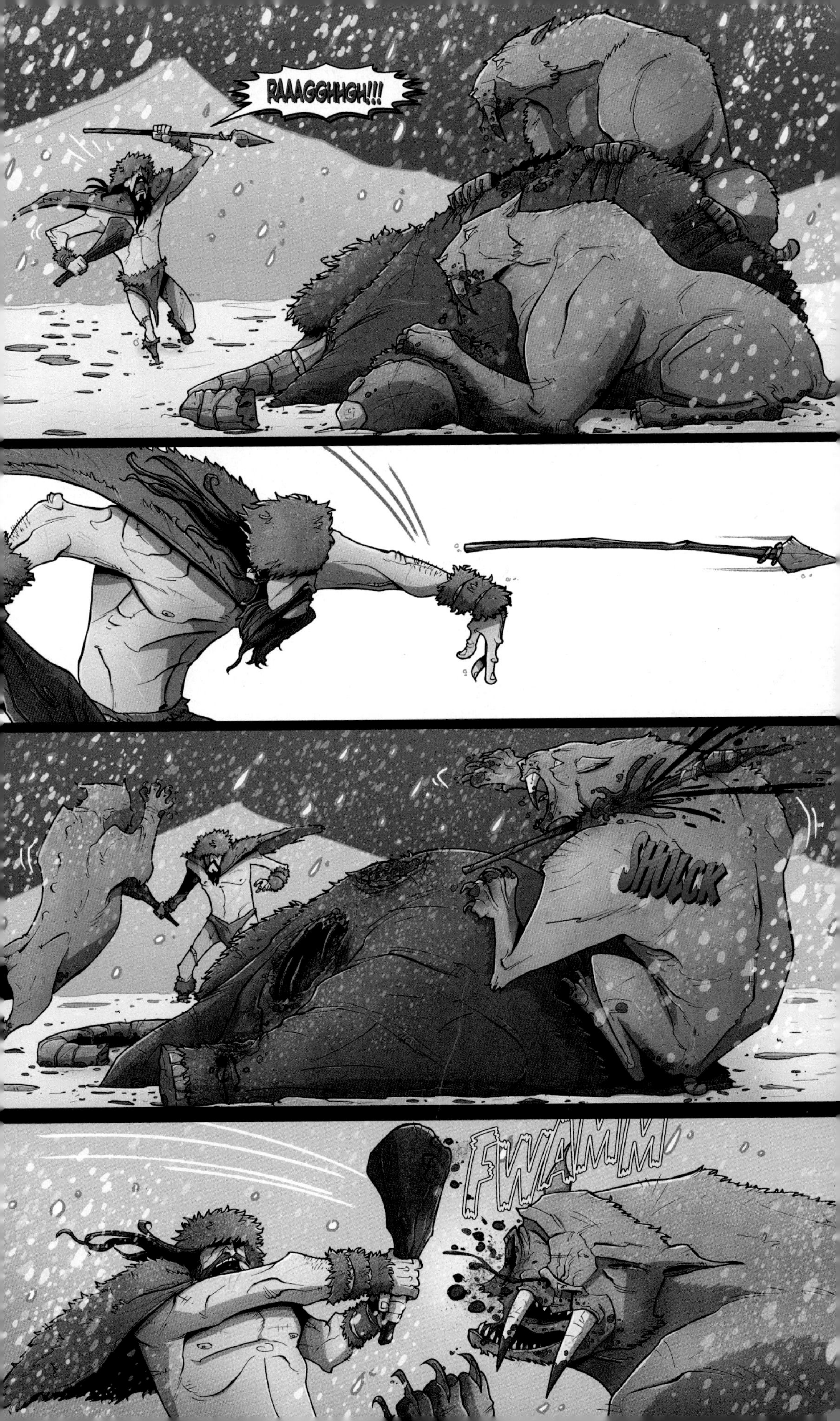
RAAAGGHHGH!!!
SHULCK
FWAMM

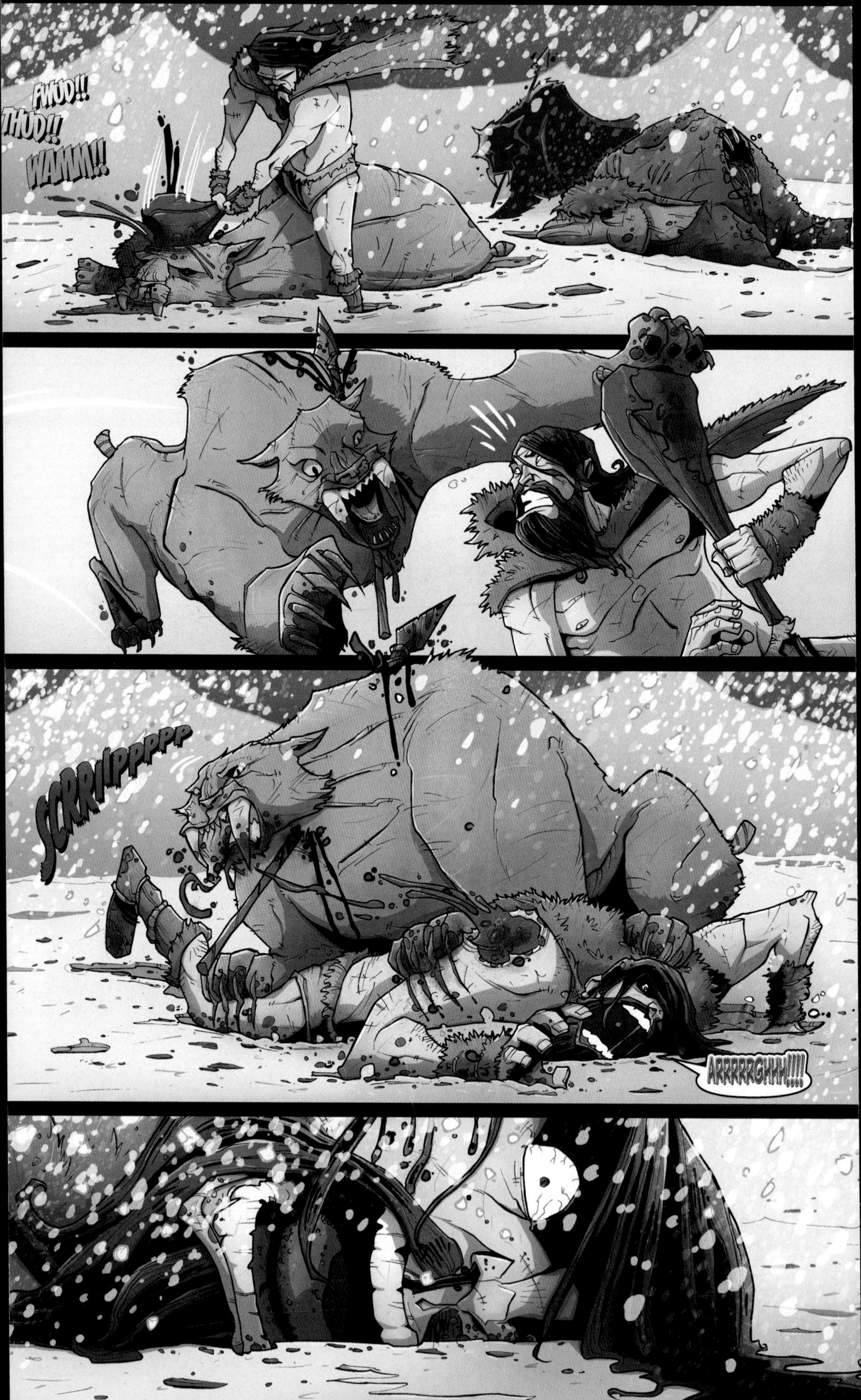
FWUD!!
THUD!!
WAMM!!
SCRRIIPPPPP
ARRRRRGHHH!!!!

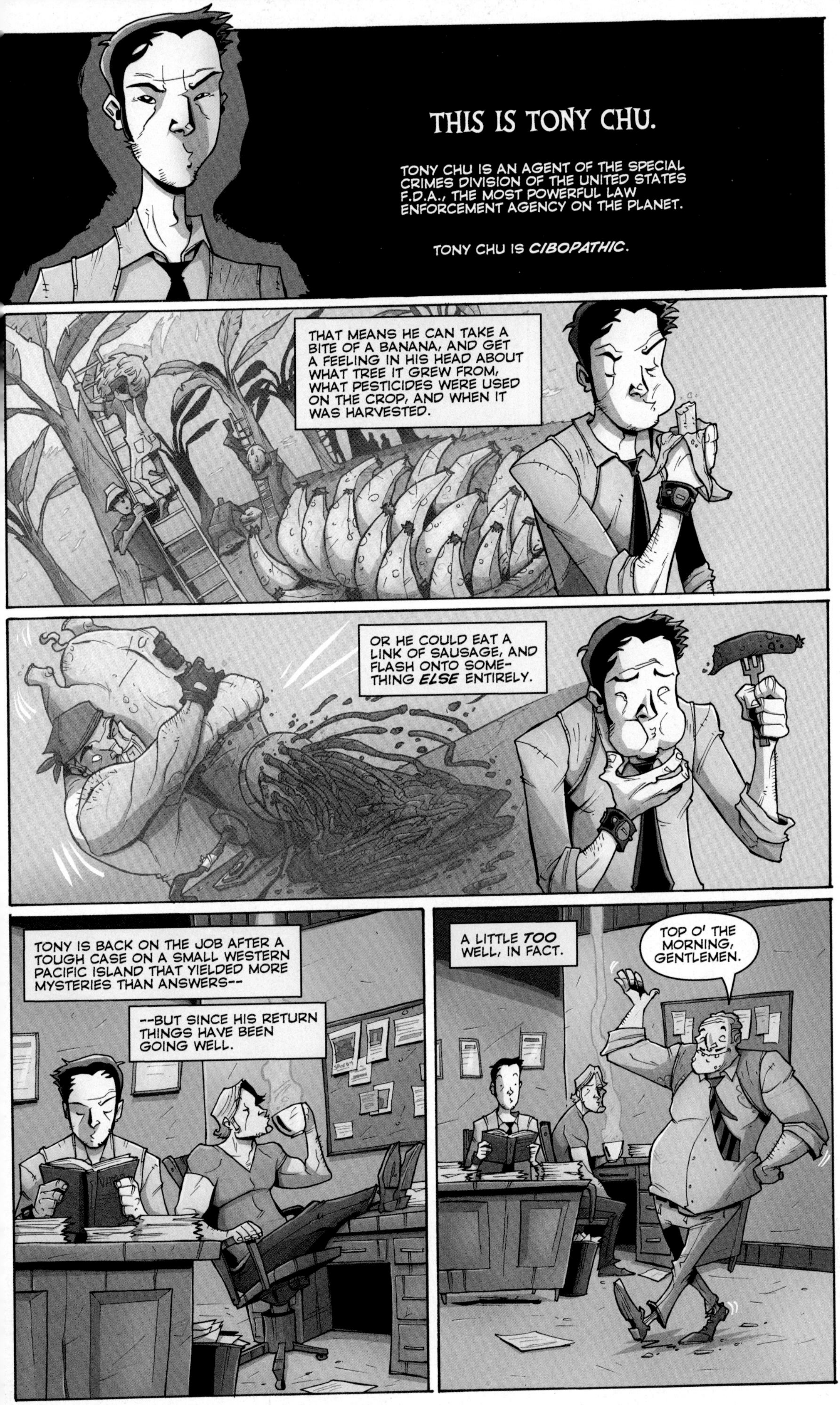

THIS IS TONY CHU.
TONY CHU IS AN AGENT OF THE SPECIAL CRIMES DIVISION OF THE UNITED STATES F.D.A., THE MOST POWERFUL LAW ENFORCEMENT AGENCY ON THE PLANET.
TONY CHU IS *CIBOPATHIC*.
THAT MEANS HE CAN TAKE A BITE OF A BANANA, AND GET A FEELING IN HIS HEAD ABOUT WHAT TREE IT GREW FROM, WHAT PESTICIDES WERE USED ON THE CROP, AND WHEN IT WAS HARVESTED.
OR HE COULD EAT A LINK OF SAUSAGE, AND FLASH ONTO SOMETHING *ELSE* ENTIRELY.
TONY IS BACK ON THE JOB AFTER A TOUGH CASE ON A SMALL WESTERN PACIFIC ISLAND THAT YIELDED MORE MYSTERIES THAN ANSWERS--
--BUT SINCE HIS RETURN THINGS HAVE BEEN GOING WELL.
A LITTLE *TOO* WELL, IN FACT.
TOP O' THE MORNING, GENTLEMEN.

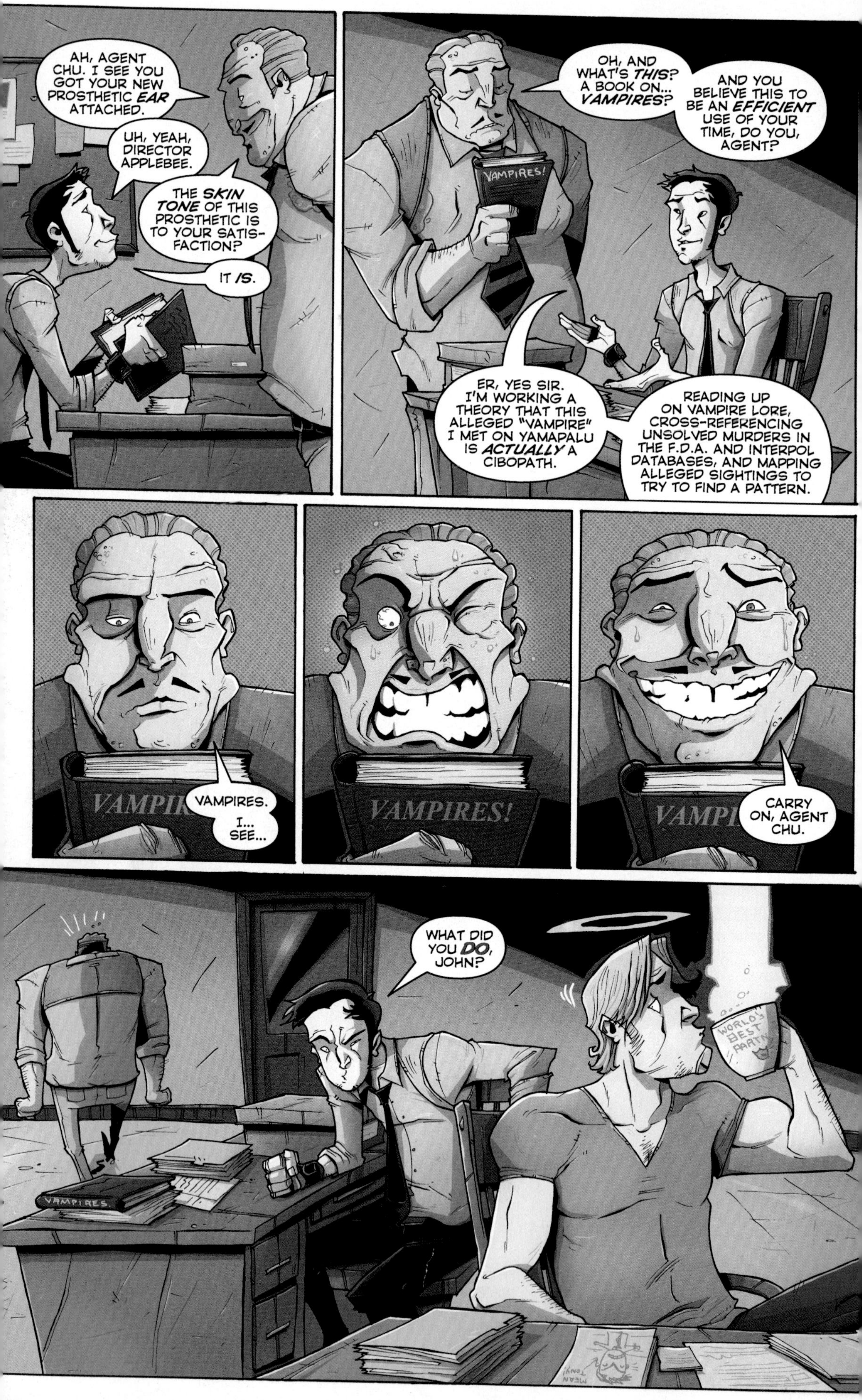
AH, AGENT CHU. I SEE YOU GOT YOUR NEW PROSTHETIC EAR ATTACHED.
UH, YEAH, DIRECTOR APPLEBEE.
THE SKIN TONE OF THIS PROSTHETIC IS TO YOUR SATIS-FACTION?
IT IS.
OH, AND WHAT'S THIS? A BOOK ON... VAMPIRES?
VAMPIRES!
AND YOU BELIEVE THIS TO BE AN EFFICIENT USE OF YOUR TIME, DO YOU, AGENT?
ER, YES SIR. I'M WORKING A THEORY THAT THIS ALLEGED "VAMPIRE" I MET ON YAMAPALU IS ACTUALLY A CIBOPATH.
READING UP ON VAMPIRE LORE, CROSS-REFERENCING UNSOLVED MURDERS IN THE F.D.A. AND INTERPOL DATABASES, AND MAPPING ALLEGED SIGHTINGS TO TRY TO FIND A PATTERN.
VAMPIRES. I... SEE...
VAMPIRES!
CARRY ON, AGENT CHU.
WHAT DID YOU DO, JOHN?
VAMPIRES.

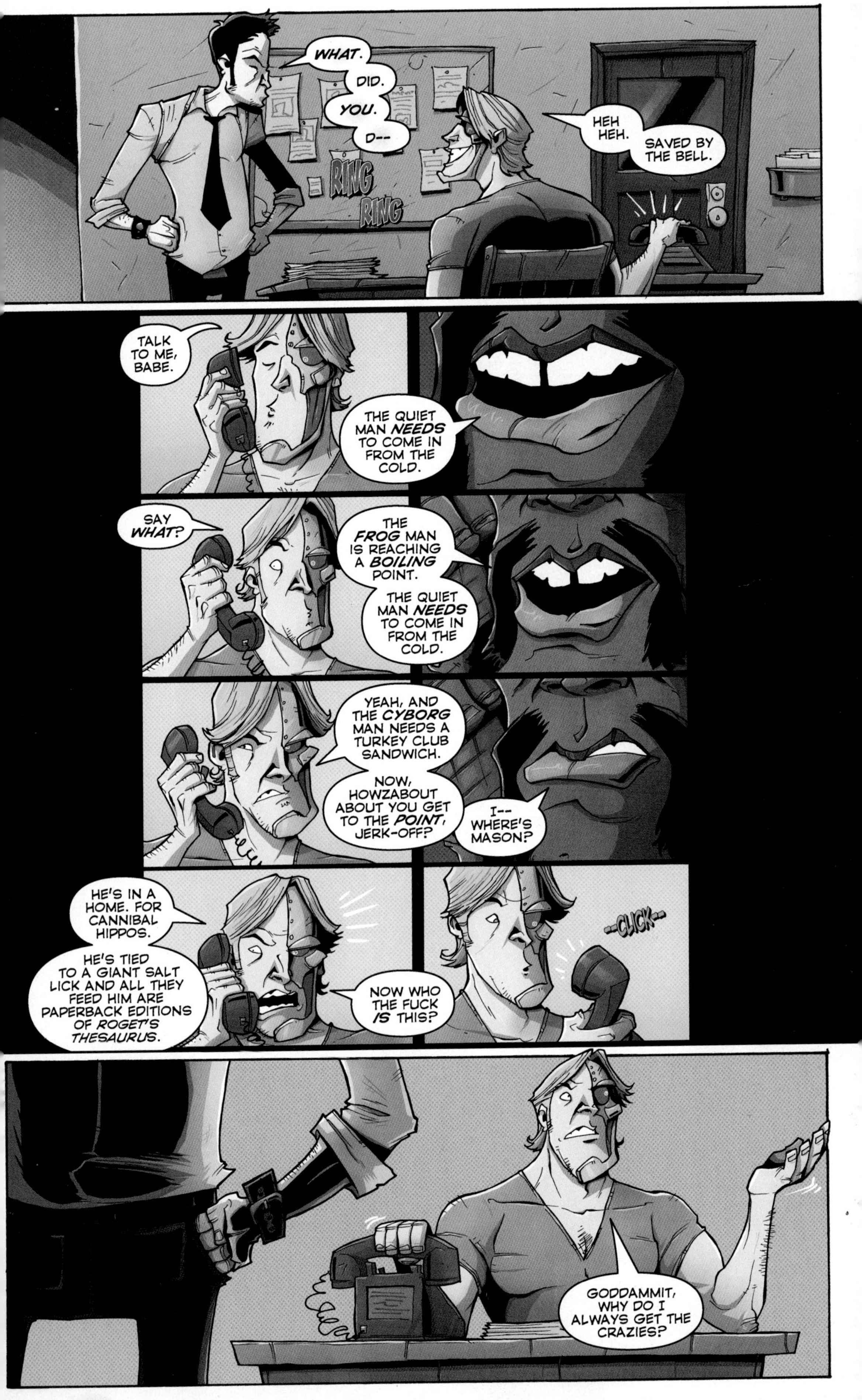

WHAT. DID. YOU. D--
RING RING
HEH HEH.
SAVED BY THE BELL.
TALK TO ME, BABE.
THE QUIET MAN NEEDS TO COME IN FROM THE COLD.
SAY WHAT?
THE FROG MAN IS REACHING A BOILING POINT.
THE QUIET MAN NEEDS TO COME IN FROM THE COLD.
YEAH, AND THE CYBORG MAN NEEDS A TURKEY CLUB SANDWICH.
NOW, HOWZABOUT ABOUT YOU GET TO THE POINT, JERK-OFF?
I-- WHERE'S MASON?
HE'S IN A HOME. FOR CANNIBAL HIPPOS.
HE'S TIED TO A GIANT SALT LICK AND ALL THEY FEED HIM ARE PAPERBACK EDITIONS OF ROGET'S THESAURUS.
NOW WHO THE FUCK IS THIS?
-CLICK-
GODDAMMIT, WHY DO I ALWAYS GET THE CRAZIES?

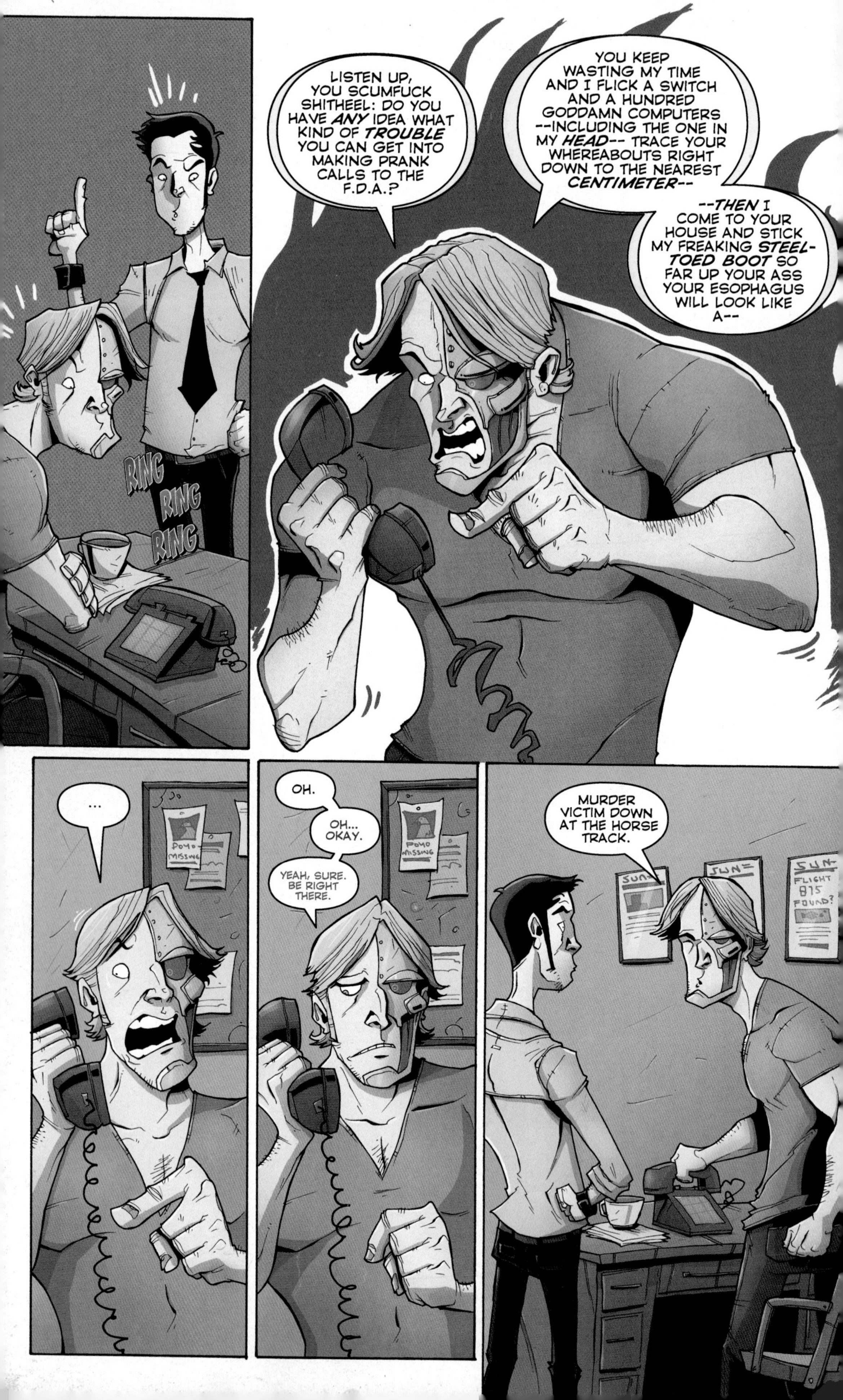
RING
RING
RING
LISTEN UP, YOU SCUMFUCK SHITHEEL: DO YOU HAVE ANY IDEA WHAT KIND OF TROUBLE YOU CAN GET INTO MAKING PRANK CALLS TO THE F.D.A.?
YOU KEEP WASTING MY TIME AND I FLICK A SWITCH AND A HUNDRED GODDAMN COMPUTERS --INCLUDING THE ONE IN MY HEAD-- TRACE YOUR WHEREABOUTS RIGHT DOWN TO THE NEAREST CENTIMETER--
--THEN I COME TO YOUR HOUSE AND STICK MY FREAKING STEEL-TOED BOOT SO FAR UP YOUR ASS YOUR ESOPHAGUS WILL LOOK LIKE A--
...
POYO MISSING
OH.
OH... OKAY.
YEAH, SURE. BE RIGHT THERE.
POYO MISSING
MURDER VICTIM DOWN AT THE HORSE TRACK.
SUN
SUN
SUN
FLIGHT 815 FOUND?

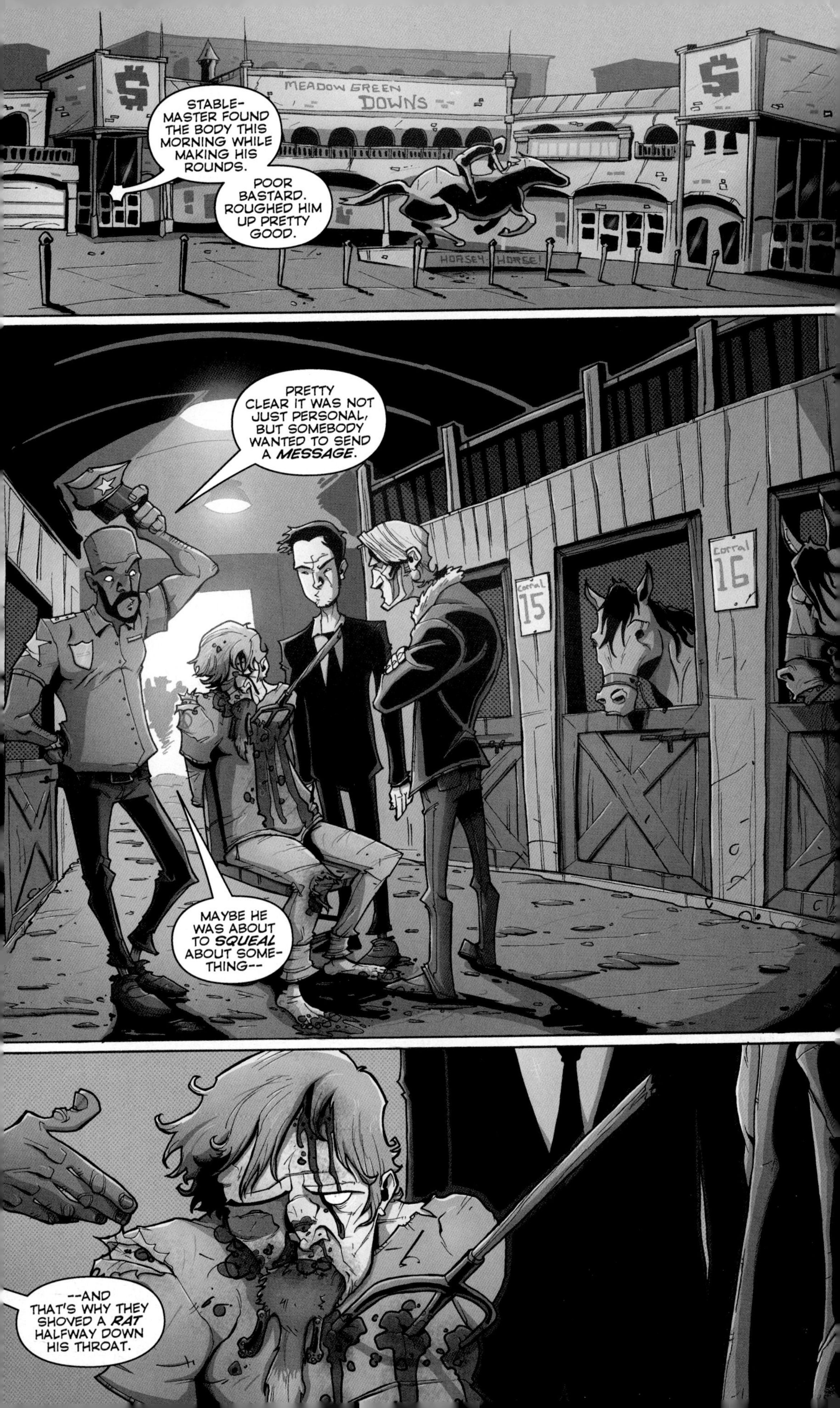

MEADOW GREEN DOWNS
STABLE-MASTER FOUND THE BODY THIS MORNING WHILE MAKING HIS ROUNDS.
POOR BASTARD. ROUGHED HIM UP PRETTY GOOD.
HORSEY HORSE!
PRETTY CLEAR IT WAS NOT JUST PERSONAL, BUT SOMEBODY WANTED TO SEND A ***MESSAGE***.
Corral 15
Corral 16
MAYBE HE WAS ABOUT TO ***SQUEAL*** ABOUT SOME-THING--
--AND THAT'S WHY THEY SHOVED A ***RAT*** HALFWAY DOWN HIS THROAT.

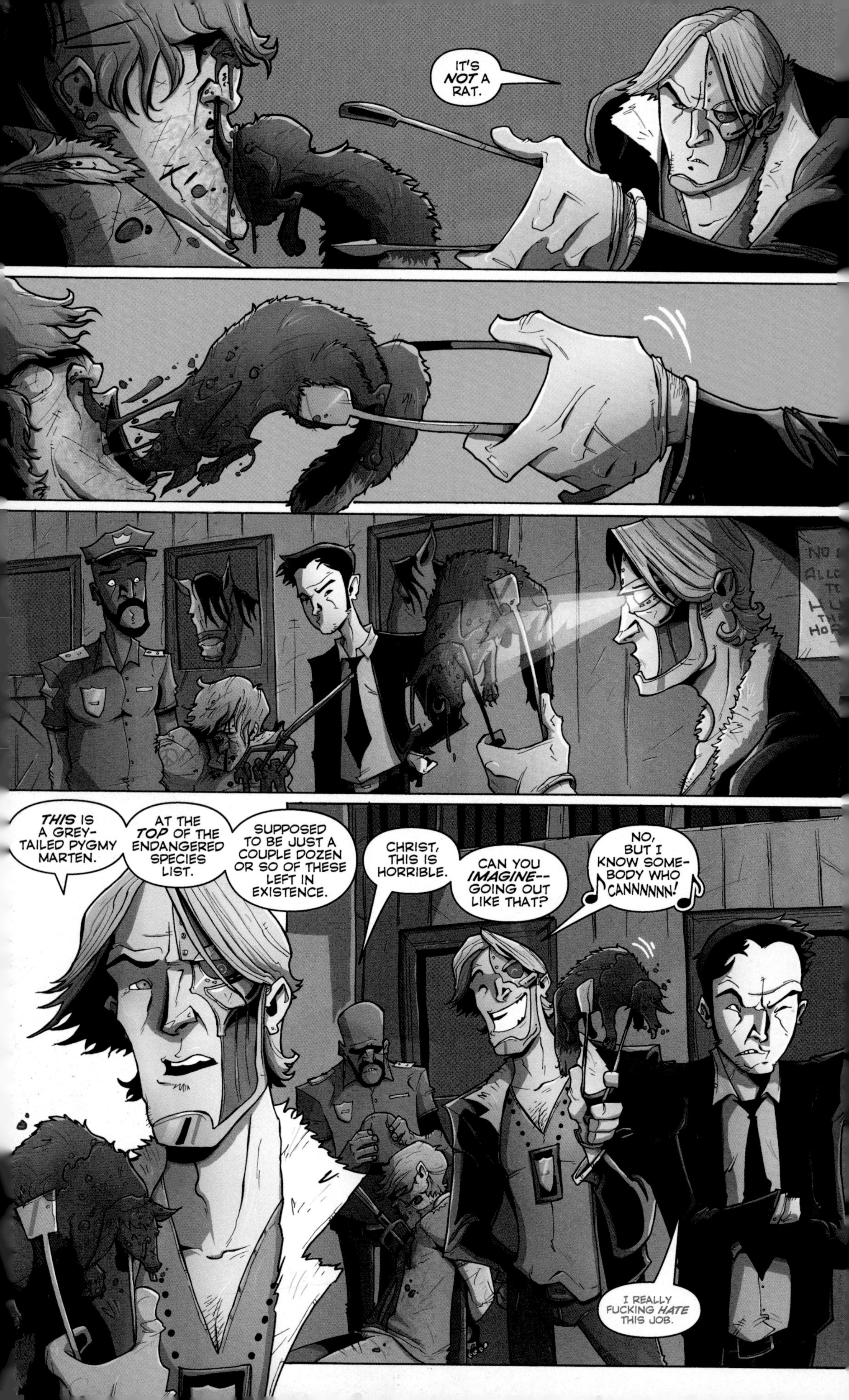
IT'S NOT A RAT.
NO ... ALL... TO H... TH... HO...
THIS IS A GREY-TAILED PYGMY MARTEN.
AT THE TOP OF THE ENDANGERED SPECIES LIST.
SUPPOSED TO BE JUST A COUPLE DOZEN OR SO OF THESE LEFT IN EXISTENCE.
CHRIST, THIS IS HORRIBLE.
CAN YOU IMAGINE-- GOING OUT LIKE THAT?
NO, BUT I KNOW SOME-BODY WHO CANNNNNN!
I REALLY FUCKING HATE THIS JOB.

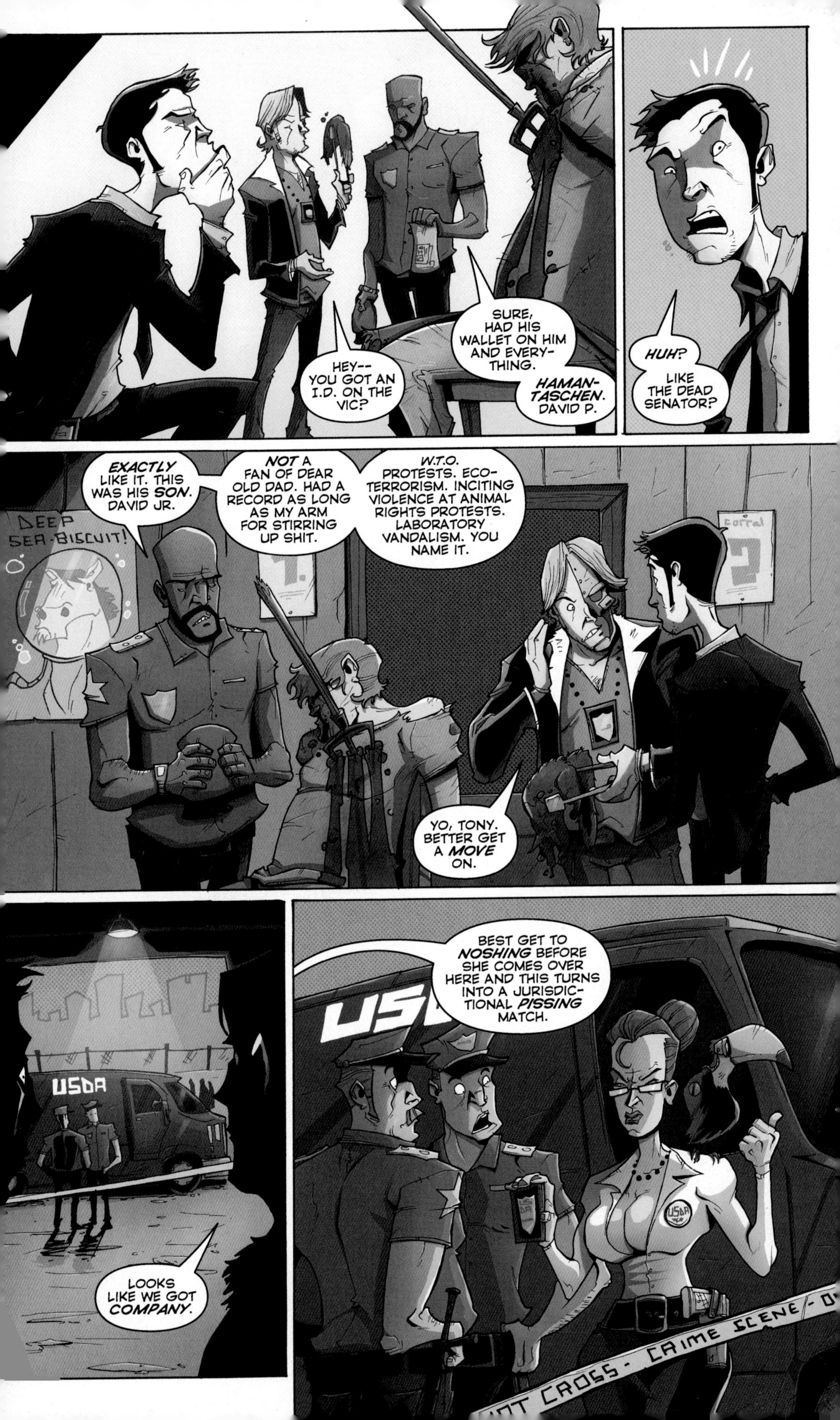

HEY-- YOU GOT AN I.D. ON THE VIC?
SURE, HAD HIS WALLET ON HIM AND EVERY-THING.
HAMAN-TASCHEN. DAVID P.
HUH?
LIKE THE DEAD SENATOR?
DEEP SEA-BISCUIT!
EXACTLY LIKE IT. THIS WAS HIS SON. DAVID JR.
NOT A FAN OF DEAR OLD DAD. HAD A RECORD AS LONG AS MY ARM FOR STIRRING UP SHIT.
W.T.O. PROTESTS. ECO-TERRORISM. INCITING VIOLENCE AT ANIMAL RIGHTS PROTESTS. LABORATORY VANDALISM. YOU NAME IT.
Corral
YO, TONY. BETTER GET A MOVE ON.
USDA
LOOKS LIKE WE GOT COMPANY.
BEST GET TO NOSHING BEFORE SHE COMES OVER HERE AND THIS TURNS INTO A JURISDIC-TIONAL PISSING MATCH.
USDA
CRIME SCENE

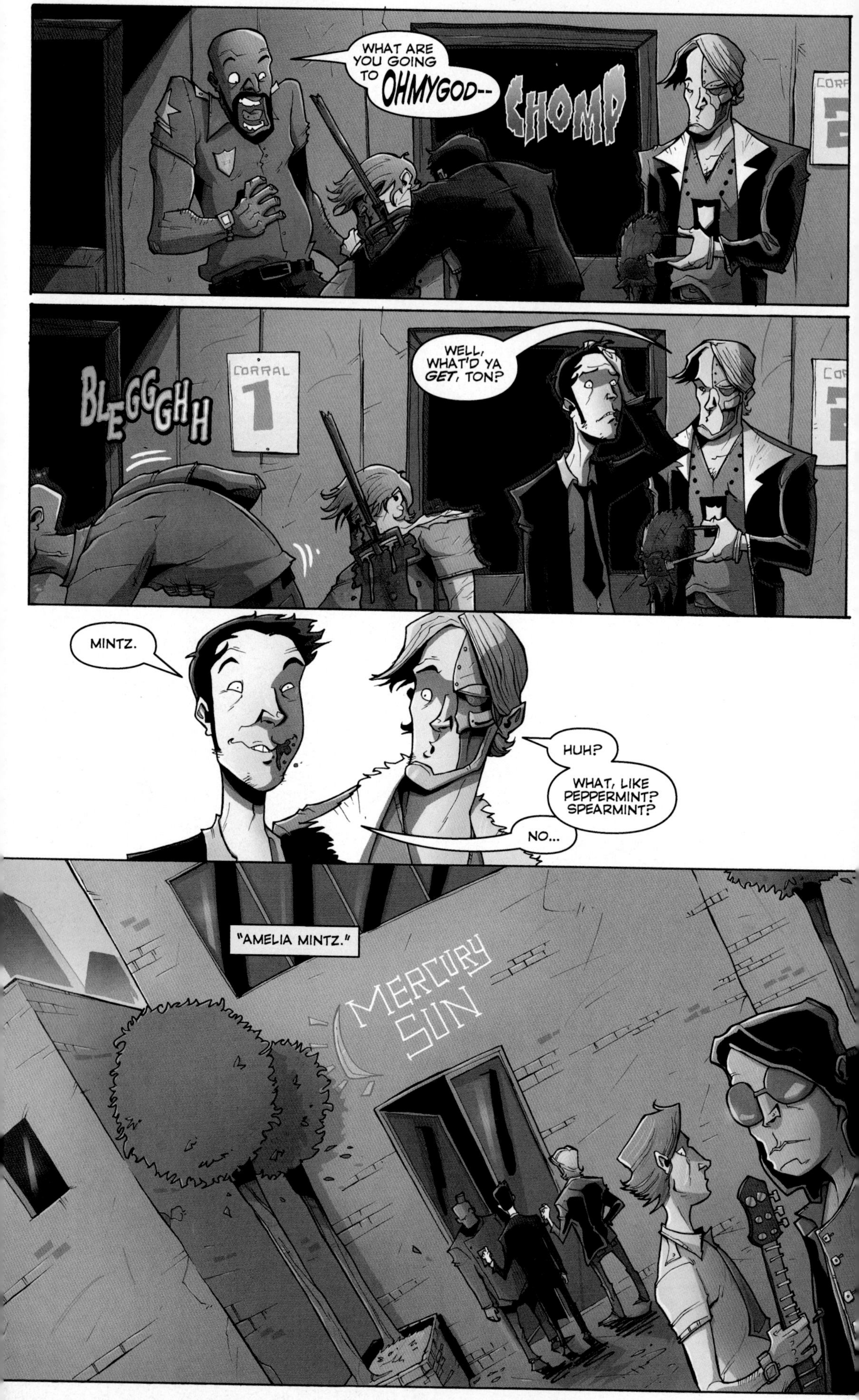
WHAT ARE YOU GOING TO OHMYGOD--
CHOMP
BLEGGGHH
CORRAL 1
WELL, WHAT'D YA GET, TON?
MINTZ.
HUH?
WHAT, LIKE PEPPERMINT? SPEARMINT?
NO...
"AMELIA MINTZ."
MERCURY SUN

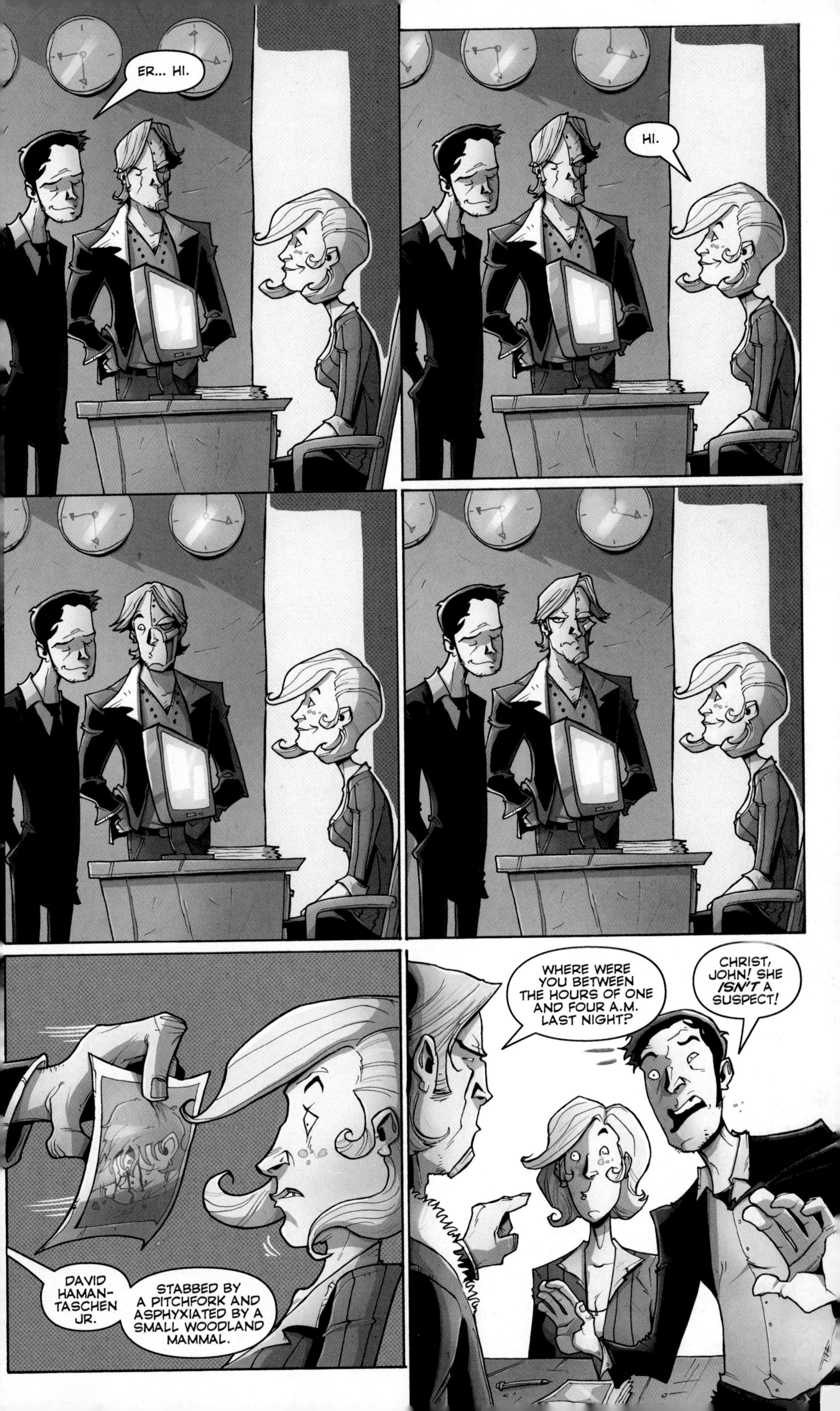
ER... HI.
HI.
DAVID HAMAN-TASCHEN JR.
STABBED BY A PITCHFORK AND ASPHYXIATED BY A SMALL WOODLAND MAMMAL.
WHERE WERE YOU BETWEEN THE HOURS OF ONE AND FOUR A.M. LAST NIGHT?
CHRIST, JOHN! SHE *ISN'T* A SUSPECT!

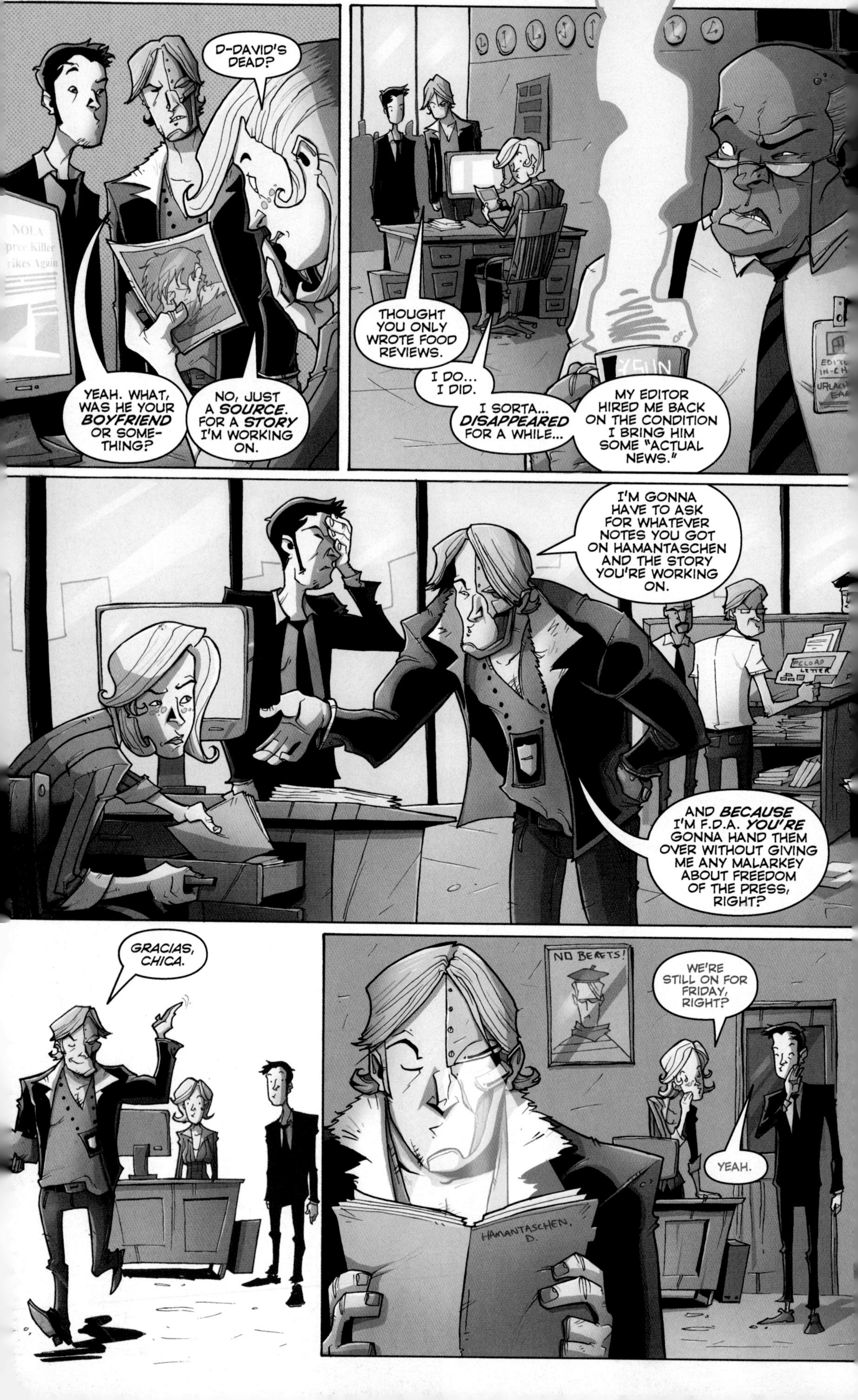
D-DAVID'S DEAD?
YEAH. WHAT, WAS HE YOUR *BOYFRIEND* OR SOME-THING?
NO, JUST A *SOURCE*. FOR A *STORY* I'M WORKING ON.
THOUGHT YOU ONLY WROTE FOOD REVIEWS.
I DO... I DID.
I SORTA... *DISAPPEARED* FOR A WHILE...
MY EDITOR HIRED ME BACK ON THE CONDITION I BRING HIM SOME "ACTUAL NEWS."
I'M GONNA HAVE TO ASK FOR WHATEVER NOTES YOU GOT ON HAMANTASCHEN AND THE STORY YOU'RE WORKING ON.
AND *BECAUSE* I'M F.D.A. *YOU'RE* GONNA HAND THEM OVER WITHOUT GIVING ME ANY MALARKEY ABOUT FREEDOM OF THE PRESS, RIGHT?
GRACIAS, CHICA.
NO BERETS!
WE'RE STILL ON FOR FRIDAY, RIGHT?
YEAH.
HAMANTASCHEN, D.

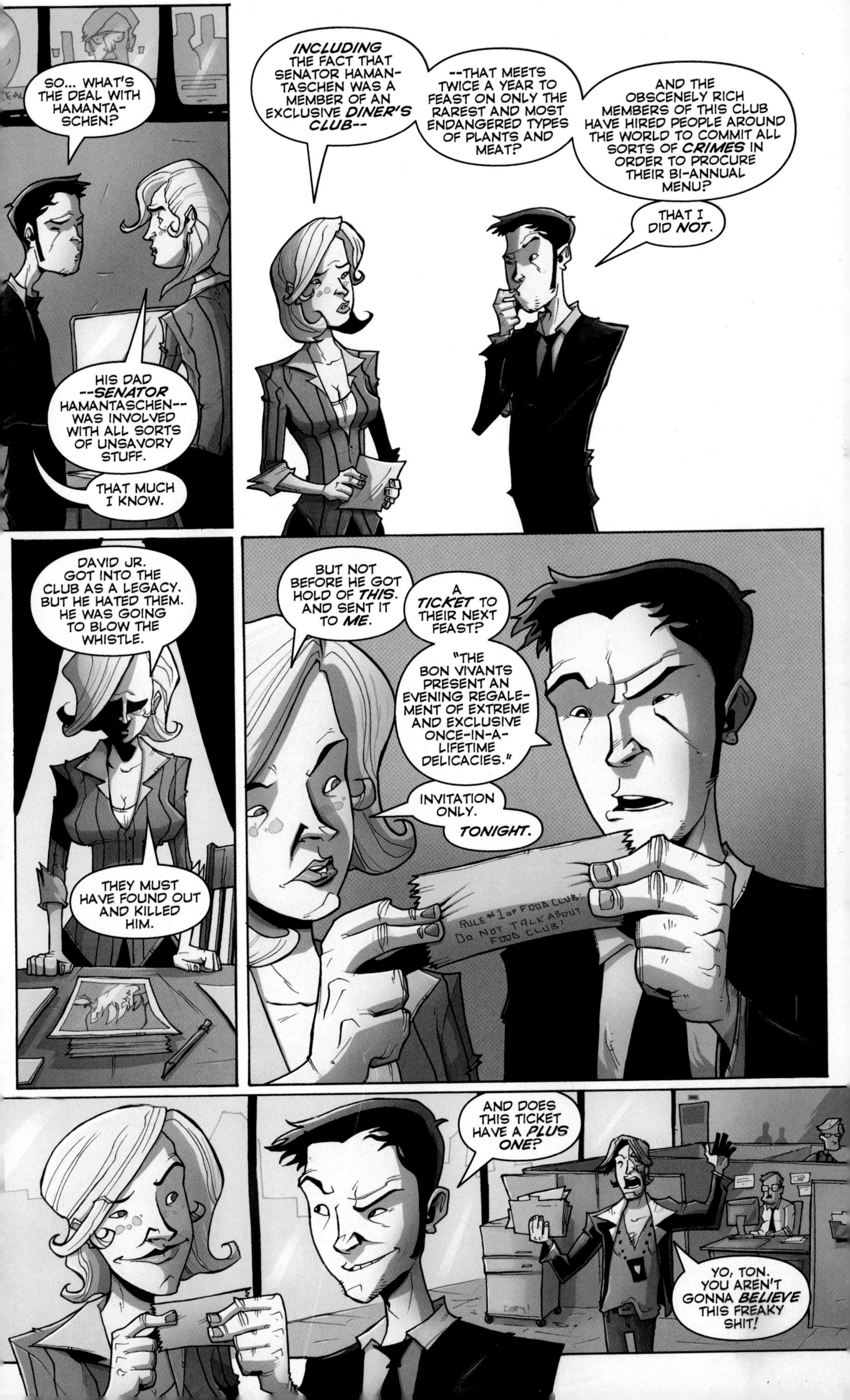
SO... WHAT'S THE DEAL WITH HAMANTASCHEN?
HIS DAD --SENATOR HAMANTASCHEN-- WAS INVOLVED WITH ALL SORTS OF UNSAVORY STUFF.
THAT MUCH I KNOW.
INCLUDING THE FACT THAT SENATOR HAMANTASCHEN WAS A MEMBER OF AN EXCLUSIVE DINER'S CLUB--
--THAT MEETS TWICE A YEAR TO FEAST ON ONLY THE RAREST AND MOST ENDANGERED TYPES OF PLANTS AND MEAT?
AND THE OBSCENELY RICH MEMBERS OF THIS CLUB HAVE HIRED PEOPLE AROUND THE WORLD TO COMMIT ALL SORTS OF CRIMES IN ORDER TO PROCURE THEIR BI-ANNUAL MENU?
THAT I DID NOT.
DAVID JR. GOT INTO THE CLUB AS A LEGACY. BUT HE HATED THEM. HE WAS GOING TO BLOW THE WHISTLE.
THEY MUST HAVE FOUND OUT AND KILLED HIM.
BUT NOT BEFORE HE GOT HOLD OF THIS. AND SENT IT TO ME.
A TICKET TO THEIR NEXT FEAST?
"THE BON VIVANTS PRESENT AN EVENING REGALEMENT OF EXTREME AND EXCLUSIVE ONCE-IN-A-LIFETIME DELICACIES."
INVITATION ONLY. TONIGHT.
RULE #1 OF FOOD CLUB: DO NOT TALK ABOUT FOOD CLUB!
AND DOES THIS TICKET HAVE A PLUS ONE?
YO, TON. YOU AREN'T GONNA BELIEVE THIS FREAKY SHIT!

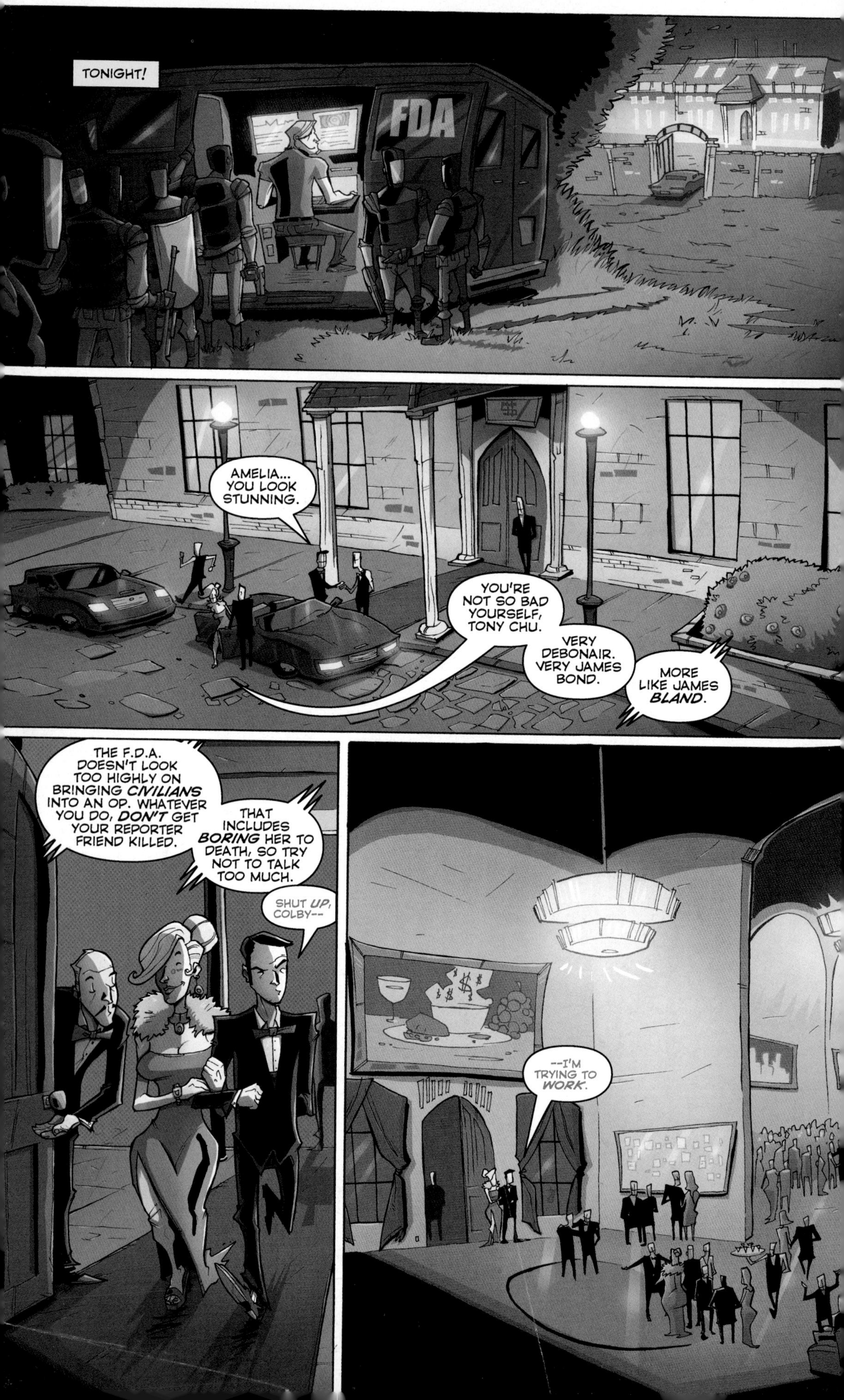
TONIGHT!
FDA
AMELIA... YOU LOOK STUNNING.
YOU'RE NOT SO BAD YOURSELF, TONY CHU.
VERY DEBONAIR. VERY JAMES BOND.
MORE LIKE JAMES *BLAND*.
THE F.D.A. DOESN'T LOOK TOO HIGHLY ON BRINGING *CIVILIANS* INTO AN OP. WHATEVER YOU DO, *DON'T* GET YOUR REPORTER FRIEND KILLED.
THAT INCLUDES *BORING* HER TO DEATH, SO TRY NOT TO TALK TOO MUCH.
SHUT *UP*, COLBY--
--I'M TRYING TO *WORK*.

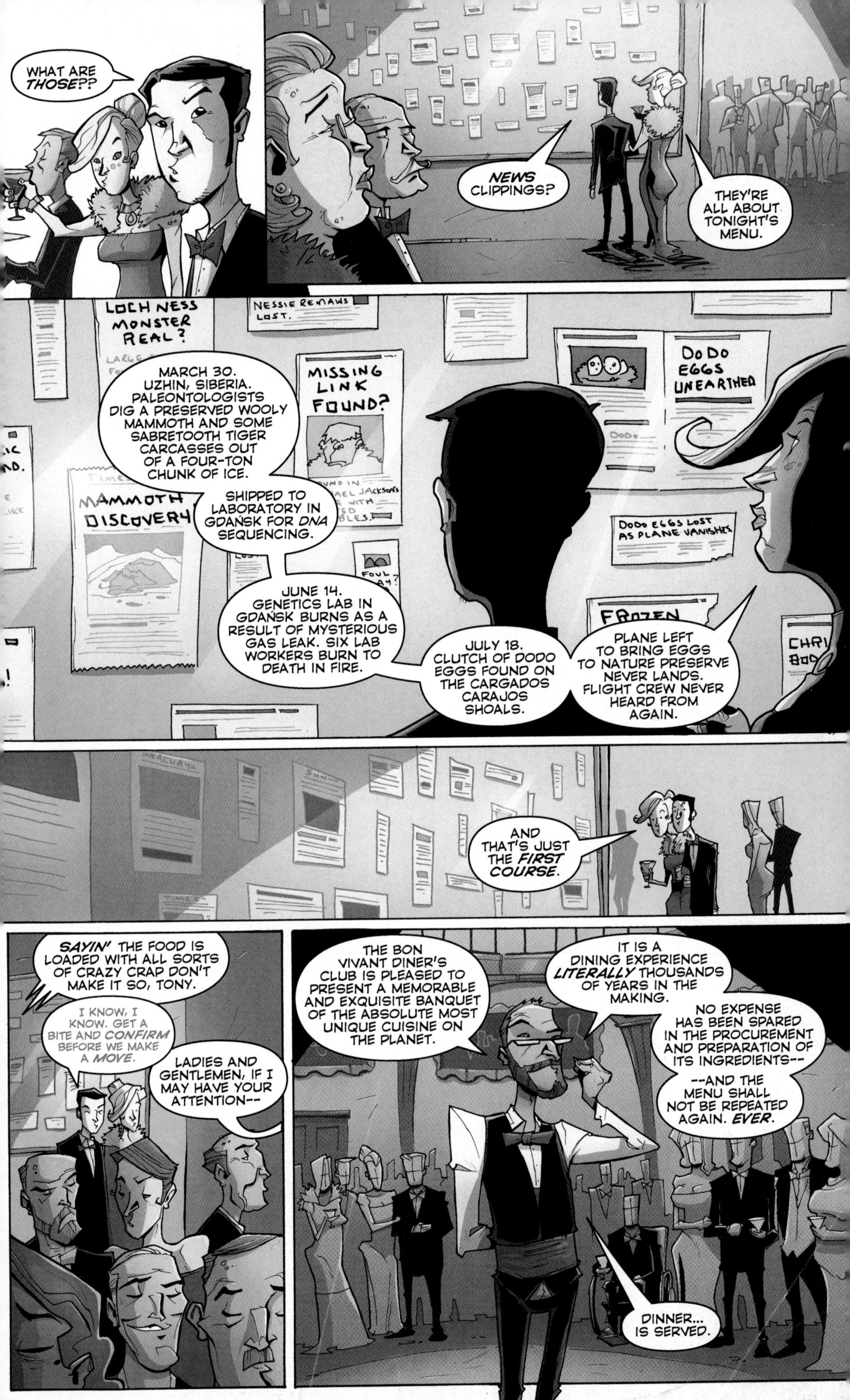

WHAT ARE *THOSE*??
NEWS CLIPPINGS?
THEY'RE ALL ABOUT TONIGHT'S MENU.
LOCH NESS MONSTER REAL?
NESSIE REMAINS LOST.
MISSING LINK FOUND?
DO DO EGGS UNEARTHED
MAMMOTH DISCOVERY
MARCH 30. UZHIN, SIBERIA. PALEONTOLOGISTS DIG A PRESERVED WOOLY MAMMOTH AND SOME SABRETOOTH TIGER CARCASSES OUT OF A FOUR-TON CHUNK OF ICE.
SHIPPED TO LABORATORY IN GDAŃSK FOR *DNA* SEQUENCING.
DODO EGGS LOST AS PLANE VANISHES
JUNE 14. GENETICS LAB IN GDAŃSK BURNS AS A RESULT OF MYSTERIOUS GAS LEAK. SIX LAB WORKERS BURN TO DEATH IN FIRE.
FROZEN
JULY 18. CLUTCH OF DODO EGGS FOUND ON THE CARGADOS CARAJOS SHOALS.
PLANE LEFT TO BRING EGGS TO NATURE PRESERVE NEVER LANDS. FLIGHT CREW NEVER HEARD FROM AGAIN.
AND THAT'S JUST THE *FIRST COURSE*.
SAYIN' THE FOOD IS LOADED WITH ALL SORTS OF CRAZY CRAP DON'T MAKE IT SO, TONY.
I KNOW, I KNOW. GET A BITE AND *CONFIRM* BEFORE WE MAKE A *MOVE*.
LADIES AND GENTLEMEN, IF I MAY HAVE YOUR ATTENTION--
THE BON VIVANT DINER'S CLUB IS PLEASED TO PRESENT A MEMORABLE AND EXQUISITE BANQUET OF THE ABSOLUTE MOST UNIQUE CUISINE ON THE PLANET.
IT IS A DINING EXPERIENCE *LITERALLY* THOUSANDS OF YEARS IN THE MAKING.
NO EXPENSE HAS BEEN SPARED IN THE PROCUREMENT AND PREPARATION OF ITS INGREDIENTS--
--AND THE MENU SHALL NOT BE REPEATED AGAIN. *EVER*.
DINNER... IS SERVED.

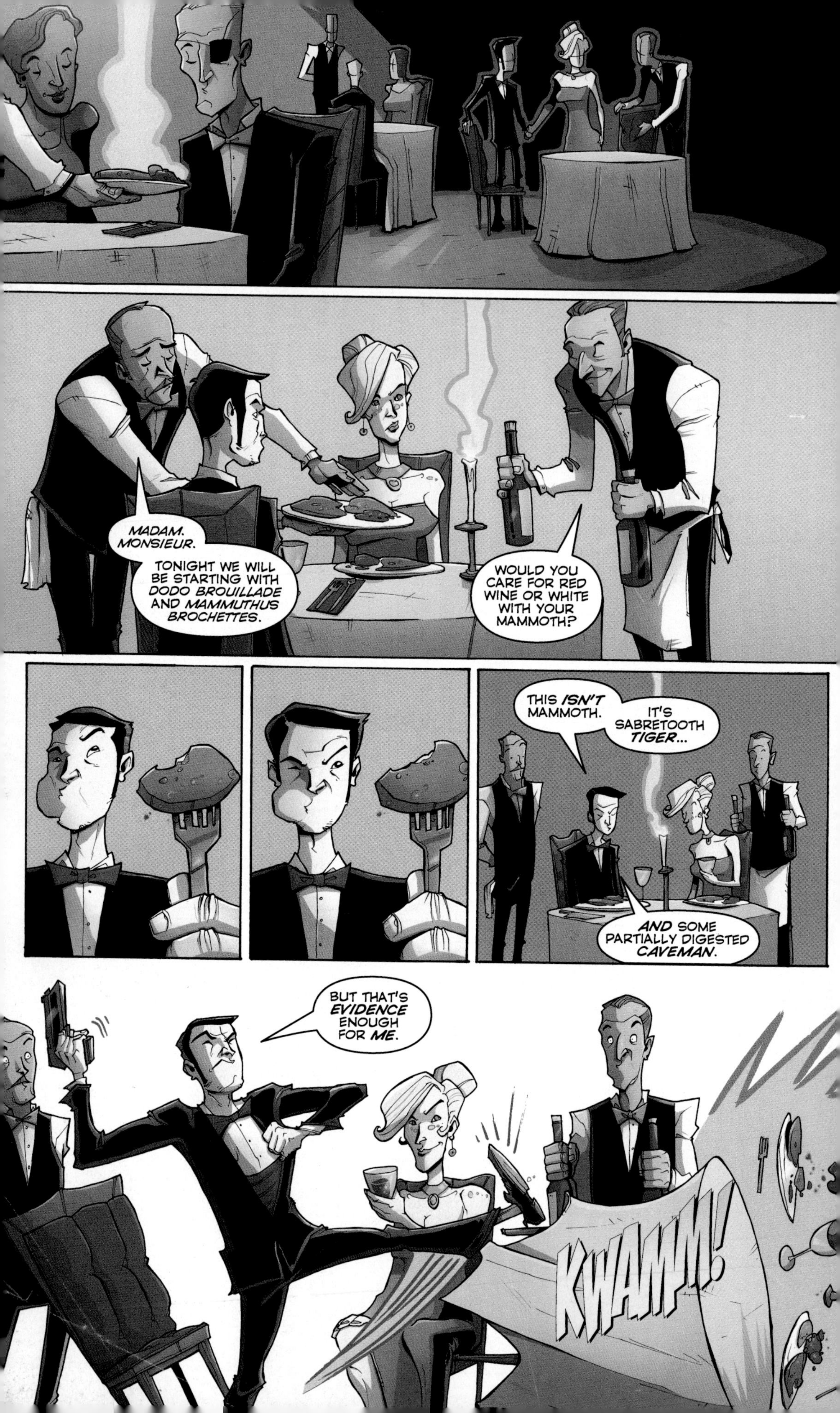
MADAM. MONSIEUR.
TONIGHT WE WILL BE STARTING WITH DODO BROUILLADE AND MAMMUTHUS BROCHETTES.
WOULD YOU CARE FOR RED WINE OR WHITE WITH YOUR MAMMOTH?
THIS ISN'T MAMMOTH.
IT'S SABRETOOTH TIGER...
AND SOME PARTIALLY DIGESTED CAVEMAN.
BUT THAT'S EVIDENCE ENOUGH FOR ME.
KWAMM!

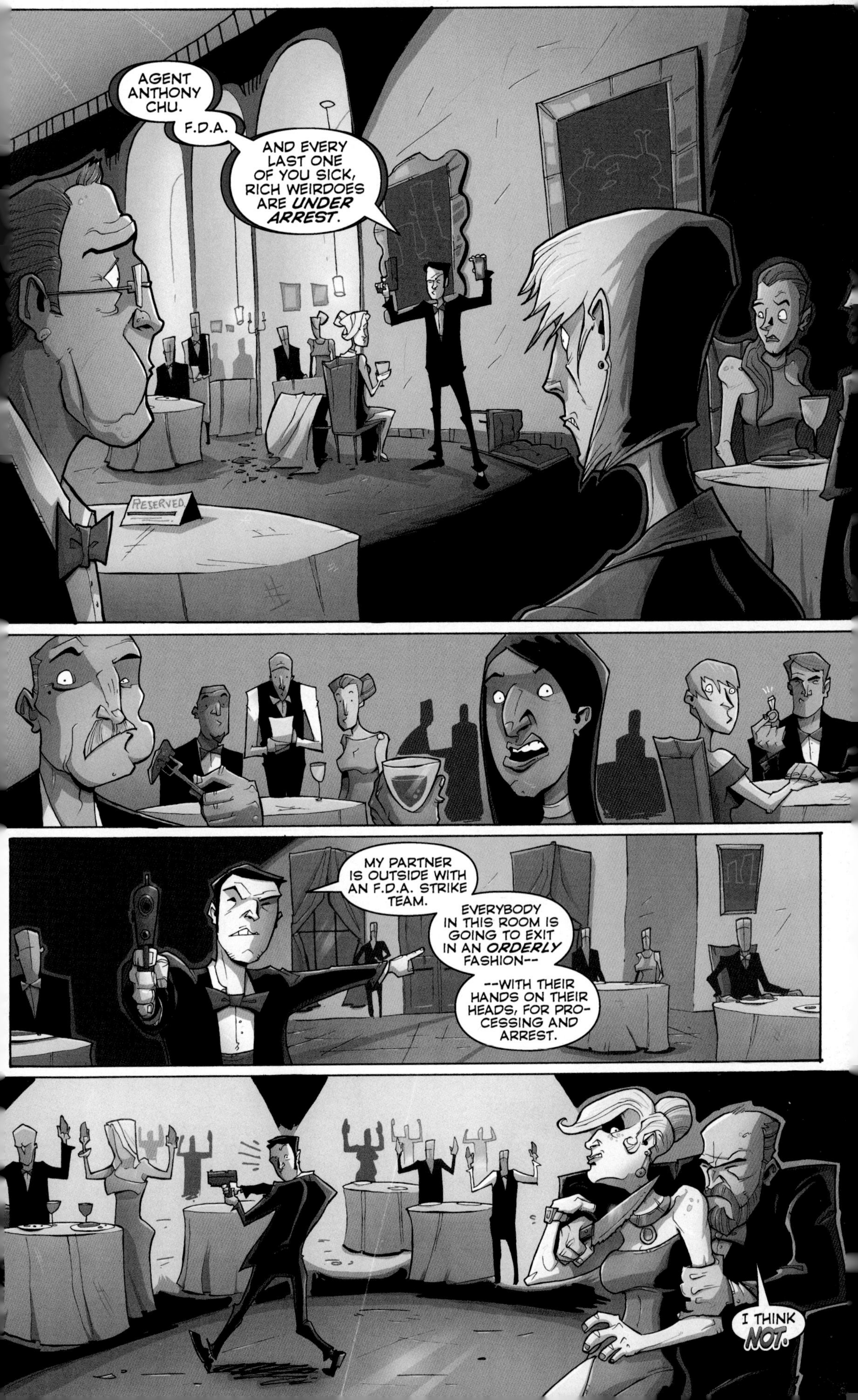
AGENT ANTHONY CHU.
F.D.A.
AND EVERY LAST ONE OF YOU SICK, RICH WEIRDOES ARE *UNDER ARREST*.
RESERVED
MY PARTNER IS OUTSIDE WITH AN F.D.A. STRIKE TEAM.
EVERYBODY IN THIS ROOM IS GOING TO EXIT IN AN *ORDERLY* FASHION--
--WITH THEIR HANDS ON THEIR HEADS, FOR PROCESSING AND ARREST.
I THINK *NOT*.

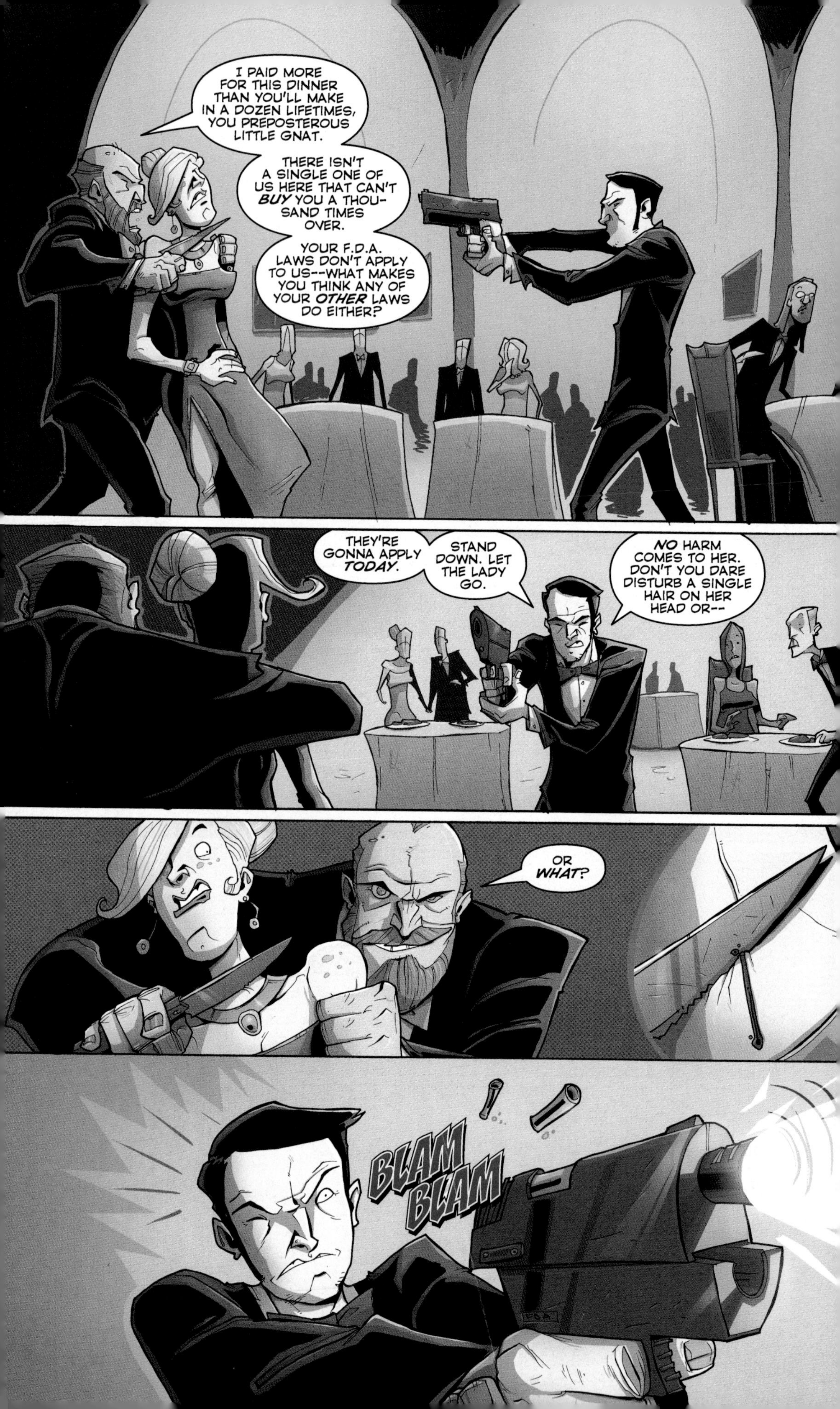
I PAID MORE FOR THIS DINNER THAN YOU'LL MAKE IN A DOZEN LIFETIMES, YOU PREPOSTEROUS LITTLE GNAT.
THERE ISN'T A SINGLE ONE OF US HERE THAT CAN'T *BUY* YOU A THOUSAND TIMES OVER.
YOUR F.D.A. LAWS DON'T APPLY TO US--WHAT MAKES YOU THINK ANY OF YOUR *OTHER* LAWS DO EITHER?
THEY'RE GONNA APPLY *TODAY*.
STAND DOWN. LET THE LADY GO.
NO HARM COMES TO HER. DON'T YOU DARE DISTURB A SINGLE HAIR ON HER HEAD OR--
OR *WHAT?*
BLAM
BLAM
F.D.A.

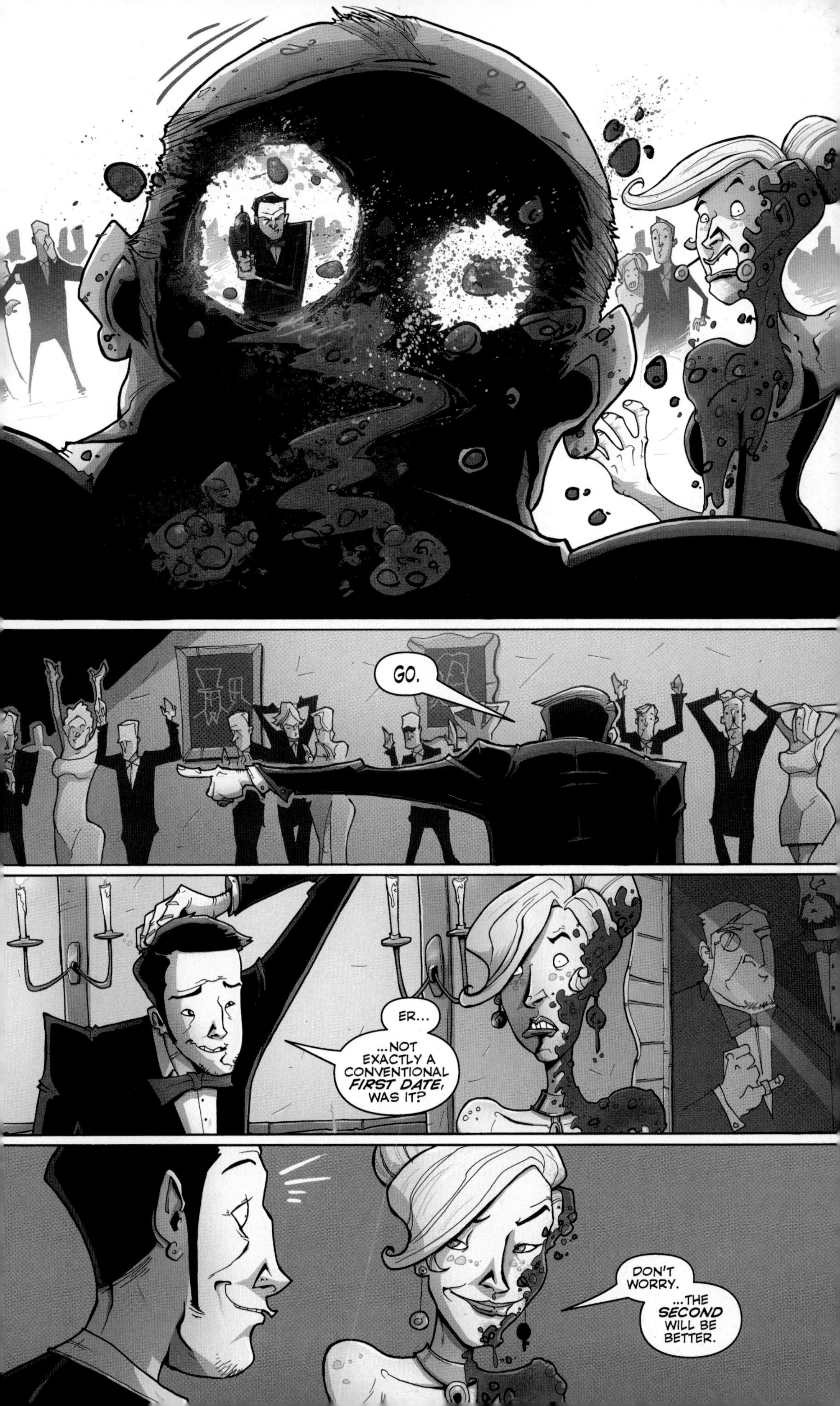
GO.
ER...
...NOT EXACTLY A CONVENTIONAL *FIRST DATE*, WAS IT?
DON'T WORRY.
...THE *SECOND* WILL BE BETTER.

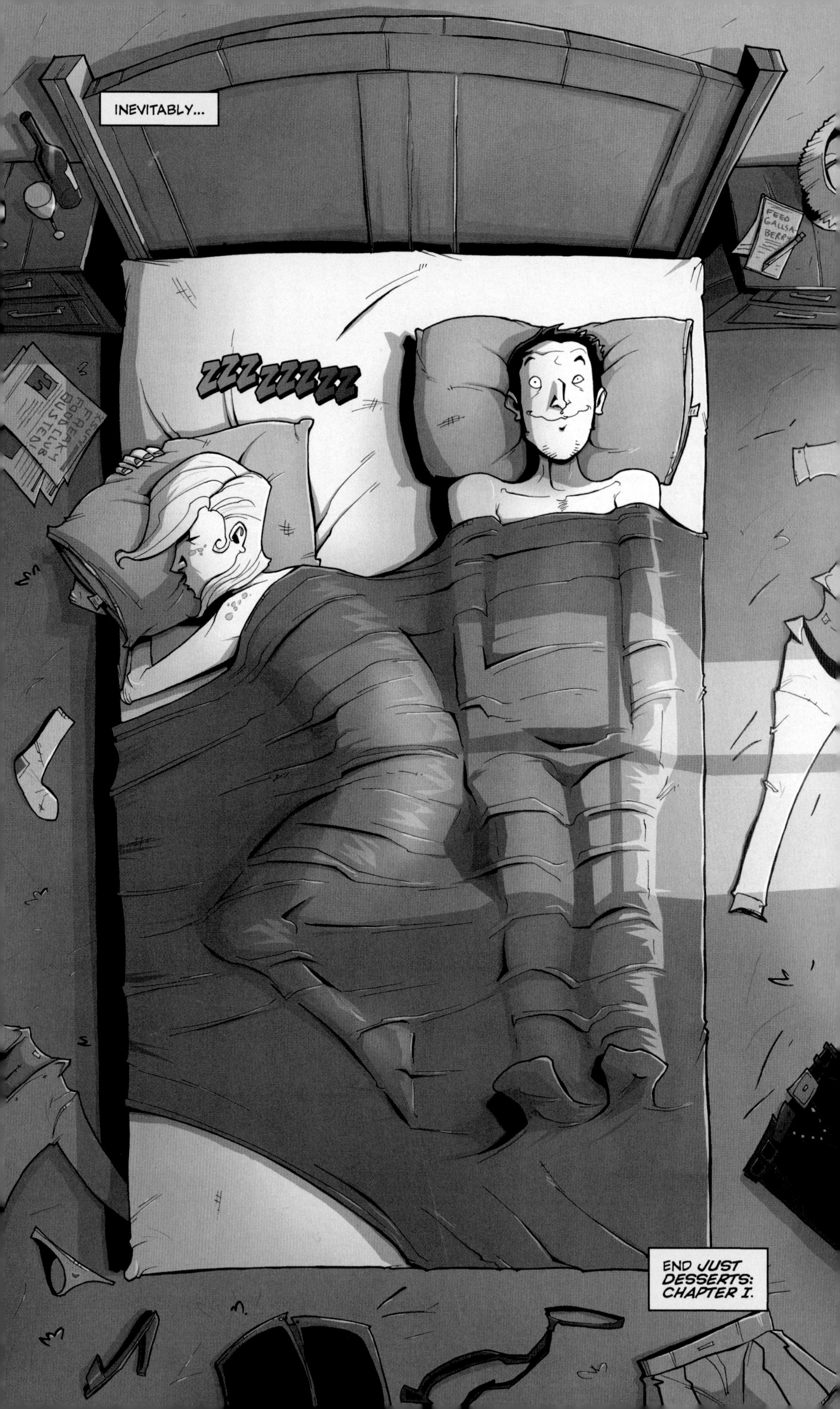
INEVITABLY...
ZZZZZZZZ
FEED GALLSABERRY
END JUST DESSERTS: CHAPTER I.

Chapter 2

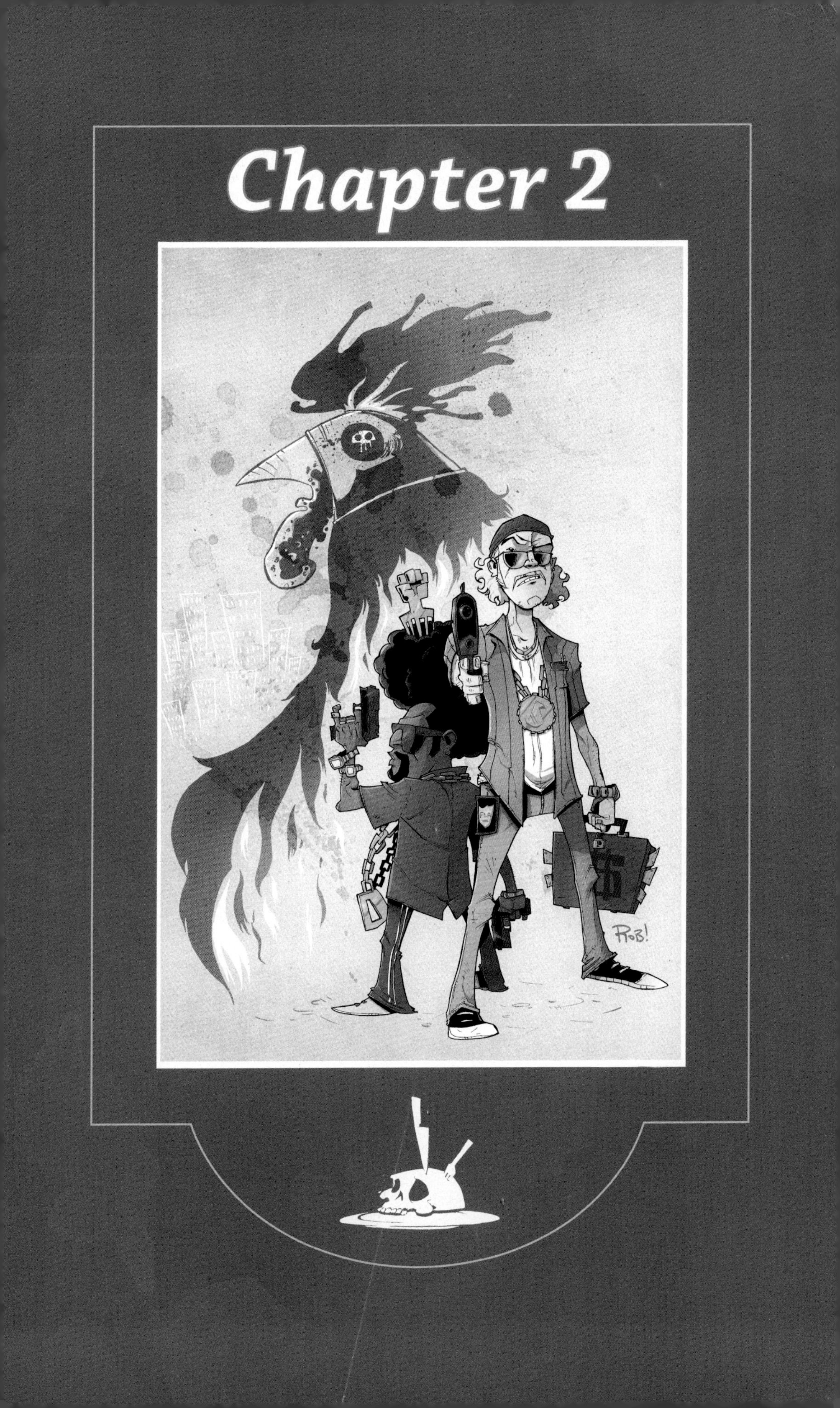
ROB!

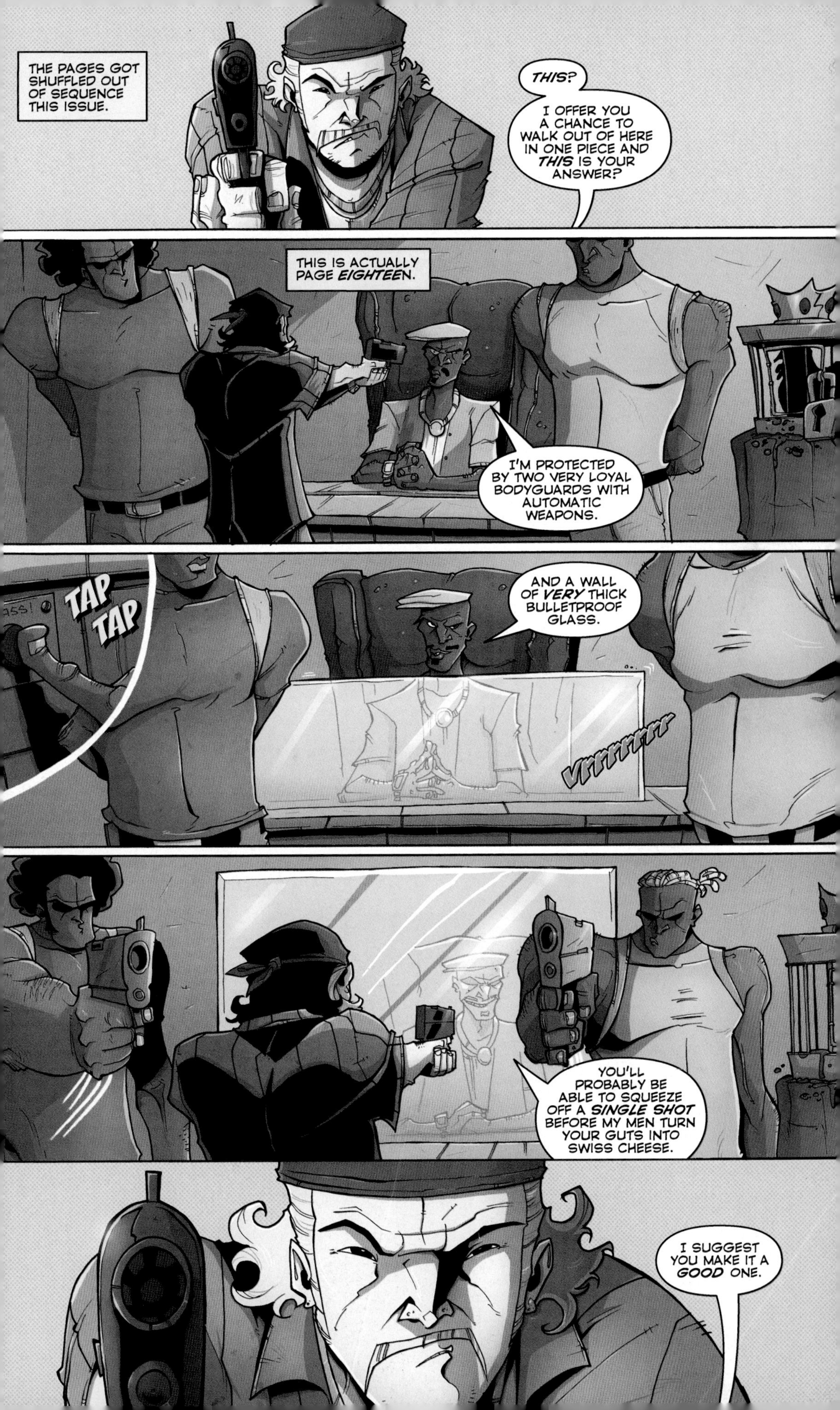
THE PAGES GOT SHUFFLED OUT OF SEQUENCE THIS ISSUE.
THIS?
I OFFER YOU A CHANCE TO WALK OUT OF HERE IN ONE PIECE AND *THIS* IS YOUR ANSWER?
THIS IS ACTUALLY PAGE *EIGHTEEN*.
I'M PROTECTED BY TWO VERY LOYAL BODYGUARDS WITH AUTOMATIC WEAPONS.
TAP
TAP
AND A WALL OF *VERY* THICK BULLETPROOF GLASS.
Vrrrrrrrr
YOU'LL PROBABLY BE ABLE TO SQUEEZE OFF A *SINGLE SHOT* BEFORE MY MEN TURN YOUR GUTS INTO SWISS CHEESE.
I SUGGEST YOU MAKE IT A *GOOD* ONE.

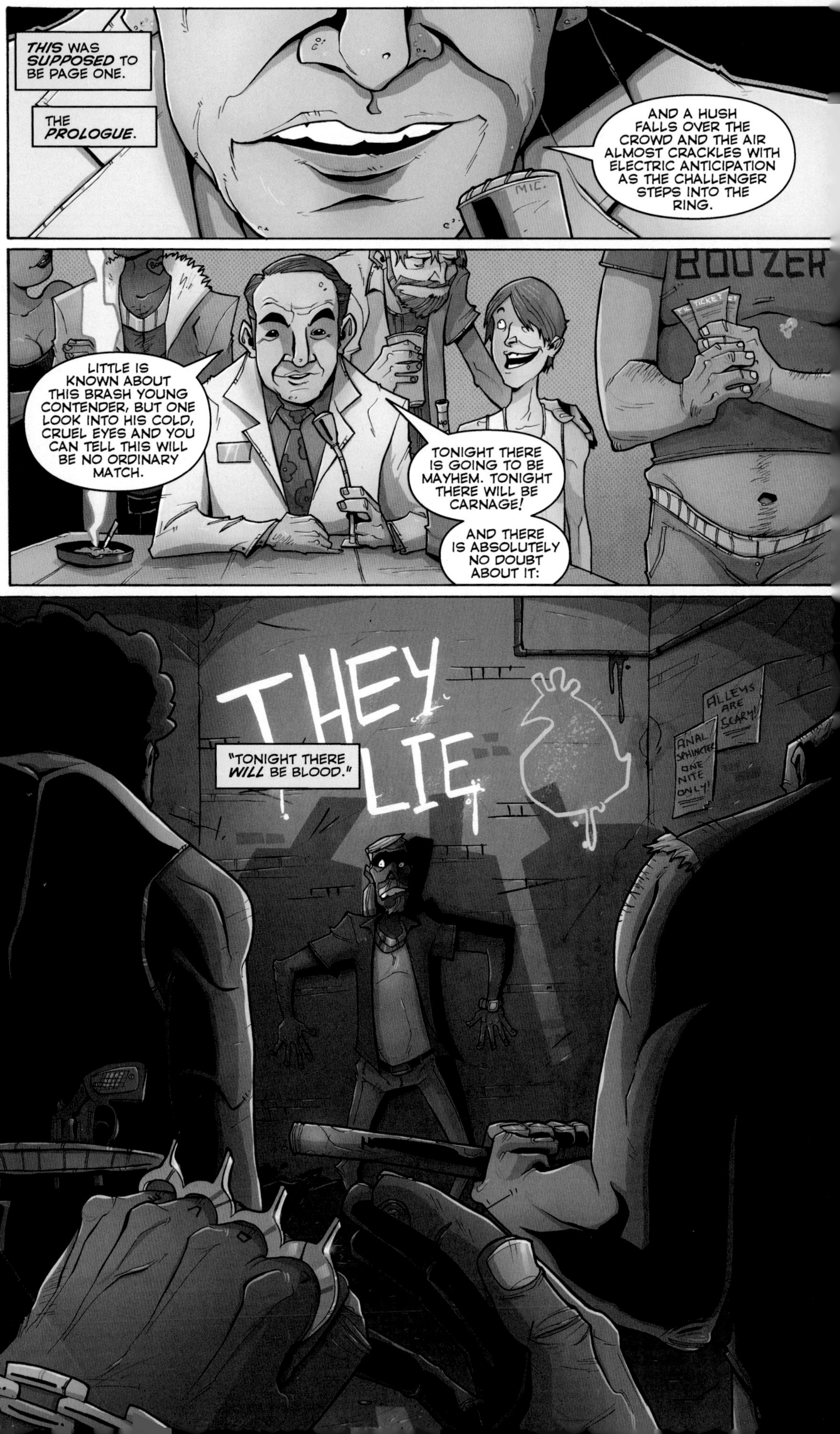
THIS WAS SUPPOSED TO BE PAGE ONE.
THE PROLOGUE.
AND A HUSH FALLS OVER THE CROWD AND THE AIR ALMOST CRACKLES WITH ELECTRIC ANTICIPATION AS THE CHALLENGER STEPS INTO THE RING.
MIC.
BOOZER
TICKET
LITTLE IS KNOWN ABOUT THIS BRASH YOUNG CONTENDER, BUT ONE LOOK INTO HIS COLD, CRUEL EYES AND YOU CAN TELL THIS WILL BE NO ORDINARY MATCH.
TONIGHT THERE IS GOING TO BE MAYHEM. TONIGHT THERE WILL BE CARNAGE!
AND THERE IS ABSOLUTELY NO DOUBT ABOUT IT:
THEY LIE
"TONIGHT THERE WILL BE BLOOD."
ALLEYS ARE SCARY!
ANAL SPHINCTER ONE NITE ONLY!

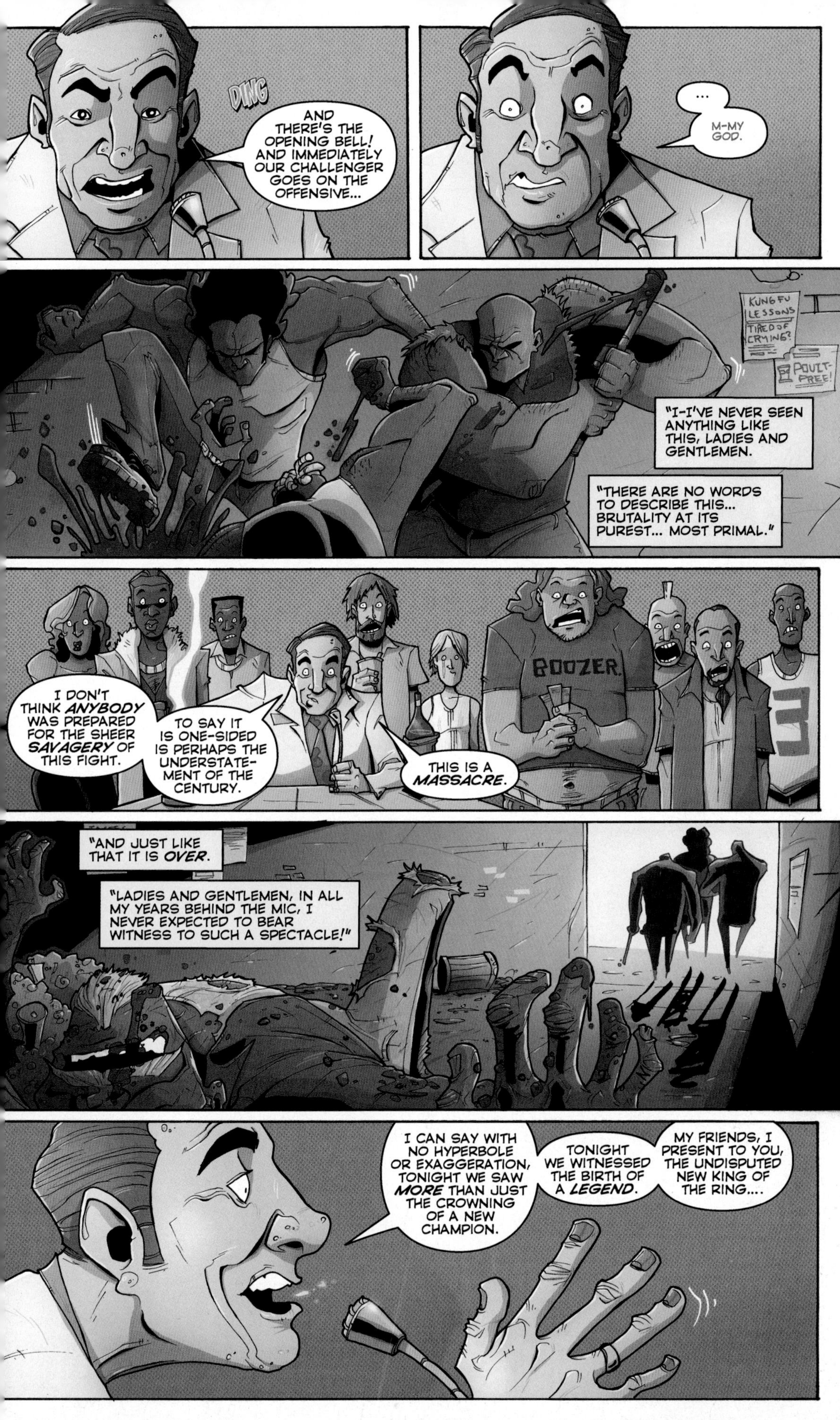
DING
AND THERE'S THE OPENING BELL! AND IMMEDIATELY OUR CHALLENGER GOES ON THE OFFENSIVE...
...
M-MY GOD.
KUNG FU LESSONS
TIRED OF CRYING?
POULT-FREE!
"I-I'VE NEVER SEEN ANYTHING LIKE THIS, LADIES AND GENTLEMEN.
"THERE ARE NO WORDS TO DESCRIBE THIS... BRUTALITY AT ITS PUREST... MOST PRIMAL."
BOOZER
I DON'T THINK *ANYBODY* WAS PREPARED FOR THE SHEER *SAVAGERY* OF THIS FIGHT.
TO SAY IT IS ONE-SIDED IS PERHAPS THE UNDERSTATEMENT OF THE CENTURY.
THIS IS A *MASSACRE*.
"AND JUST LIKE THAT IT IS *OVER*.
"LADIES AND GENTLEMEN, IN ALL MY YEARS BEHIND THE MIC, I NEVER EXPECTED TO BEAR WITNESS TO SUCH A SPECTACLE!"
I CAN SAY WITH NO HYPERBOLE OR EXAGGERATION, TONIGHT WE SAW *MORE* THAN JUST THE CROWNING OF A NEW CHAMPION.
TONIGHT WE WITNESSED THE BIRTH OF A *LEGEND*.
MY FRIENDS, I PRESENT TO YOU, THE UNDISPUTED NEW KING OF THE RING....

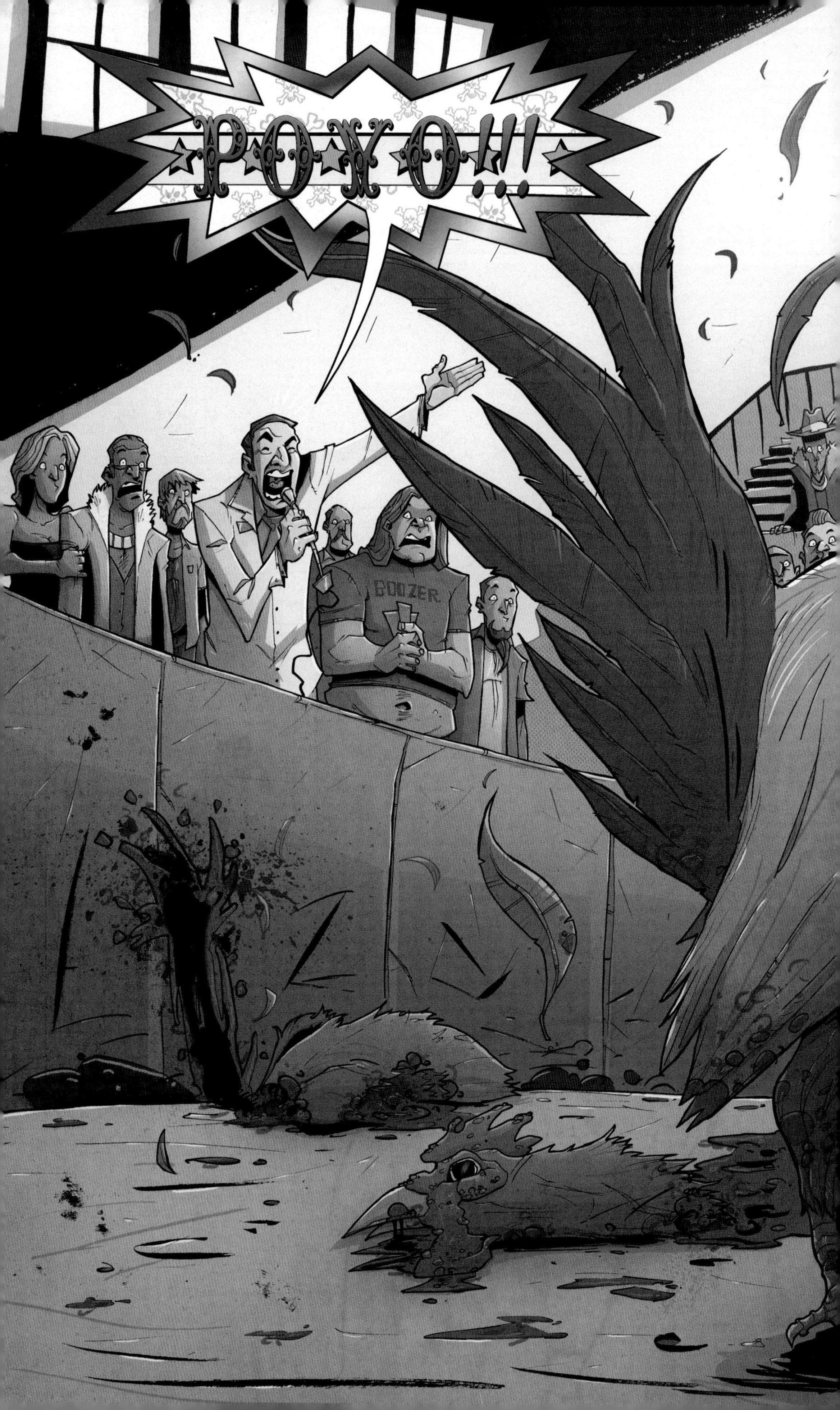
POYO!!!
BOOZER

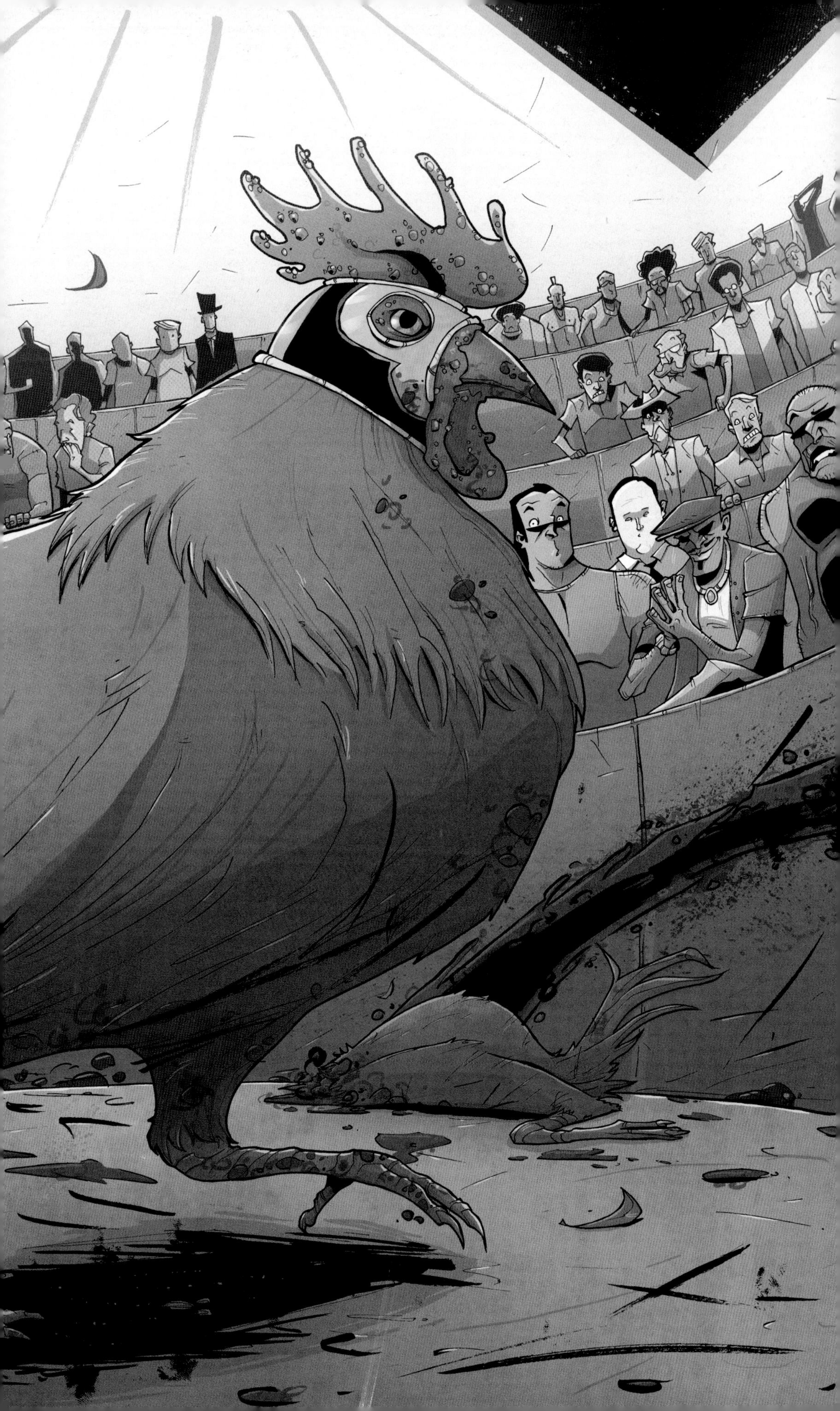

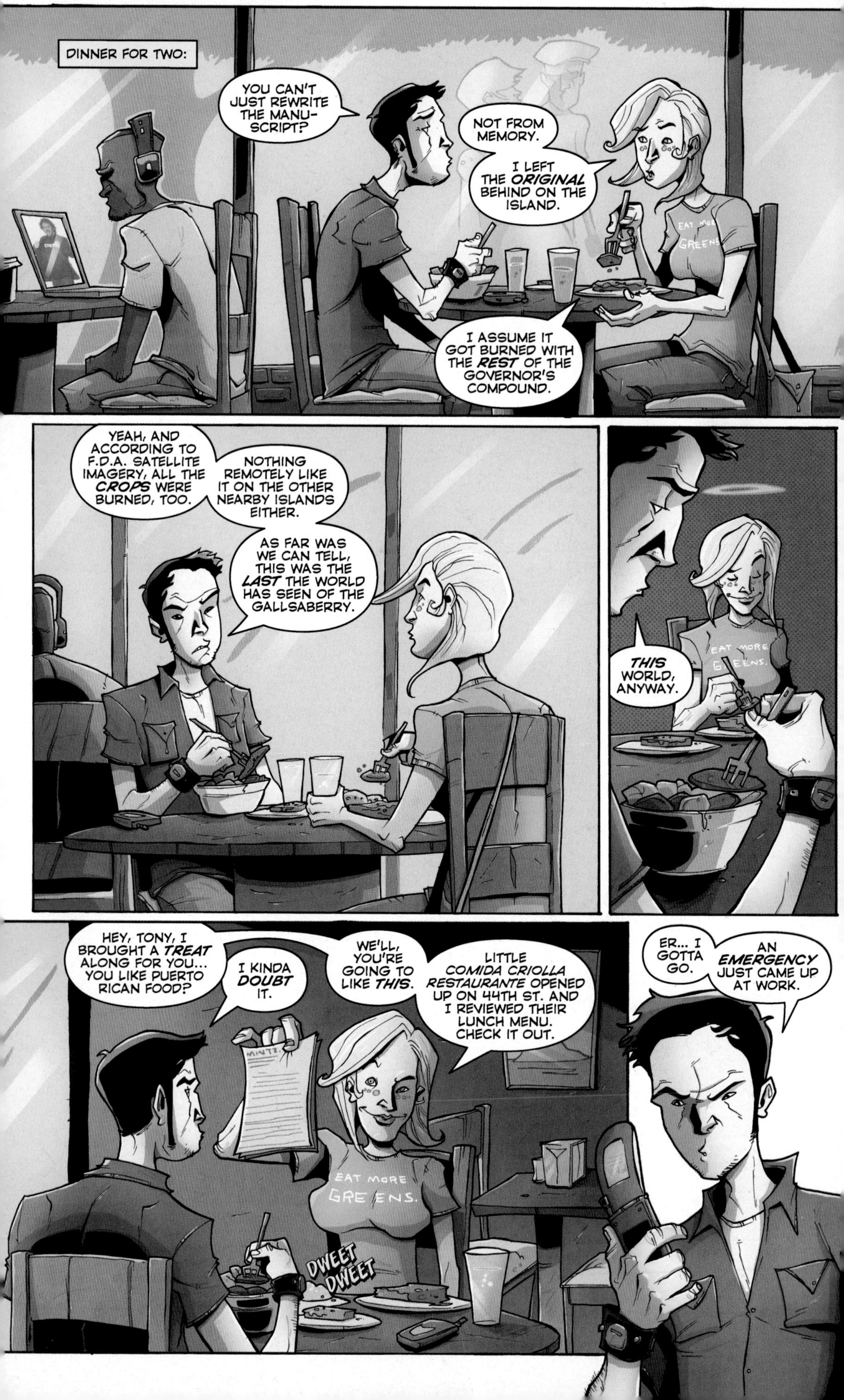
DINNER FOR TWO:
YOU CAN'T JUST REWRITE THE MANU-SCRIPT?
NOT FROM MEMORY.
I LEFT THE ORIGINAL BEHIND ON THE ISLAND.
I ASSUME IT GOT BURNED WITH THE REST OF THE GOVERNOR'S COMPOUND.
YEAH, AND ACCORDING TO F.D.A. SATELLITE IMAGERY, ALL THE CROPS WERE BURNED, TOO.
NOTHING REMOTELY LIKE IT ON THE OTHER NEARBY ISLANDS EITHER.
AS FAR WAS WE CAN TELL, THIS WAS THE LAST THE WORLD HAS SEEN OF THE GALLSABERRY.
THIS WORLD, ANYWAY.
HEY, TONY, I BROUGHT A TREAT ALONG FOR YOU... YOU LIKE PUERTO RICAN FOOD?
I KINDA DOUBT IT.
WE'LL, YOU'RE GOING TO LIKE THIS.
LITTLE COMIDA CRIOLLA RESTAURANTE OPENED UP ON 44TH ST. AND I REVIEWED THEIR LUNCH MENU. CHECK IT OUT.
DWEET DWEET
ER... I GOTTA GO.
AN EMERGENCY JUST CAME UP AT WORK.

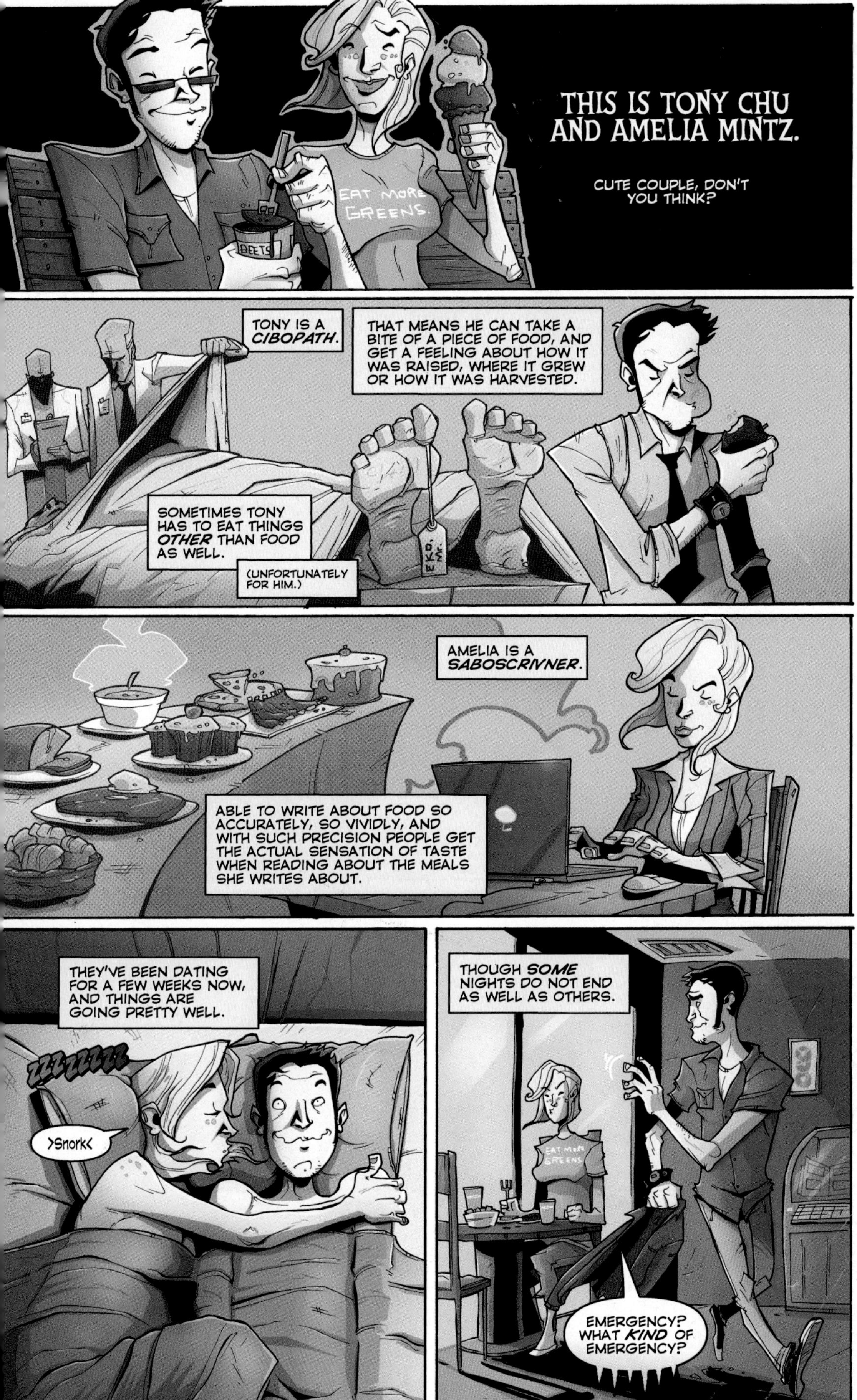

THIS IS TONY CHU AND AMELIA MINTZ.
CUTE COUPLE, DON'T YOU THINK?
BEETS
EAT MORE GREENS.
TONY IS A *CIBOPATH*.
THAT MEANS HE CAN TAKE A BITE OF A PIECE OF FOOD, AND GET A FEELING ABOUT HOW IT WAS RAISED, WHERE IT GREW OR HOW IT WAS HARVESTED.
SOMETIMES TONY HAS TO EAT THINGS *OTHER* THAN FOOD AS WELL.
(UNFORTUNATELY FOR HIM.)
AMELIA IS A *SABOSCRIVNER*.
ABLE TO WRITE ABOUT FOOD SO ACCURATELY, SO VIVIDLY, AND WITH SUCH PRECISION PEOPLE GET THE ACTUAL SENSATION OF TASTE WHEN READING ABOUT THE MEALS SHE WRITES ABOUT.
THEY'VE BEEN DATING FOR A FEW WEEKS NOW, AND THINGS ARE GOING PRETTY WELL.
ZZZZZZZ
>Snork<
THOUGH *SOME* NIGHTS DO NOT END AS WELL AS OTHERS.
EAT MORE GREENS
EMERGENCY? WHAT *KIND* OF EMERGENCY?

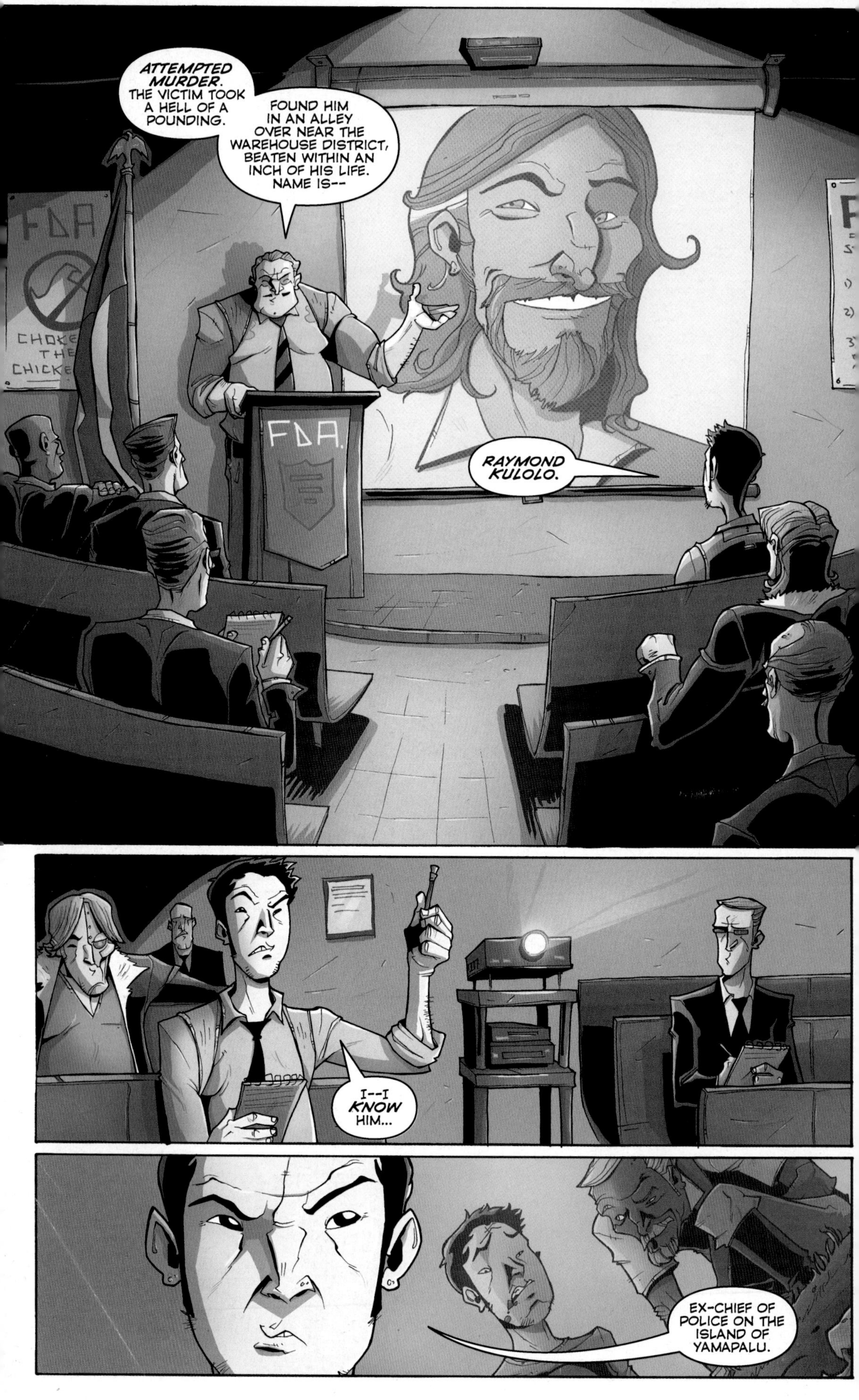
ATTEMPTED MURDER. THE VICTIM TOOK A HELL OF A POUNDING.
FOUND HIM IN AN ALLEY OVER NEAR THE WAREHOUSE DISTRICT, BEATEN WITHIN AN INCH OF HIS LIFE. NAME IS--
FDA
CHOKE THE CHICKE
F.D.A.
RAYMOND KULOLO.
I--I KNOW HIM...
EX-CHIEF OF POLICE ON THE ISLAND OF YAMAPALU.

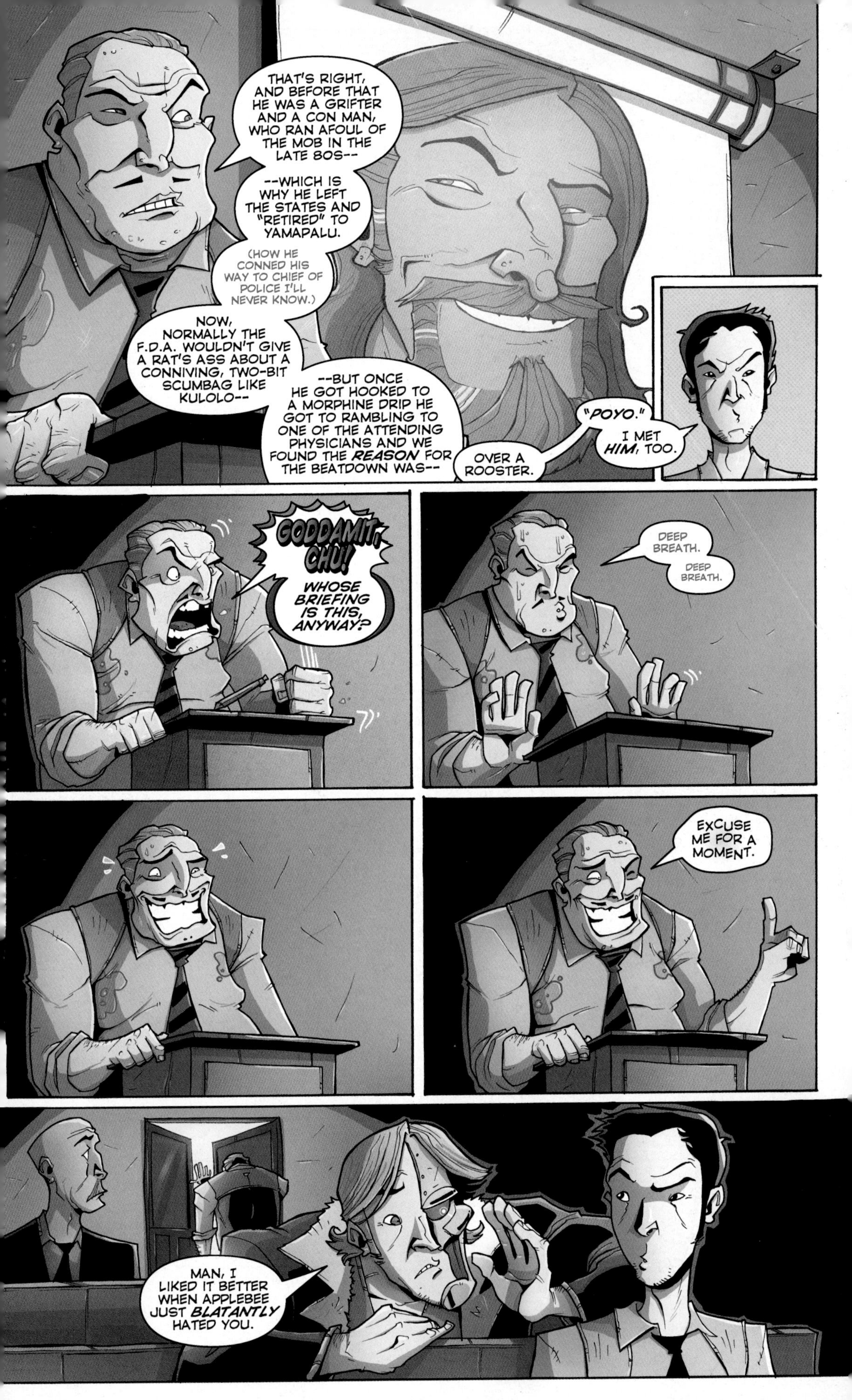

THAT'S RIGHT, AND BEFORE THAT HE WAS A GRIFTER AND A CON MAN, WHO RAN AFOUL OF THE MOB IN THE LATE 80S--
--WHICH IS WHY HE LEFT THE STATES AND "RETIRED" TO YAMAPALU.
(HOW HE CONNED HIS WAY TO CHIEF OF POLICE I'LL NEVER KNOW.)
NOW, NORMALLY THE F.D.A. WOULDN'T GIVE A RAT'S ASS ABOUT A CONNIVING, TWO-BIT SCUMBAG LIKE KULOLO--
--BUT ONCE HE GOT HOOKED TO A MORPHINE DRIP HE GOT TO RAMBLING TO ONE OF THE ATTENDING PHYSICIANS AND WE FOUND THE *REASON* FOR THE BEATDOWN WAS--
OVER A ROOSTER.
"*POYO.*"
I MET *HIM*, TOO.
GODDAMIT, CHU!
WHOSE BRIEFING IS THIS, ANYWAY?
DEEP BREATH.
DEEP BREATH.
EXCUSE ME FOR A MOMENT.
MAN, I LIKED IT BETTER WHEN APPLEBEE JUST *BLATANTLY* HATED YOU.

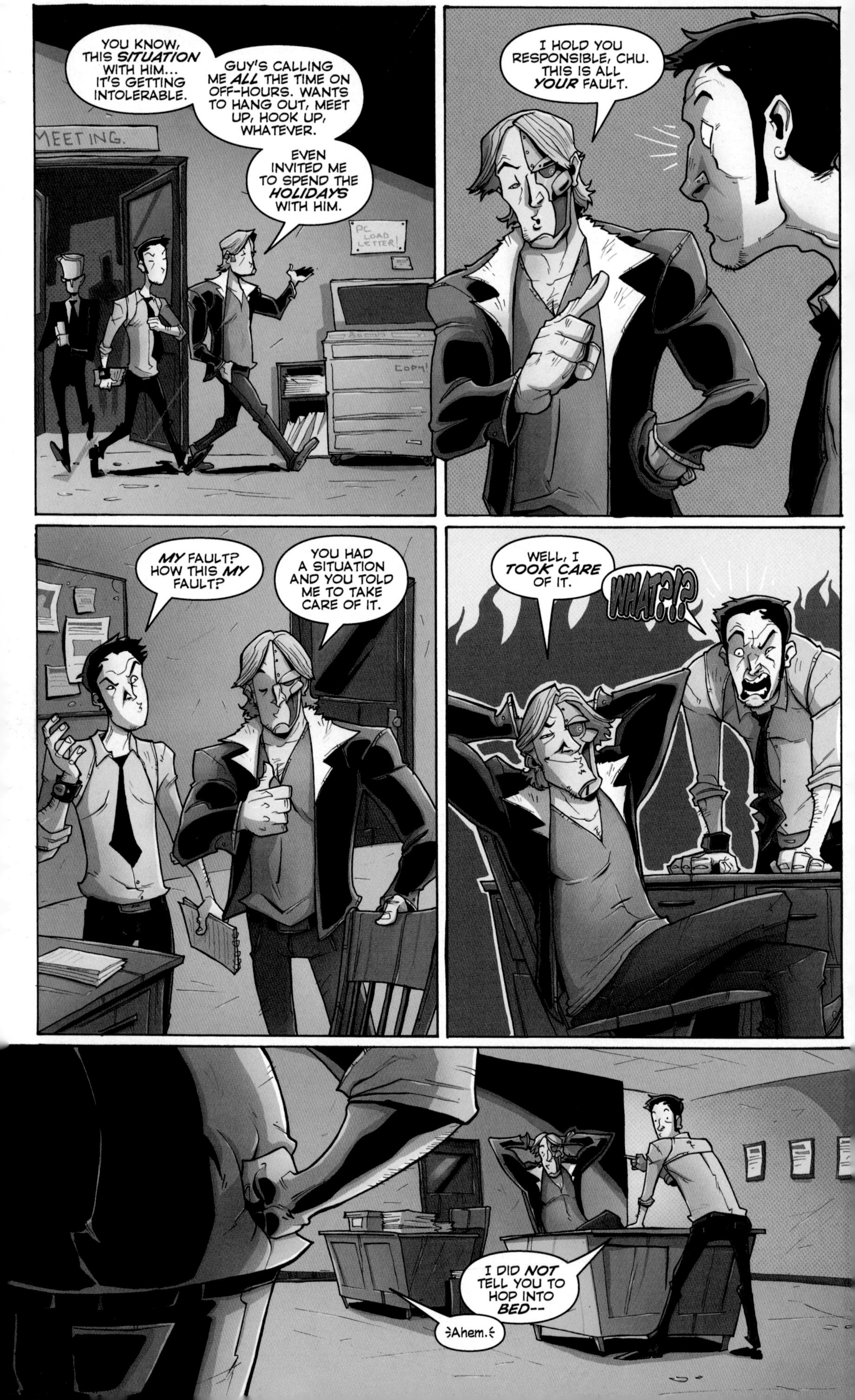
MEETING.
YOU KNOW, THIS SITUATION WITH HIM... IT'S GETTING INTOLERABLE.
GUY'S CALLING ME ALL THE TIME ON OFF-HOURS. WANTS TO HANG OUT, MEET UP, HOOK UP, WHATEVER.
EVEN INVITED ME TO SPEND THE HOLIDAYS WITH HIM.
PC LOAD LETTER!
COPY!
I HOLD YOU RESPONSIBLE, CHU. THIS IS ALL YOUR FAULT.
MY FAULT? HOW THIS MY FAULT?
YOU HAD A SITUATION AND YOU TOLD ME TO TAKE CARE OF IT.
WELL, I TOOK CARE OF IT.
WHAT?!?
I DID NOT TELL YOU TO HOP INTO BED--
Ahem.

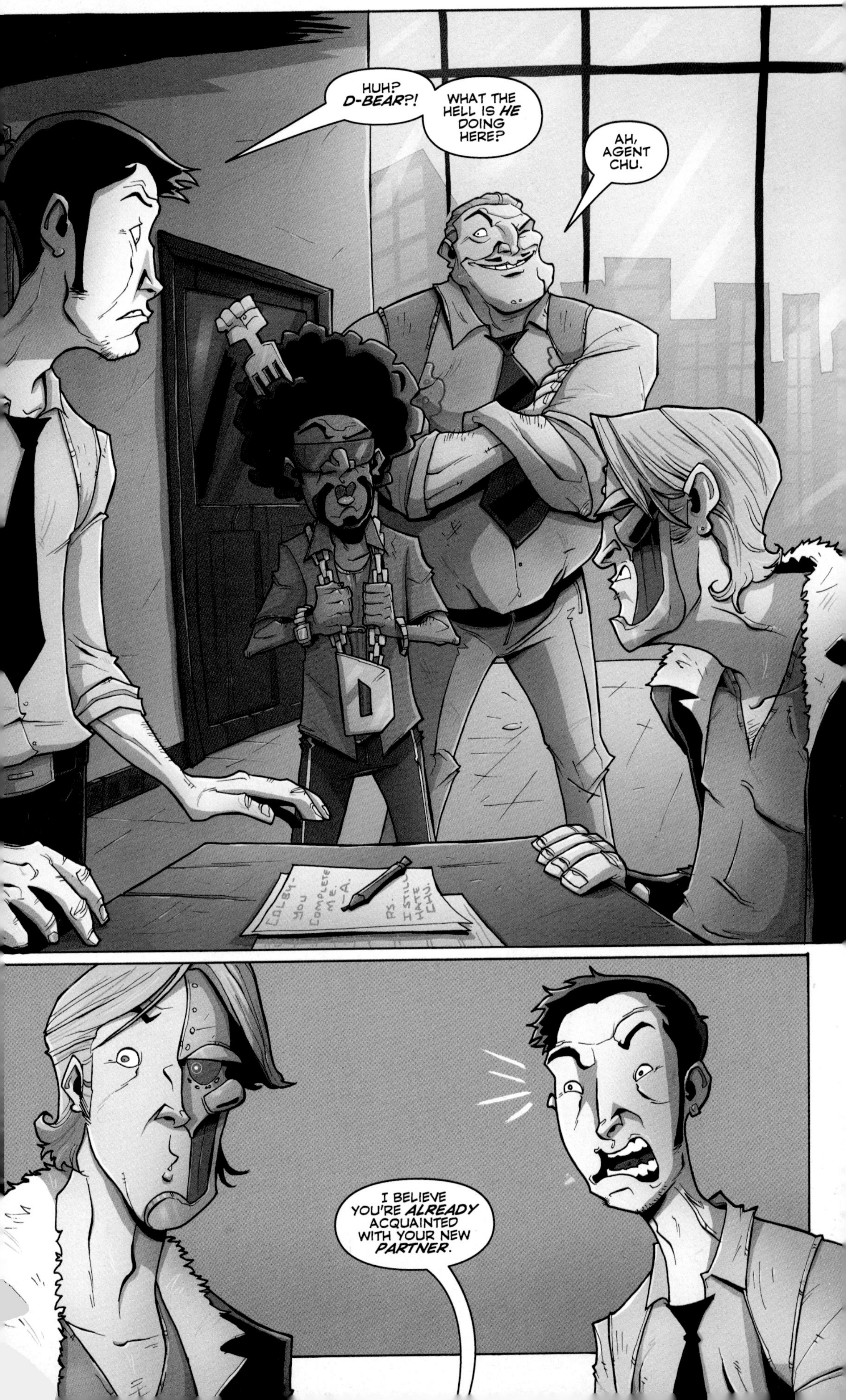
HUH? D-BEAR?!
WHAT THE HELL IS HE DOING HERE?
AH, AGENT CHU.
COLBY- YOU COMPLETE ME. —A.
P.S. I STILL HATE CHU.
I BELIEVE YOU'RE ALREADY ACQUAINTED WITH YOUR NEW PARTNER.

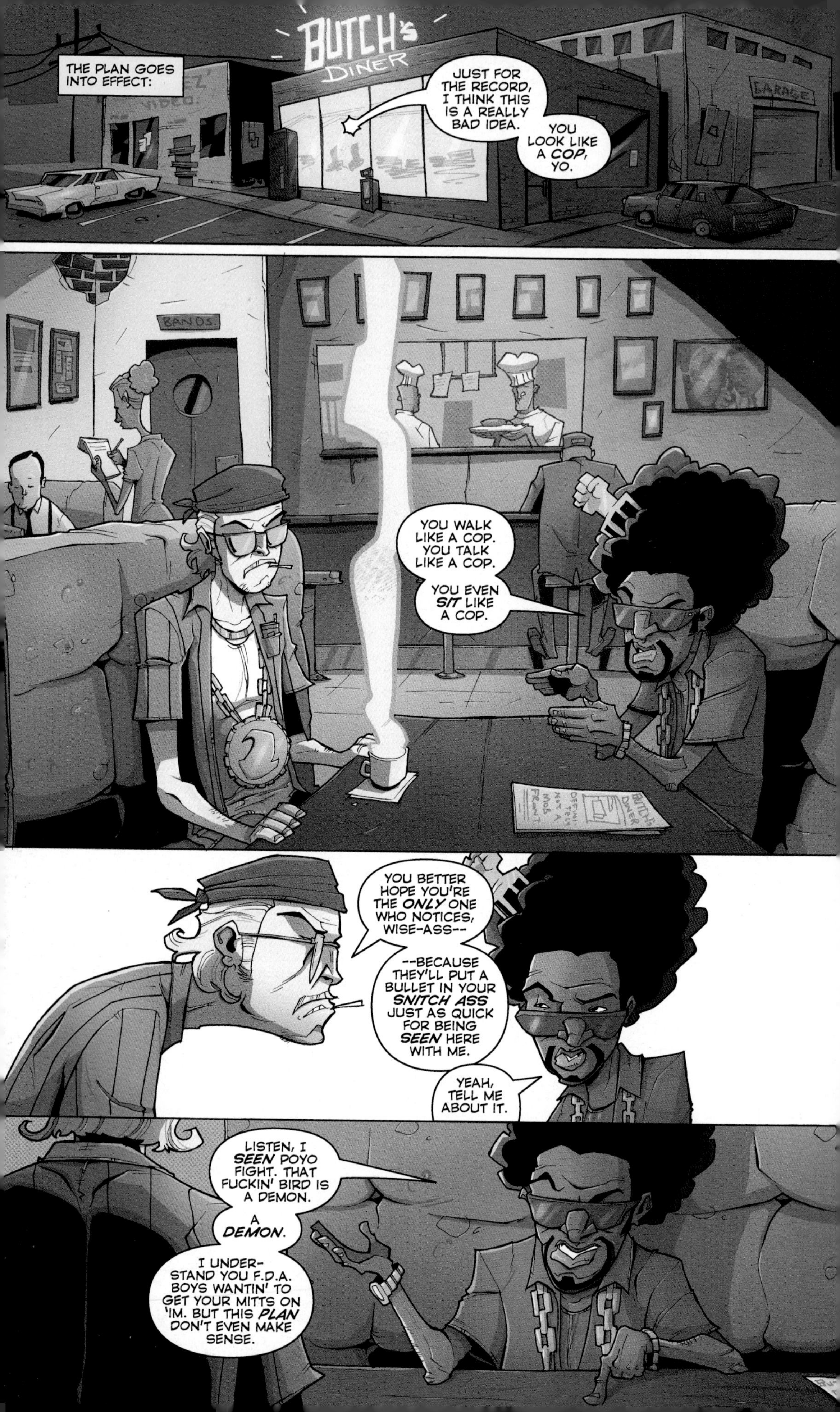
BUTCH'S DINER
THE PLAN GOES INTO EFFECT:
GARAGE
JUST FOR THE RECORD, I THINK THIS IS A REALLY BAD IDEA.
YOU LOOK LIKE A COP, YO.
BAND.S.
YOU WALK LIKE A COP. YOU TALK LIKE A COP.
YOU EVEN SIT LIKE A COP.
BUTCH'S DINER
DEFINITELY NOT A MOB FRONT.
YOU BETTER HOPE YOU'RE THE ONLY ONE WHO NOTICES, WISE-ASS--
--BECAUSE THEY'LL PUT A BULLET IN YOUR SNITCH ASS JUST AS QUICK FOR BEING SEEN HERE WITH ME.
YEAH, TELL ME ABOUT IT.
LISTEN, I SEEN POYO FIGHT. THAT FUCKIN' BIRD IS A DEMON.
A DEMON.
I UNDER-STAND YOU F.D.A. BOYS WANTIN' TO GET YOUR MITTS ON 'IM. BUT THIS PLAN DON'T EVEN MAKE SENSE.

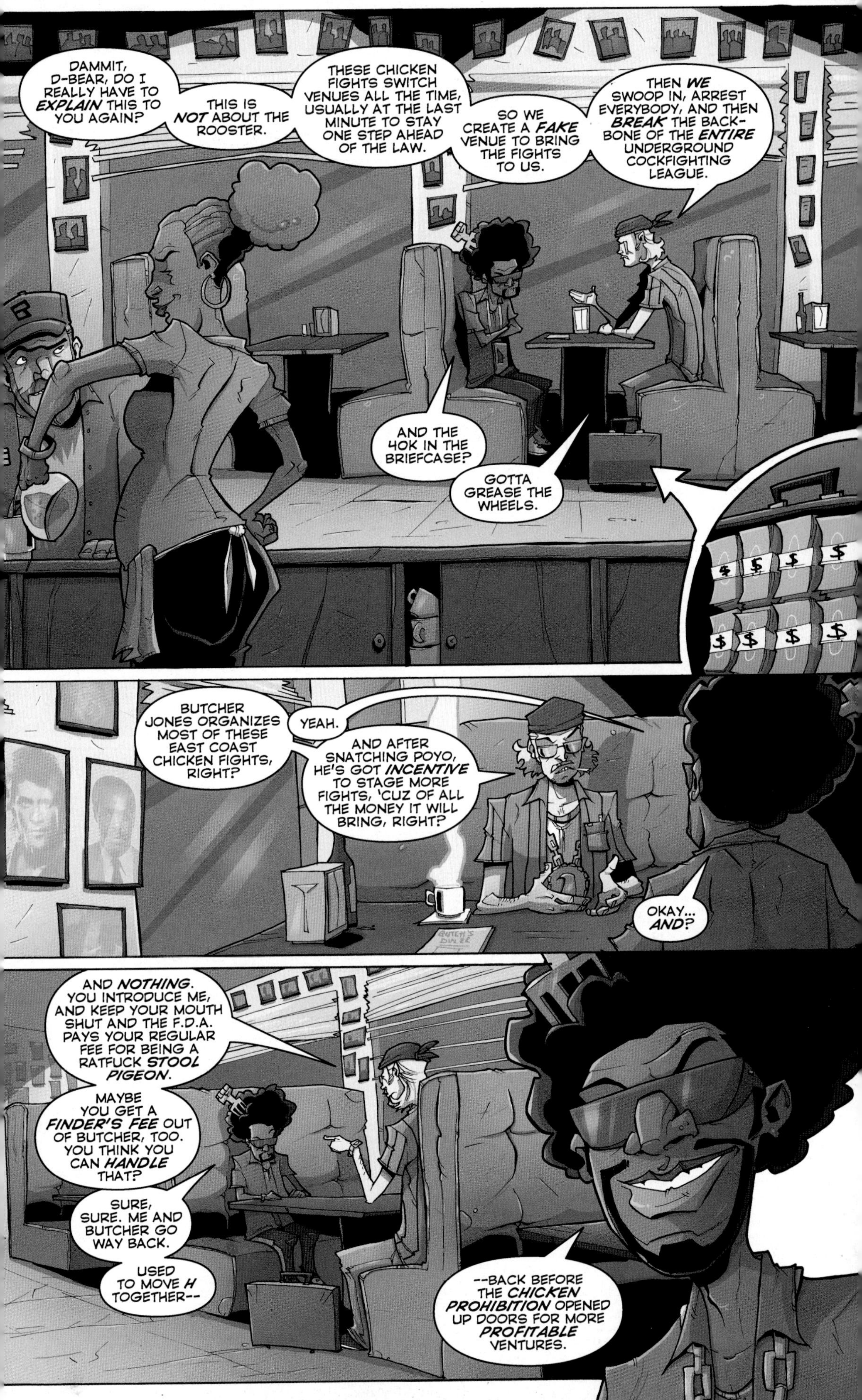
DAMMIT, D-BEAR, DO I REALLY HAVE TO EXPLAIN THIS TO YOU AGAIN?
THIS IS NOT ABOUT THE ROOSTER.
THESE CHICKEN FIGHTS SWITCH VENUES ALL THE TIME, USUALLY AT THE LAST MINUTE TO STAY ONE STEP AHEAD OF THE LAW.
SO WE CREATE A FAKE VENUE TO BRING THE FIGHTS TO US.
THEN WE SWOOP IN, ARREST EVERYBODY, AND THEN BREAK THE BACK-BONE OF THE ENTIRE UNDERGROUND COCKFIGHTING LEAGUE.
AND THE 40K IN THE BRIEFCASE?
GOTTA GREASE THE WHEELS.
BUTCHER JONES ORGANIZES MOST OF THESE EAST COAST CHICKEN FIGHTS, RIGHT?
YEAH.
AND AFTER SNATCHING POYO, HE'S GOT INCENTIVE TO STAGE MORE FIGHTS, 'CUZ OF ALL THE MONEY IT WILL BRING, RIGHT?
OKAY... AND?
BUTCH'S DINER
AND NOTHING. YOU INTRODUCE ME, AND KEEP YOUR MOUTH SHUT AND THE F.D.A. PAYS YOUR REGULAR FEE FOR BEING A RATFUCK STOOL PIGEON.
MAYBE YOU GET A FINDER'S FEE OUT OF BUTCHER, TOO. YOU THINK YOU CAN HANDLE THAT?
SURE, SURE. ME AND BUTCHER GO WAY BACK.
USED TO MOVE H TOGETHER--
--BACK BEFORE THE CHICKEN PROHIBITION OPENED UP DOORS FOR MORE PROFITABLE VENTURES.

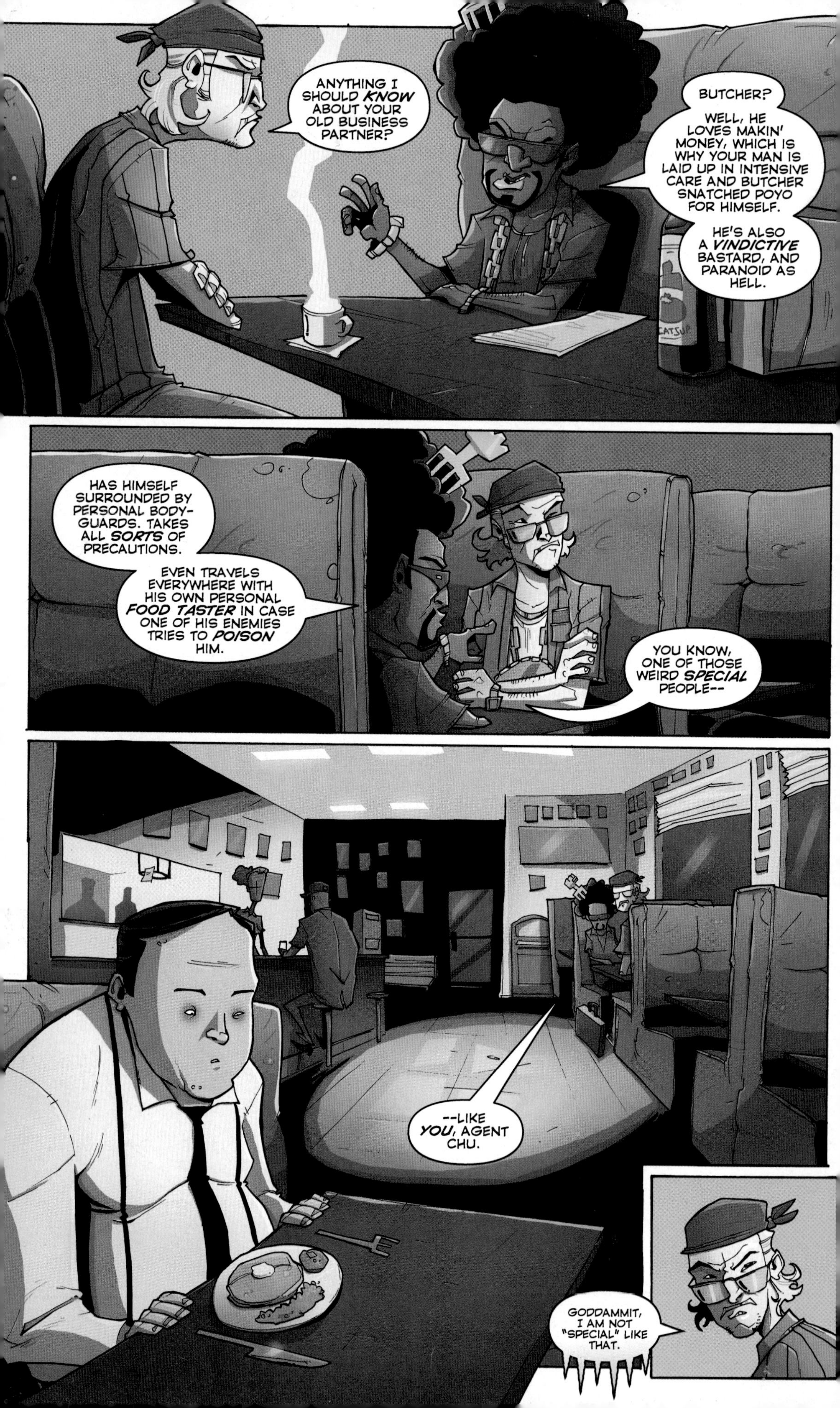
ANYTHING I SHOULD KNOW ABOUT YOUR OLD BUSINESS PARTNER?
BUTCHER?
WELL, HE LOVES MAKIN' MONEY, WHICH IS WHY YOUR MAN IS LAID UP IN INTENSIVE CARE AND BUTCHER SNATCHED POYO FOR HIMSELF.
HE'S ALSO A VINDICTIVE BASTARD, AND PARANOID AS HELL.
CATSUP
HAS HIMSELF SURROUNDED BY PERSONAL BODY-GUARDS. TAKES ALL SORTS OF PRECAUTIONS.
EVEN TRAVELS EVERYWHERE WITH HIS OWN PERSONAL FOOD TASTER IN CASE ONE OF HIS ENEMIES TRIES TO POISON HIM.
YOU KNOW, ONE OF THOSE WEIRD SPECIAL PEOPLE--
--LIKE YOU, AGENT CHU.
GODDAMMIT, I AM NOT "SPECIAL" LIKE THAT.

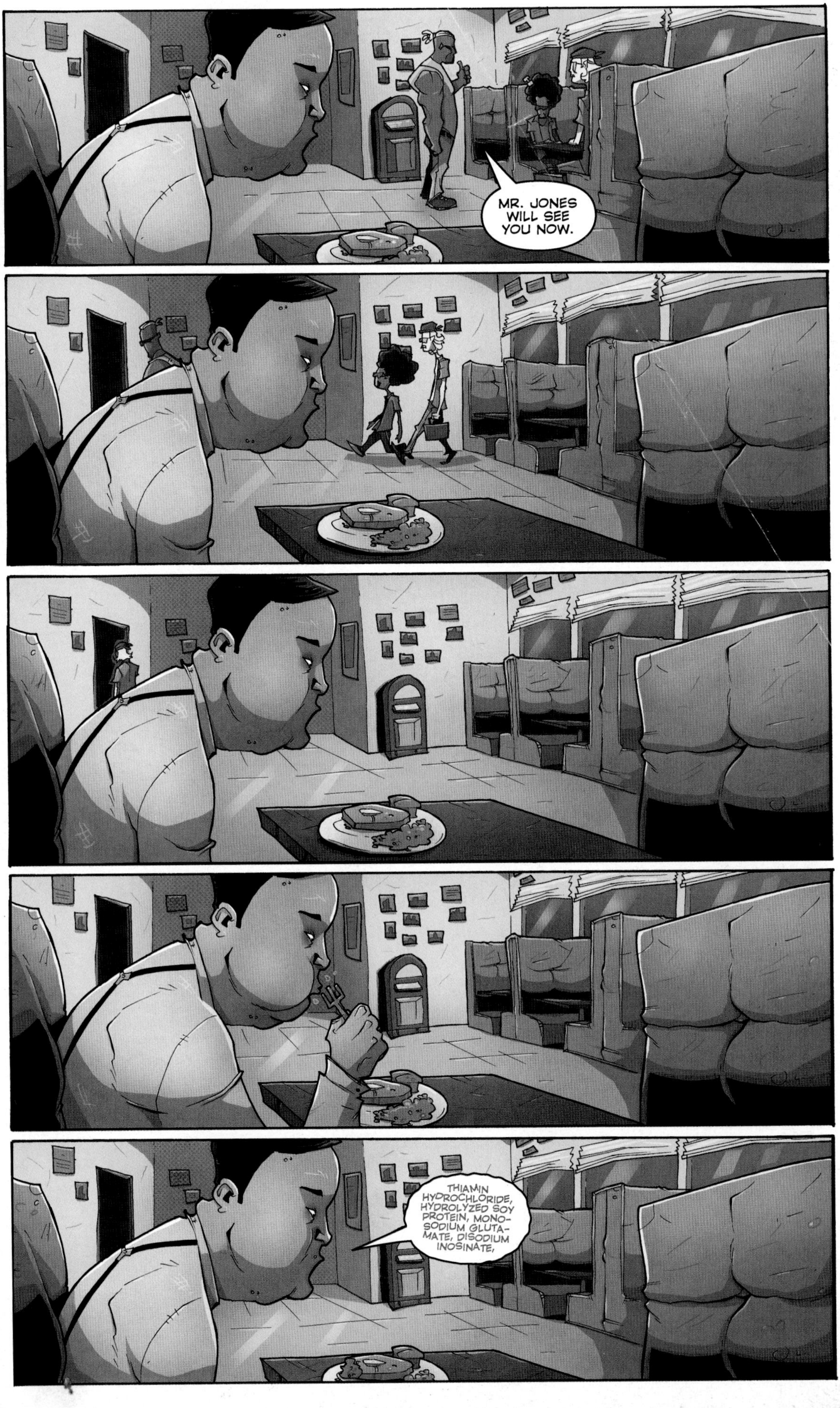
MR. JONES WILL SEE YOU NOW.
THIAMIN HYDROCHLORIDE, HYDROLYZED SOY PROTEIN, MONO-SODIUM GLUTA-MATE, DISODIUM INOSINATE,

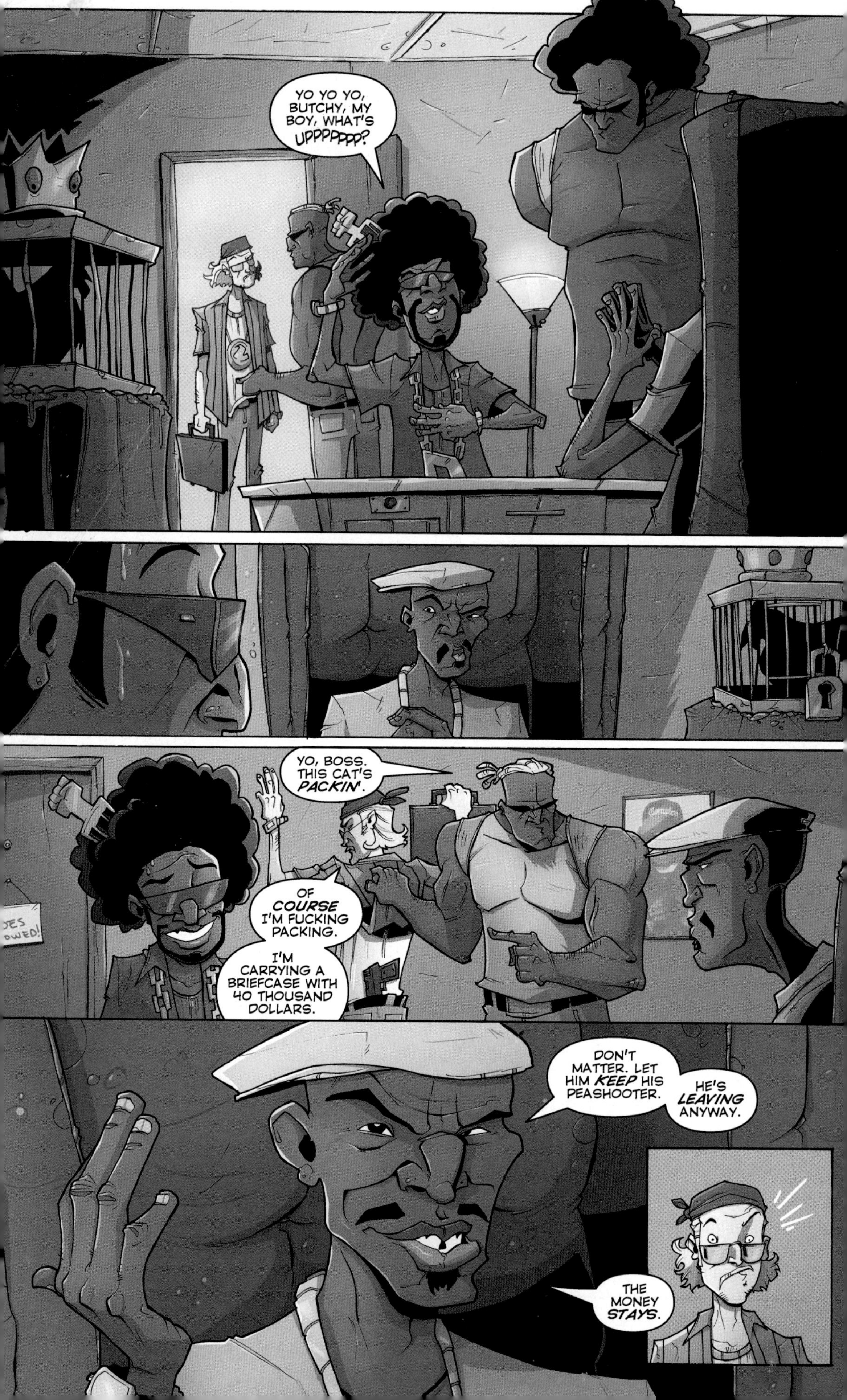
YO YO YO, BUTCHY, MY BOY, WHAT'S UPPPPPPP?
YO, BOSS. THIS CAT'S PACKIN'.
OF COURSE I'M FUCKING PACKING.
I'M CARRYING A BRIEFCASE WITH 40 THOUSAND DOLLARS.
DON'T MATTER. LET HIM KEEP HIS PEASHOOTER.
HE'S LEAVING ANYWAY.
THE MONEY STAYS.

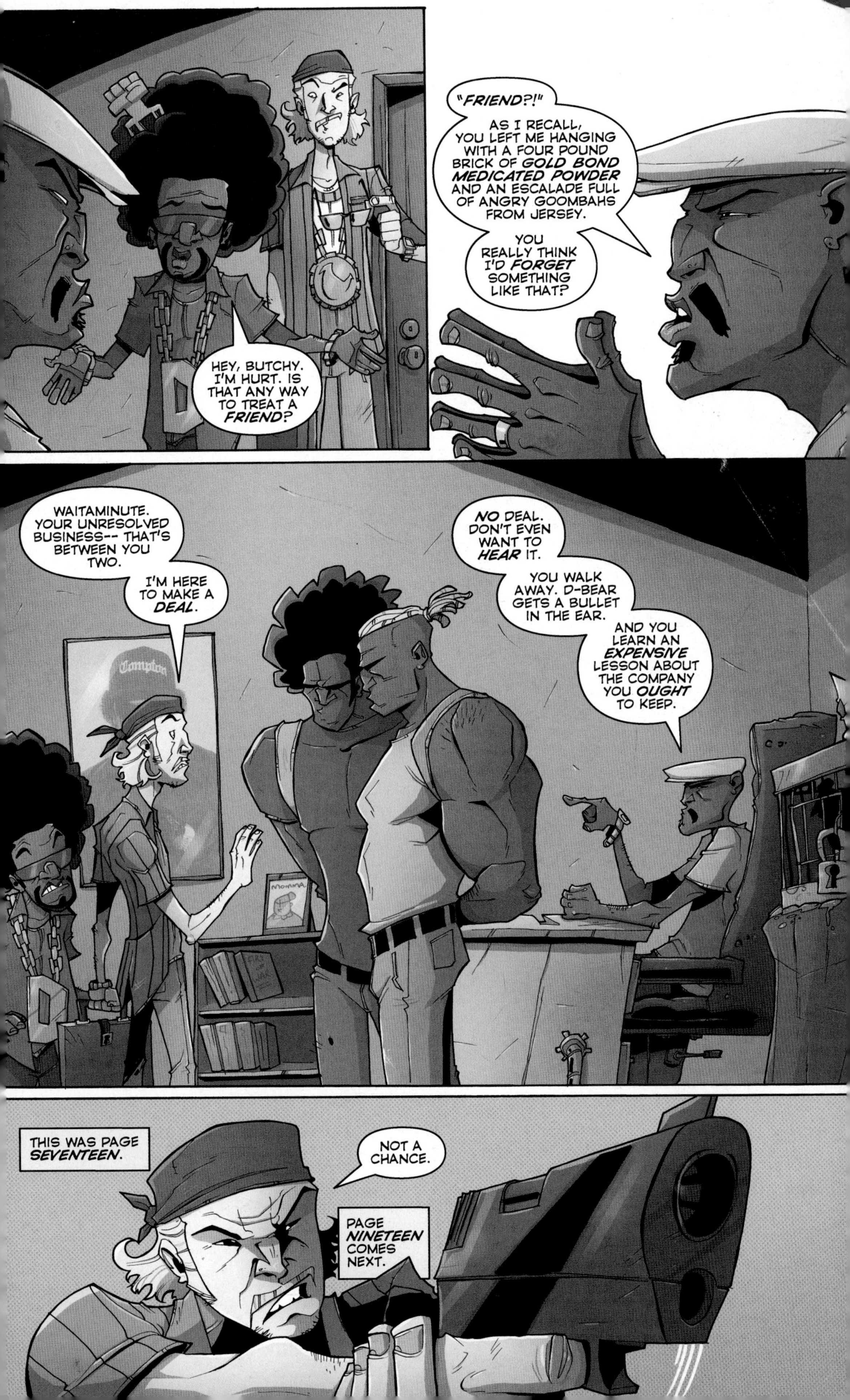
HEY, BUTCHY. I'M HURT. IS THAT ANY WAY TO TREAT A FRIEND?
"FRIEND?!" AS I RECALL, YOU LEFT ME HANGING WITH A FOUR POUND BRICK OF GOLD BOND MEDICATED POWDER AND AN ESCALADE FULL OF ANGRY GOOMBAHS FROM JERSEY.
YOU REALLY THINK I'D FORGET SOMETHING LIKE THAT?
WAITAMINUTE. YOUR UNRESOLVED BUSINESS-- THAT'S BETWEEN YOU TWO.
I'M HERE TO MAKE A DEAL.
NO DEAL. DON'T EVEN WANT TO HEAR IT.
YOU WALK AWAY. D-BEAR GETS A BULLET IN THE EAR.
AND YOU LEARN AN EXPENSIVE LESSON ABOUT THE COMPANY YOU OUGHT TO KEEP.
Compton
MOMMA
THIS WAS PAGE SEVENTEEN.
NOT A CHANCE.
PAGE NINETEEN COMES NEXT.

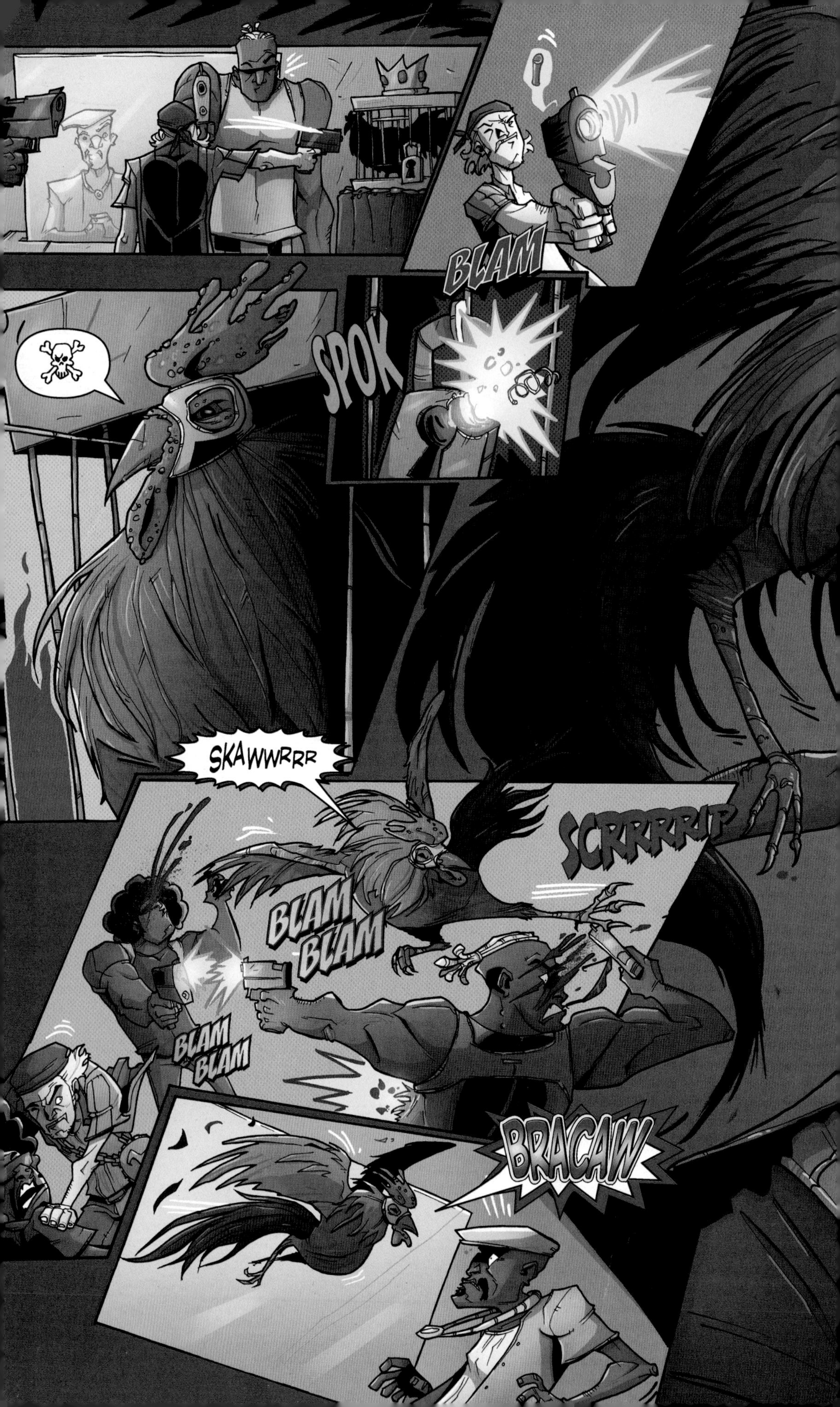
BLAM
SPOK
SKAWWRRR
SCRRRRIP
BLAM BLAM
BLAM BLAM
BRACAW

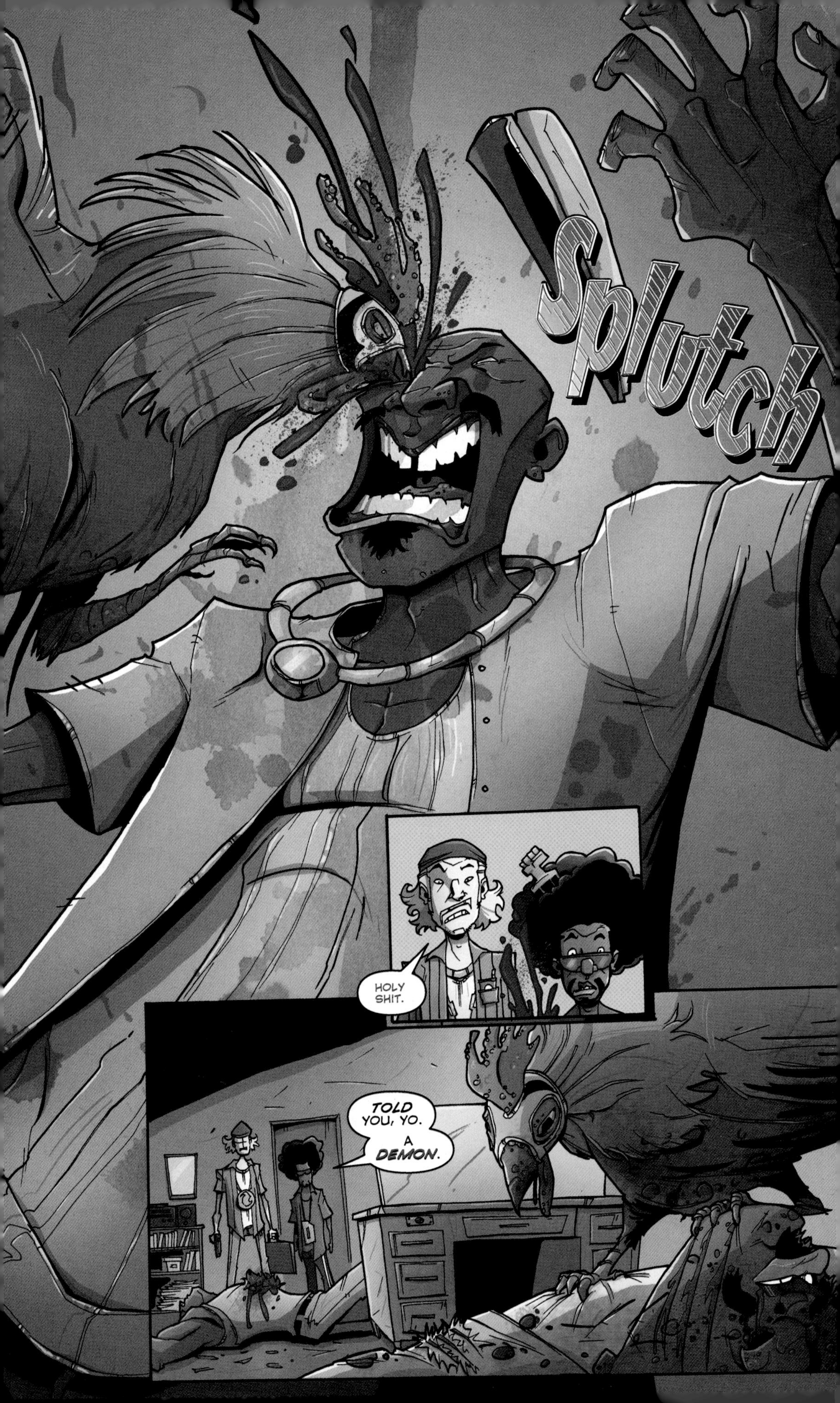
SPLUTCH
HOLY SHIT.
TOLD YOU, YO. A DEMON.

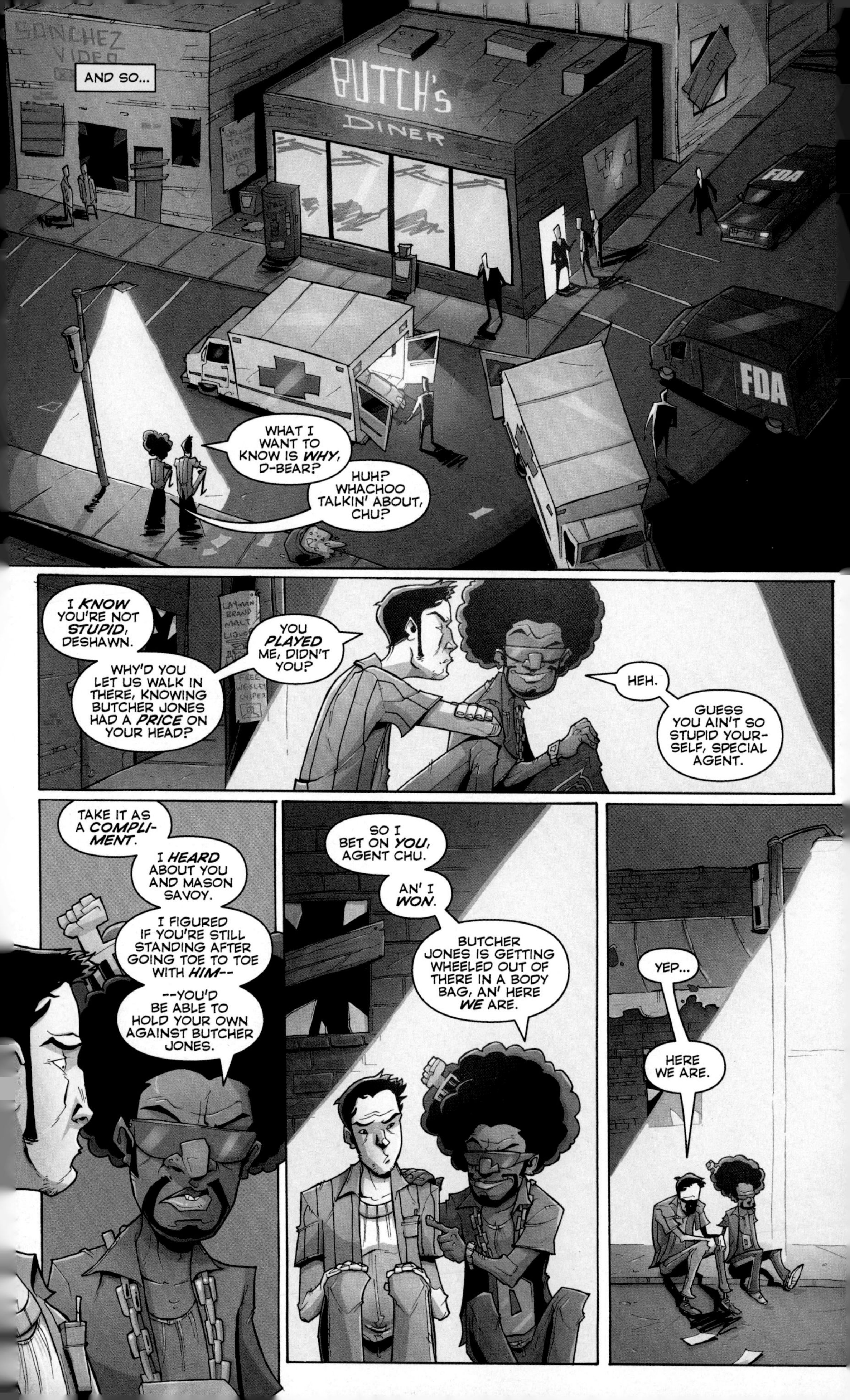
SANCHEZ VIDEO
AND SO...
BUTCH's
DINER
FDA
FDA
WHAT I WANT TO KNOW IS *WHY*, D-BEAR?
HUH? WHACHOO TALKIN' ABOUT, CHU?
I *KNOW* YOU'RE NOT *STUPID*, DESHAWN.
WHY'D YOU LET US WALK IN THERE, KNOWING BUTCHER JONES HAD A *PRICE* ON YOUR HEAD?
YOU *PLAYED* ME, DIDN'T YOU?
HEH.
GUESS YOU AIN'T SO STUPID YOUR-SELF, SPECIAL AGENT.
TAKE IT AS A *COMPLI-MENT*.
I *HEARD* ABOUT YOU AND MASON SAVOY.
I FIGURED IF YOU'RE STILL STANDING AFTER GOING TOE TO TOE WITH *HIM*--
--YOU'D BE ABLE TO HOLD YOUR OWN AGAINST BUTCHER JONES.
SO I BET ON *YOU*, AGENT CHU.
AN' I *WON*.
BUTCHER JONES IS GETTING WHEELED OUT OF THERE IN A BODY BAG, AN' HERE *WE* ARE.
YEP...
HERE WE ARE.

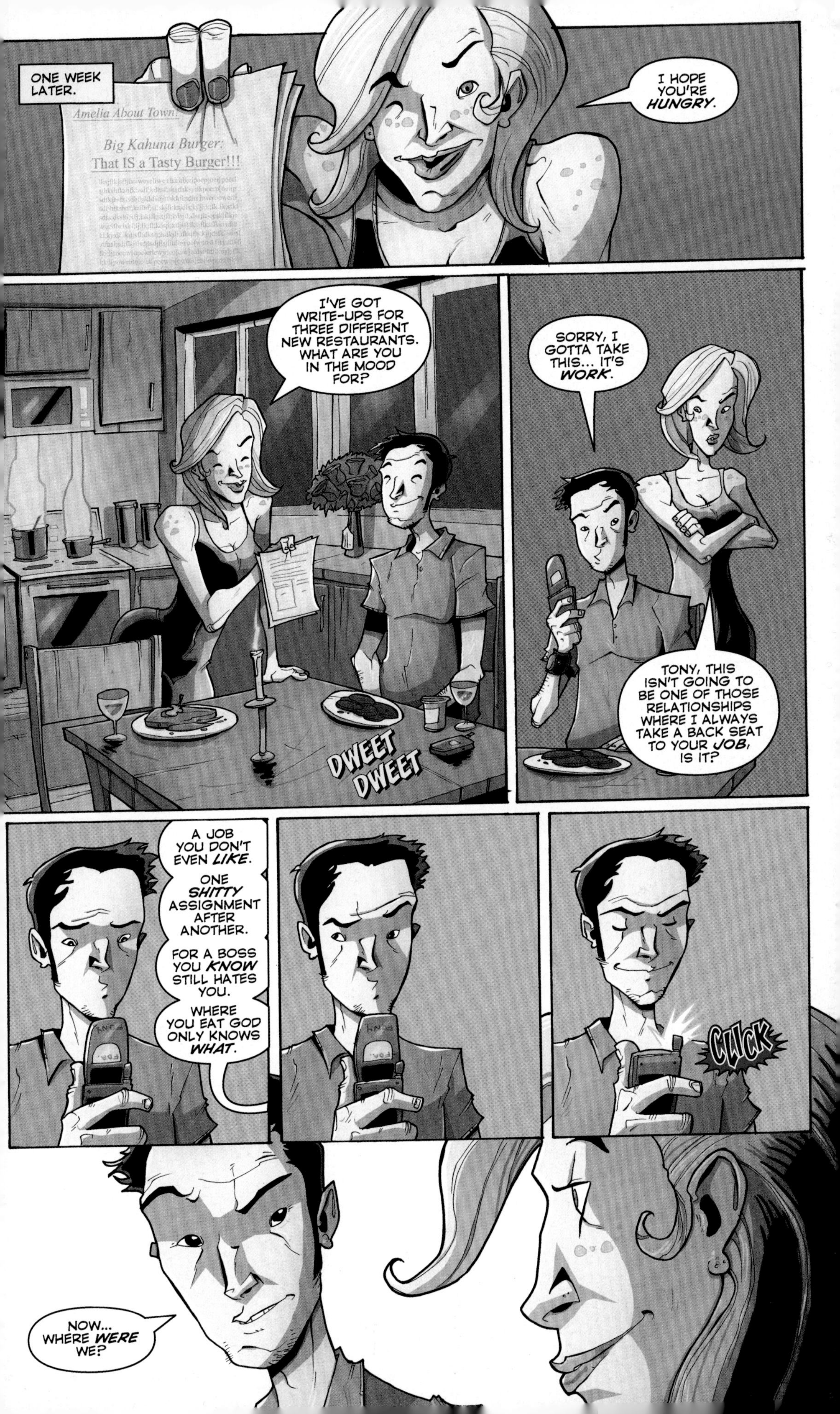

ONE WEEK LATER.
Amelia About Town!
Big Kahuna Burger:
That IS a Tasty Burger!!!
I HOPE YOU'RE *HUNGRY*.
I'VE GOT WRITE-UPS FOR THREE DIFFERENT NEW RESTAURANTS. WHAT ARE YOU IN THE MOOD FOR?
DWEET DWEET
SORRY, I GOTTA TAKE THIS... IT'S *WORK*.
TONY, THIS ISN'T GOING TO BE ONE OF THOSE RELATIONSHIPS WHERE I ALWAYS TAKE A BACK SEAT TO YOUR *JOB*, IS IT?
A JOB YOU DON'T EVEN *LIKE*.
ONE *SHITTY* ASSIGNMENT AFTER ANOTHER.
FOR A BOSS YOU *KNOW* STILL HATES YOU.
WHERE YOU EAT GOD ONLY KNOWS *WHAT*.
CLICK
NOW... WHERE *WERE* WE?

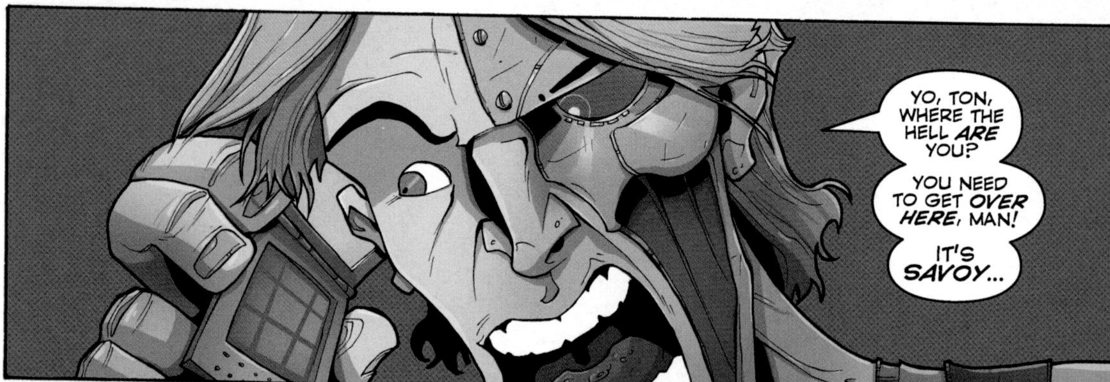
YO, TON, WHERE THE HELL *ARE* YOU?
YOU NEED TO GET *OVER HERE*, MAN!
IT'S *SAVOY*...

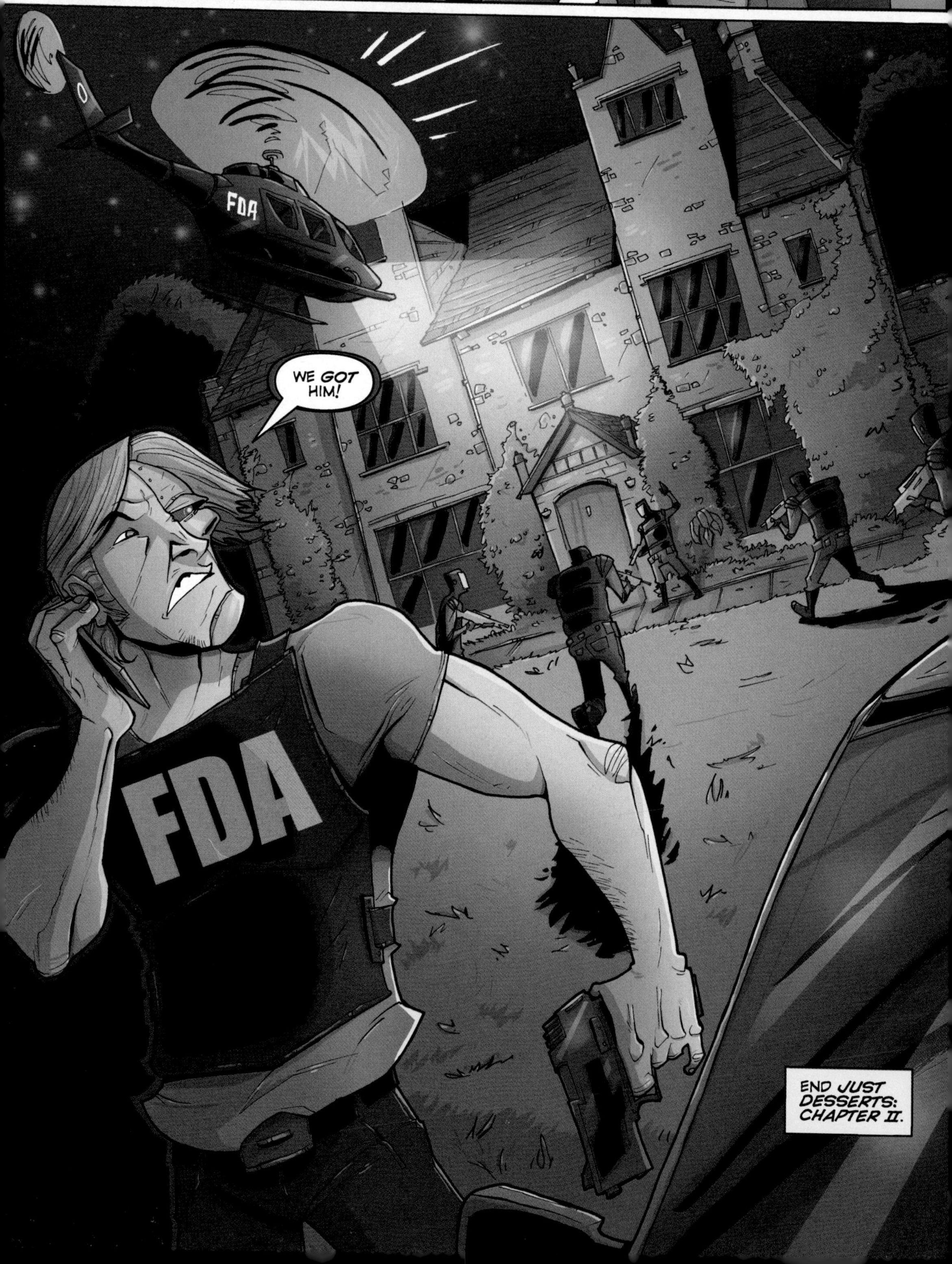
FDA
WE *GOT* HIM!
FDA
END *JUST DESSERTS: CHAPTER II*.

Chapter 3

CHEW presents
PULLET FICTION
THEY LIE.

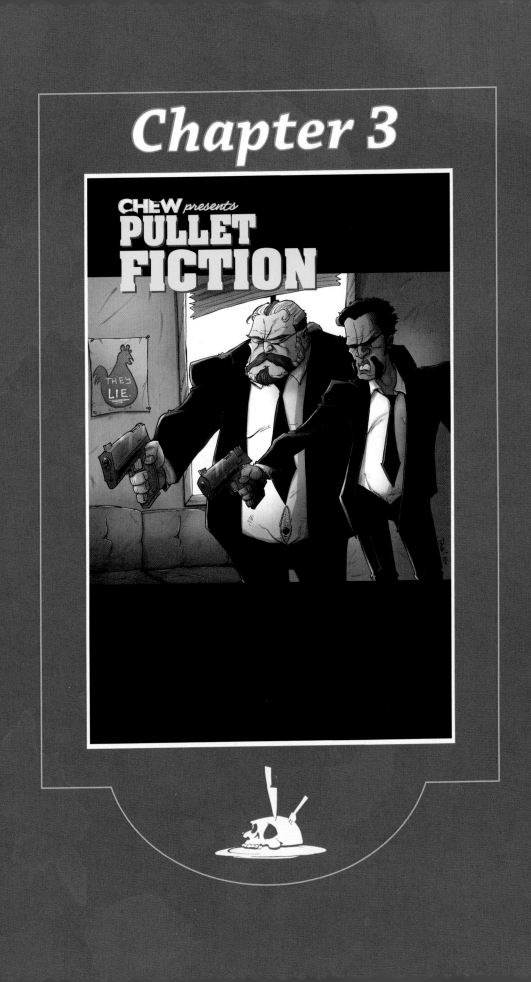

reservoir
chogs

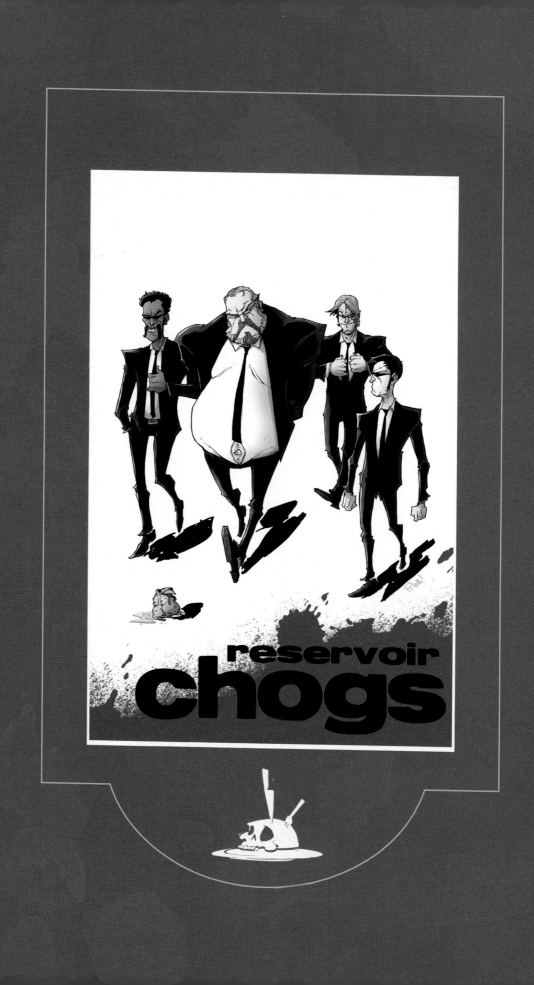

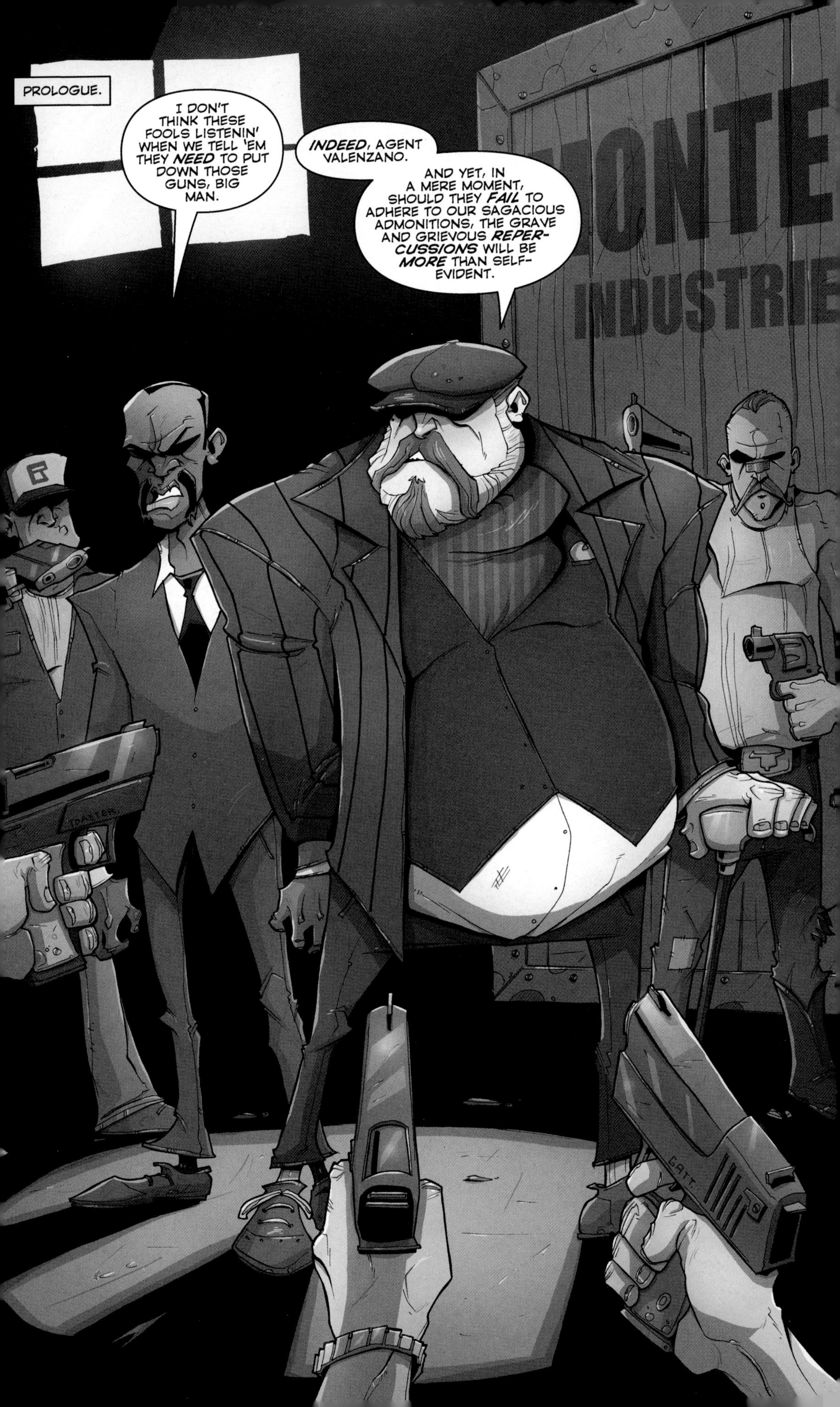
PROLOGUE.
I DON'T THINK THESE FOOLS LISTENIN' WHEN WE TELL 'EM THEY NEED TO PUT DOWN THOSE GUNS, BIG MAN.
INDEED, AGENT VALENZANO.
AND YET, IN A MERE MOMENT, SHOULD THEY FAIL TO ADHERE TO OUR SAGACIOUS ADMONITIONS, THE GRAVE AND GRIEVOUS REPERCUSSIONS WILL BE MORE THAN SELF-EVIDENT.
MONTE
INDUSTRIE

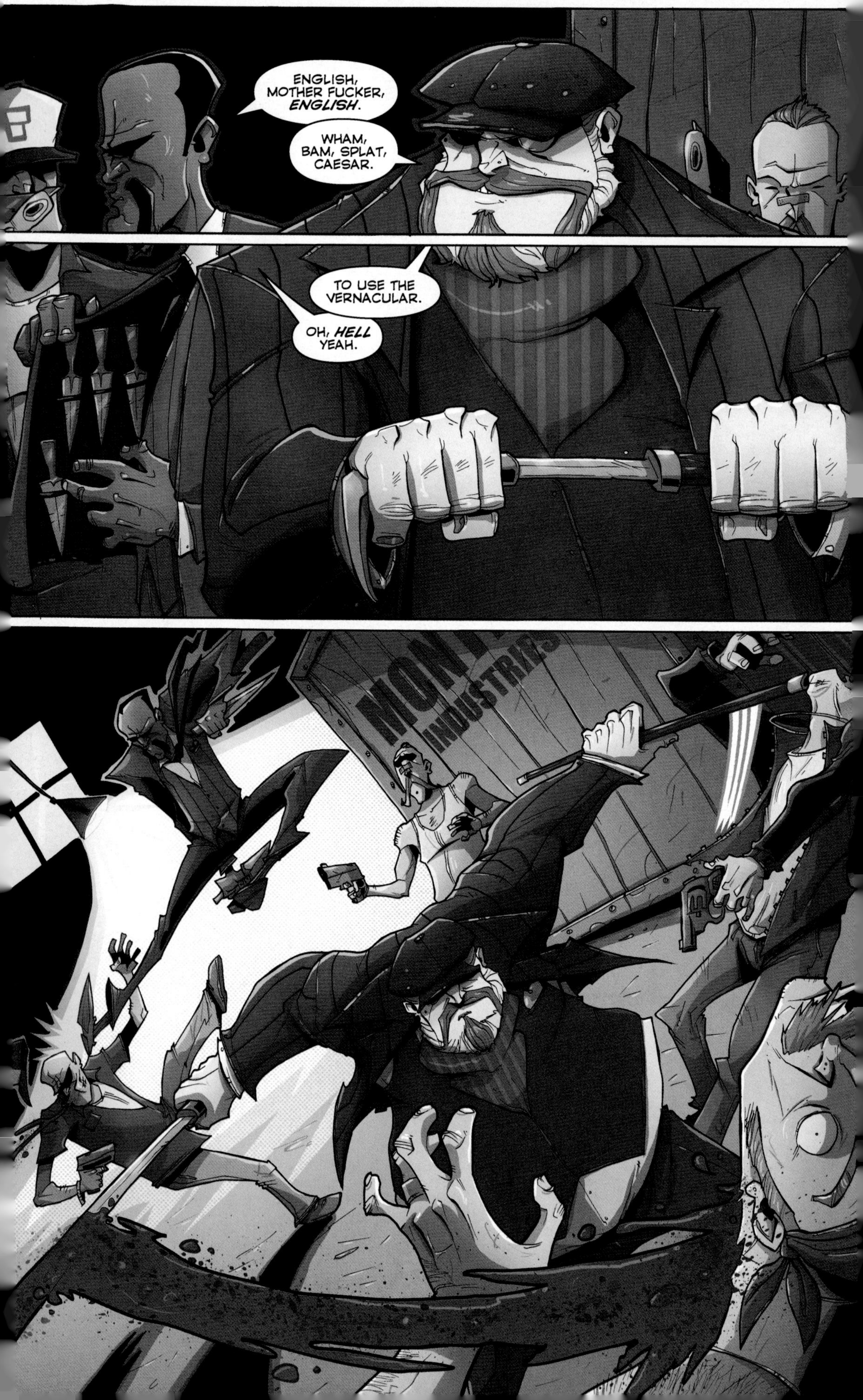
ENGLISH, MOTHER FUCKER, ENGLISH.
WHAM, BAM, SPLAT, CAESAR.
TO USE THE VERNACULAR.
OH, HELL YEAH.

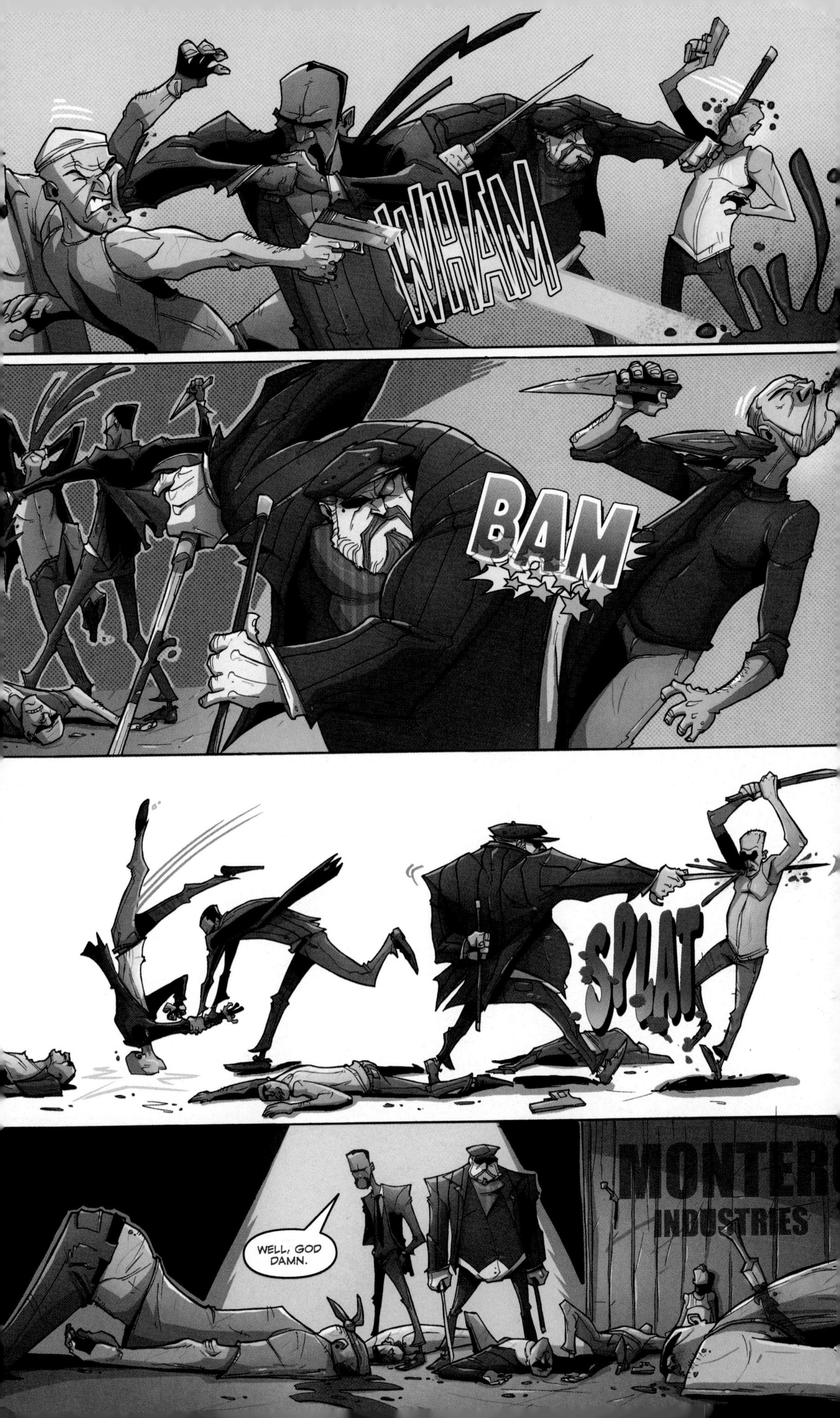
WHAM
BAM
SPLAT
MONTER
INDUSTRIES
WELL, GOD DAMN.

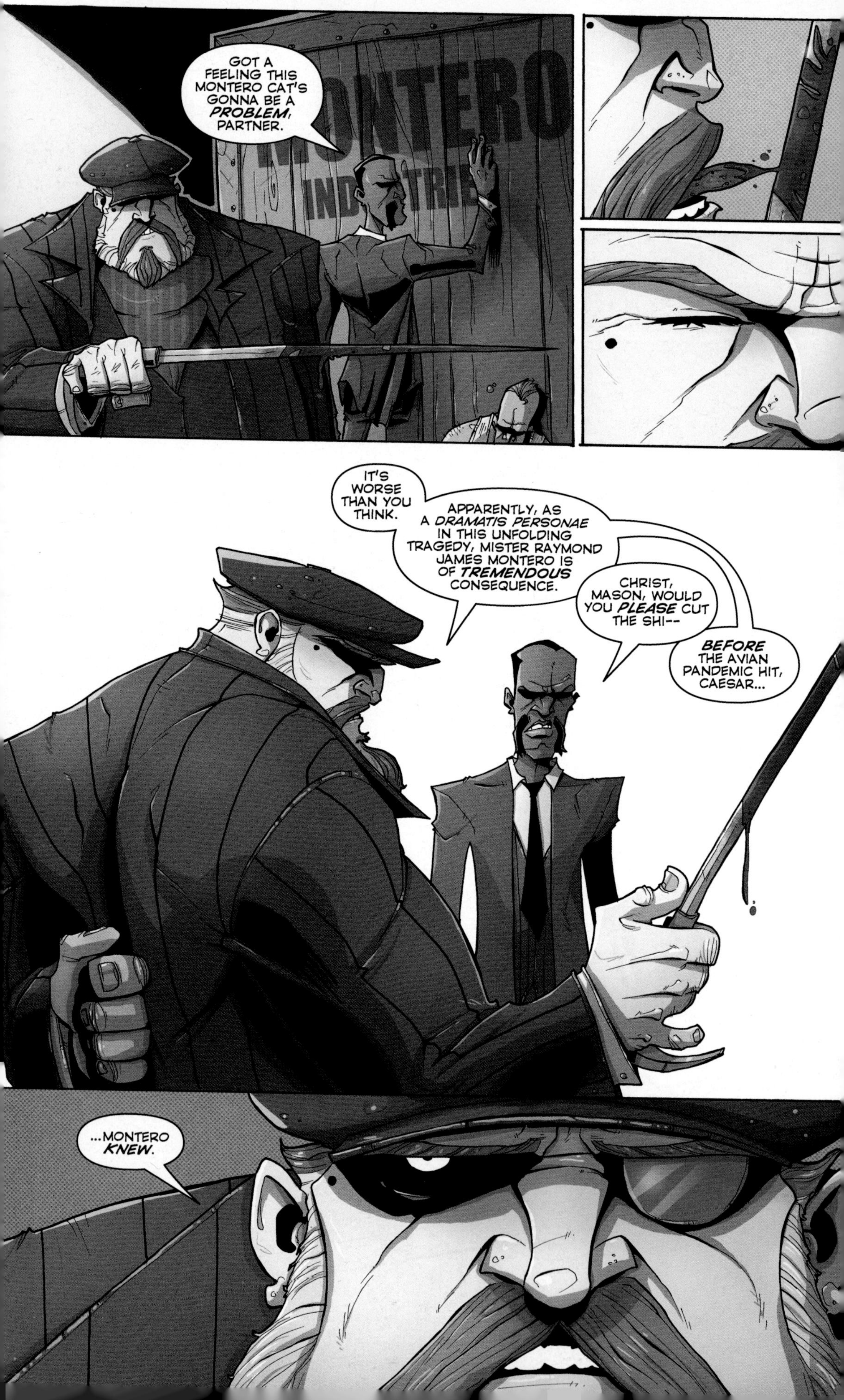
GOT A FEELING THIS MONTERO CAT'S GONNA BE A *PROBLEM*, PARTNER.
IT'S WORSE THAN YOU THINK.
APPARENTLY, AS A *DRAMATIS PERSONAE* IN THIS UNFOLDING TRAGEDY, MISTER RAYMOND JAMES MONTERO IS OF ***TREMENDOUS*** CONSEQUENCE.
CHRIST, MASON, WOULD YOU ***PLEASE*** CUT THE SHI--
BEFORE THE AVIAN PANDEMIC HIT, CAESAR...
...MONTERO ***KNEW***.

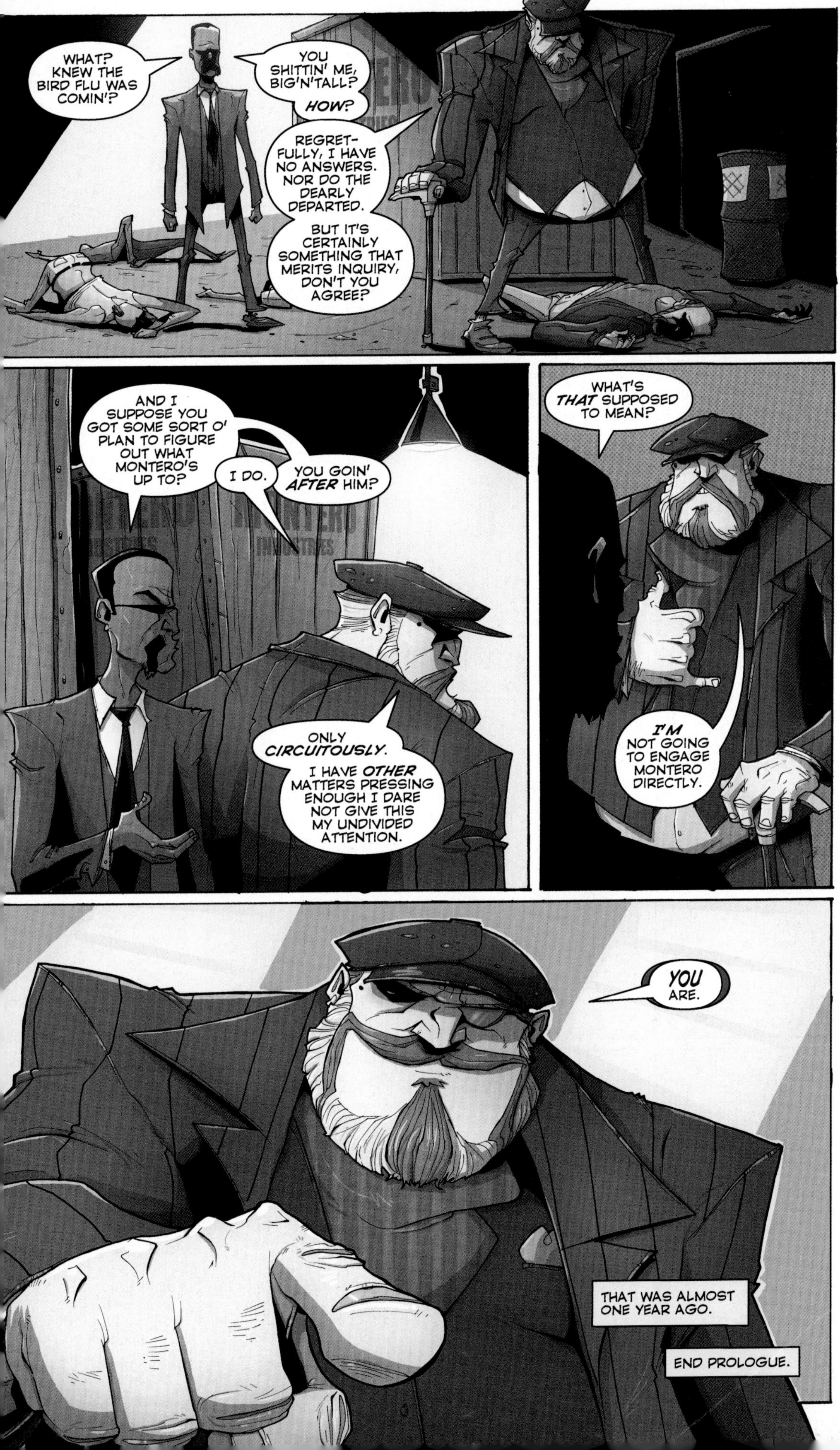
WHAT? KNEW THE BIRD FLU WAS COMIN'?
YOU SHITTIN' ME, BIG'N'TALL? *HOW?*
REGRET-FULLY, I HAVE NO ANSWERS. NOR DO THE DEARLY DEPARTED.
BUT IT'S CERTAINLY SOMETHING THAT MERITS INQUIRY, DON'T YOU AGREE?
AND I SUPPOSE YOU GOT SOME SORT O' PLAN TO FIGURE OUT WHAT MONTERO'S UP TO?
I DO.
YOU GOIN' *AFTER* HIM?
ONLY *CIRCUITOUSLY*.
I HAVE *OTHER* MATTERS PRESSING ENOUGH I DARE NOT GIVE THIS MY UNDIVIDED ATTENTION.
WHAT'S *THAT* SUPPOSED TO MEAN?
I'M NOT GOING TO ENGAGE MONTERO DIRECTLY.
YOU ARE.
THAT WAS ALMOST ONE YEAR AGO.
END PROLOGUE.

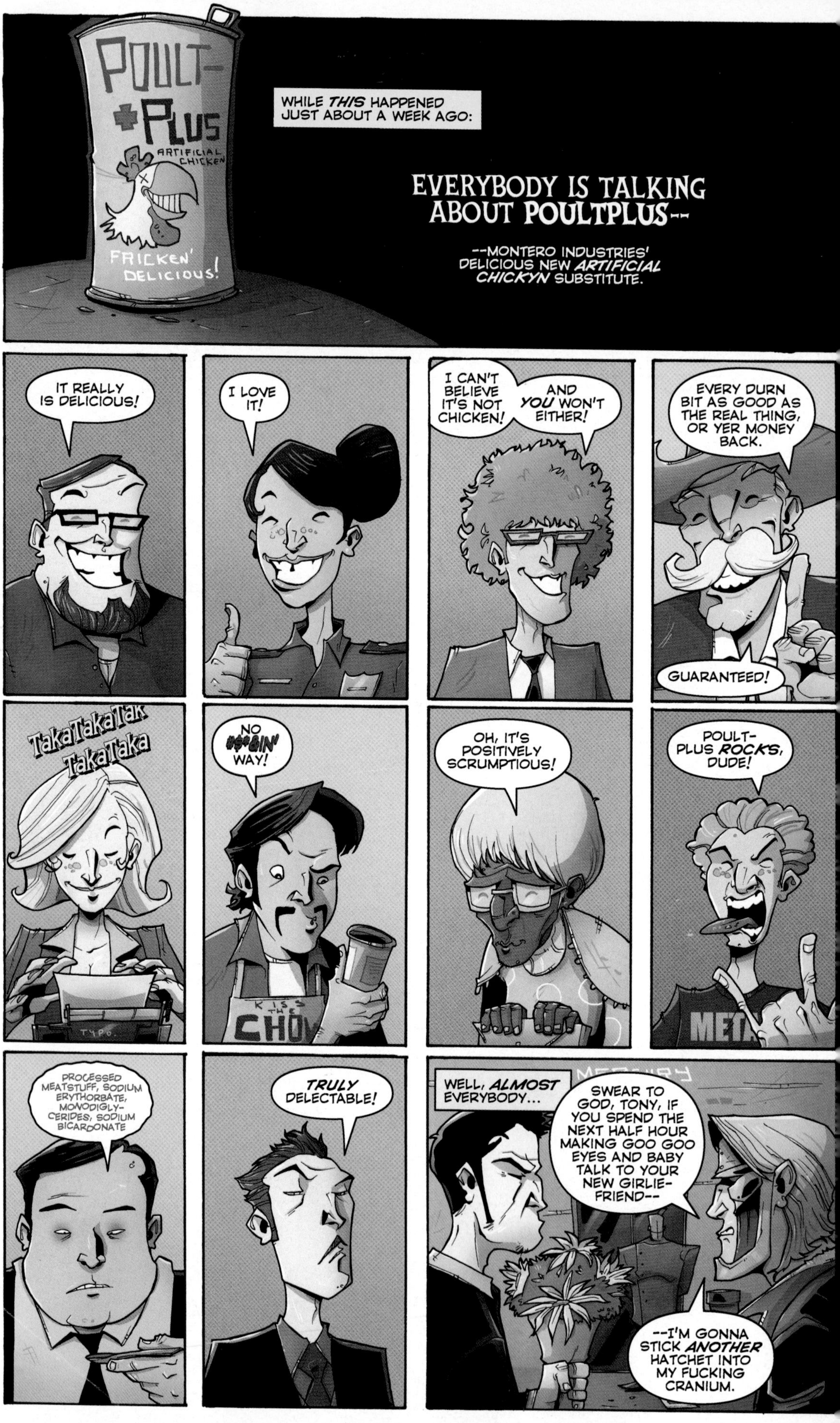
POULT-
+PLUS
ARTIFICIAL CHICKEN
FRICKEN' DELICIOUS!
WHILE *THIS* HAPPENED JUST ABOUT A WEEK AGO:
EVERYBODY IS TALKING ABOUT **POULTPLUS**--
--MONTERO INDUSTRIES' DELICIOUS NEW ***ARTIFICIAL CHICKYN*** SUBSTITUTE.
IT REALLY IS DELICIOUS!
I LOVE IT!
I CAN'T BELIEVE IT'S NOT CHICKEN!
AND ***YOU*** WON'T EITHER!
EVERY DURN BIT AS GOOD AS THE REAL THING, OR YER MONEY BACK.
GUARANTEED!
TakaTakaTak TakaTaka
TYPO.
NO #$*&IN' WAY!
KISS THE CHO
OH, IT'S POSITIVELY SCRUMPTIOUS!
POULT-PLUS ***ROCKS***, DUDE!
META
PROCESSED MEATSTUFF, SODIUM ERYTHORBATE, MONODIGLY-CERIDES, SODIUM BICARDONATE
TRULY DELECTABLE!
WELL, ***ALMOST*** EVERYBODY...
SWEAR TO GOD, TONY, IF YOU SPEND THE NEXT HALF HOUR MAKING GOO GOO EYES AND BABY TALK TO YOUR NEW GIRLIE-FRIEND--
--I'M GONNA STICK ***ANOTHER*** HATCHET INTO MY FUCKING CRANIUM.

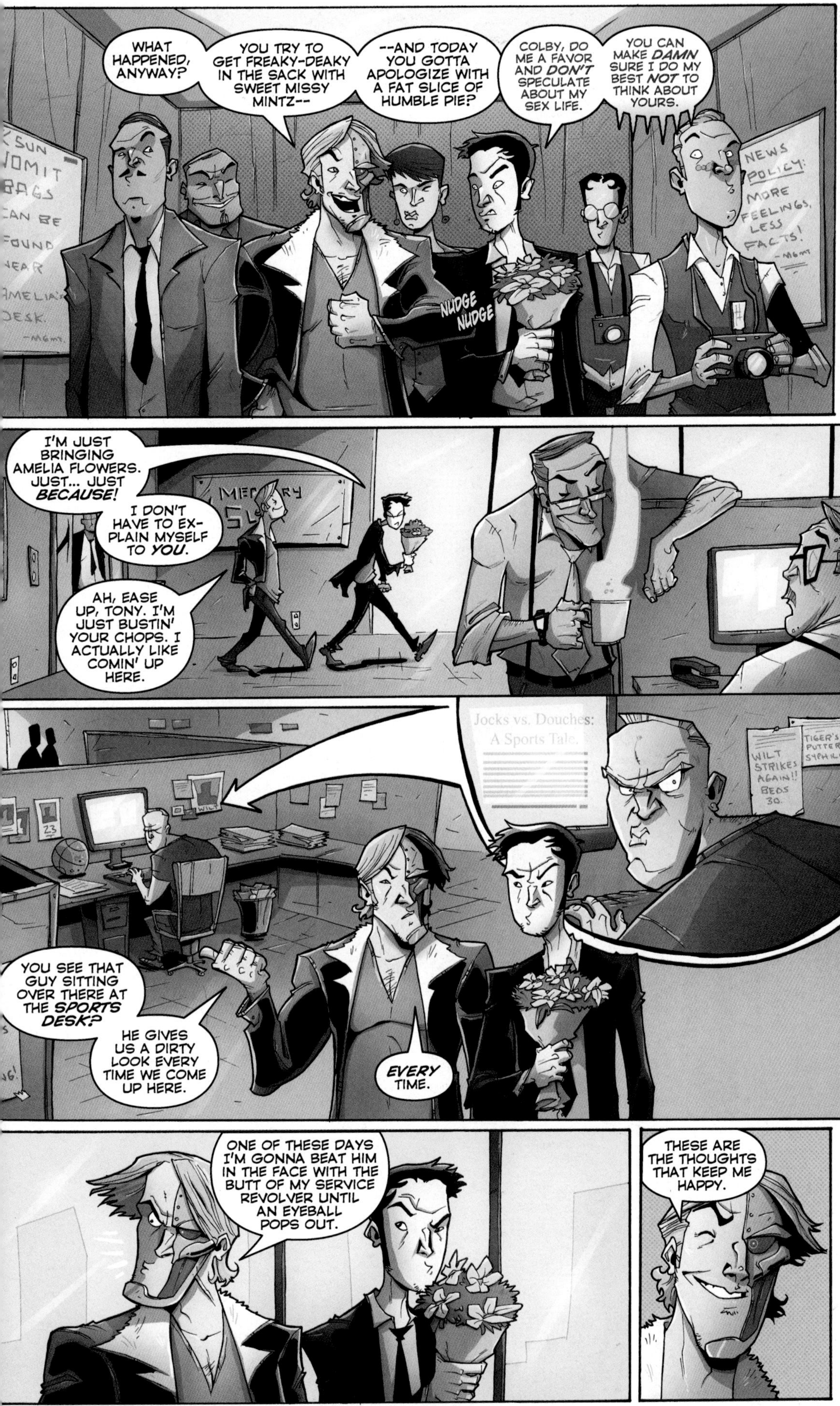

WHAT HAPPENED, ANYWAY?
YOU TRY TO GET FREAKY-DEAKY IN THE SACK WITH SWEET MISSY MINTZ--
--AND TODAY YOU GOTTA APOLOGIZE WITH A FAT SLICE OF HUMBLE PIE?
COLBY, DO ME A FAVOR AND DON'T SPECULATE ABOUT MY SEX LIFE.
YOU CAN MAKE DAMN SURE I DO MY BEST NOT TO THINK ABOUT YOURS.
NUDGE NUDGE
NEWS POLICY: MORE FEELINGS, LESS FACTS! —MGMT
I'M JUST BRINGING AMELIA FLOWERS. JUST... JUST BECAUSE!
I DON'T HAVE TO EXPLAIN MYSELF TO YOU.
AH, EASE UP, TONY. I'M JUST BUSTIN' YOUR CHOPS. I ACTUALLY LIKE COMIN' UP HERE.
Jocks vs. Douches: A Sports Tale.
TIGER'S PUTTER HAS SYPHILLIS.
WILT STRIKES AGAIN!! BEDS 30.
YOU SEE THAT GUY SITTING OVER THERE AT THE SPORTS DESK?
HE GIVES US A DIRTY LOOK EVERY TIME WE COME UP HERE.
EVERY TIME.
ONE OF THESE DAYS I'M GONNA BEAT HIM IN THE FACE WITH THE BUTT OF MY SERVICE REVOLVER UNTIL AN EYEBALL POPS OUT.
THESE ARE THE THOUGHTS THAT KEEP ME HAPPY.

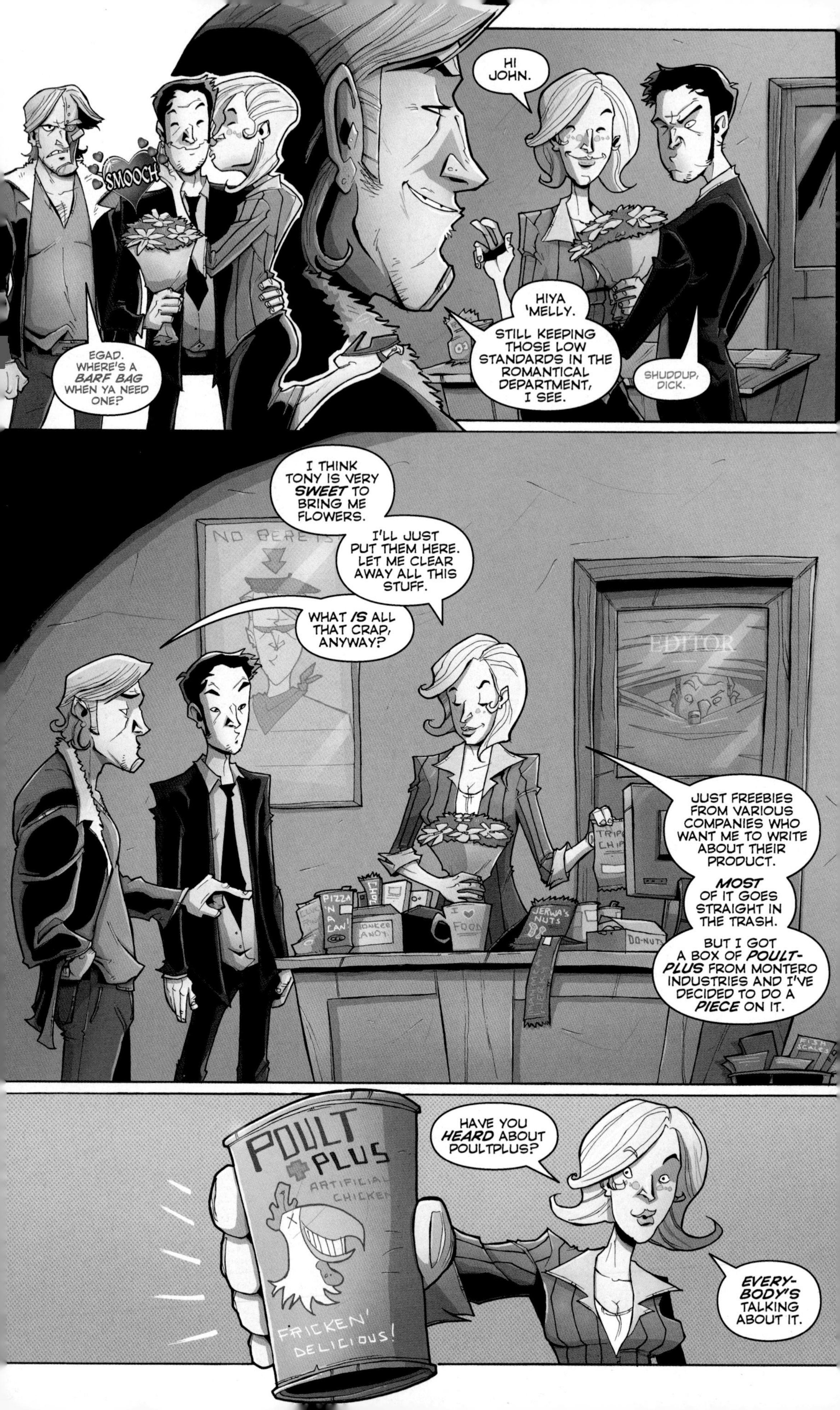
SMOOCH
HI JOHN.
EGAD. WHERE'S A BARF BAG WHEN YA NEED ONE?
HIYA 'MELLY.
STILL KEEPING THOSE LOW STANDARDS IN THE ROMANTICAL DEPARTMENT, I SEE.
SHUDDUP, DICK.
I THINK TONY IS VERY SWEET TO BRING ME FLOWERS.
I'LL JUST PUT THEM HERE. LET ME CLEAR AWAY ALL THIS STUFF.
NO BERETS
WHAT IS ALL THAT CRAP, ANYWAY?
EDITOR
JUST FREEBIES FROM VARIOUS COMPANIES WHO WANT ME TO WRITE ABOUT THEIR PRODUCT.
MOST OF IT GOES STRAIGHT IN THE TRASH.
BUT I GOT A BOX OF POULT-PLUS FROM MONTERO INDUSTRIES AND I'VE DECIDED TO DO A PIECE ON IT.
PIZZA 'N A CAN
JERWA'S NUTS
DO-NUTS
HAVE YOU HEARD ABOUT POULTPLUS?
POULT PLUS
ARTIFICIAL CHICKEN
FRICKEN' DELICIOUS!
EVERY-BODY'S TALKING ABOUT IT.

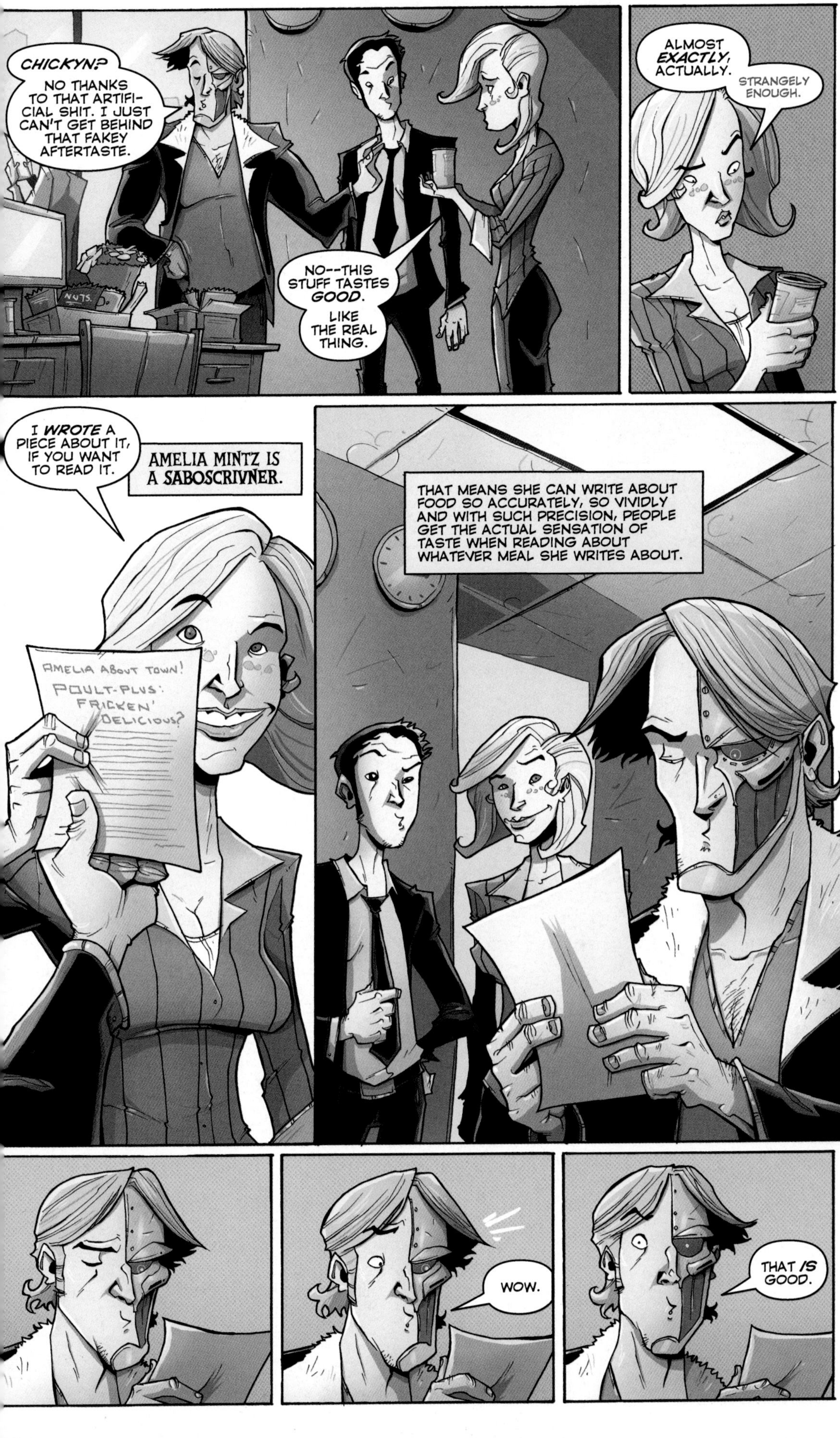
CHICKYN?
NO THANKS TO THAT ARTIFI-CIAL SHIT. I JUST CAN'T GET BEHIND THAT FAKEY AFTERTASTE.
N.U.T.S.
NO--THIS STUFF TASTES GOOD.
LIKE THE REAL THING.
ALMOST EXACTLY, ACTUALLY.
STRANGELY ENOUGH.
I WROTE A PIECE ABOUT IT, IF YOU WANT TO READ IT.
AMELIA MINTZ IS A SABOSCRIVNER.
AMELIA ABOUT TOWN!
POULT-PLUS: FRICKEN' DELICIOUS?
THAT MEANS SHE CAN WRITE ABOUT FOOD SO ACCURATELY, SO VIVIDLY AND WITH SUCH PRECISION, PEOPLE GET THE ACTUAL SENSATION OF TASTE WHEN READING ABOUT WHATEVER MEAL SHE WRITES ABOUT.
WOW.
THAT IS GOOD.

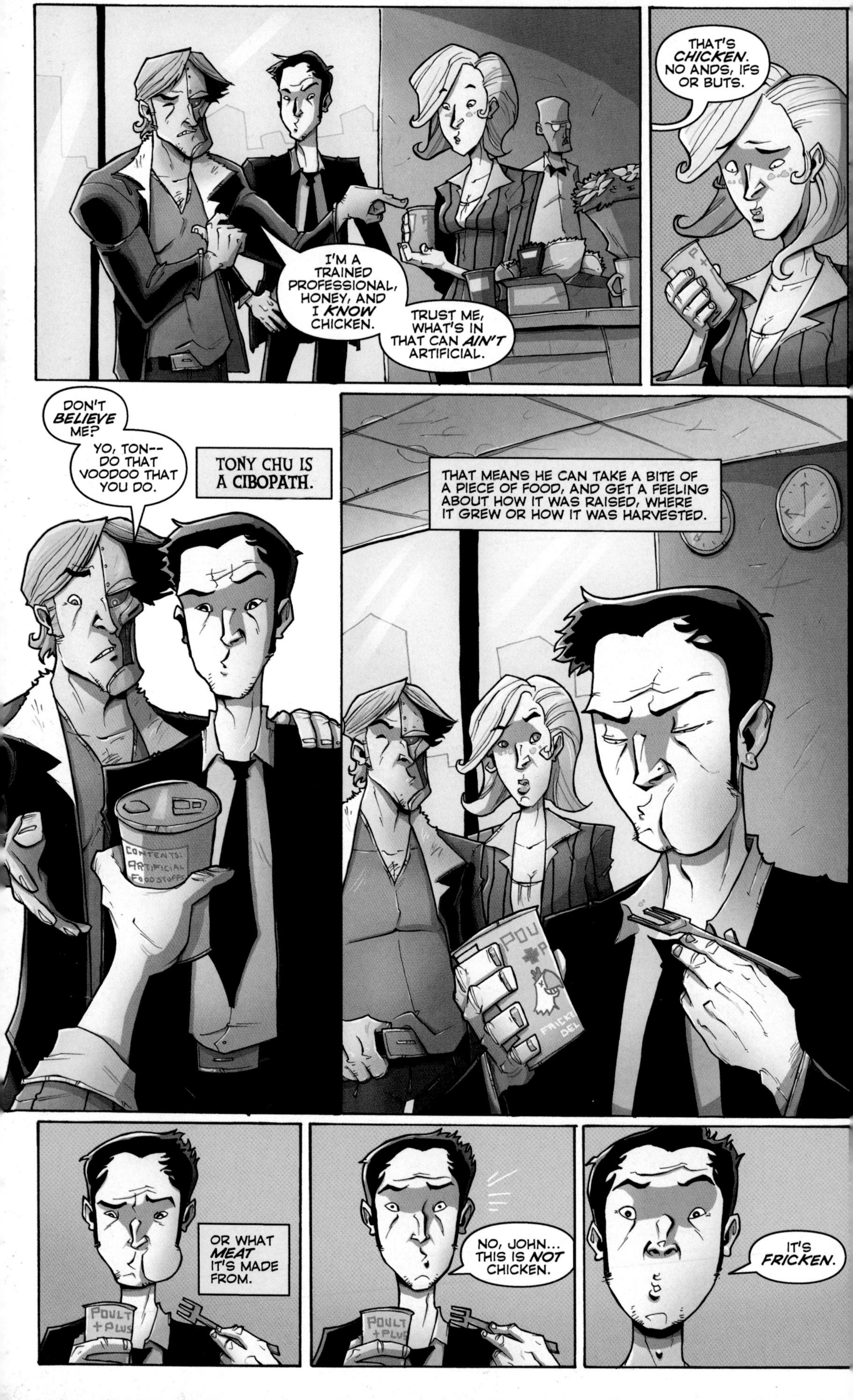
I'M A TRAINED PROFESSIONAL, HONEY, AND I *KNOW* CHICKEN.
TRUST ME, WHAT'S IN THAT CAN *AIN'T* ARTIFICIAL.
THAT'S *CHICKEN*. NO ANDS, IFS OR BUTS.
DON'T *BELIEVE* ME?
YO, TON-- DO THAT VOODOO THAT YOU DO.
TONY CHU IS A CIBOPATH.
CONTENTS: ARTIFICIAL FOOD STUFFS
THAT MEANS HE CAN TAKE A BITE OF A PIECE OF FOOD, AND GET A FEELING ABOUT HOW IT WAS RAISED, WHERE IT GREW OR HOW IT WAS HARVESTED.
OR WHAT *MEAT* IT'S MADE FROM.
POULT +PLUS
NO, JOHN... THIS IS *NOT* CHICKEN.
POULT +PLUS
IT'S *FRICKEN*.

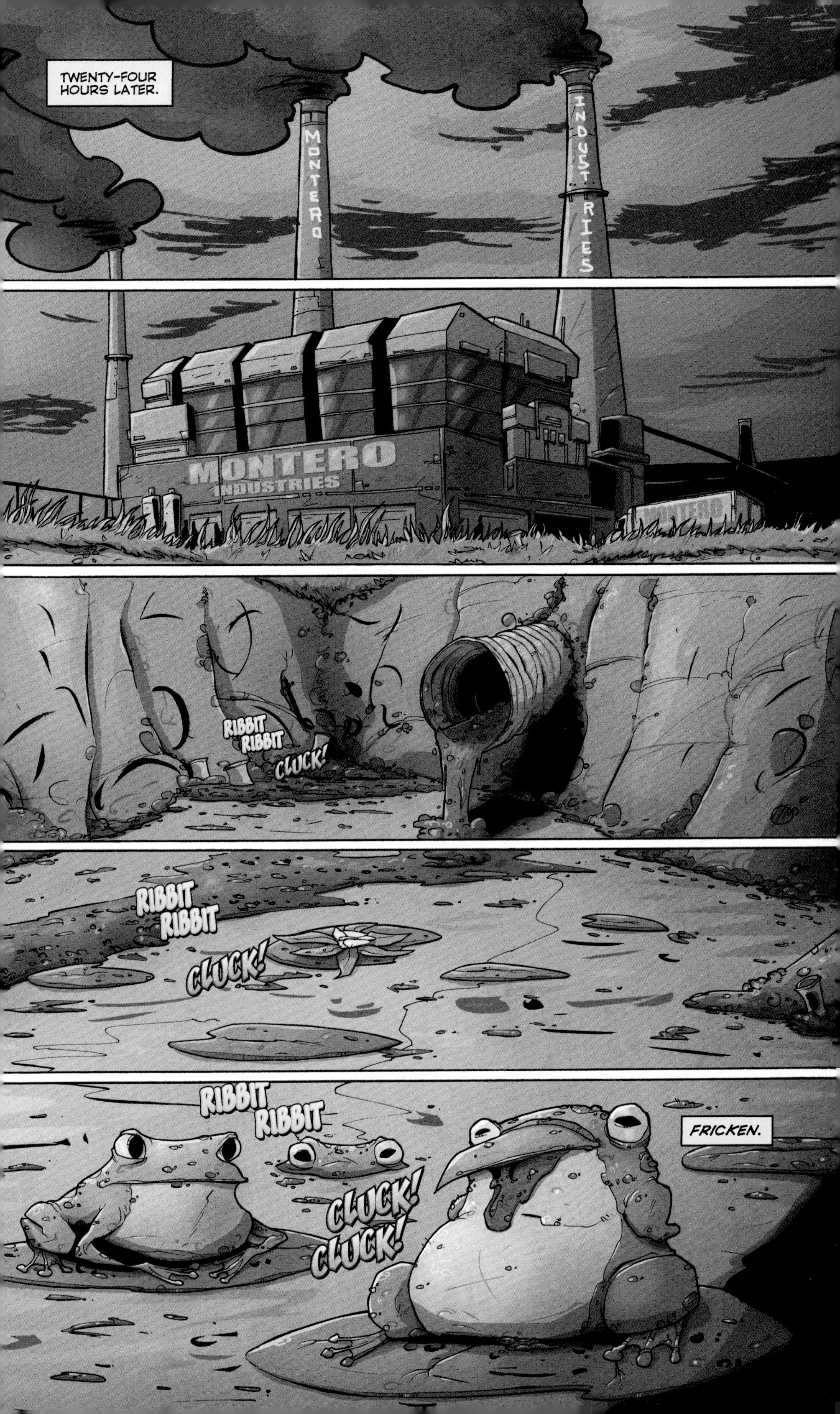
TWENTY-FOUR HOURS LATER.
MONTERO
INDUSTRIES
MONTERO
INDUSTRIES
MONTERO
RIBBIT RIBBIT
CLUCK!
RIBBIT RIBBIT
CLUCK!
RIBBIT RIBBIT
CLUCK! CLUCK!
FRICKEN.

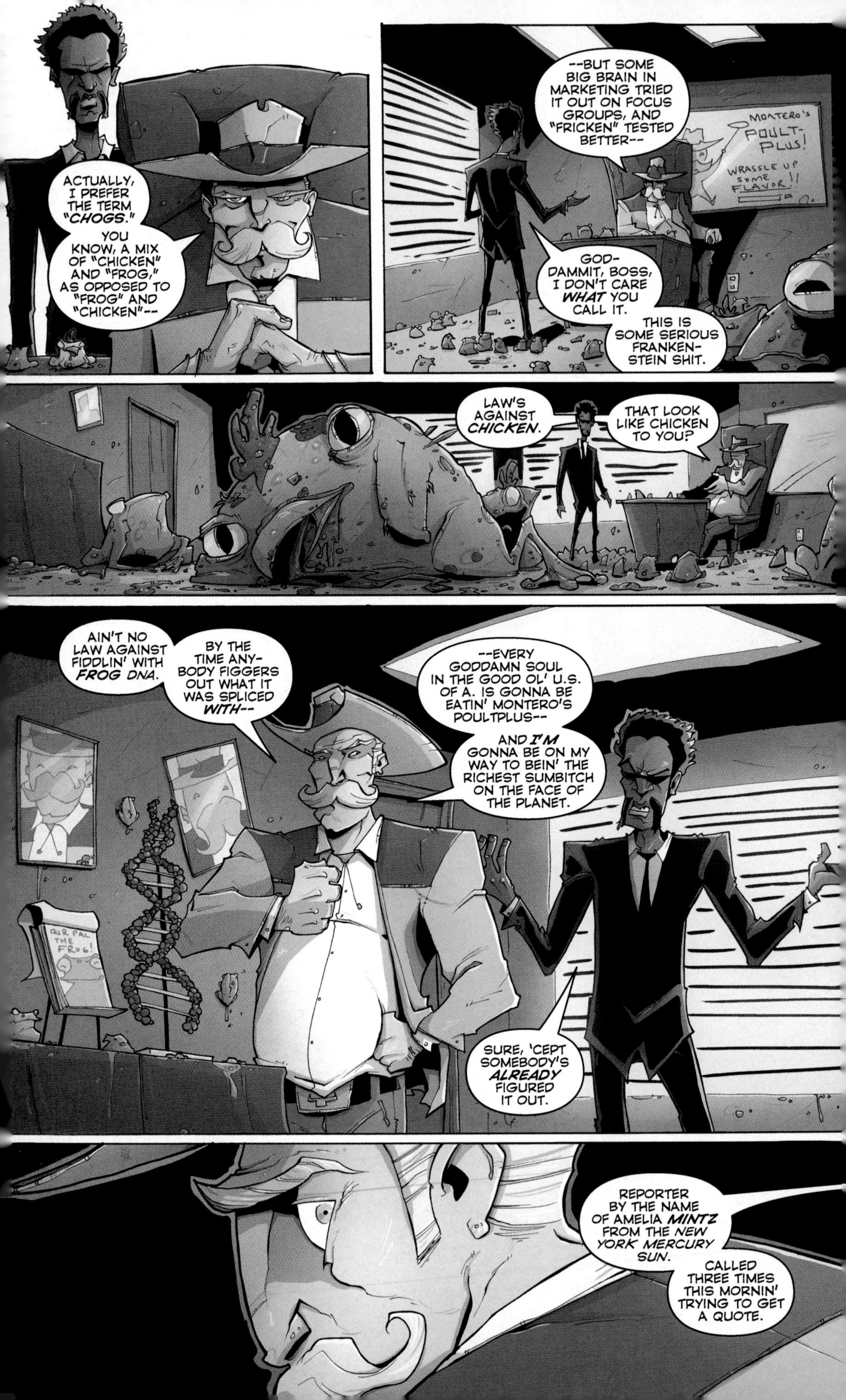
ACTUALLY, I PREFER THE TERM "CHOGS."
YOU KNOW, A MIX OF "CHICKEN" AND "FROG," AS OPPOSED TO "FROG" AND "CHICKEN"--
--BUT SOME BIG BRAIN IN MARKETING TRIED IT OUT ON FOCUS GROUPS, AND "FRICKEN" TESTED BETTER--
MONTERO'S POULT-PLUS! WRASSLE UP SOME FLAVOR!!
GOD-DAMMIT, BOSS, I DON'T CARE WHAT YOU CALL IT.
THIS IS SOME SERIOUS FRANKEN-STEIN SHIT.
LAW'S AGAINST CHICKEN.
THAT LOOK LIKE CHICKEN TO YOU?
AIN'T NO LAW AGAINST FIDDLIN' WITH FROG DNA.
BY THE TIME ANY-BODY FIGGERS OUT WHAT IT WAS SPLICED WITH--
--EVERY GODDAMN SOUL IN THE GOOD OL' U.S. OF A. IS GONNA BE EATIN' MONTERO'S POULTPLUS--
AND I'M GONNA BE ON MY WAY TO BEIN' THE RICHEST SUMBITCH ON THE FACE OF THE PLANET.
OUR PAL THE FROG!
SURE, 'CEPT SOMEBODY'S ALREADY FIGURED IT OUT.
REPORTER BY THE NAME OF AMELIA MINTZ FROM THE NEW YORK MERCURY SUN.
CALLED THREE TIMES THIS MORNIN' TRYING TO GET A QUOTE.

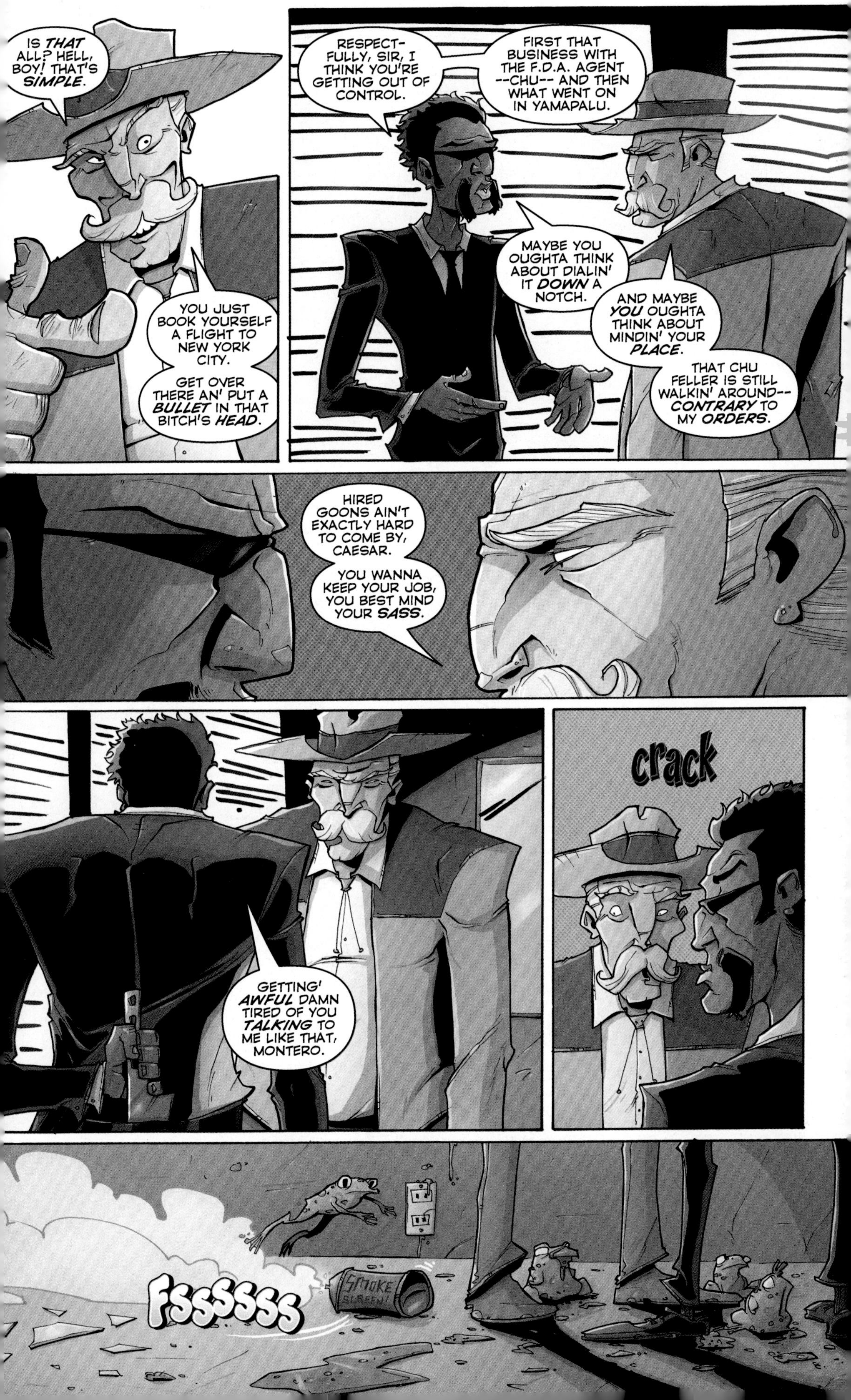

IS THAT ALL? HELL, BOY! THAT'S SIMPLE.
YOU JUST BOOK YOURSELF A FLIGHT TO NEW YORK CITY.
GET OVER THERE AN' PUT A BULLET IN THAT BITCH'S HEAD.
RESPECT-FULLY, SIR, I THINK YOU'RE GETTING OUT OF CONTROL.
FIRST THAT BUSINESS WITH THE F.D.A. AGENT --CHU-- AND THEN WHAT WENT ON IN YAMAPALU.
MAYBE YOU OUGHTA THINK ABOUT DIALIN' IT DOWN A NOTCH.
AND MAYBE YOU OUGHTA THINK ABOUT MINDIN' YOUR PLACE.
THAT CHU FELLER IS STILL WALKIN' AROUND-- CONTRARY TO MY ORDERS.
HIRED GOONS AIN'T EXACTLY HARD TO COME BY, CAESAR.
YOU WANNA KEEP YOUR JOB, YOU BEST MIND YOUR SASS.
GETTING' AWFUL DAMN TIRED OF YOU TALKING TO ME LIKE THAT, MONTERO.
crack
SMOKE SCREEN!
FSSSSSS

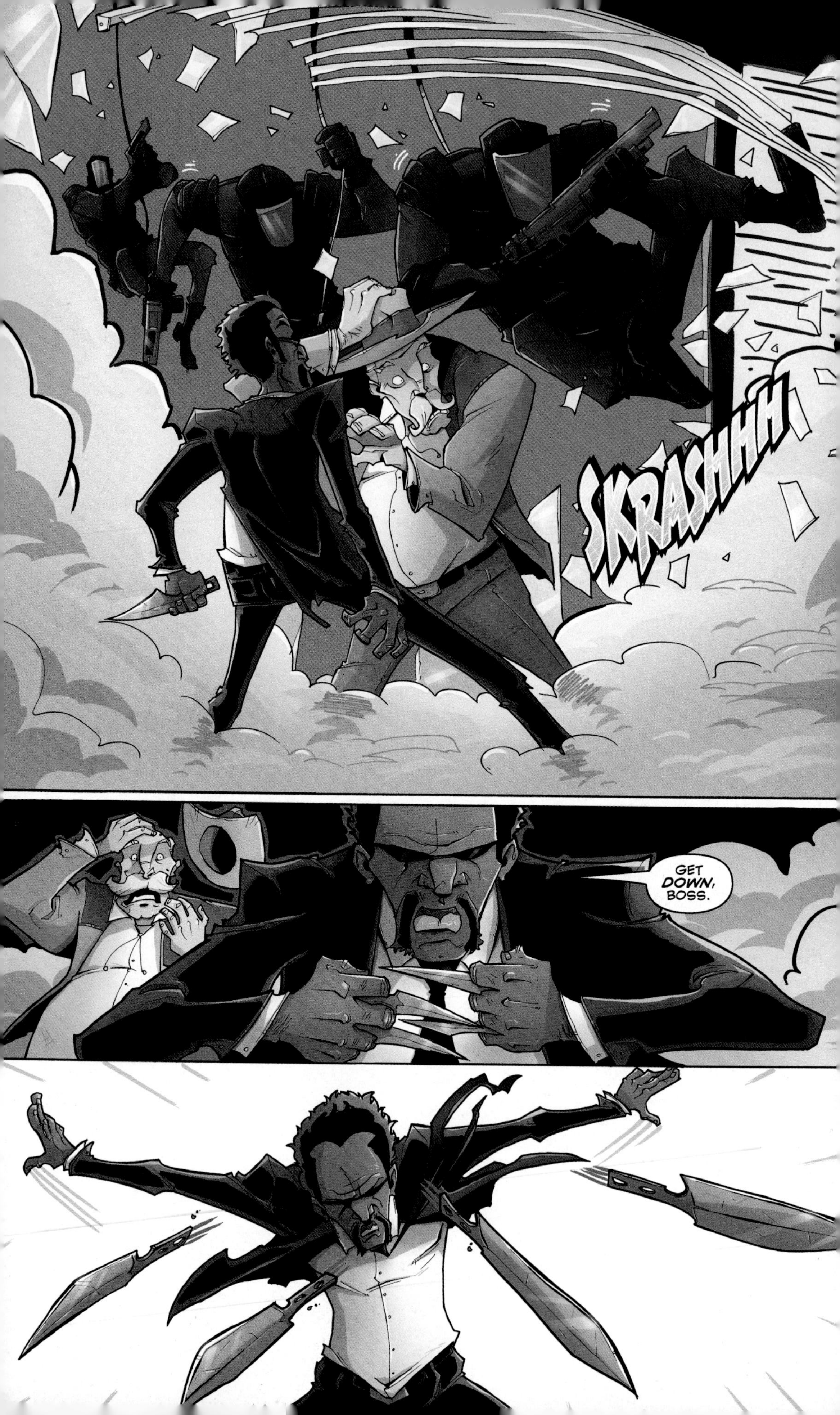
SKRASHHH
GET DOWN, BOSS.

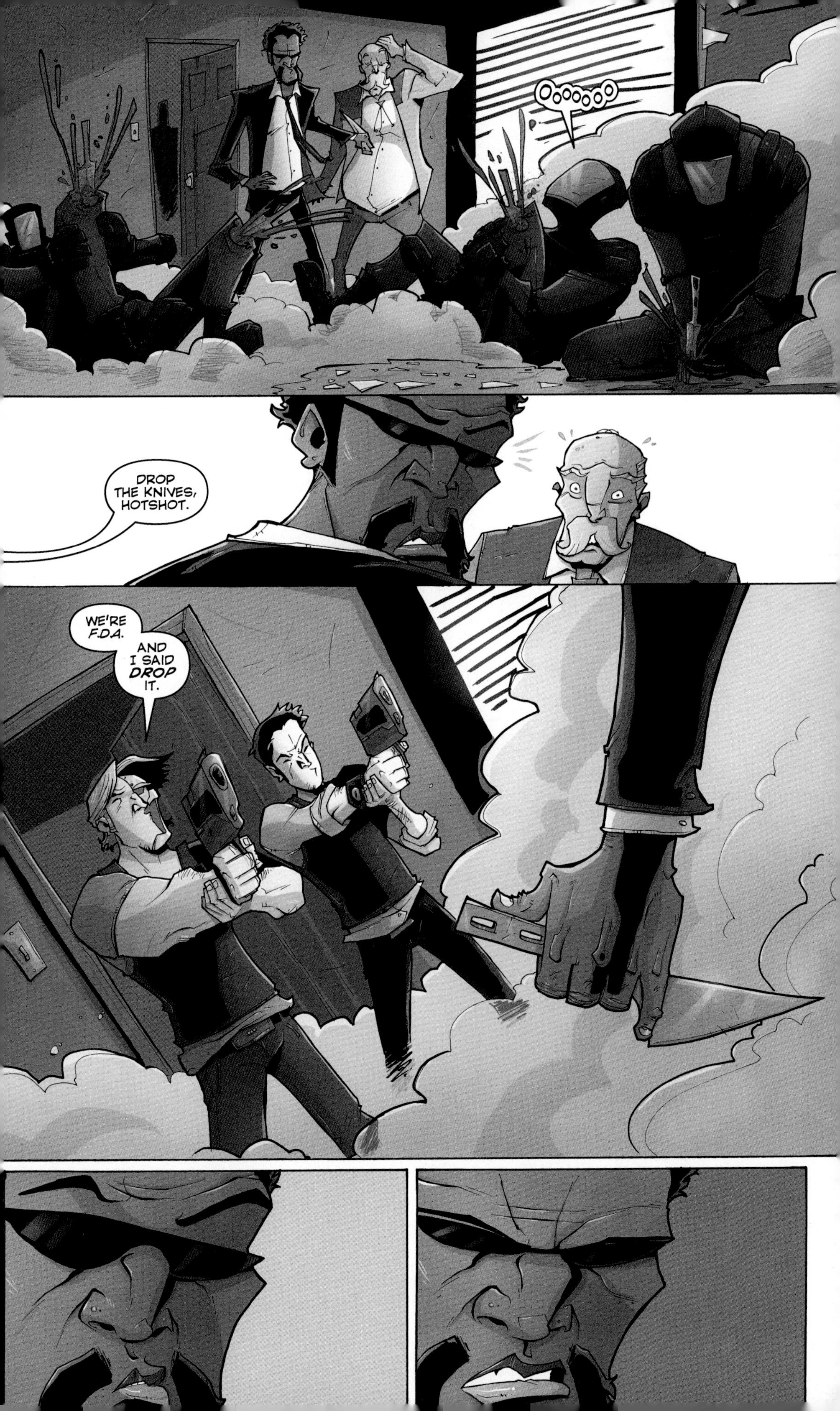
Ooooooo
DROP THE KNIVES, HOTSHOT.
WE'RE *F.D.A.*
AND I SAID ***DROP*** IT.

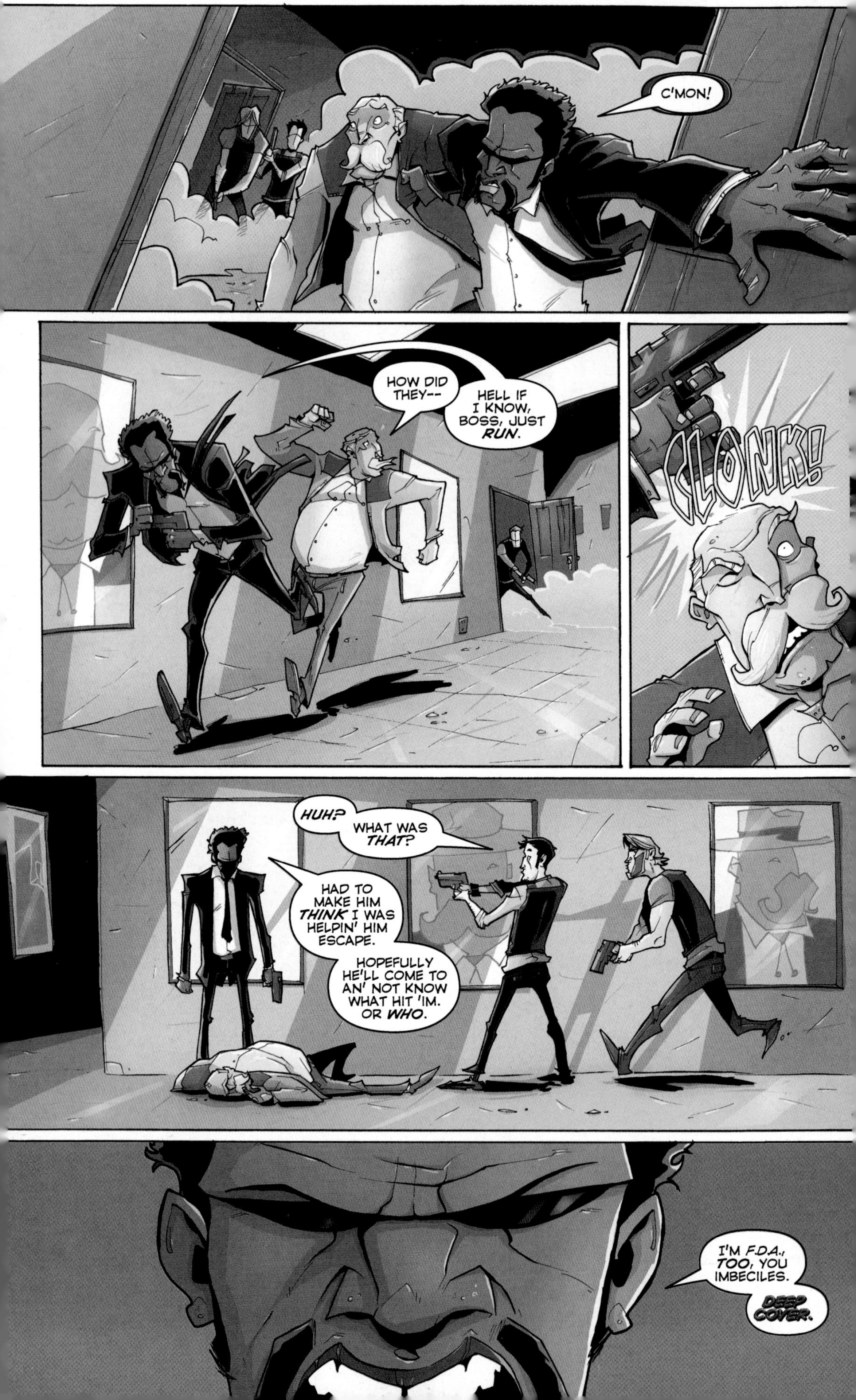
C'MON!
HOW DID THEY--
HELL IF I KNOW, BOSS, JUST RUN.
CLONK!
HUH?
WHAT WAS THAT?
HAD TO MAKE HIM THINK I WAS HELPIN' HIM ESCAPE.
HOPEFULLY HE'LL COME TO AN' NOT KNOW WHAT HIT 'IM. OR WHO.
I'M F.D.A., TOO, YOU IMBECILES.
DEEP COVER.

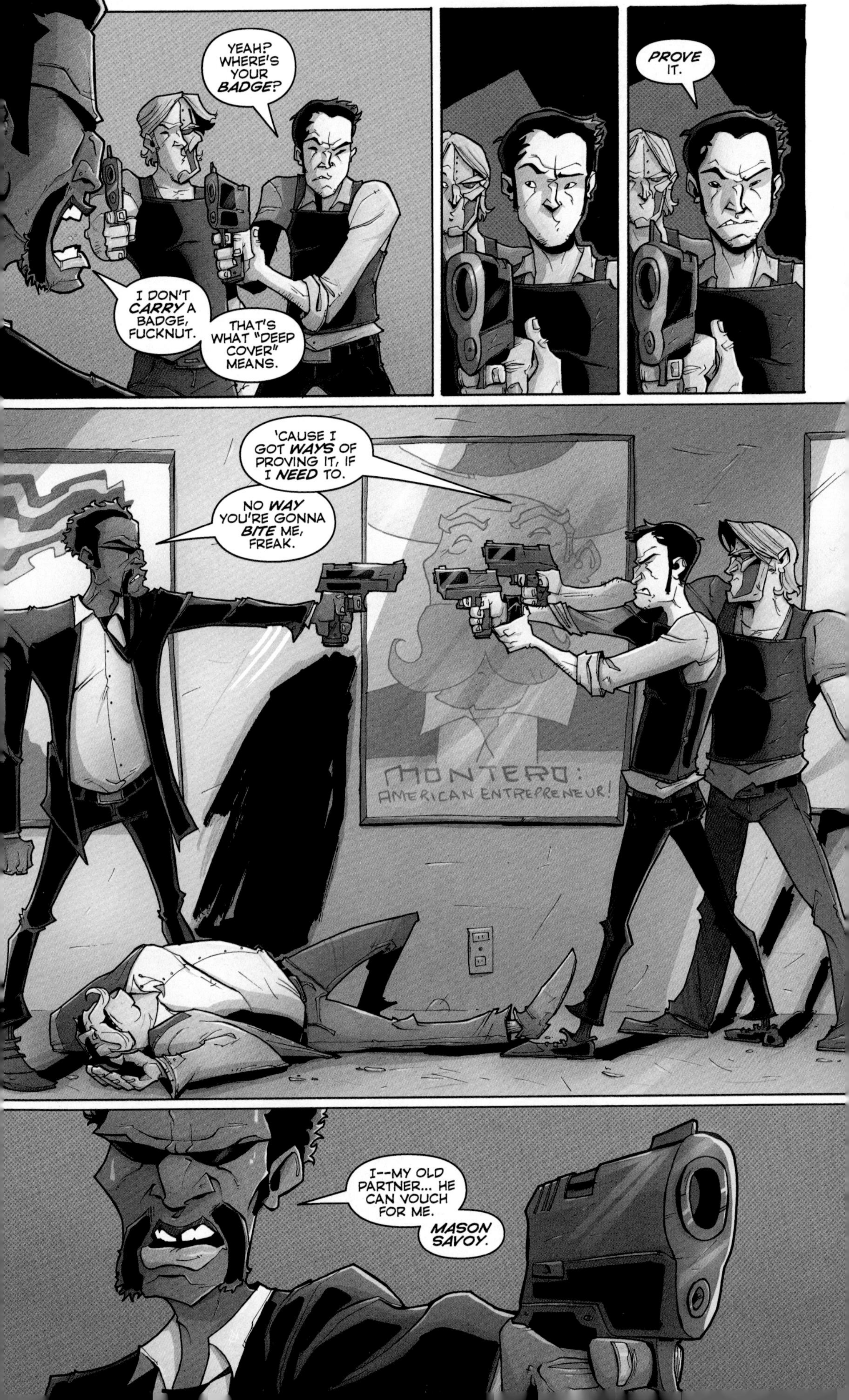
YEAH? WHERE'S YOUR BADGE?
I DON'T CARRY A BADGE, FUCKNUT.
THAT'S WHAT "DEEP COVER" MEANS.
PROVE IT.
'CAUSE I GOT WAYS OF PROVING IT, IF I NEED TO.
NO WAY YOU'RE GONNA BITE ME, FREAK.
MONTERO: AMERICAN ENTREPRENEUR!
I--MY OLD PARTNER... HE CAN VOUCH FOR ME.
MASON SAVOY.

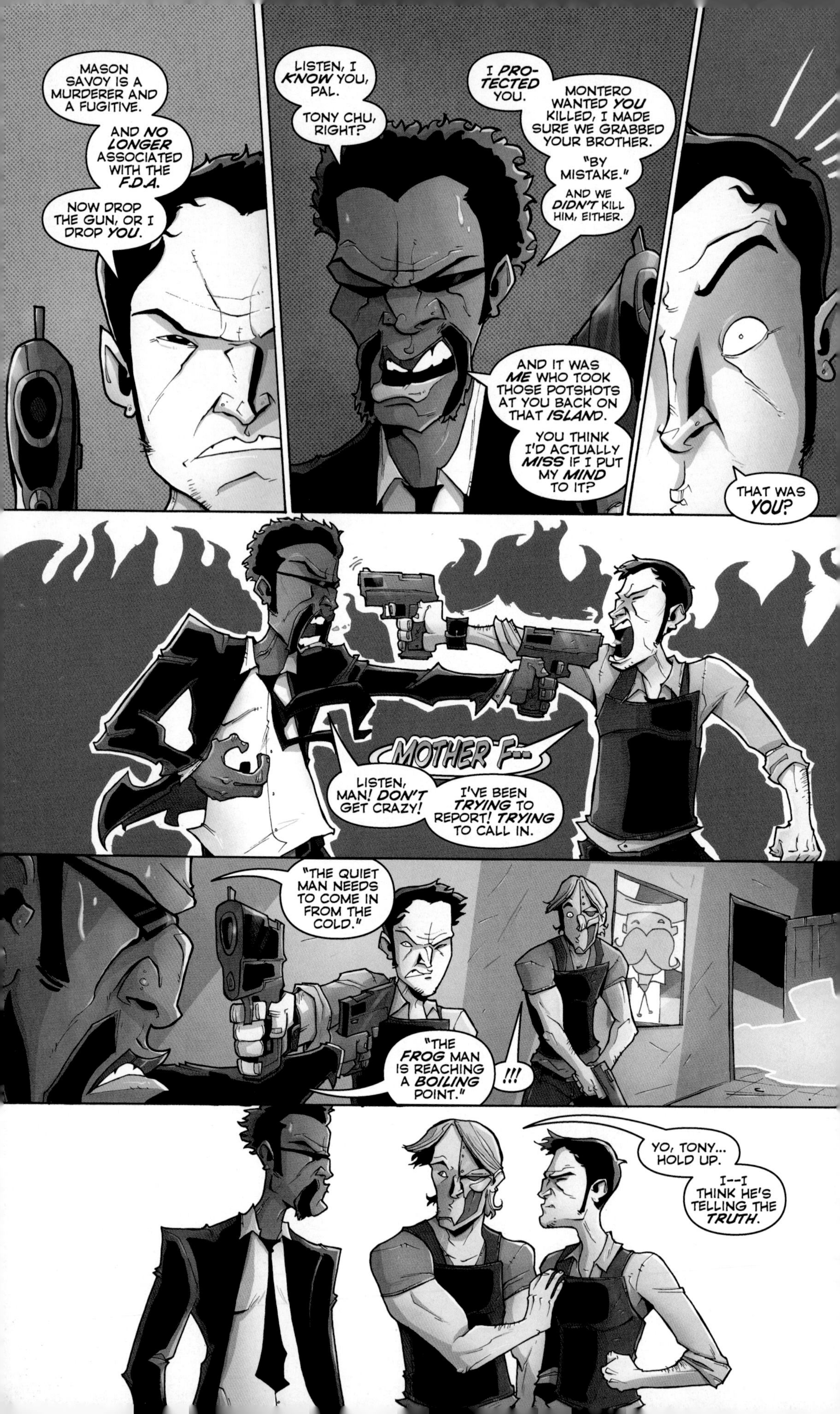
MASON SAVOY IS A MURDERER AND A FUGITIVE.
AND NO LONGER ASSOCIATED WITH THE F.D.A.
NOW DROP THE GUN, OR I DROP YOU.
LISTEN, I KNOW YOU, PAL.
TONY CHU, RIGHT?
AND IT WAS ME WHO TOOK THOSE POTSHOTS AT YOU BACK ON THAT ISLAND.
YOU THINK I'D ACTUALLY MISS IF I PUT MY MIND TO IT?
I PROTECTED YOU.
MONTERO WANTED YOU KILLED, I MADE SURE WE GRABBED YOUR BROTHER.
"BY MISTAKE."
AND WE DIDN'T KILL HIM, EITHER.
THAT WAS YOU?
MOTHER F--
LISTEN, MAN! DON'T GET CRAZY!
I'VE BEEN TRYING TO REPORT! TRYING TO CALL IN.
"THE QUIET MAN NEEDS TO COME IN FROM THE COLD."
"THE FROG MAN IS REACHING A BOILING POINT."
!!!
YO, TONY... HOLD UP.
I--I THINK HE'S TELLING THE TRUTH.

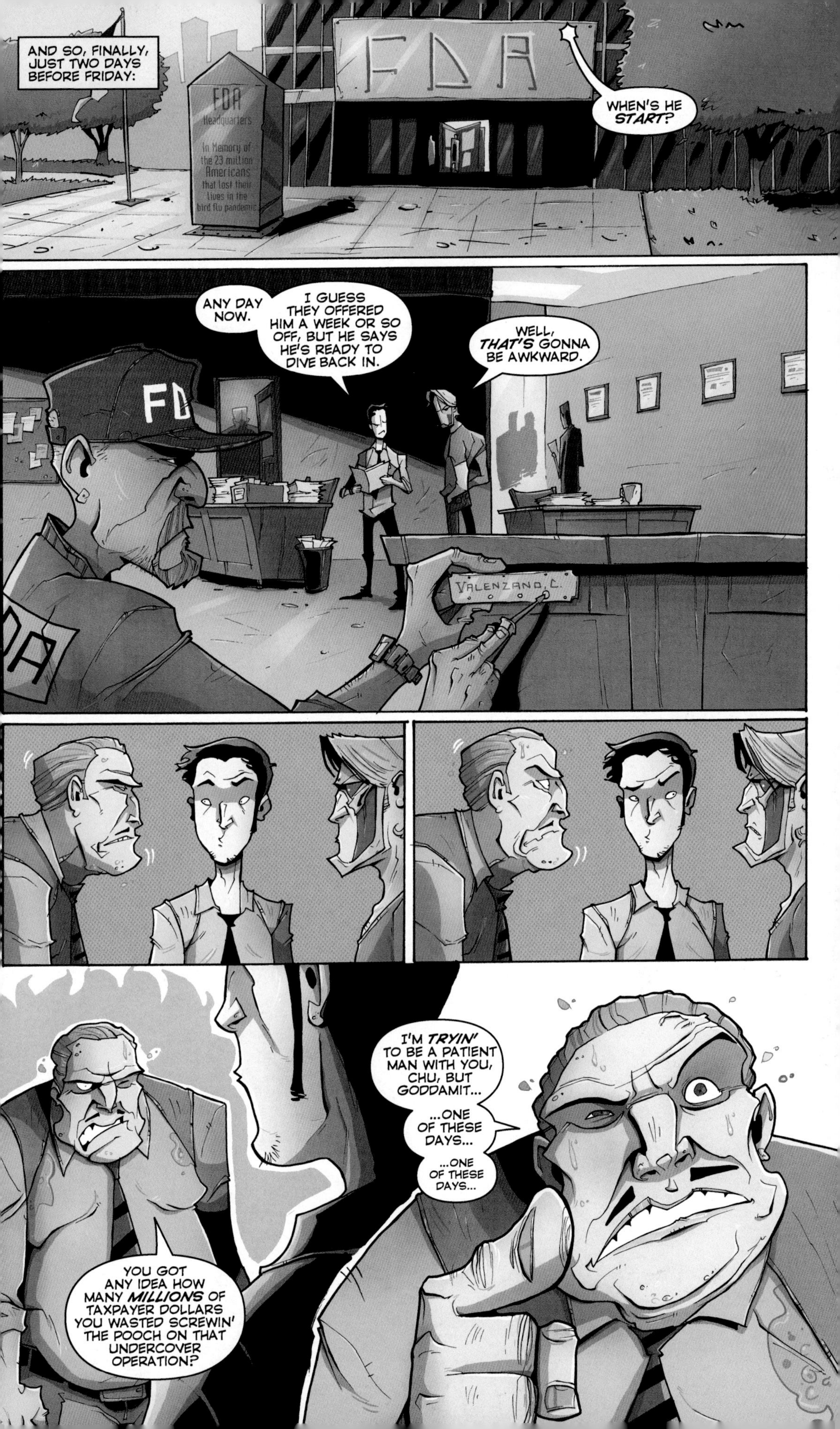
AND SO, FINALLY, JUST TWO DAYS BEFORE FRIDAY:
FDA
FDA Headquarters
In Memory of the 23 million Americans that lost their lives in the bird flu pandemic
WHEN'S HE *START?*
ANY DAY NOW.
I GUESS THEY OFFERED HIM A WEEK OR SO OFF, BUT HE SAYS HE'S READY TO DIVE BACK IN.
WELL, *THAT'S* GONNA BE AWKWARD.
FD
VALENZANO, C.
I'M *TRYIN'* TO BE A PATIENT MAN WITH YOU, CHU, BUT GODDAMIT...
...ONE OF THESE DAYS...
...ONE OF THESE DAYS...
YOU GOT ANY IDEA HOW MANY *MILLIONS* OF TAXPAYER DOLLARS YOU WASTED SCREWIN' THE POOCH ON THAT UNDERCOVER OPERATION?

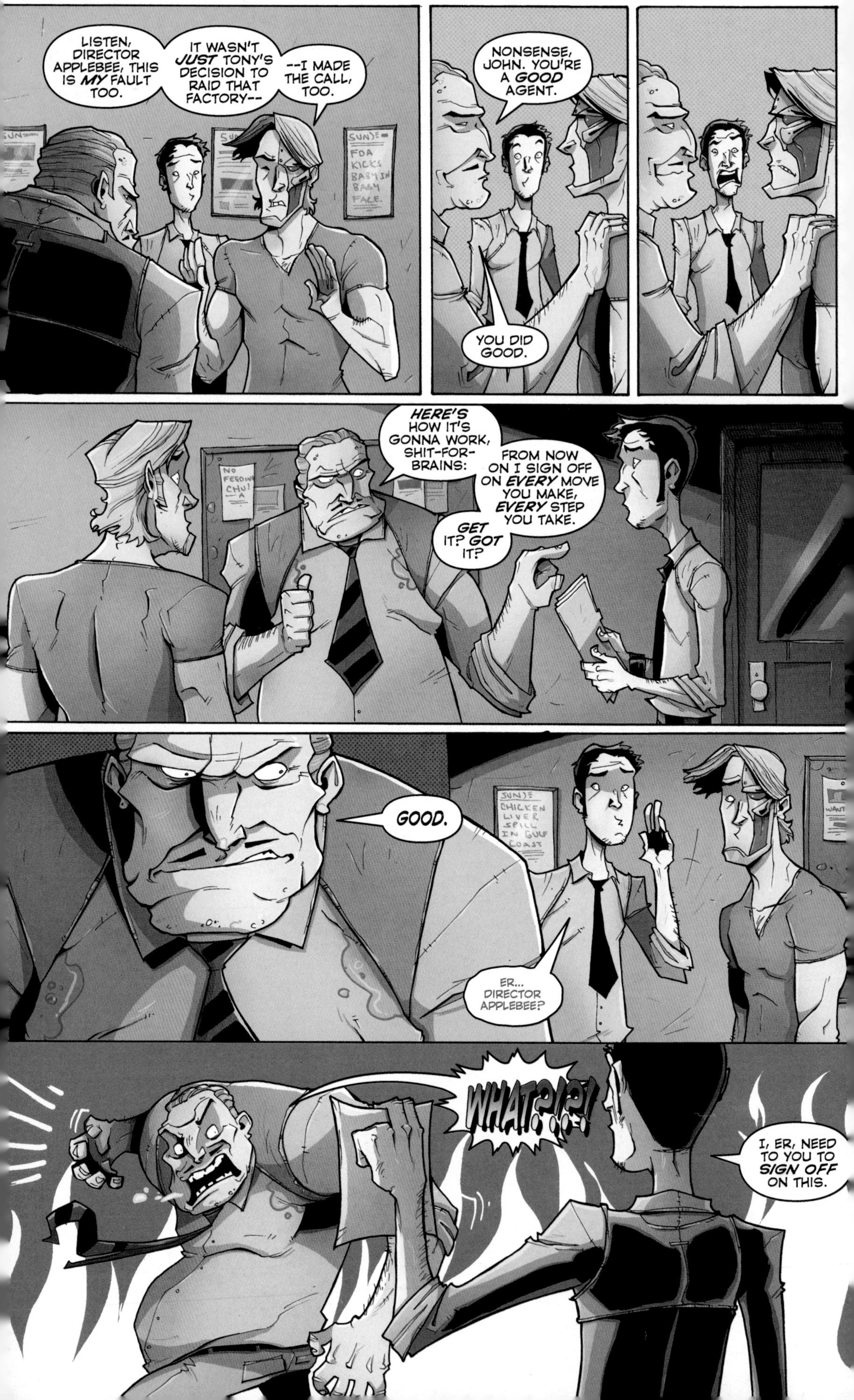
LISTEN, DIRECTOR APPLEBEE, THIS IS *MY* FAULT TOO.
IT WASN'T *JUST* TONY'S DECISION TO RAID THAT FACTORY--
--I MADE THE CALL, TOO.
SUN
FDA KICKS BABY IN BABY FACE.
NONSENSE, JOHN. YOU'RE A *GOOD* AGENT.
YOU DID GOOD.
HERE'S HOW IT'S GONNA WORK, SHIT-FOR-BRAINS:
FROM NOW ON I SIGN OFF ON *EVERY* MOVE YOU MAKE, *EVERY* STEP YOU TAKE.
GET IT? *GOT* IT?
NO FEEDING CHU
GOOD.
SUN
CHICKEN LIVER SPILL IN GULF COAST
ER... DIRECTOR APPLEBEE?
WHAT?!?!
I, ER, NEED TO YOU TO *SIGN OFF* ON THIS.

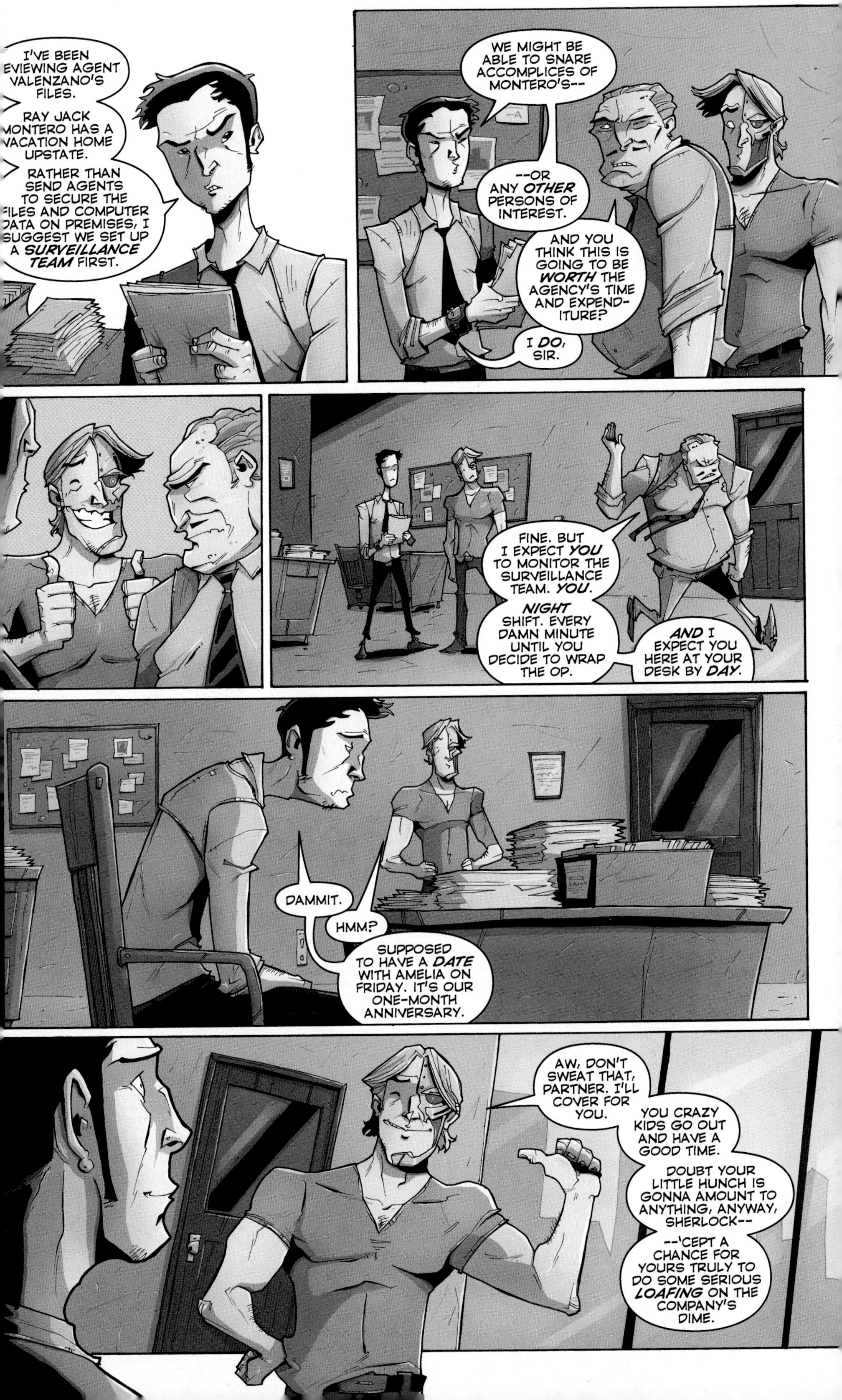
I'VE BEEN EVIEWING AGENT VALENZANO'S FILES.
RAY JACK MONTERO HAS A VACATION HOME UPSTATE.
RATHER THAN SEND AGENTS TO SECURE THE FILES AND COMPUTER DATA ON PREMISES, I SUGGEST WE SET UP A SURVEILLANCE TEAM FIRST.
WE MIGHT BE ABLE TO SNARE ACCOMPLICES OF MONTERO'S--
--OR ANY OTHER PERSONS OF INTEREST.
AND YOU THINK THIS IS GOING TO BE WORTH THE AGENCY'S TIME AND EXPEND-ITURE?
I DO, SIR.
FINE. BUT I EXPECT YOU TO MONITOR THE SURVEILLANCE TEAM. YOU.
NIGHT SHIFT. EVERY DAMN MINUTE UNTIL YOU DECIDE TO WRAP THE OP.
AND I EXPECT YOU HERE AT YOUR DESK BY DAY.
DAMMIT.
HMM?
SUPPOSED TO HAVE A DATE WITH AMELIA ON FRIDAY. IT'S OUR ONE-MONTH ANNIVERSARY.
AW, DON'T SWEAT THAT, PARTNER. I'LL COVER FOR YOU.
YOU CRAZY KIDS GO OUT AND HAVE A GOOD TIME.
DOUBT YOUR LITTLE HUNCH IS GONNA AMOUNT TO ANYTHING, ANYWAY, SHERLOCK--
--'CEPT A CHANCE FOR YOURS TRULY TO DO SOME SERIOUS LOAFING ON THE COMPANY'S DIME.

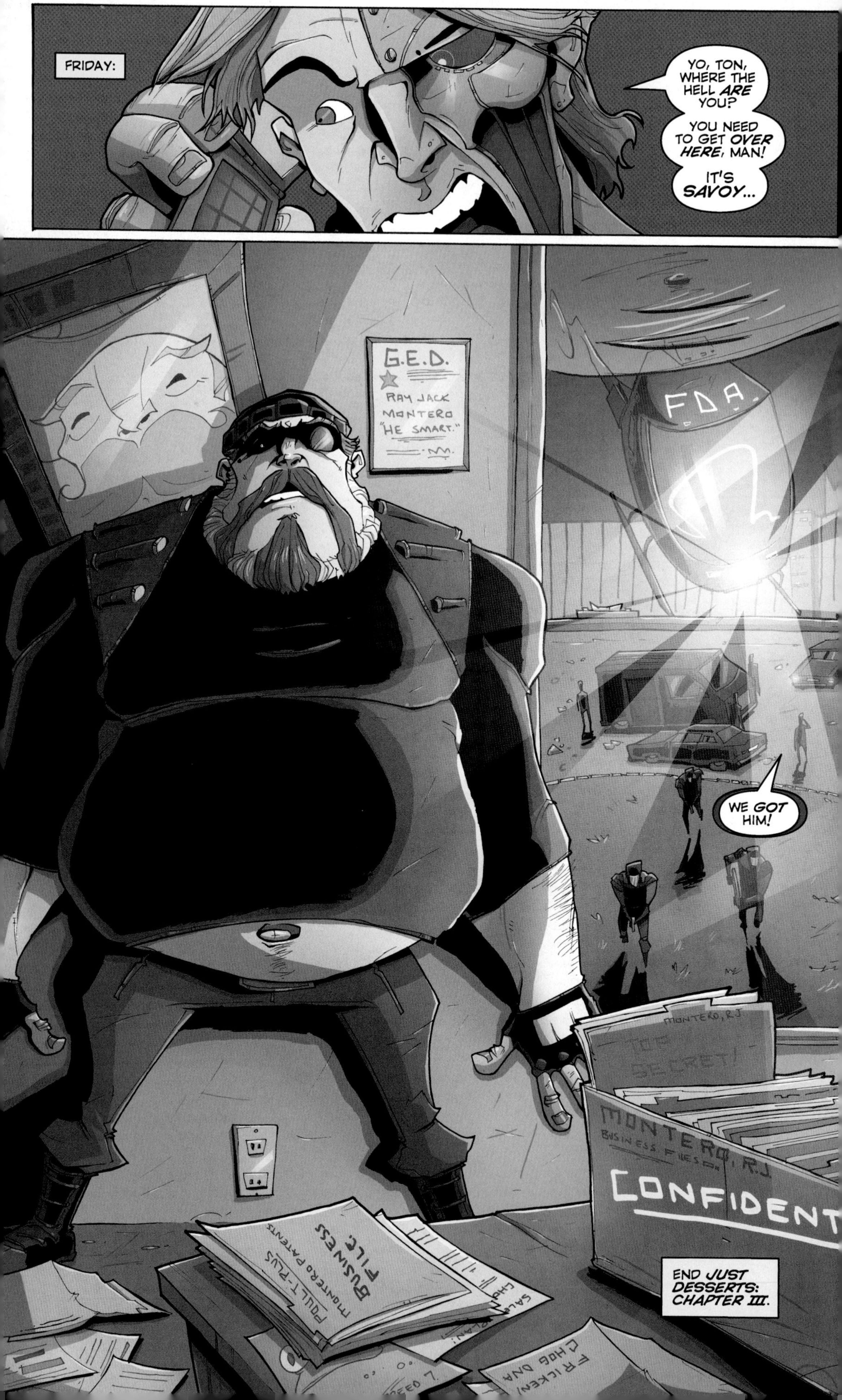
FRIDAY:
YO, TON, WHERE THE HELL *ARE* YOU?
YOU NEED TO GET *OVER HERE*, MAN!
IT'S *SAVOY...*
G.E.D.
RAY JACK MONTERO
"HE SMART."
F.D.A.
WE *GOT* HIM!
MONTERO, R.J.
TOP SECRET!
MONTERO, R.J.
BUSINESS FILES
CONFIDENT
POULT-PLUS
MONTERO PATENTS
BUSINESS FILE
FRICKEN CHOG DNA
END *JUST DESSERTS:* CHAPTER III.

Chapter 4

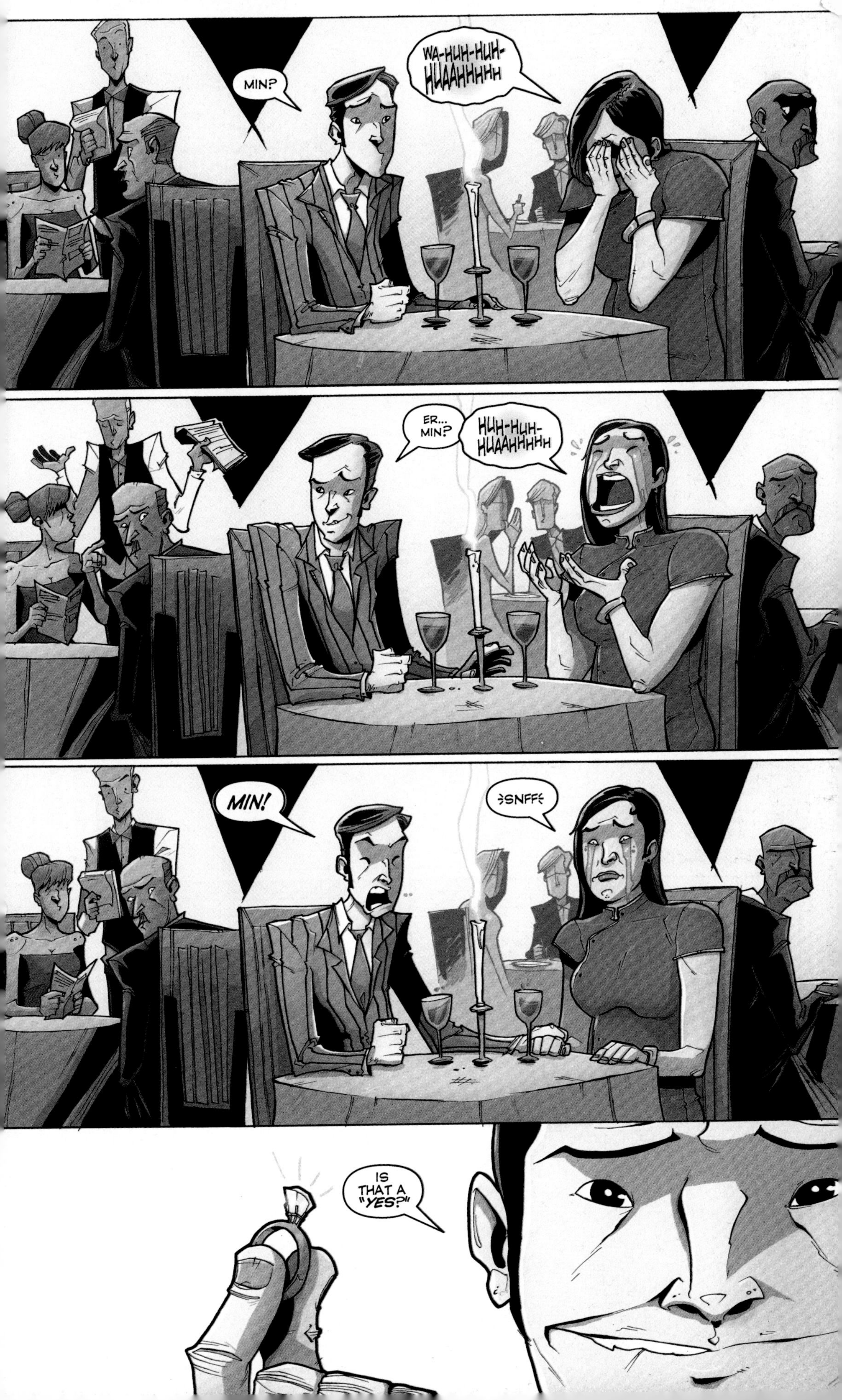
MIN?
WA-HUH-HUH-HUAAHHHHH
ER... MIN?
HUH-HUH-HUAAHHHHH
MIN!
SNFF
IS THAT A "YES?"

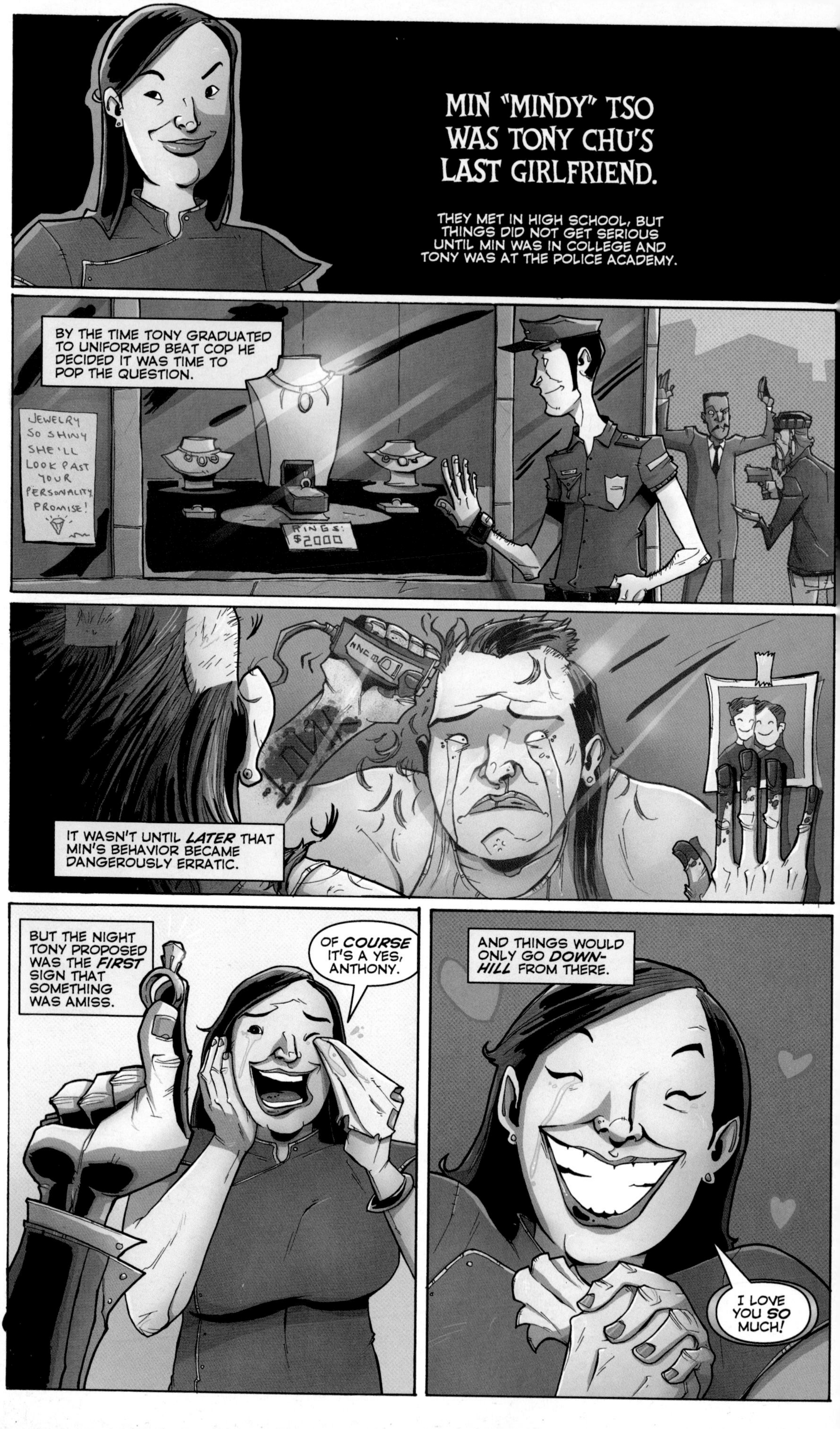
MIN "MINDY" TSO WAS TONY CHU'S LAST GIRLFRIEND.
THEY MET IN HIGH SCHOOL, BUT THINGS DID NOT GET SERIOUS UNTIL MIN WAS IN COLLEGE AND TONY WAS AT THE POLICE ACADEMY.
BY THE TIME TONY GRADUATED TO UNIFORMED BEAT COP HE DECIDED IT WAS TIME TO POP THE QUESTION.
JEWELRY SO SHINY SHE'LL LOOK PAST YOUR PERSONALITY. PROMISE!
RINGS: $2000
IT WASN'T UNTIL LATER THAT MIN'S BEHAVIOR BECAME DANGEROUSLY ERRATIC.
BUT THE NIGHT TONY PROPOSED WAS THE FIRST SIGN THAT SOMETHING WAS AMISS.
OF COURSE IT'S A YES, ANTHONY.
AND THINGS WOULD ONLY GO DOWN-HILL FROM THERE.
I LOVE YOU SO MUCH!

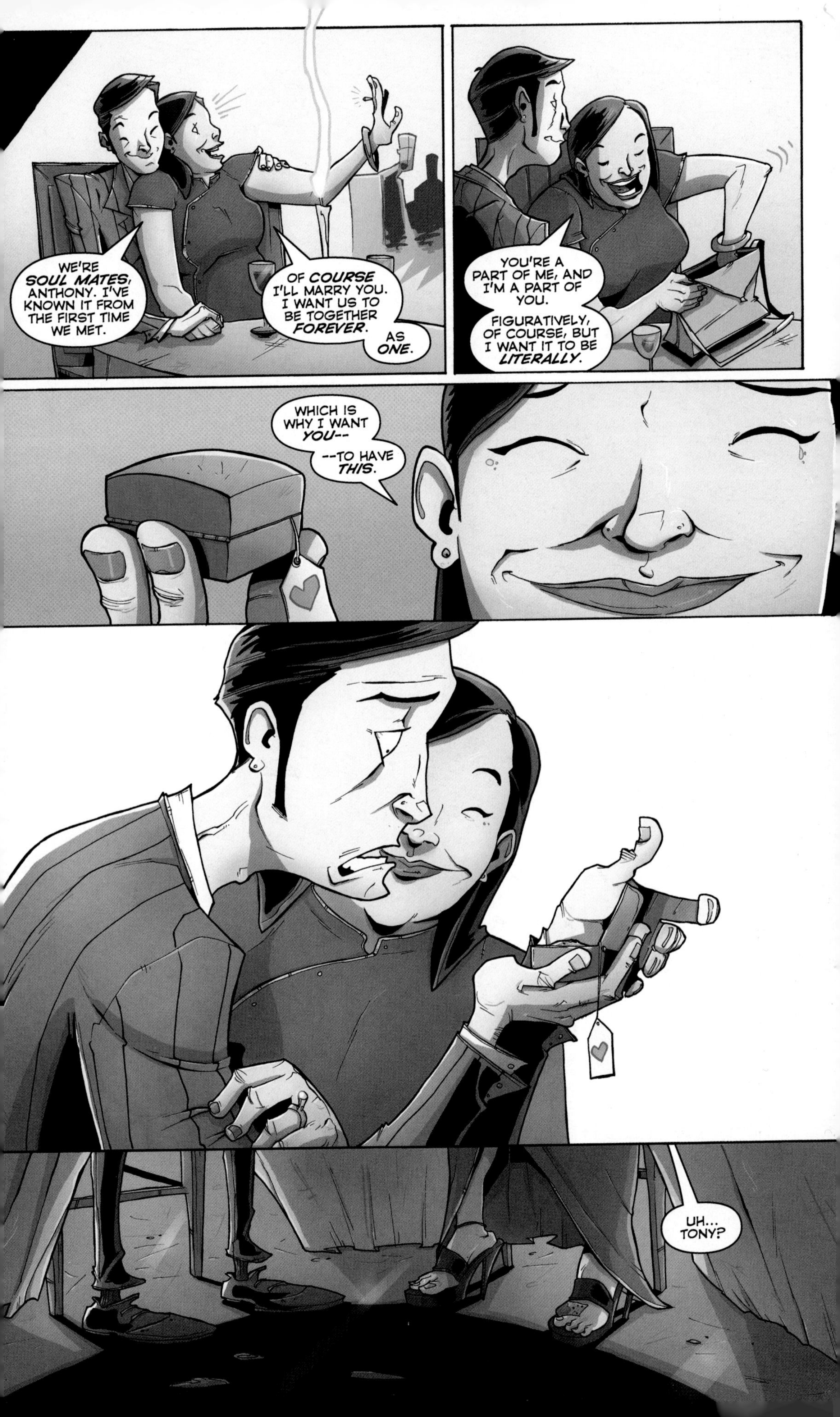
WE'RE SOUL MATES, ANTHONY. I'VE KNOWN IT FROM THE FIRST TIME WE MET.
OF COURSE I'LL MARRY YOU. I WANT US TO BE TOGETHER FOREVER.
AS ONE.
YOU'RE A PART OF ME, AND I'M A PART OF YOU.
FIGURATIVELY, OF COURSE, BUT I WANT IT TO BE LITERALLY.
WHICH IS WHY I WANT YOU--
--TO HAVE THIS.
UH... TONY?

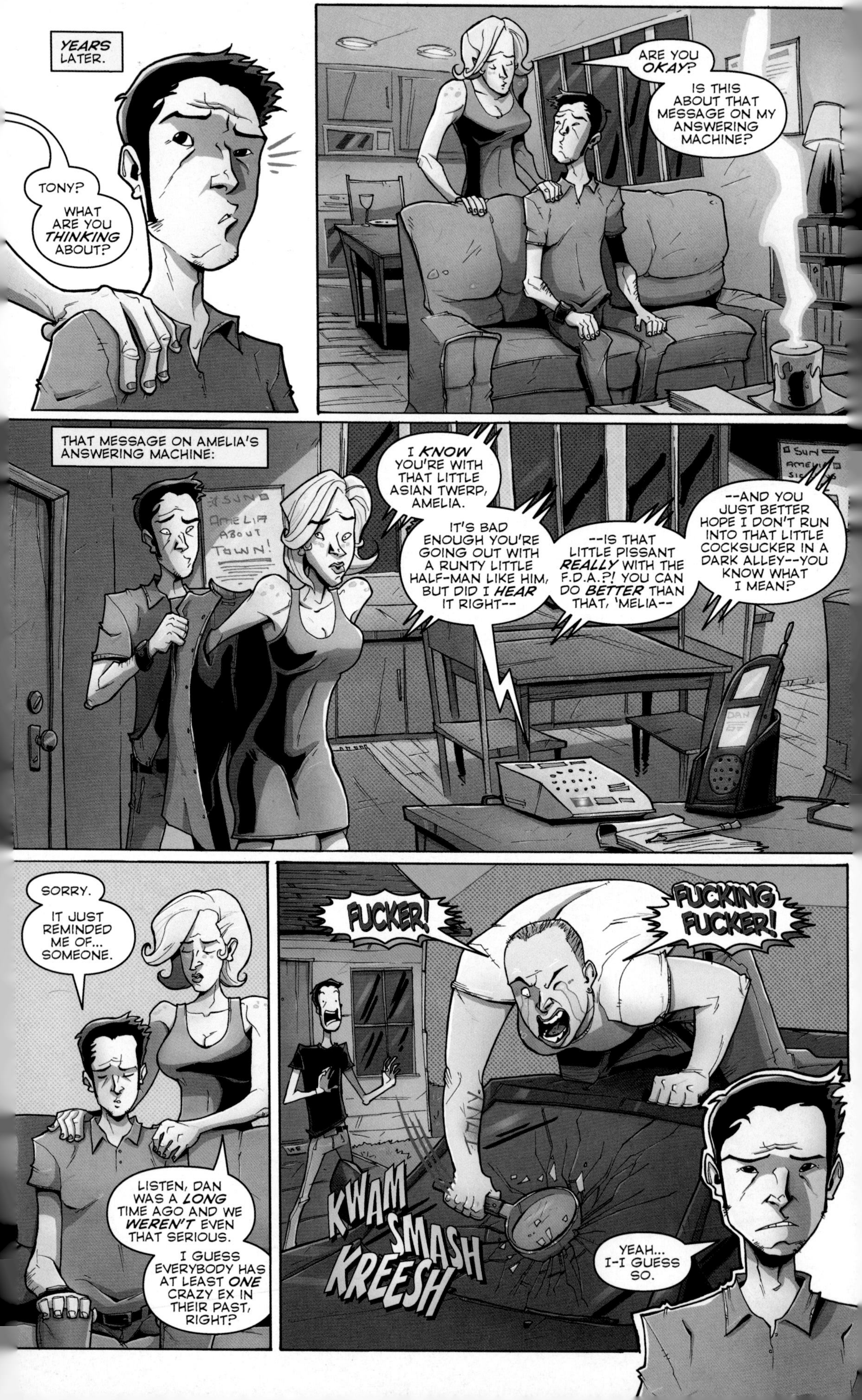
YEARS LATER.
TONY?
WHAT ARE YOU THINKING ABOUT?
ARE YOU OKAY?
IS THIS ABOUT THAT MESSAGE ON MY ANSWERING MACHINE?
THAT MESSAGE ON AMELIA'S ANSWERING MACHINE:
I KNOW YOU'RE WITH THAT LITTLE ASIAN TWERP, AMELIA.
IT'S BAD ENOUGH YOU'RE GOING OUT WITH A RUNTY LITTLE HALF-MAN LIKE HIM, BUT DID I HEAR IT RIGHT--
--IS THAT LITTLE PISSANT REALLY WITH THE F.D.A.?! YOU CAN DO BETTER THAN THAT, 'MELIA--
--AND YOU JUST BETTER HOPE I DON'T RUN INTO THAT LITTLE COCKSUCKER IN A DARK ALLEY--YOU KNOW WHAT I MEAN?
SORRY.
IT JUST REMINDED ME OF... SOMEONE.
LISTEN, DAN WAS A LONG TIME AGO AND WE WEREN'T EVEN THAT SERIOUS.
I GUESS EVERYBODY HAS AT LEAST ONE CRAZY EX IN THEIR PAST, RIGHT?
FUCKER!
FUCKING FUCKER!
KWAM
SMASH
KREESH
YEAH... I-I GUESS SO.

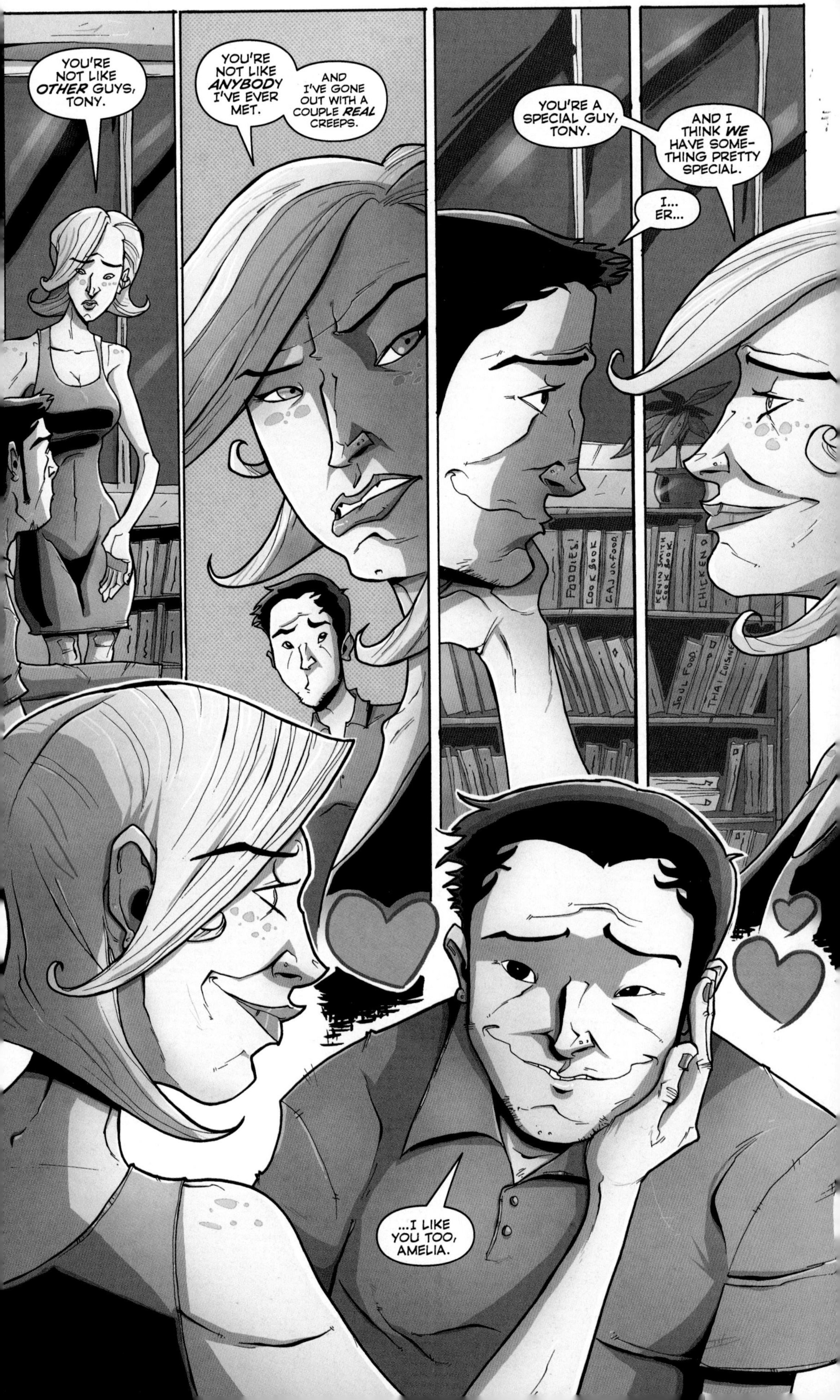
YOU'RE NOT LIKE *OTHER* GUYS, TONY.
YOU'RE NOT LIKE *ANYBODY* I'VE EVER MET.
AND I'VE GONE OUT WITH A COUPLE *REAL* CREEPS.
YOU'RE A SPECIAL GUY, TONY.
AND I THINK *WE* HAVE SOMETHING PRETTY SPECIAL.
I... ER...
FOODIES!
LOOK BOOK
CAJUN FOOD
KEVIN SMITH COOK BOOK
CHICKEN
SOUL FOOD
THAI CUISINE
...I LIKE YOU TOO, AMELIA.

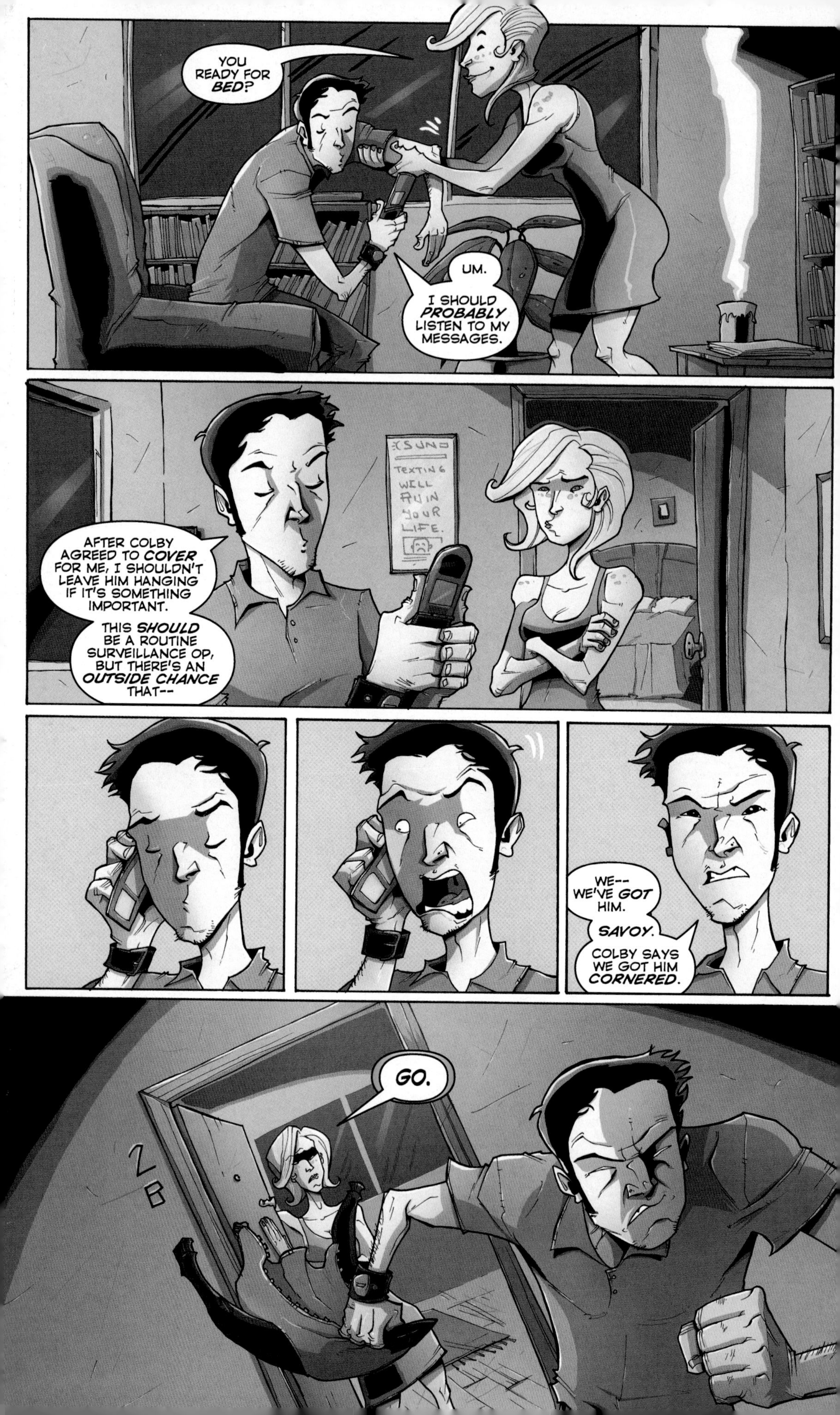
YOU READY FOR *BED?*
UM.
I SHOULD *PROBABLY* LISTEN TO MY MESSAGES.
TEXTING WELL RUIN YOUR LIFE.
AFTER COLBY AGREED TO *COVER* FOR ME, I SHOULDN'T LEAVE HIM HANGING IF IT'S SOMETHING IMPORTANT.
THIS *SHOULD* BE A ROUTINE SURVEILLANCE OP, BUT THERE'S AN *OUTSIDE CHANCE* THAT--
WE-- WE'VE *GOT* HIM.
SAVOY.
COLBY SAYS WE GOT HIM *CORNERED*.
GO.
2B

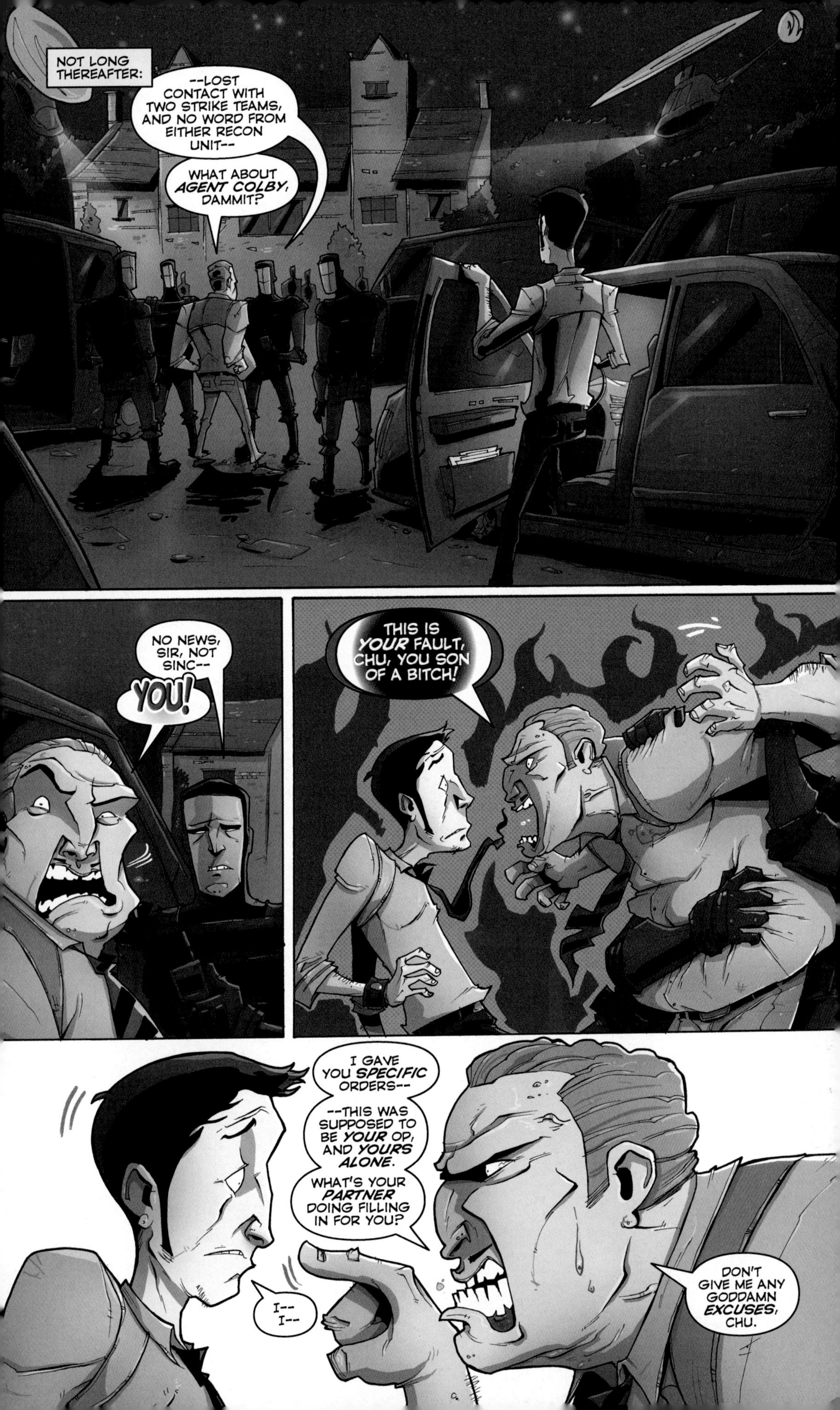
NOT LONG THEREAFTER:
--LOST CONTACT WITH TWO STRIKE TEAMS, AND NO WORD FROM EITHER RECON UNIT--
WHAT ABOUT AGENT COLBY, DAMMIT?
NO NEWS, SIR, NOT SINC--
YOU!
THIS IS YOUR FAULT, CHU, YOU SON OF A BITCH!
I GAVE YOU SPECIFIC ORDERS--
--THIS WAS SUPPOSED TO BE YOUR OP, AND YOURS ALONE.
WHAT'S YOUR PARTNER DOING FILLING IN FOR YOU?
I-- I--
DON'T GIVE ME ANY GODDAMN EXCUSES, CHU.

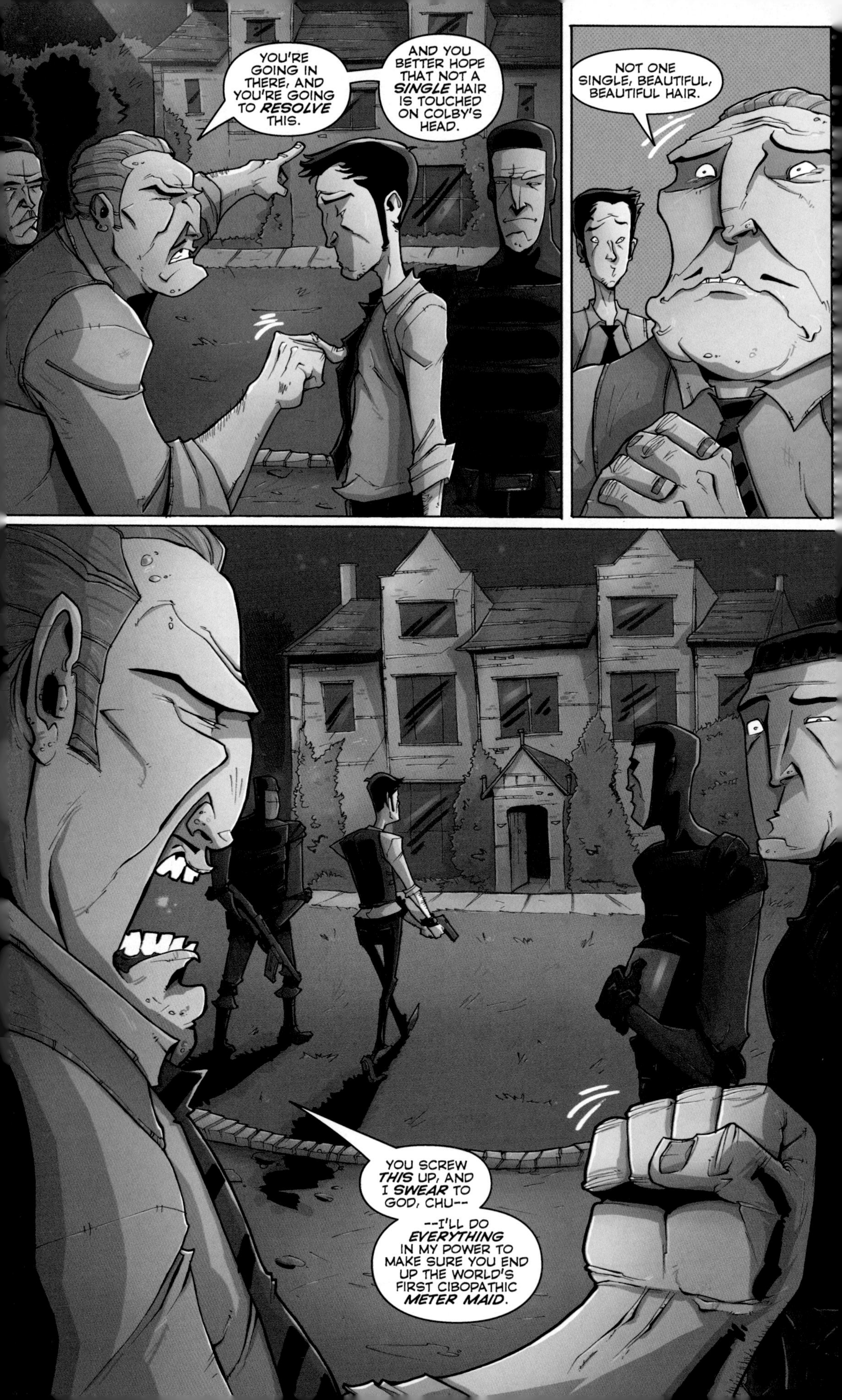
YOU'RE GOING IN THERE, AND YOU'RE GOING TO *RESOLVE* THIS.
AND YOU BETTER HOPE THAT NOT A *SINGLE* HAIR IS TOUCHED ON COLBY'S HEAD.
NOT ONE SINGLE, BEAUTIFUL, BEAUTIFUL HAIR.
YOU SCREW *THIS* UP, AND I *SWEAR* TO GOD, CHU--
--I'LL DO *EVERYTHING* IN MY POWER TO MAKE SURE YOU END UP THE WORLD'S FIRST CIBOPATHIC *METER MAID*.

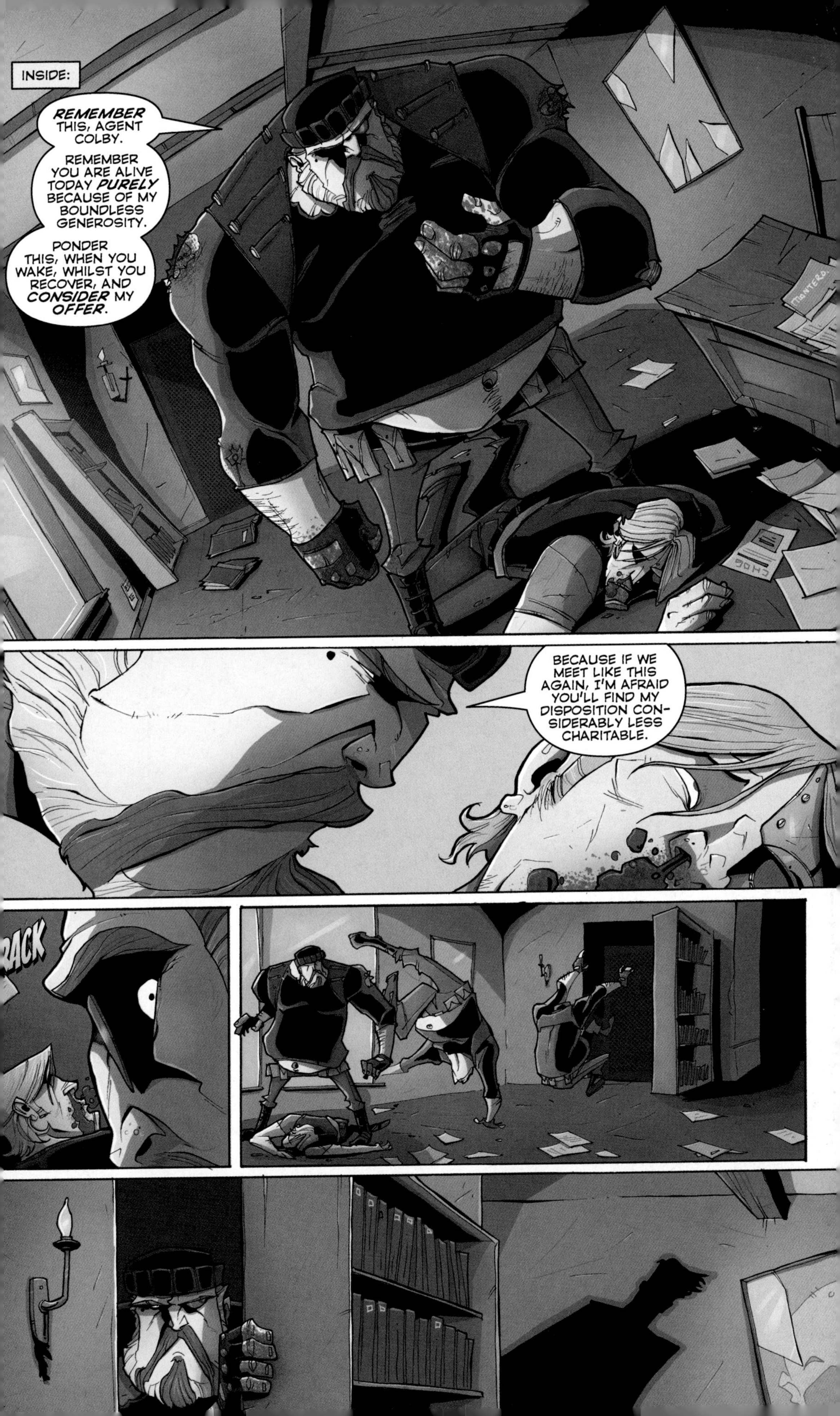
INSIDE:
REMEMBER THIS, AGENT COLBY.
REMEMBER YOU ARE ALIVE TODAY PURELY BECAUSE OF MY BOUNDLESS GENEROSITY.
PONDER THIS, WHEN YOU WAKE, WHILST YOU RECOVER, AND CONSIDER MY OFFER.
BECAUSE IF WE MEET LIKE THIS AGAIN, I'M AFRAID YOU'LL FIND MY DISPOSITION CONSIDERABLY LESS CHARITABLE.
RACK

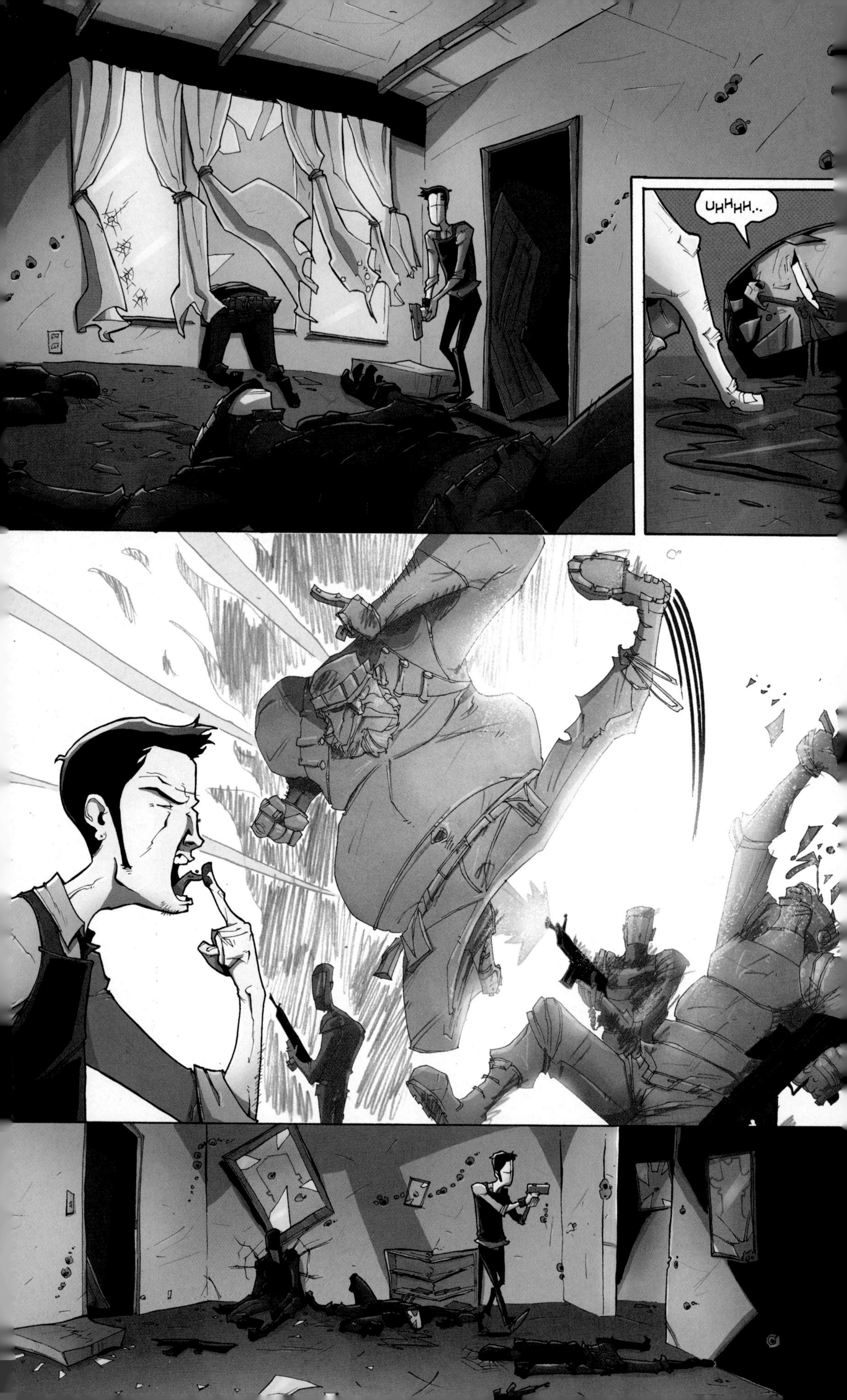
UHHHH..

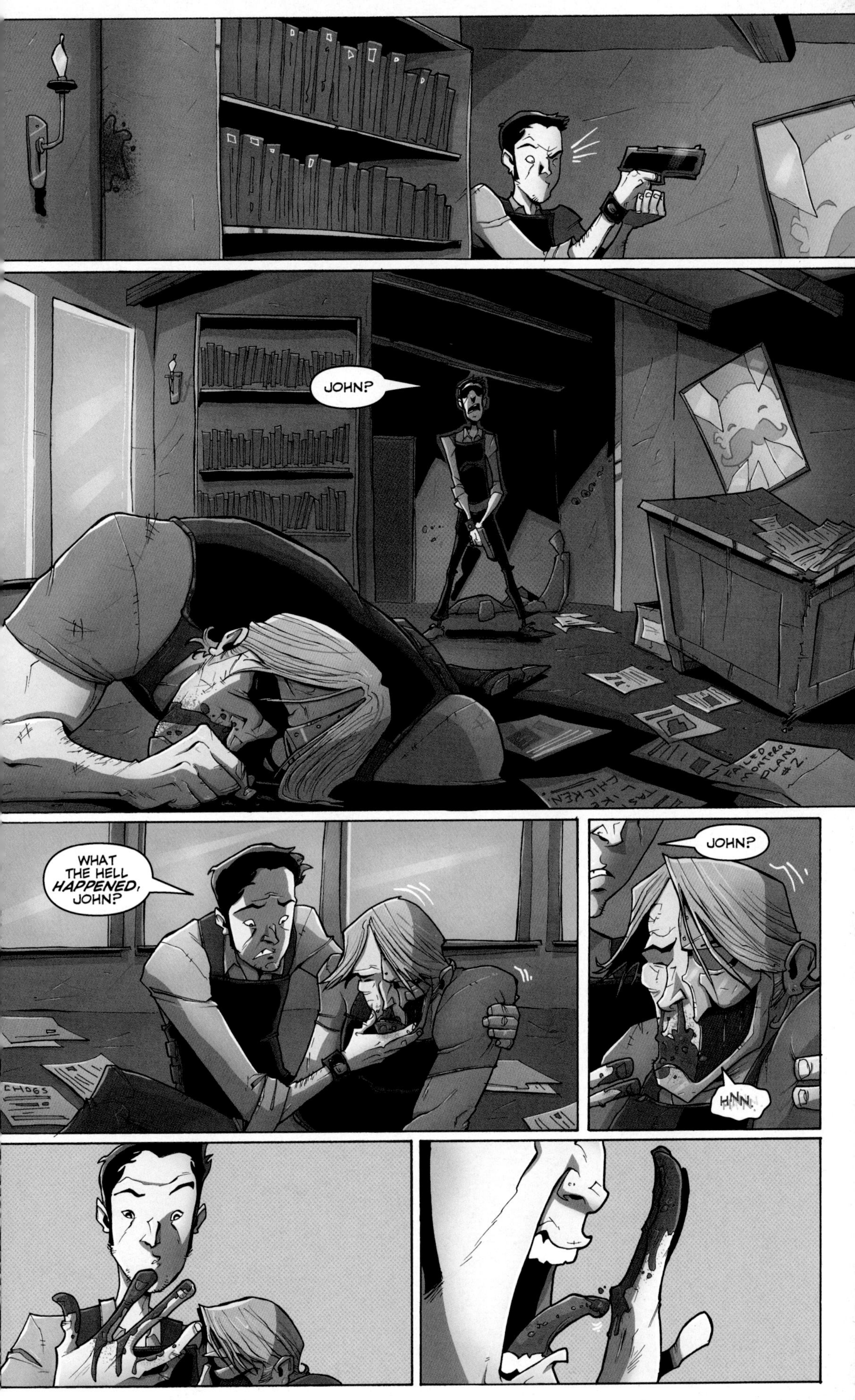
JOHN?
FAILED MONTERO PLANS #2
WHAT THE HELL HAPPENED, JOHN?
JOHN?
HNNN.

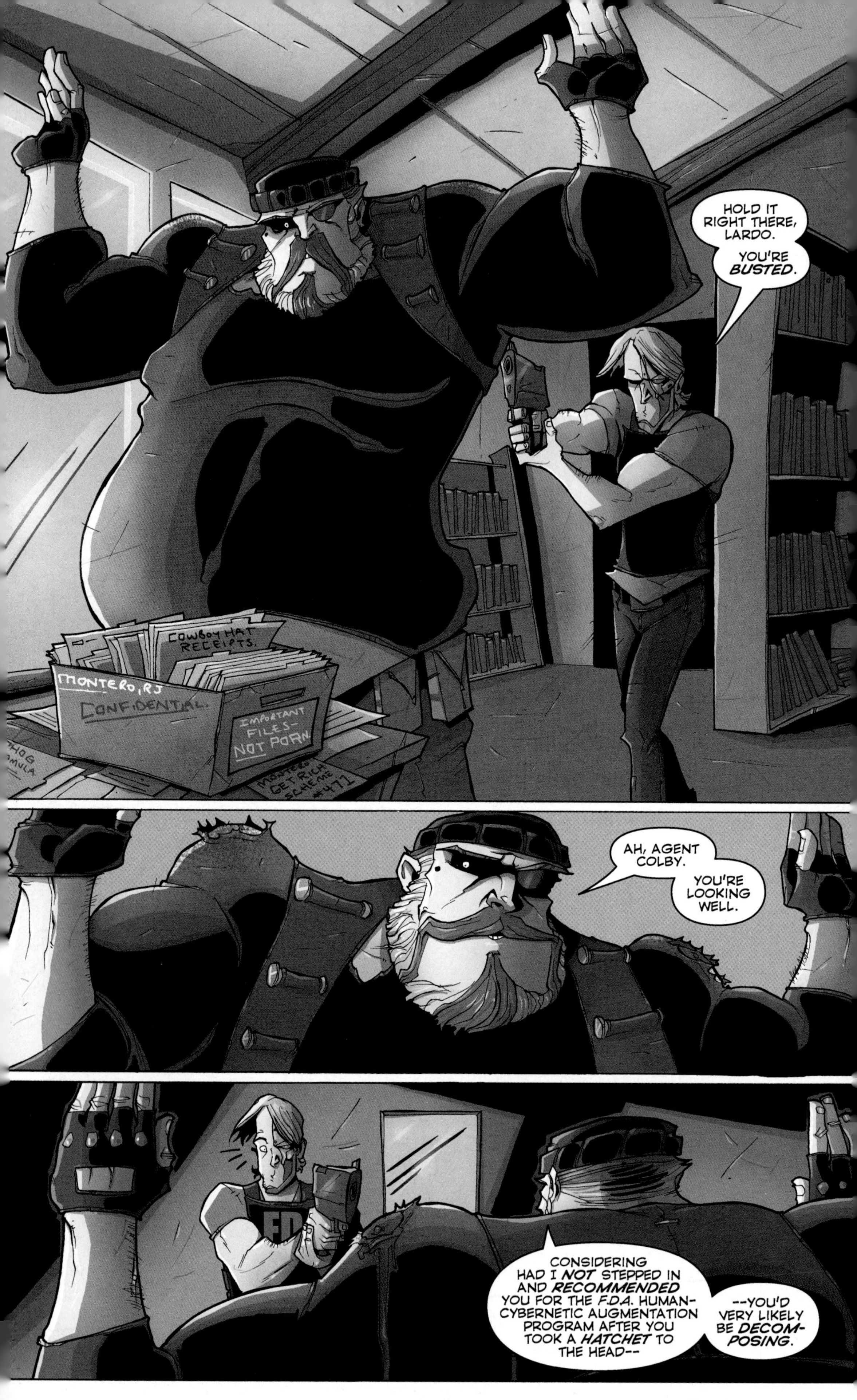
COWBOY HAT RECEIPTS.
MONTERO, RJ
CONFIDENTIAL
IMPORTANT FILES- NOT PORN
MONTERO GET RICH SCHEME #471
HOLD IT RIGHT THERE, LARDO.
YOU'RE ***BUSTED***.
AH, AGENT COLBY.
YOU'RE LOOKING WELL.
CONSIDERING HAD I ***NOT*** STEPPED IN AND ***RECOMMENDED*** YOU FOR THE *F.D.A.* HUMAN-CYBERNETIC AUGMENTATION PROGRAM AFTER YOU TOOK A ***HATCHET*** TO THE HEAD--
--YOU'D VERY LIKELY BE ***DECOMPOSING***.

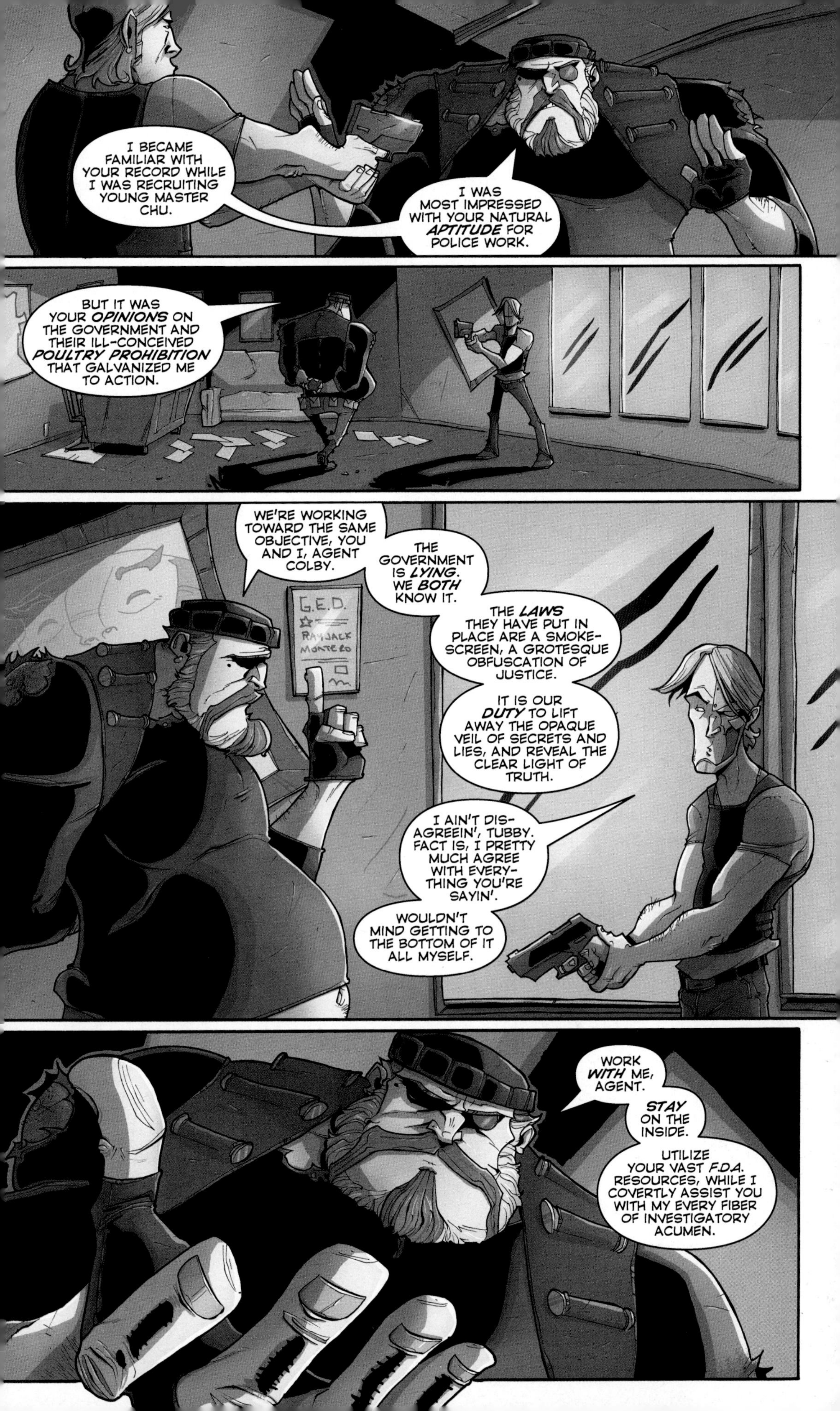

I BECAME FAMILIAR WITH YOUR RECORD WHILE I WAS RECRUITING YOUNG MASTER CHU.
I WAS MOST IMPRESSED WITH YOUR NATURAL APTITUDE FOR POLICE WORK.
BUT IT WAS YOUR OPINIONS ON THE GOVERNMENT AND THEIR ILL-CONCEIVED POULTRY PROHIBITION THAT GALVANIZED ME TO ACTION.
WE'RE WORKING TOWARD THE SAME OBJECTIVE, YOU AND I, AGENT COLBY.
G.E.D.
RAYJACK MONTERO
THE GOVERNMENT IS LYING. WE BOTH KNOW IT.
THE LAWS THEY HAVE PUT IN PLACE ARE A SMOKE-SCREEN, A GROTESQUE OBFUSCATION OF JUSTICE.
IT IS OUR DUTY TO LIFT AWAY THE OPAQUE VEIL OF SECRETS AND LIES, AND REVEAL THE CLEAR LIGHT OF TRUTH.
I AIN'T DIS-AGREEIN', TUBBY. FACT IS, I PRETTY MUCH AGREE WITH EVERY-THING YOU'RE SAYIN'.
WOULDN'T MIND GETTING TO THE BOTTOM OF IT ALL MYSELF.
WORK WITH ME, AGENT.
STAY ON THE INSIDE.
UTILIZE YOUR VAST F.D.A. RESOURCES, WHILE I COVERTLY ASSIST YOU WITH MY EVERY FIBER OF INVESTIGATORY ACUMEN.

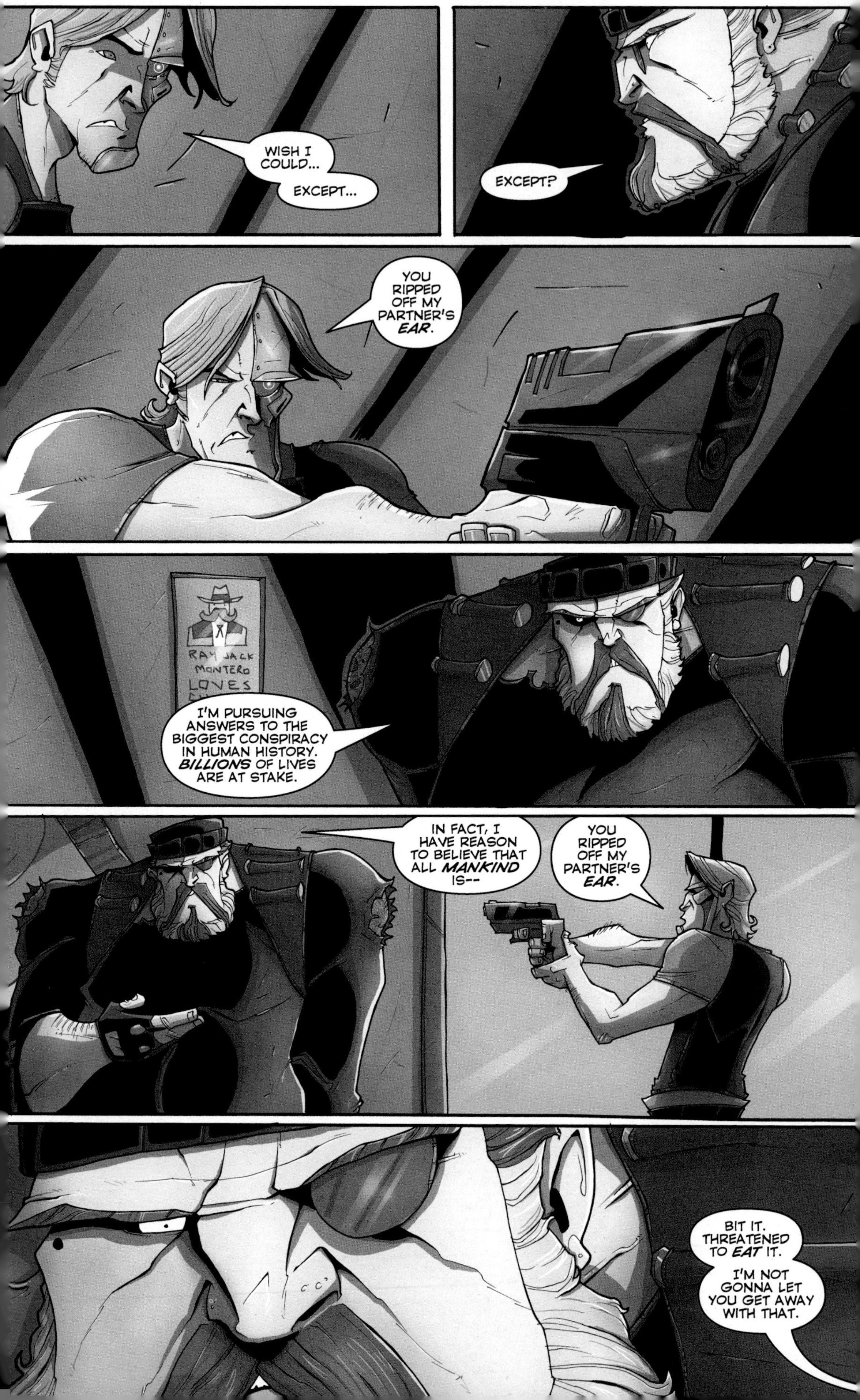

WISH I COULD...
EXCEPT...
EXCEPT?
YOU RIPPED OFF MY PARTNER'S *EAR*.
RAY JACK MONTERO LOVES
I'M PURSUING ANSWERS TO THE BIGGEST CONSPIRACY IN HUMAN HISTORY. *BILLIONS* OF LIVES ARE AT STAKE.
IN FACT, I HAVE REASON TO BELIEVE THAT ALL *MANKIND* IS--
YOU RIPPED OFF MY PARTNER'S *EAR*.
BIT IT. THREATENED TO *EAT* IT.
I'M NOT GONNA LET YOU GET AWAY WITH THAT.

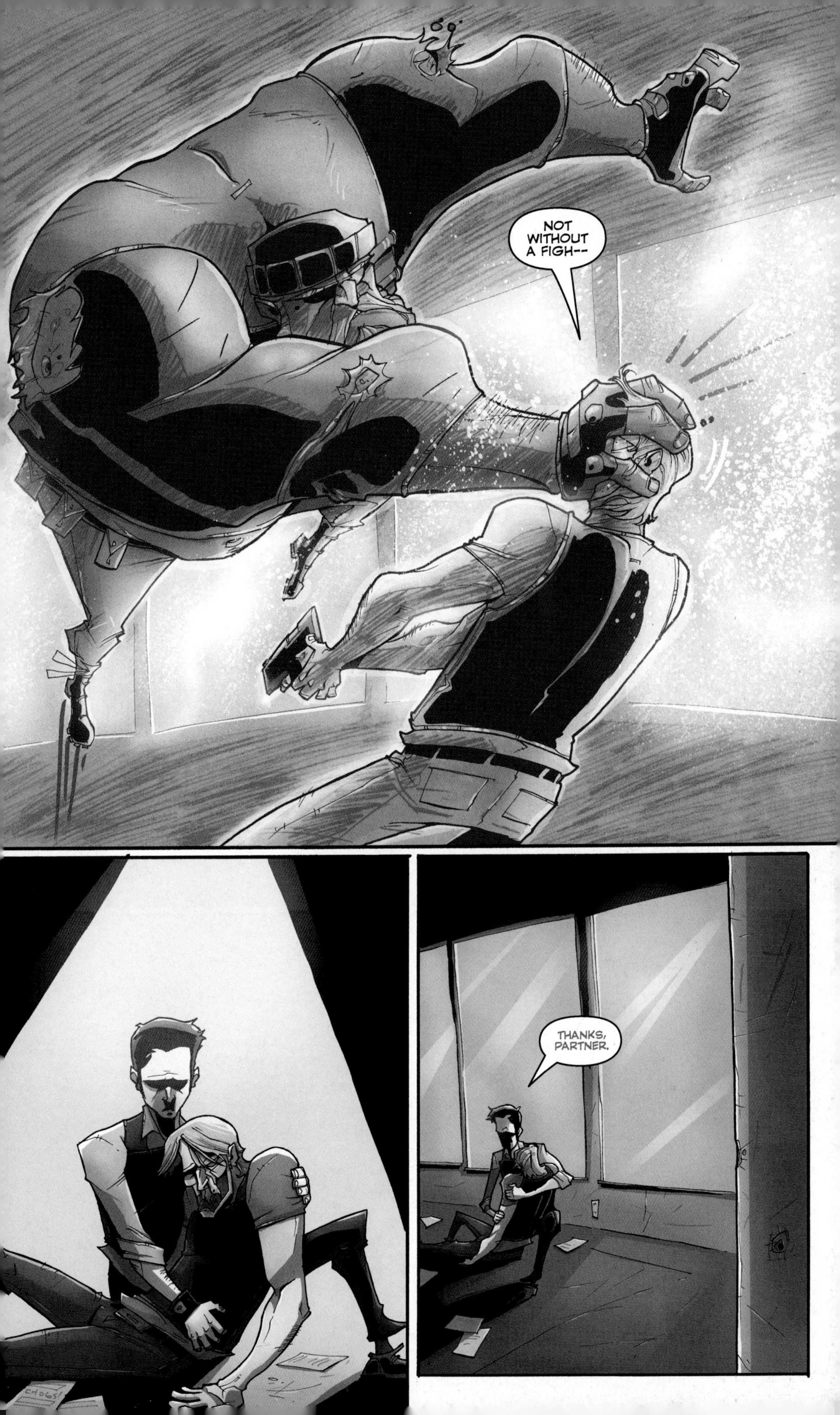
NOT WITHOUT A FIGH--
THANKS, PARTNER.

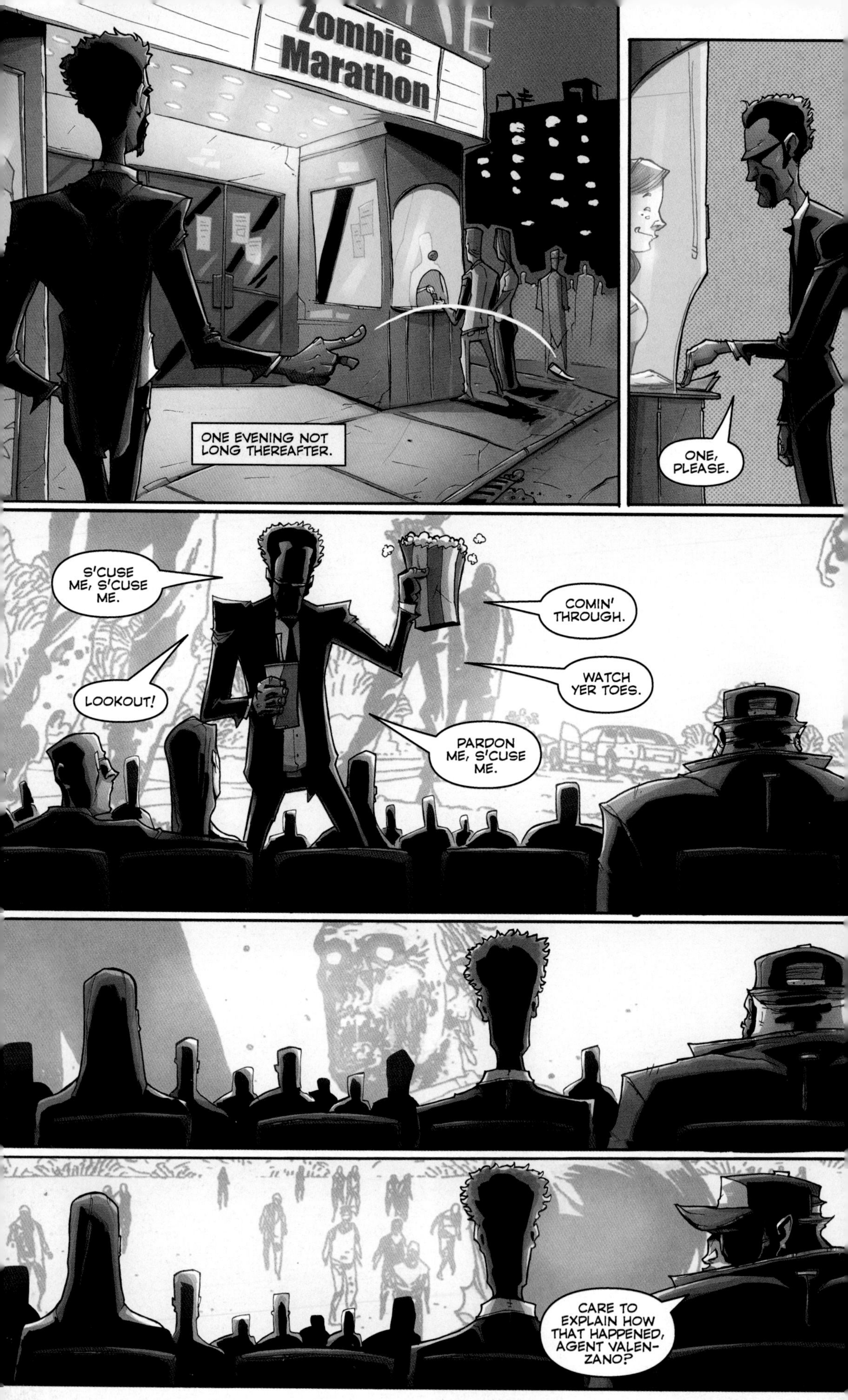
Zombie Marathon
ONE EVENING NOT LONG THEREAFTER.
ONE, PLEASE.
S'CUSE ME, S'CUSE ME.
COMIN' THROUGH.
LOOKOUT!
WATCH YER TOES.
PARDON ME, S'CUSE ME.
CARE TO EXPLAIN HOW THAT HAPPENED, AGENT VALEN-ZANO?

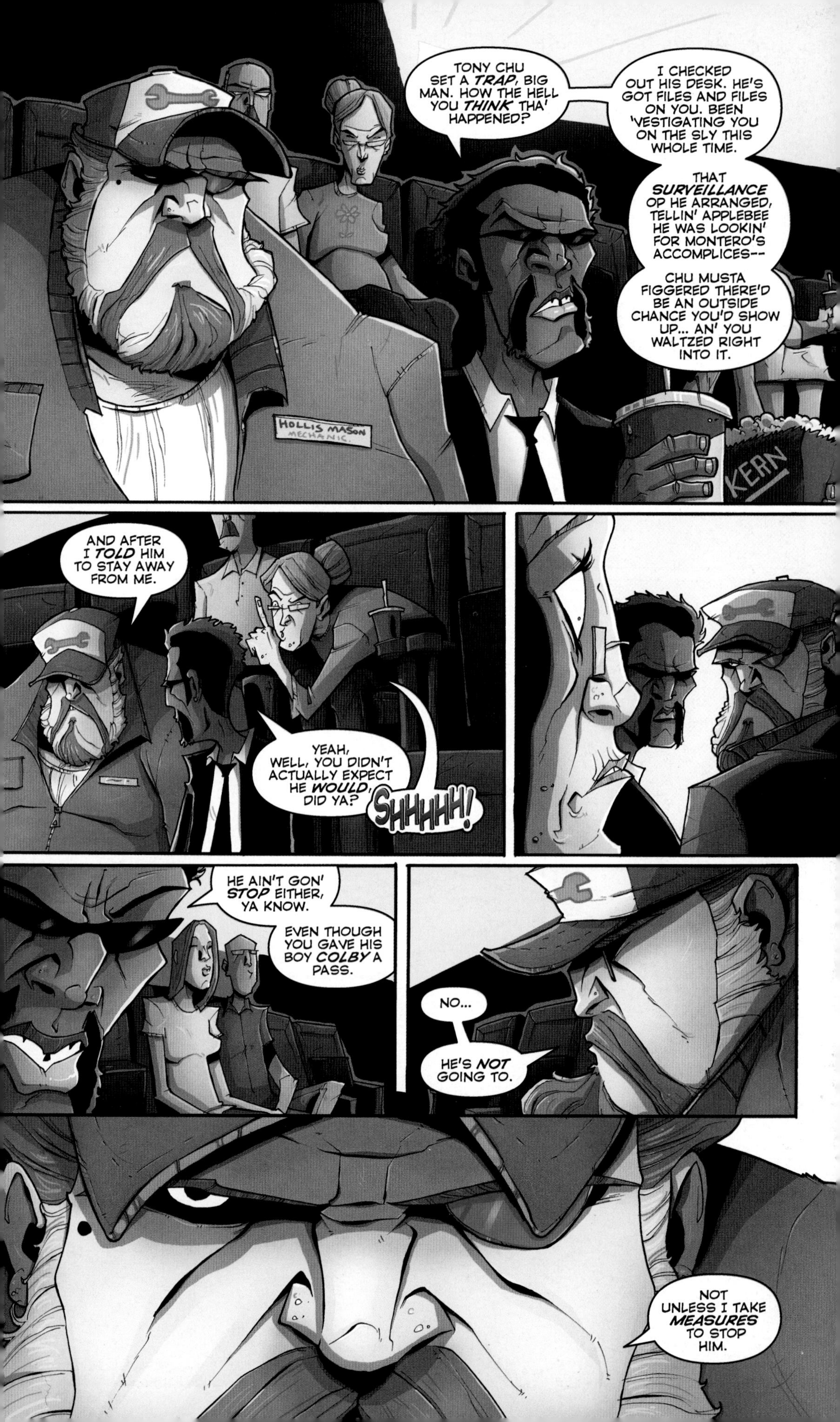

TONY CHU SET A *TRAP*, BIG MAN. HOW THE HELL YOU *THINK* THA' HAPPENED?
I CHECKED OUT HIS DESK. HE'S GOT FILES AND FILES ON YOU. BEEN 'VESTIGATING YOU ON THE SLY THIS WHOLE TIME.
THAT *SURVEILLANCE* OP HE ARRANGED, TELLIN' APPLEBEE HE WAS LOOKIN' FOR MONTERO'S ACCOMPLICES--
CHU MUSTA FIGGERED THERE'D BE AN OUTSIDE CHANCE YOU'D SHOW UP... AN' YOU WALTZED RIGHT INTO IT.
HOLLIS MASON MECHANIC
KERN
AND AFTER I *TOLD* HIM TO STAY AWAY FROM ME.
YEAH, WELL, YOU DIDN'T ACTUALLY EXPECT HE *WOULD*, DID YA?
SHHHHH!
HE AIN'T GON' *STOP* EITHER, YA KNOW.
EVEN THOUGH YOU GAVE HIS BOY *COLBY* A PASS.
NO...
HE'S *NOT* GOING TO.
NOT UNLESS I TAKE *MEASURES* TO STOP HIM.

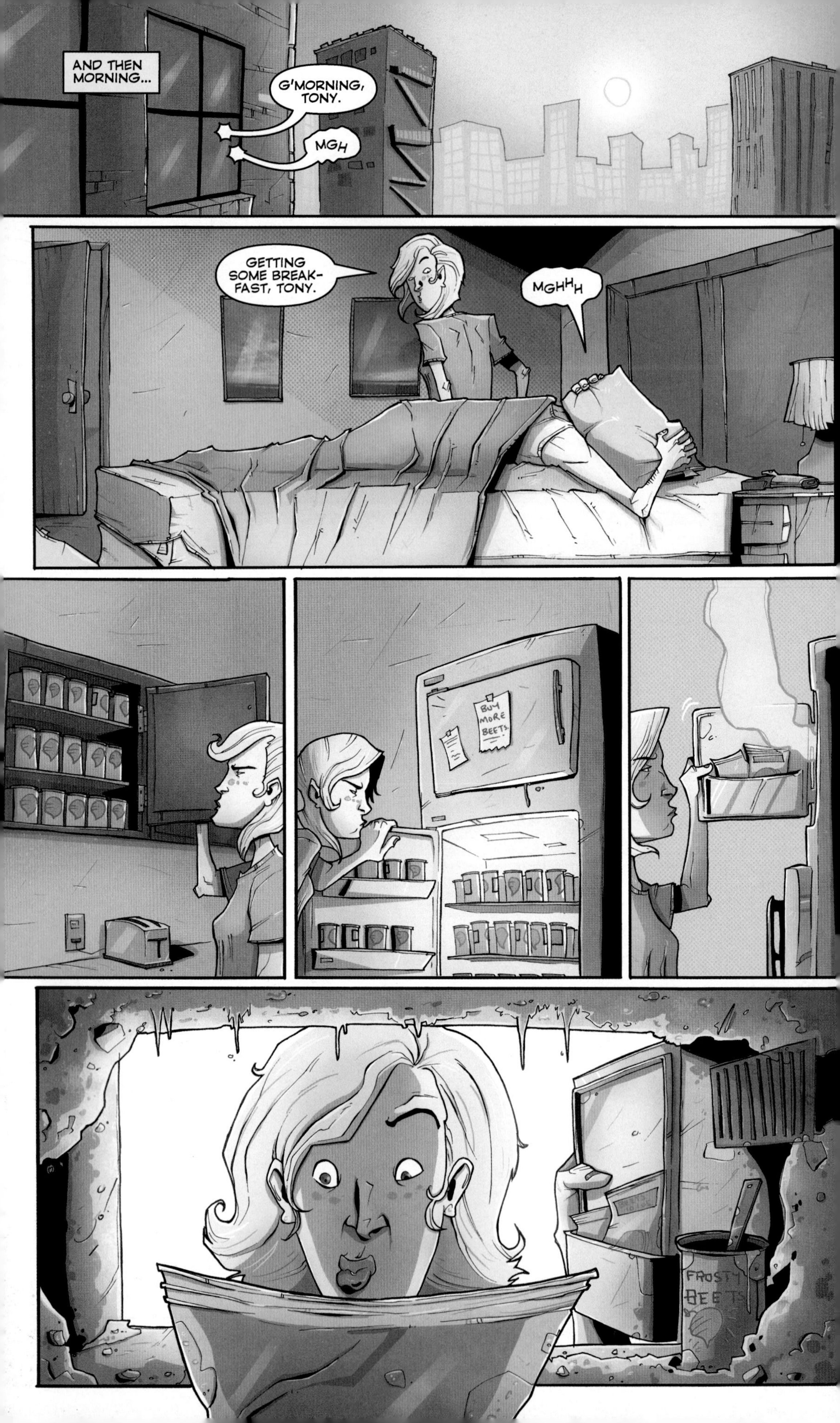
AND THEN MORNING...
G'MORNING, TONY.
MGH
GETTING SOME BREAK-FAST, TONY.
MGHHH
BUY MORE BEETS
FROSTY BEETS

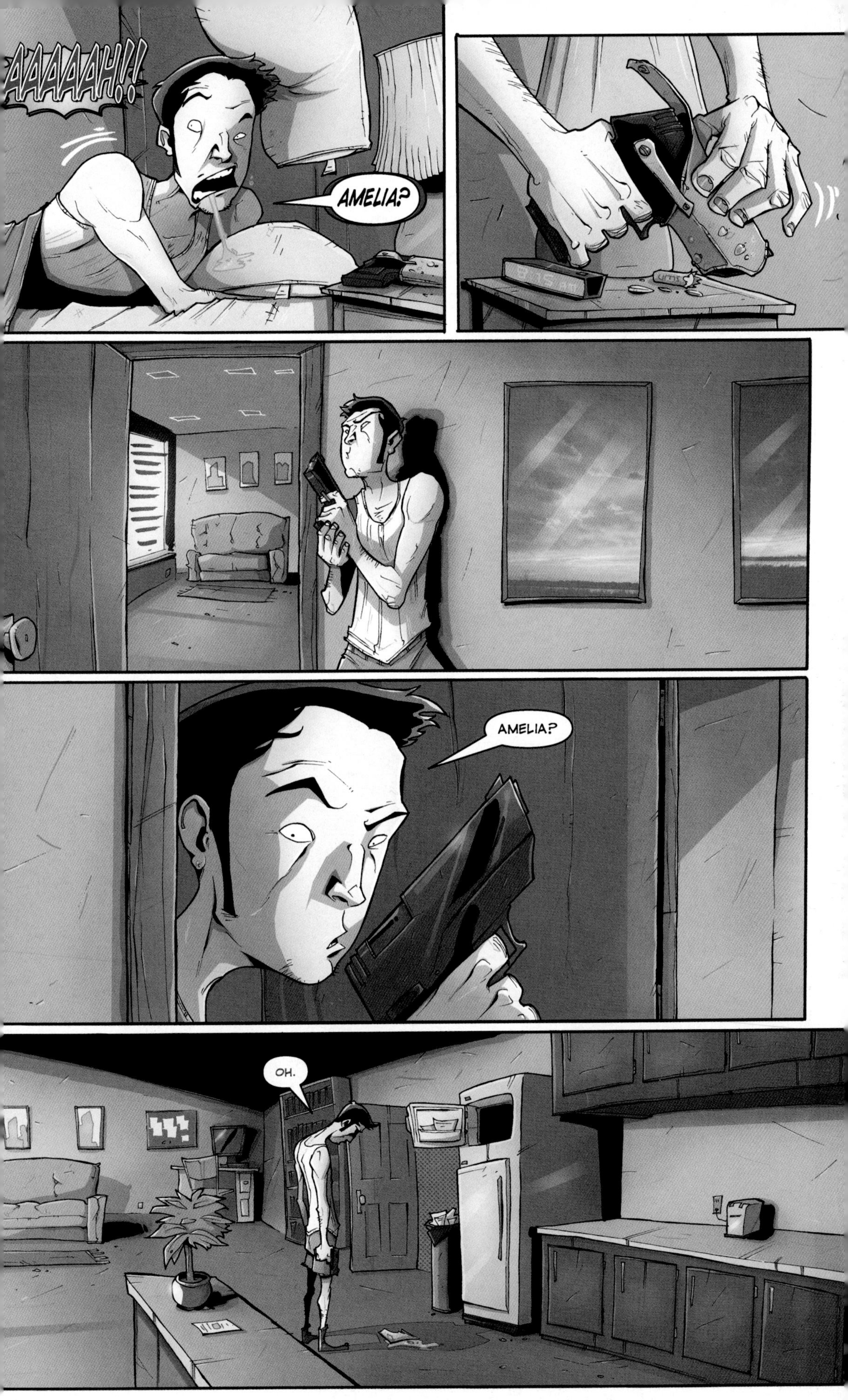
AAAAAH!!
AMELIA?
AMELIA?
OH.

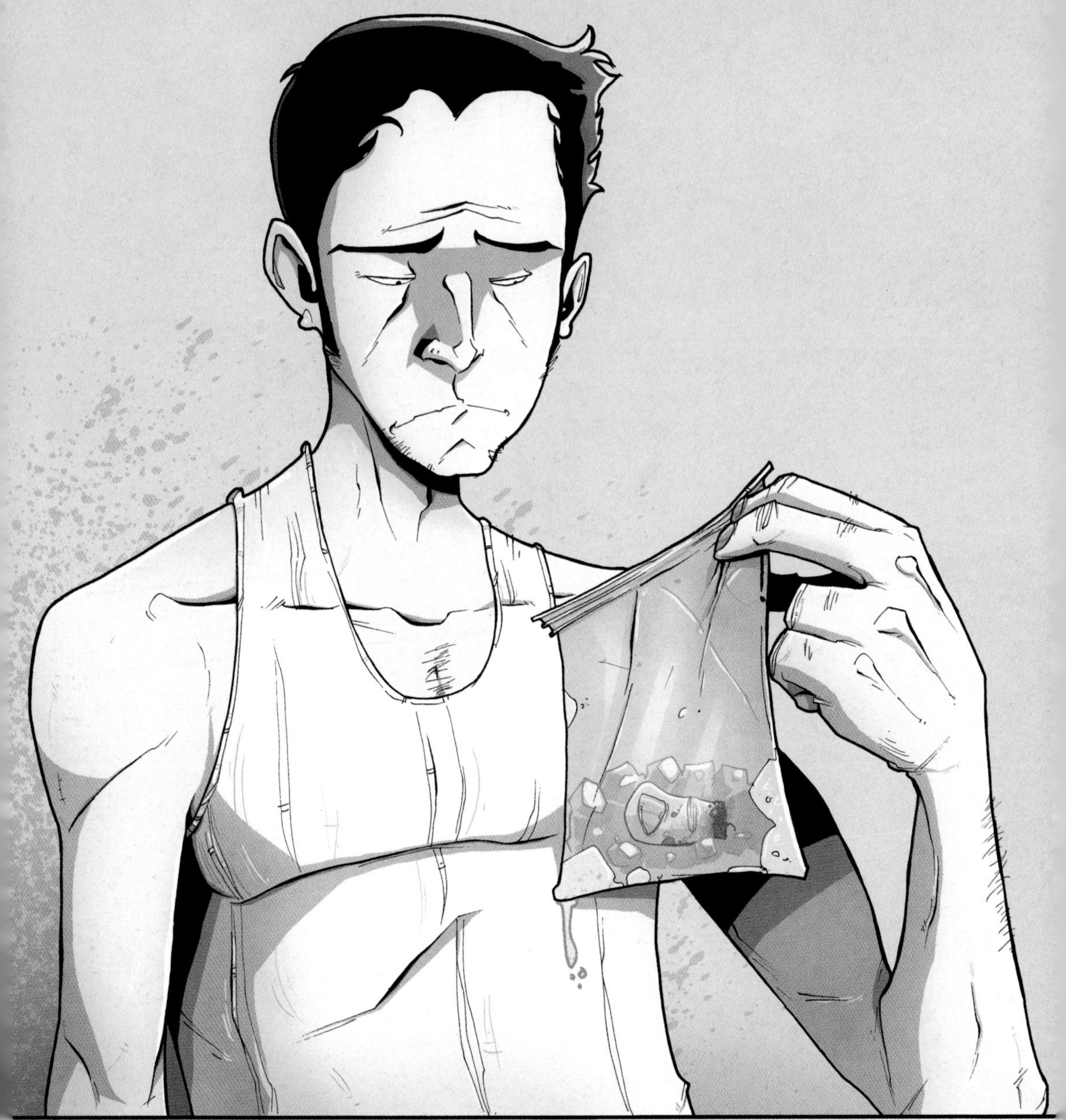

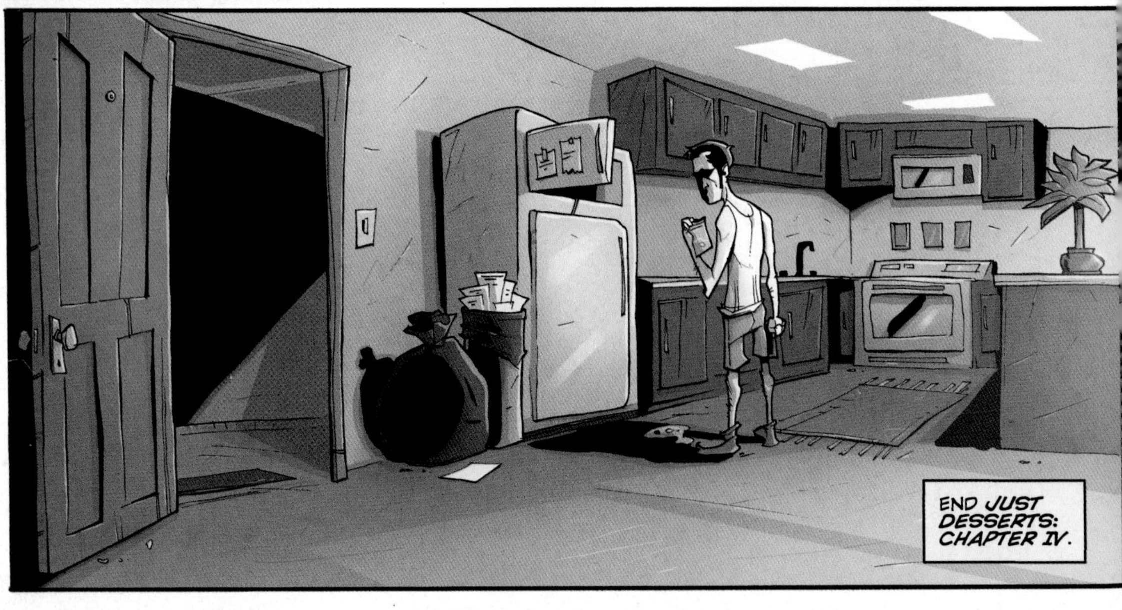
END JUST DESSERTS: CHAPTER IV.

Chapter 5

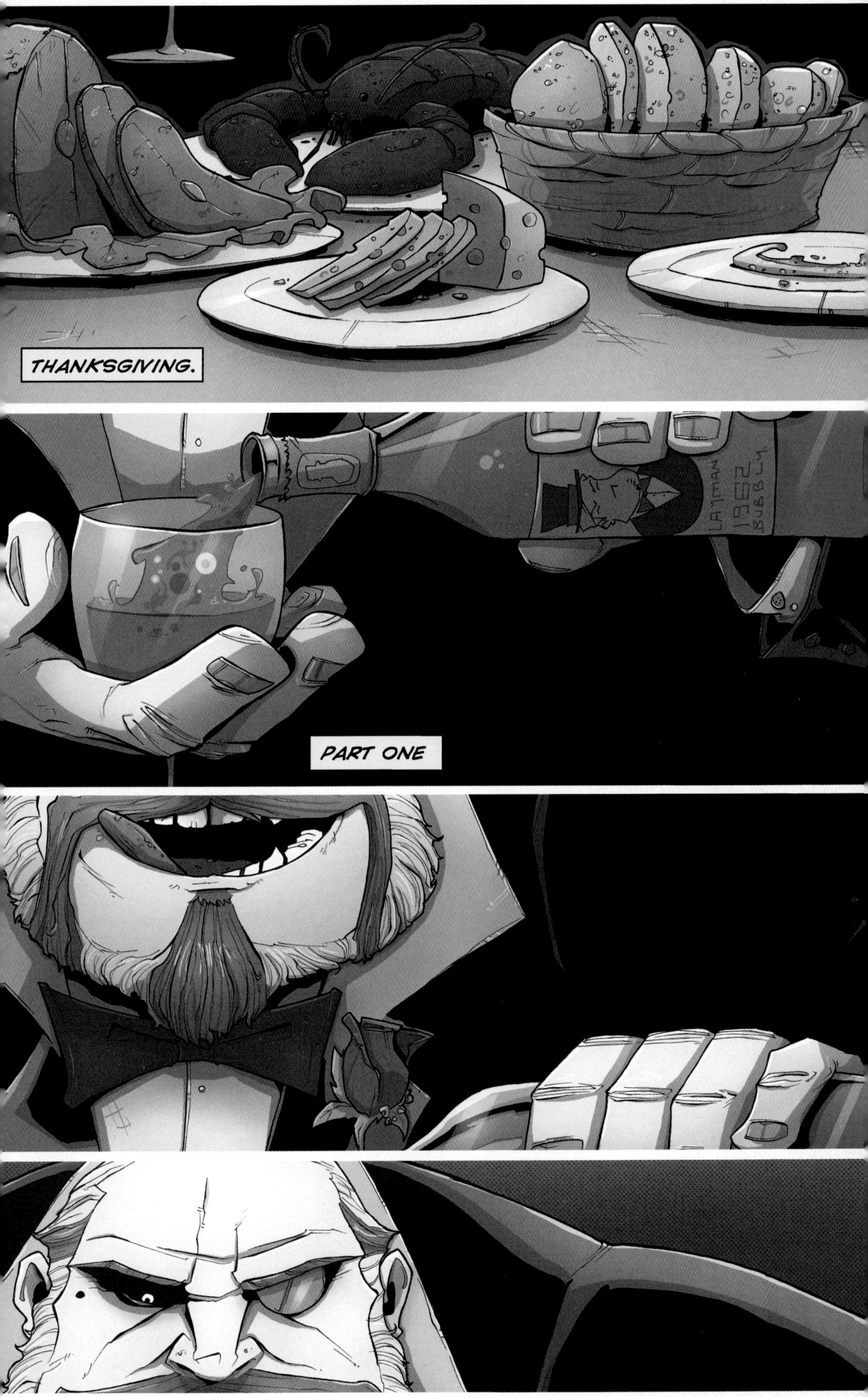
THANKSGIVING.
LAYMAN
1962
BUBBLY
PART ONE

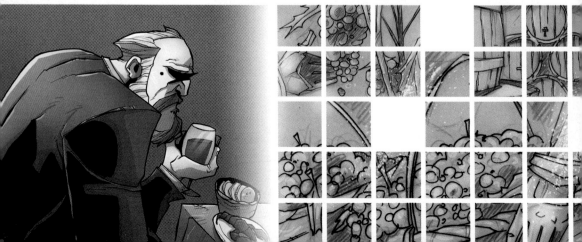

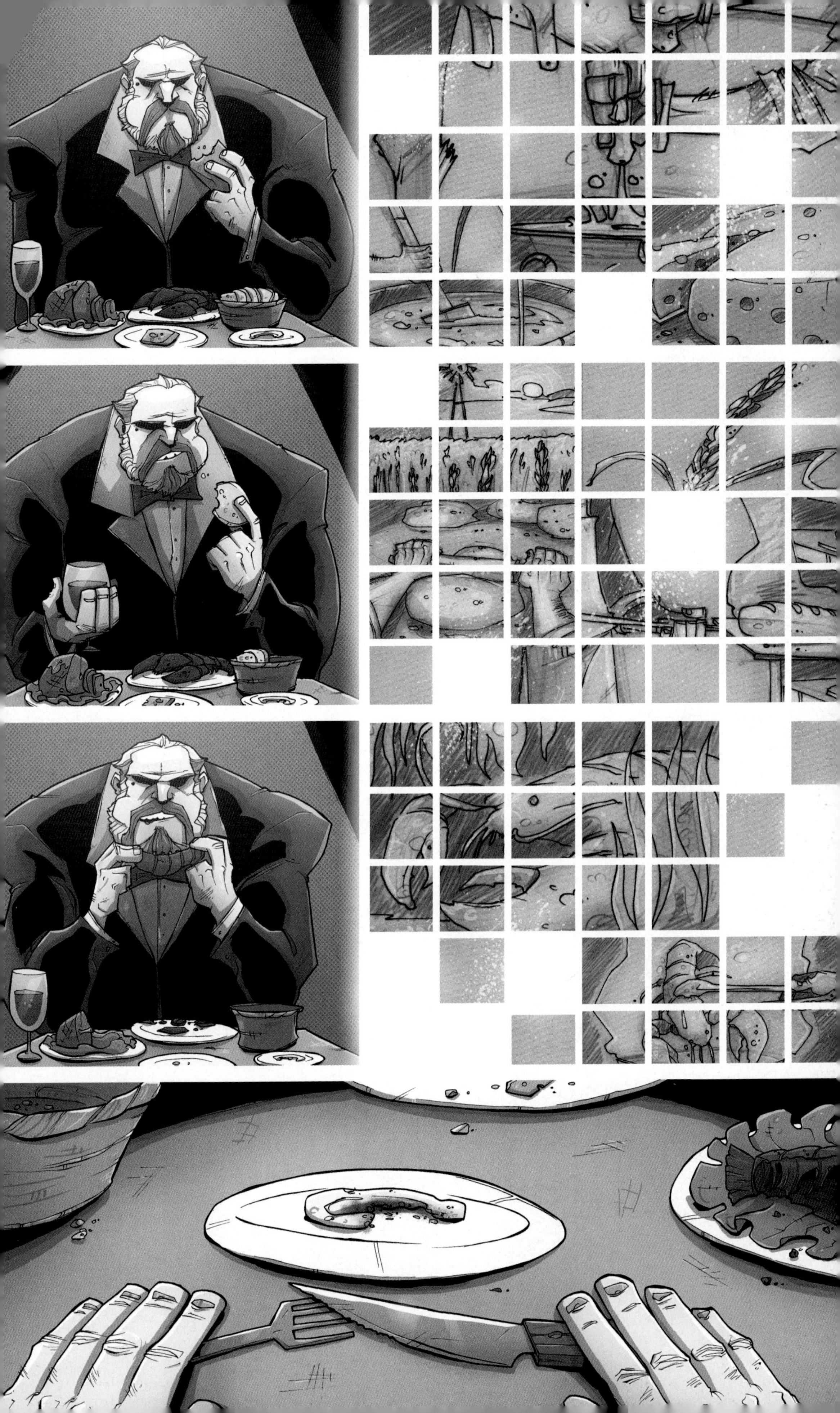

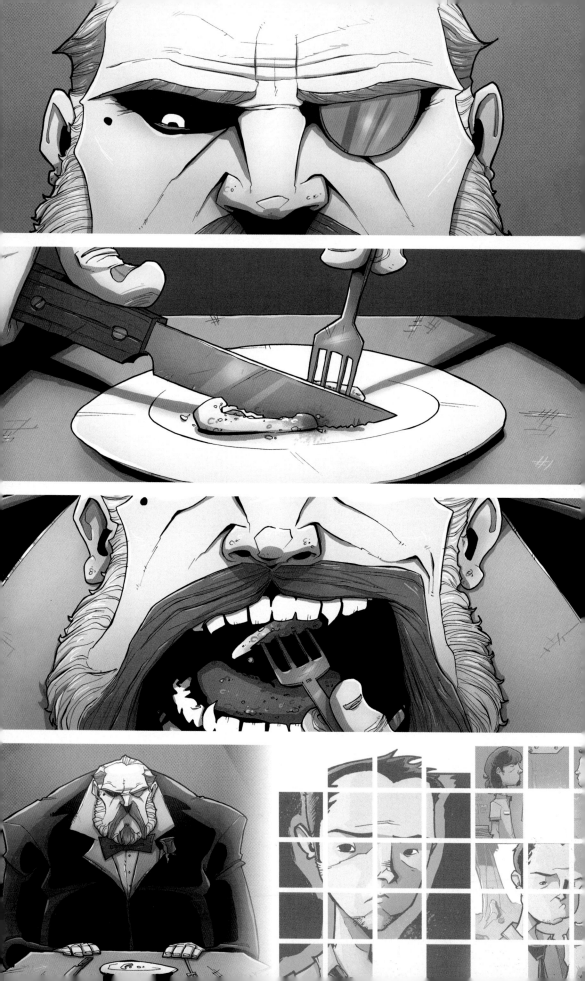

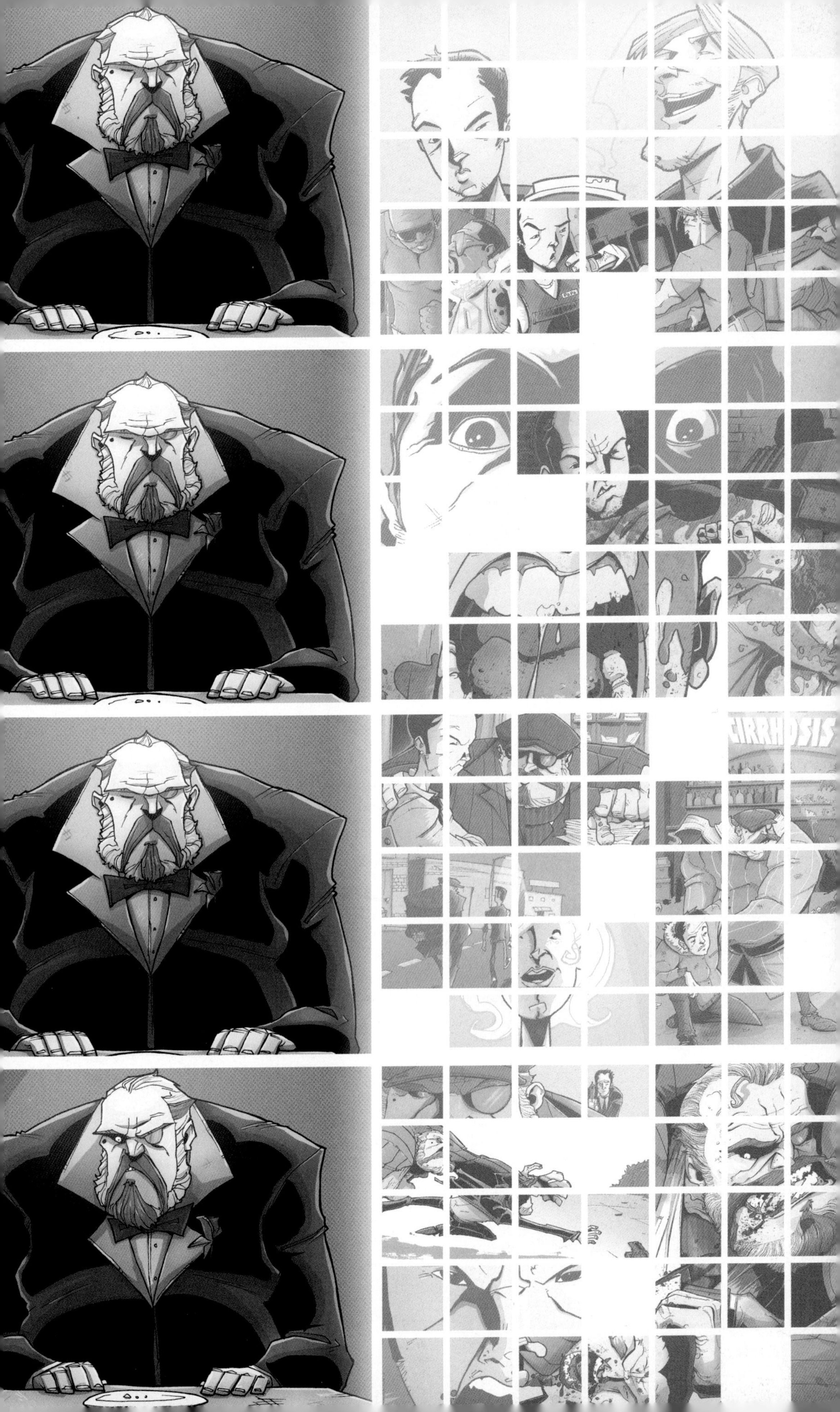
CIRRHOSIS

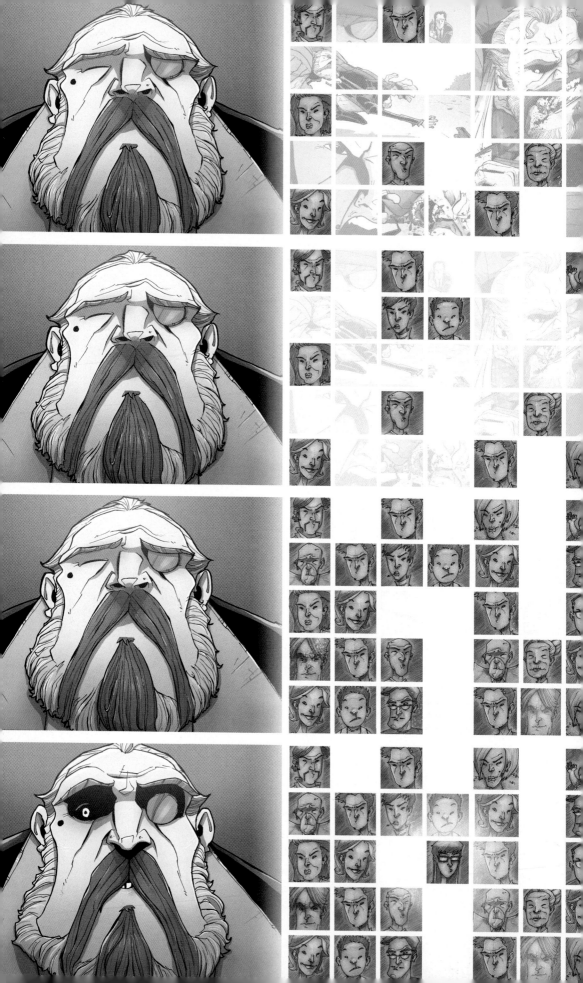

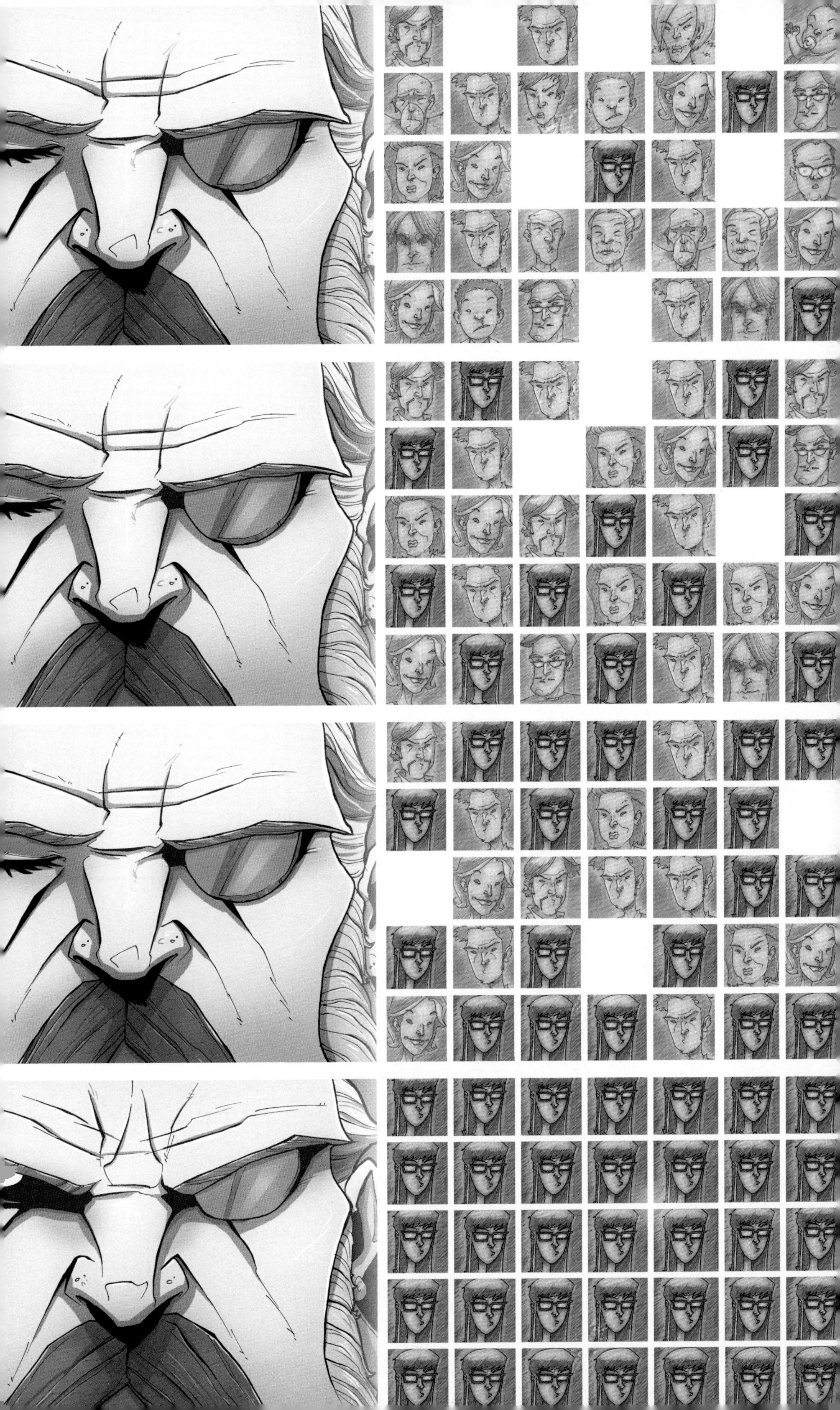

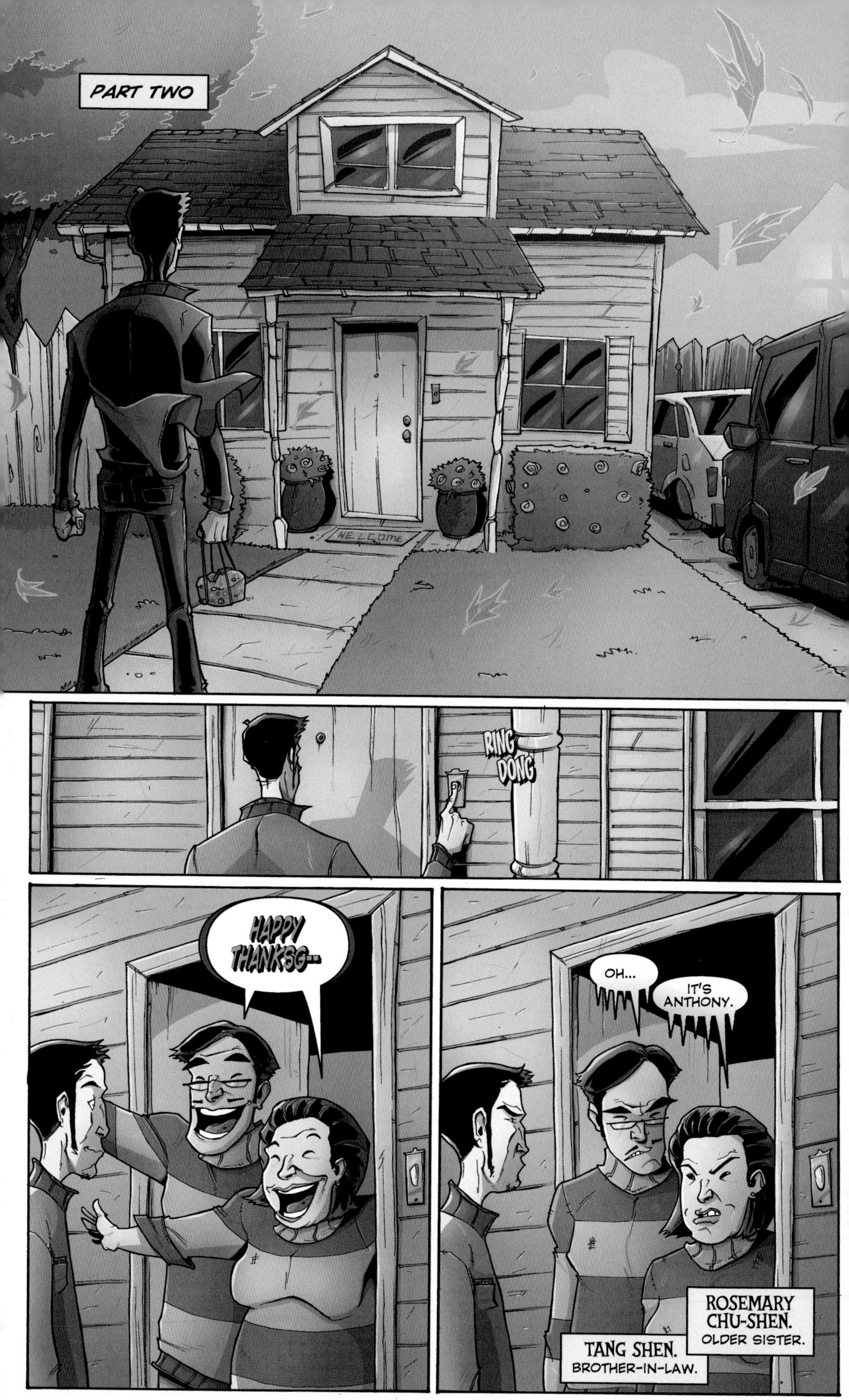
PART TWO
WELCOME
RING DONG
HAPPY THANKSG--
OH...
IT'S ANTHONY.
ROSEMARY CHU-SHEN.
OLDER SISTER.
TANG SHEN.
BROTHER-IN-LAW.

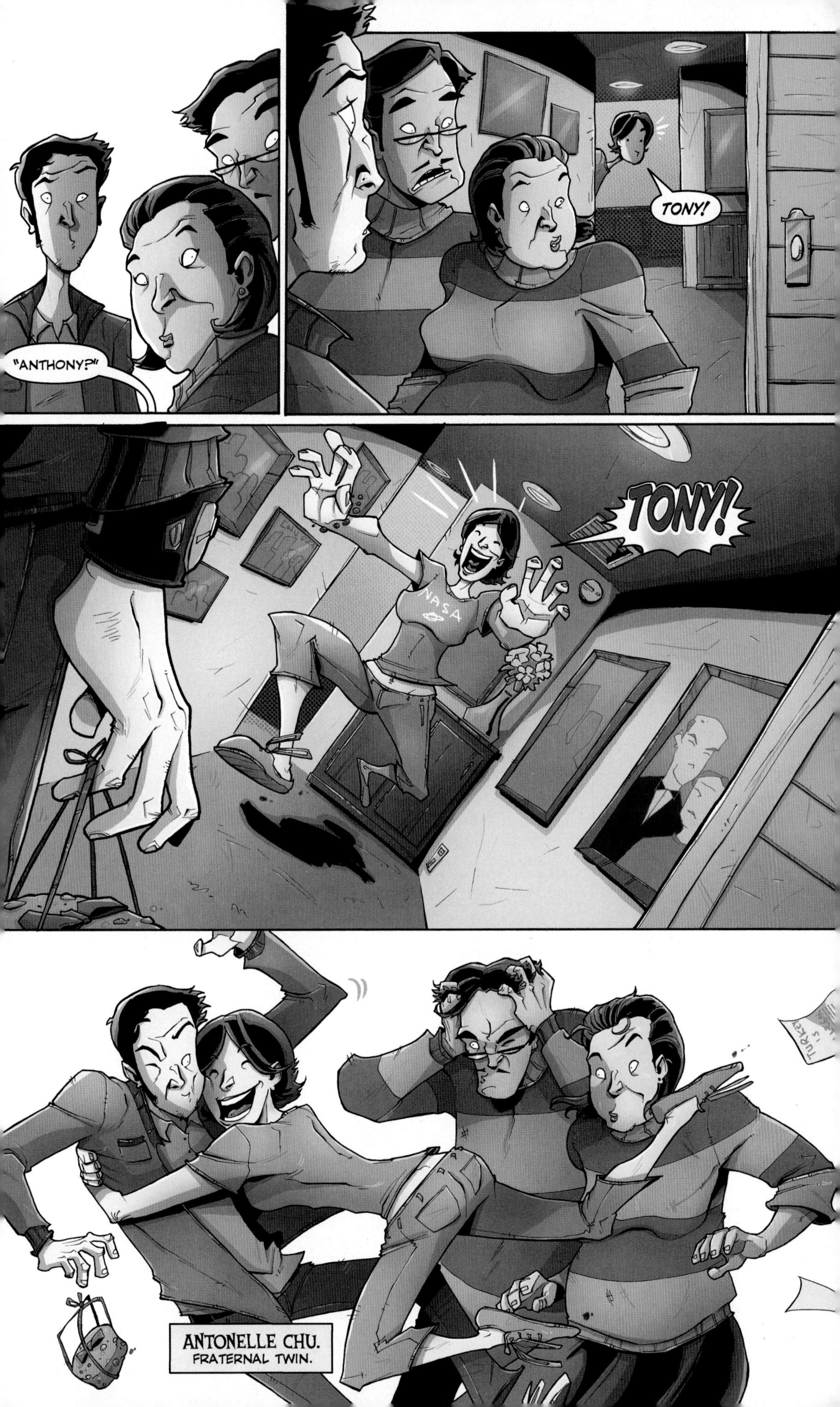
"ANTHONY?"
TONY!
TONY!
ANTONELLE CHU.
FRATERNAL TWIN.

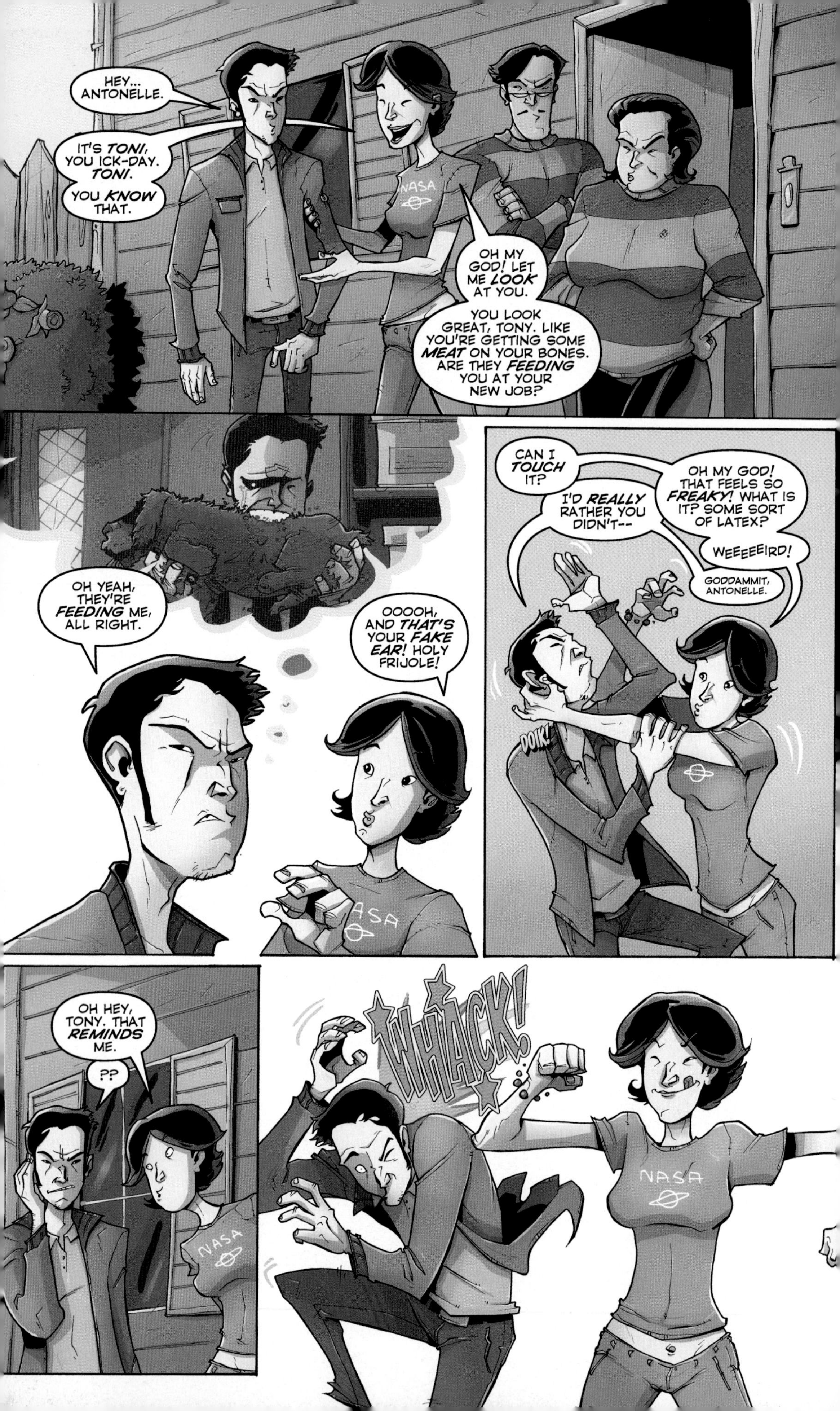
HEY... ANTONELLE.
IT'S TONI, YOU ICK-DAY. TONI.
YOU KNOW THAT.
OH MY GOD! LET ME LOOK AT YOU.
YOU LOOK GREAT, TONY. LIKE YOU'RE GETTING SOME MEAT ON YOUR BONES. ARE THEY FEEDING YOU AT YOUR NEW JOB?
OH YEAH, THEY'RE FEEDING ME, ALL RIGHT.
OOOOH, AND THAT'S YOUR FAKE EAR! HOLY FRIJOLE!
CAN I TOUCH IT?
I'D REALLY RATHER YOU DIDN'T--
OH MY GOD! THAT FEELS SO FREAKY! WHAT IS IT? SOME SORT OF LATEX?
WEEEEEIRD!
GODDAMMIT, ANTONELLE.
DOIK!
OH HEY, TONY. THAT REMINDS ME.
??
WHACK!

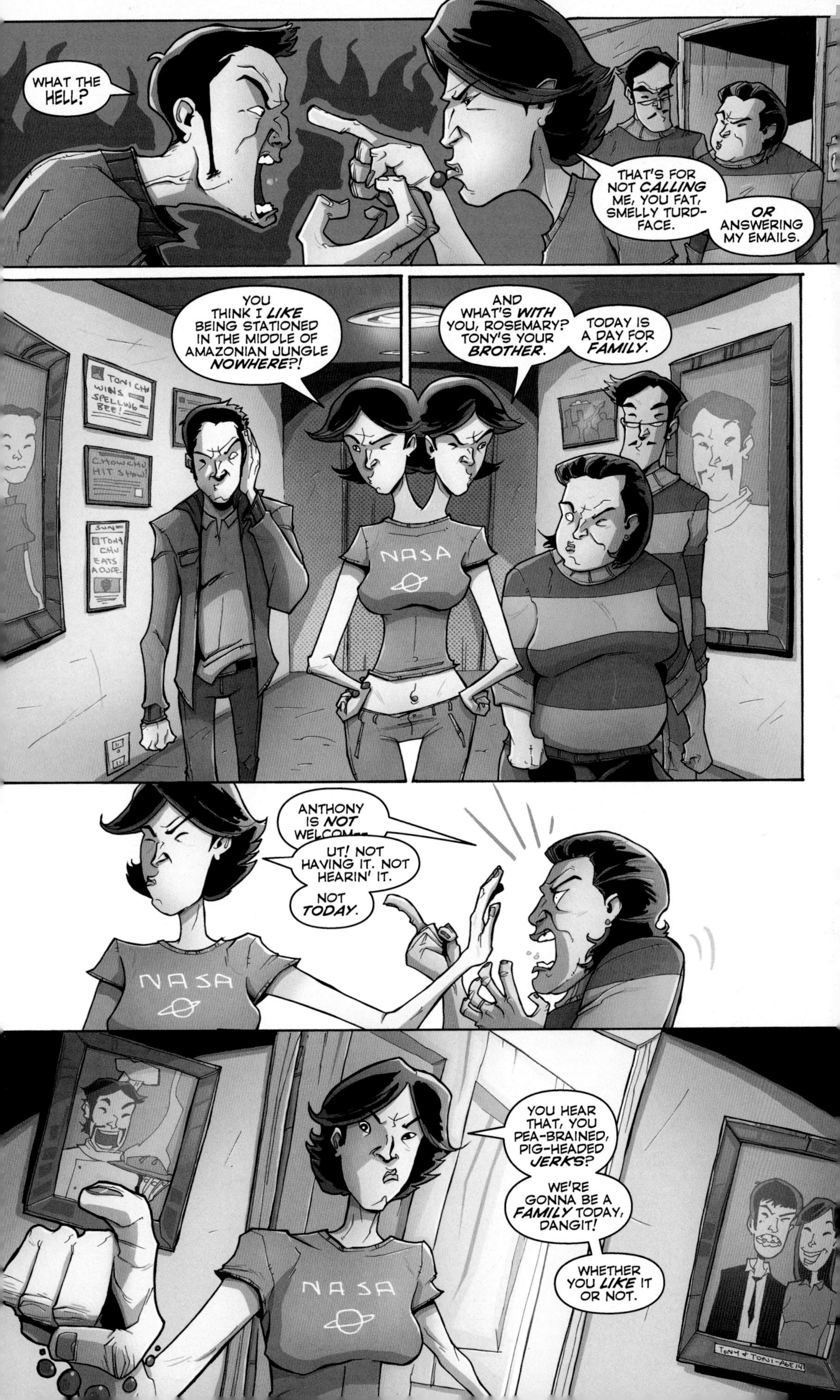
WHAT THE HELL?
THAT'S FOR NOT CALLING ME, YOU FAT, SMELLY TURD-FACE.
OR ANSWERING MY EMAILS.
YOU THINK I LIKE BEING STATIONED IN THE MIDDLE OF AMAZONIAN JUNGLE NOWHERE?!
AND WHAT'S WITH YOU, ROSEMARY? TONY'S YOUR BROTHER.
TODAY IS A DAY FOR FAMILY.
TONI CHU WINS SPELLING BEE!
CHOW CHU HIT SHOW!
TONY CHU EATS A DOPE.
ANTHONY IS NOT WELCOM--
UT! NOT HAVING IT. NOT HEARIN' IT.
NOT TODAY.
NASA
YOU HEAR THAT, YOU PEA-BRAINED, PIG-HEADED JERKS?
WE'RE GONNA BE A FAMILY TODAY, DANGIT!
WHETHER YOU LIKE IT OR NOT.
TONY & TONI - AGE 14

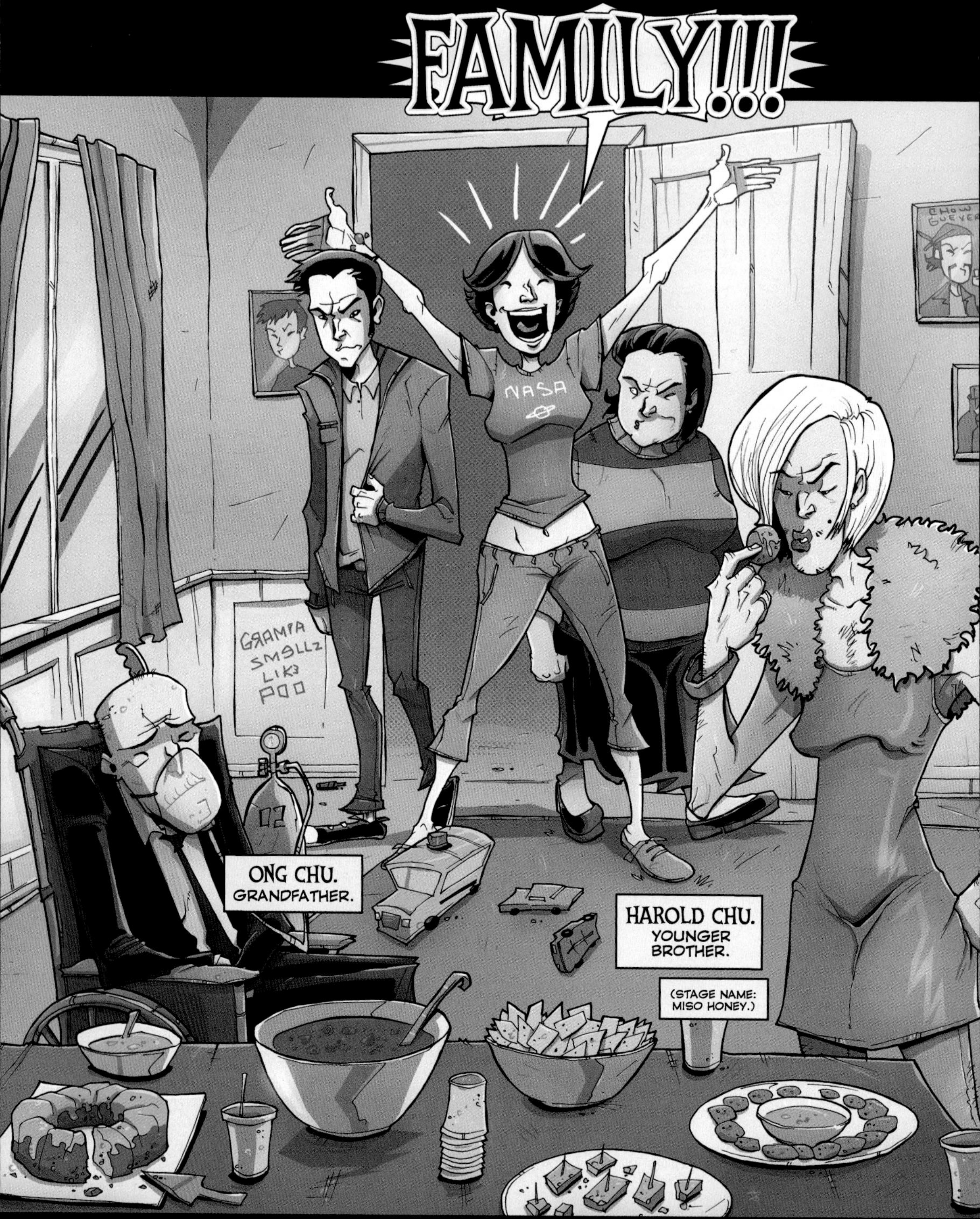
FAMILY!!!
CHOW GUEVERA
NASA
GRAMPA SMELLZ LIKE POO
ONG CHU.
GRANDFATHER.
HAROLD CHU.
YOUNGER BROTHER.
(STAGE NAME: MISO HONEY.)

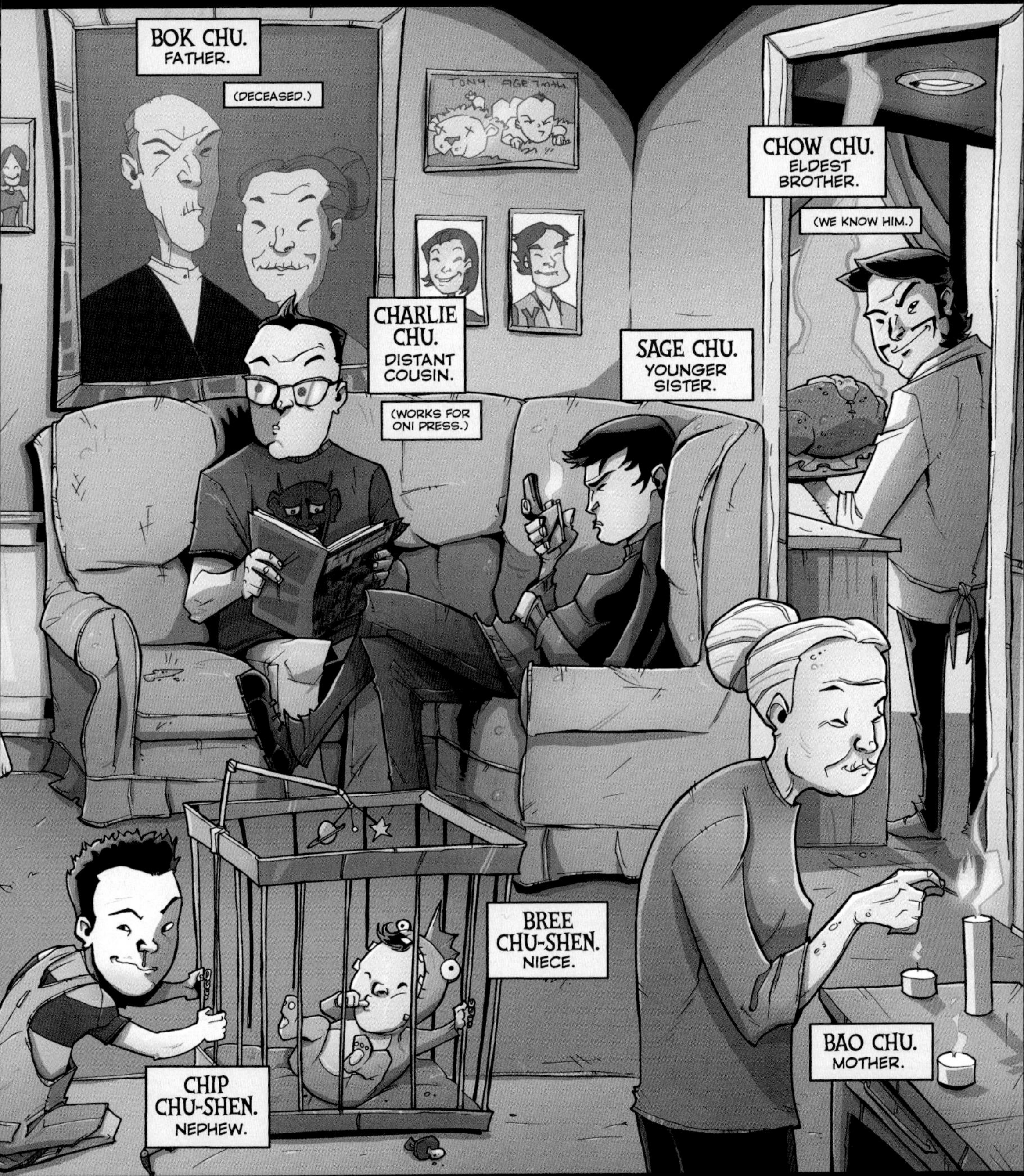
BOK CHU.
FATHER.
(DECEASED.)
CHOW CHU.
ELDEST BROTHER.
(WE KNOW HIM.)
CHARLIE CHU.
DISTANT COUSIN.
(WORKS FOR ONI PRESS.)
SAGE CHU.
YOUNGER SISTER.
BREE CHU-SHEN.
NIECE.
CHIP CHU-SHEN.
NEPHEW.
BAO CHU.
MOTHER.

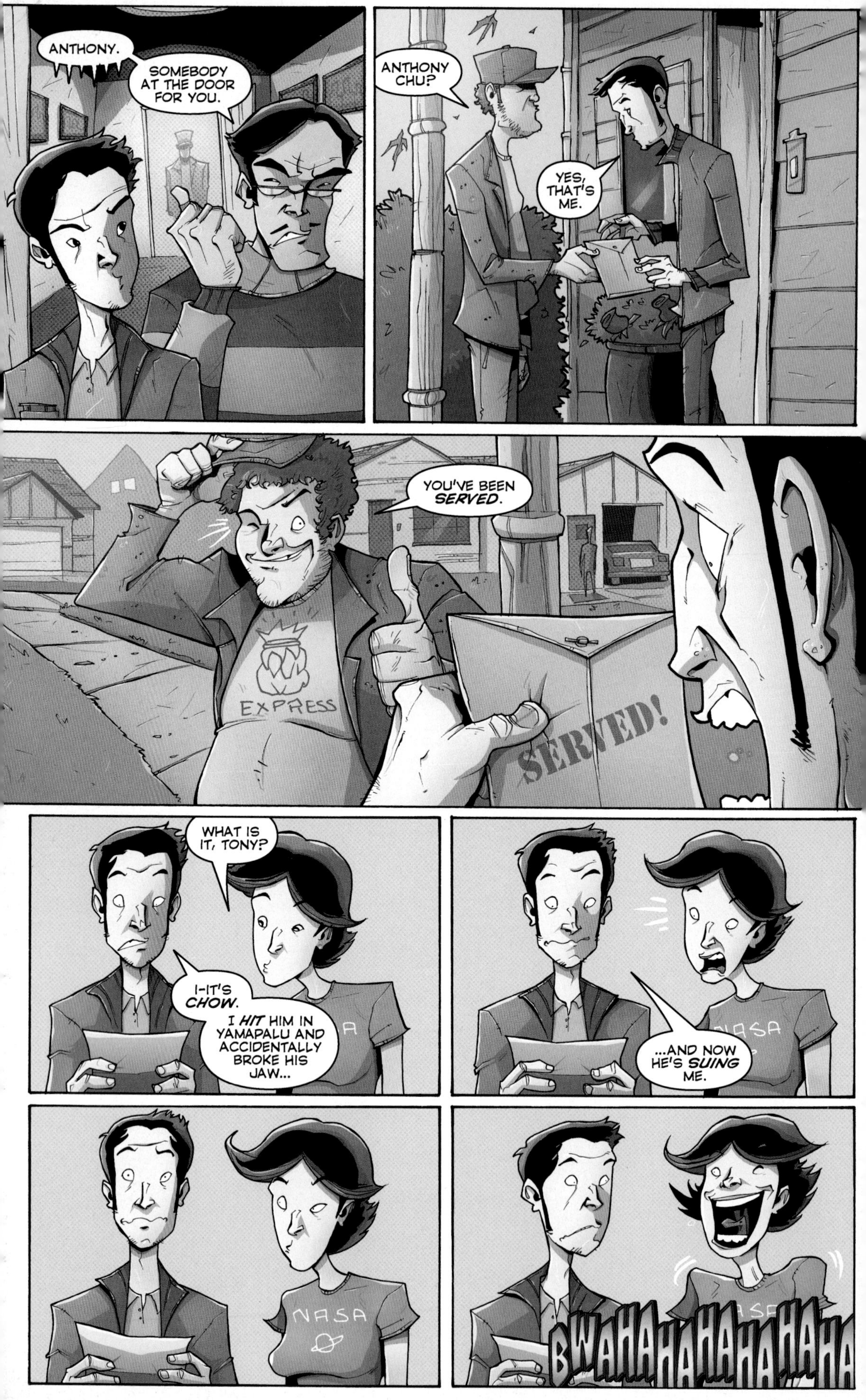
ANTHONY.
SOMEBODY AT THE DOOR FOR YOU.
ANTHONY CHU?
YES, THAT'S ME.
YOU'VE BEEN *SERVED*.
EXPRESS
SERVED!
WHAT IS IT, TONY?
I-IT'S *CHOW*.
I *HIT* HIM IN YAMAPALU AND ACCIDENTALLY BROKE HIS JAW...
NASA
...AND NOW HE'S *SUING* ME.
NASA
BWAHAHAHAHAHAHAHA

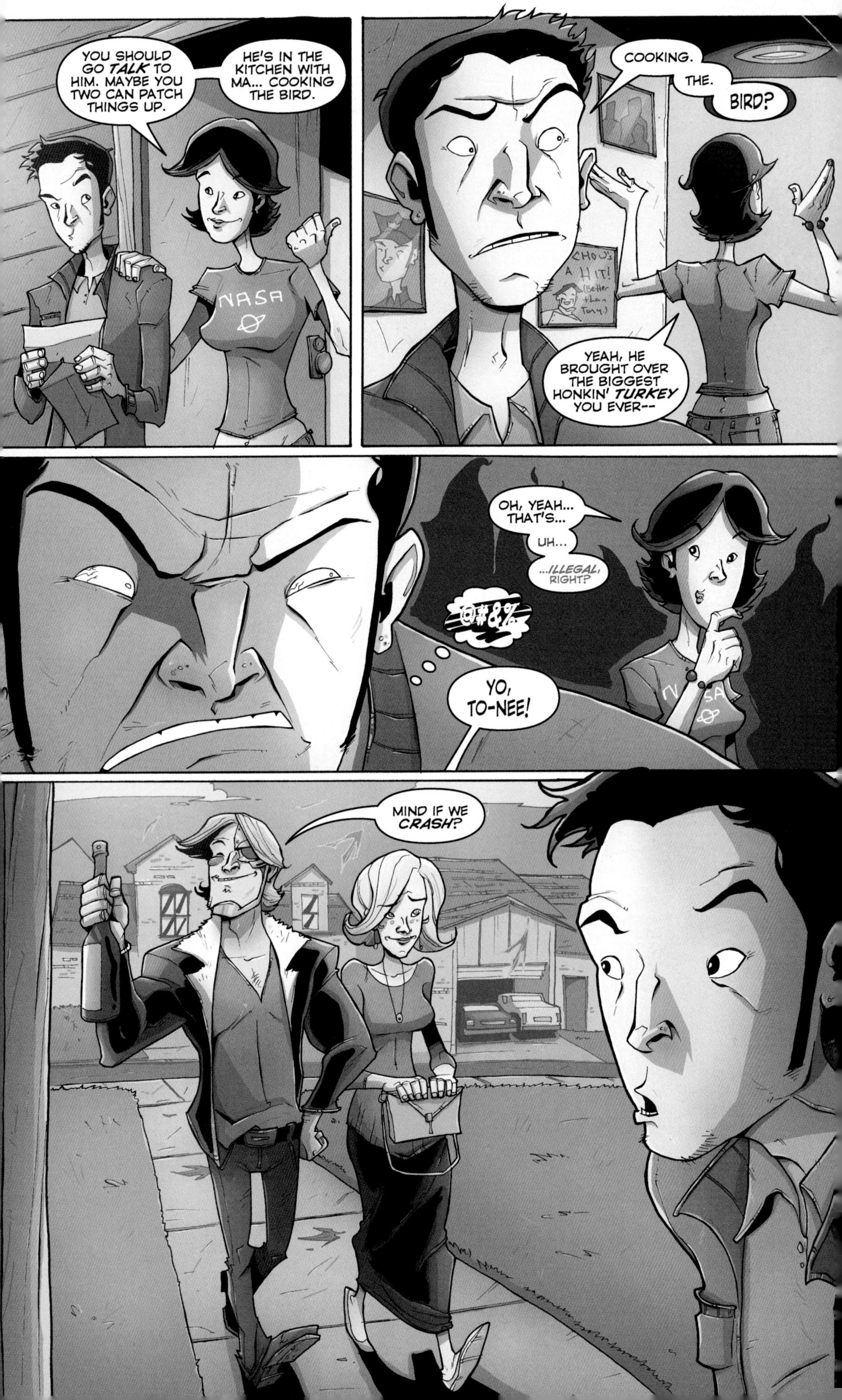

YOU SHOULD GO TALK TO HIM. MAYBE YOU TWO CAN PATCH THINGS UP.
HE'S IN THE KITCHEN WITH MA... COOKING THE BIRD.
CHOU'S A HIT! (Better than Tony.)
COOKING.
THE.
BIRD?
YEAH, HE BROUGHT OVER THE BIGGEST HONKIN' TURKEY YOU EVER--
OH, YEAH... THAT'S...
UH...
...ILLEGAL, RIGHT?
@#&%
YO, TO-NEE!
MIND IF WE CRASH?

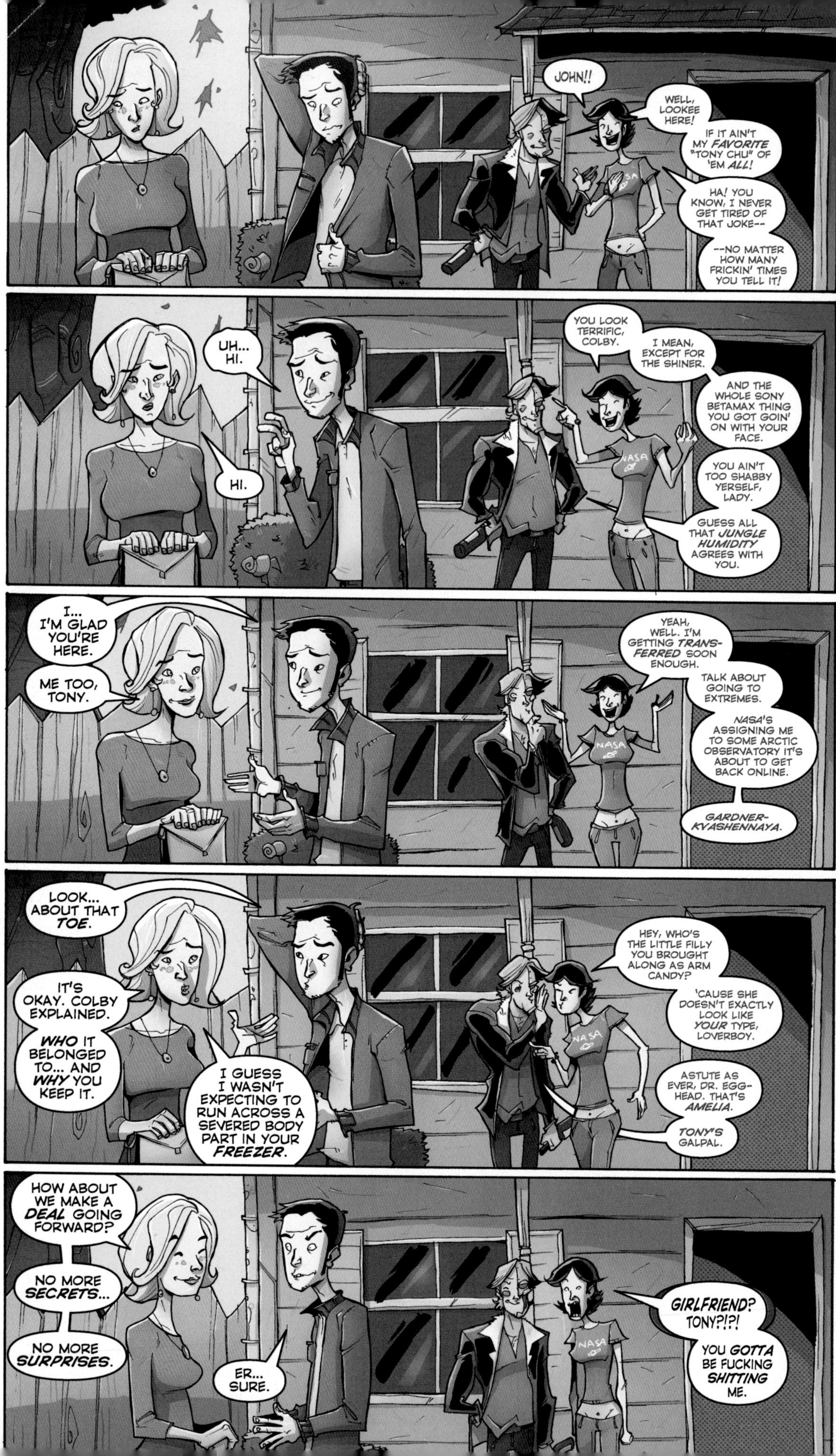
JOHN!!
WELL, LOOKEE HERE!
IF IT AIN'T MY FAVORITE "TONY CHU" OF 'EM ALL!
HA! YOU KNOW, I NEVER GET TIRED OF THAT JOKE--
--NO MATTER HOW MANY FRICKIN' TIMES YOU TELL IT!
UH... HI.
HI.
YOU LOOK TERRIFIC, COLBY.
I MEAN, EXCEPT FOR THE SHINER.
AND THE WHOLE SONY BETAMAX THING YOU GOT GOIN' ON WITH YOUR FACE.
YOU AIN'T TOO SHABBY YERSELF, LADY.
GUESS ALL THAT JUNGLE HUMIDITY AGREES WITH YOU.
I... I'M GLAD YOU'RE HERE.
ME TOO, TONY.
YEAH, WELL. I'M GETTING TRANS-FERRED SOON ENOUGH.
TALK ABOUT GOING TO EXTREMES.
NASA'S ASSIGNING ME TO SOME ARCTIC OBSERVATORY IT'S ABOUT TO GET BACK ONLINE.
GARDNER-KVASHENNAYA.
LOOK... ABOUT THAT TOE.
IT'S OKAY. COLBY EXPLAINED.
WHO IT BELONGED TO... AND WHY YOU KEEP IT.
I GUESS I WASN'T EXPECTING TO RUN ACROSS A SEVERED BODY PART IN YOUR FREEZER.
HEY, WHO'S THE LITTLE FILLY YOU BROUGHT ALONG AS ARM CANDY?
'CAUSE SHE DOESN'T EXACTLY LOOK LIKE YOUR TYPE, LOVERBOY.
ASTUTE AS EVER, DR. EGG-HEAD. THAT'S AMELIA.
TONY'S GALPAL.
HOW ABOUT WE MAKE A DEAL GOING FORWARD?
NO MORE SECRETS...
NO MORE SURPRISES.
ER... SURE.
GIRLFRIEND? TONY?!?!
YOU GOTTA BE FUCKING SHITTING ME.

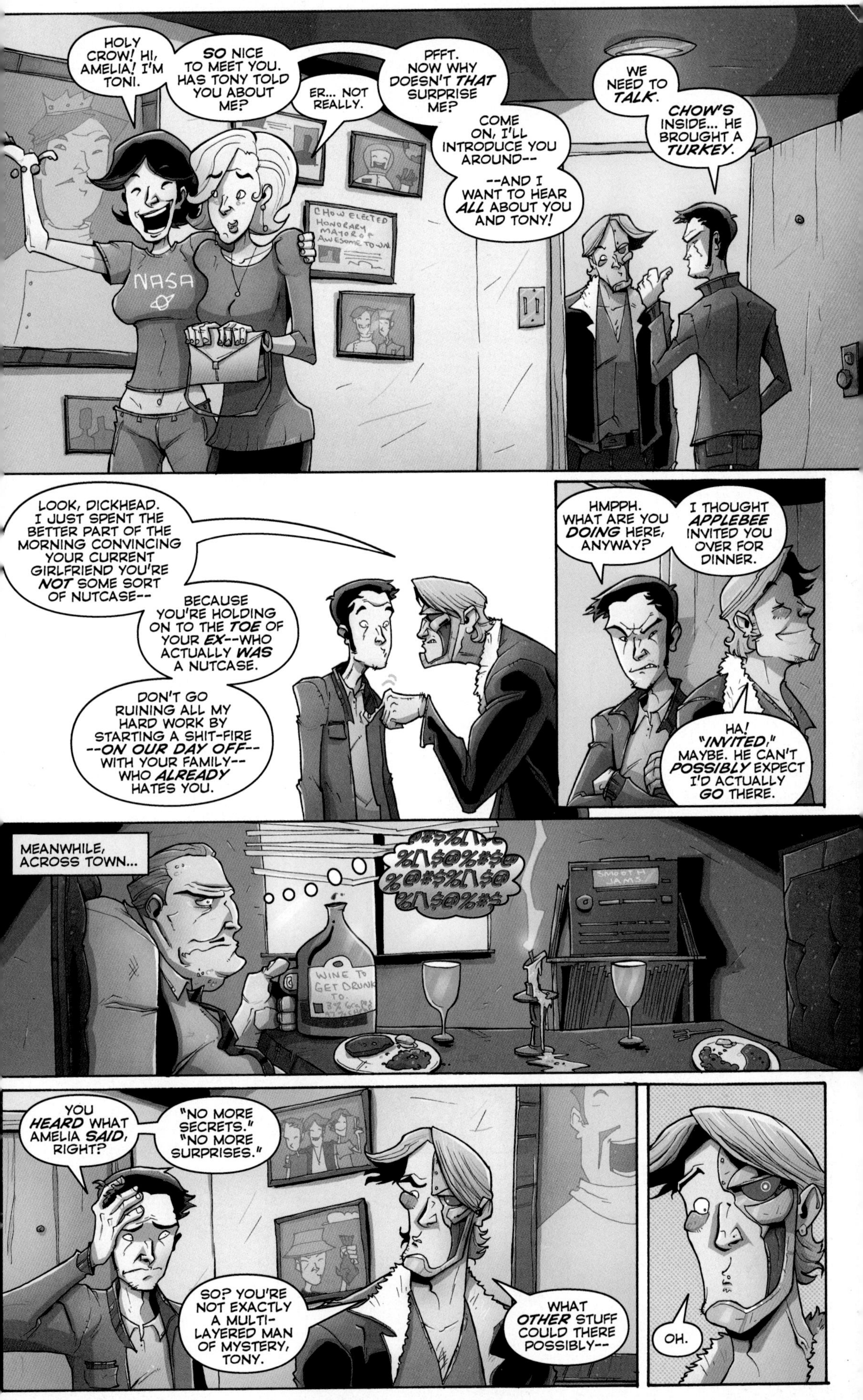

HOLY CROW! HI, AMELIA! I'M TONI.
SO NICE TO MEET YOU. HAS TONY TOLD YOU ABOUT ME?
ER... NOT REALLY.
PFFT. NOW WHY DOESN'T THAT SURPRISE ME?
COME ON, I'LL INTRODUCE YOU AROUND--
--AND I WANT TO HEAR ALL ABOUT YOU AND TONY!
CHOW ELECTED HONORARY MAYOR OF AWESOME TOWN
NASA
WE NEED TO TALK.
CHOW'S INSIDE... HE BROUGHT A TURKEY.
LOOK, DICKHEAD. I JUST SPENT THE BETTER PART OF THE MORNING CONVINCING YOUR CURRENT GIRLFRIEND YOU'RE NOT SOME SORT OF NUTCASE--
BECAUSE YOU'RE HOLDING ON TO THE TOE OF YOUR EX--WHO ACTUALLY WAS A NUTCASE.
DON'T GO RUINING ALL MY HARD WORK BY STARTING A SHIT-FIRE --ON OUR DAY OFF-- WITH YOUR FAMILY-- WHO ALREADY HATES YOU.
HMPPH. WHAT ARE YOU DOING HERE, ANYWAY?
I THOUGHT APPLEBEE INVITED YOU OVER FOR DINNER.
HA! "INVITED," MAYBE. HE CAN'T POSSIBLY EXPECT I'D ACTUALLY GO THERE.
MEANWHILE, ACROSS TOWN...
#*$%[\$@%#$@ %@#$%[\$@ %[\$@%#$
SMOOTH JAMS
WINE TO GET DRUNK TO.
YOU HEARD WHAT AMELIA SAID, RIGHT?
"NO MORE SECRETS." "NO MORE SURPRISES."
SO? YOU'RE NOT EXACTLY A MULTI-LAYERED MAN OF MYSTERY, TONY.
WHAT OTHER STUFF COULD THERE POSSIBLY--
OH.

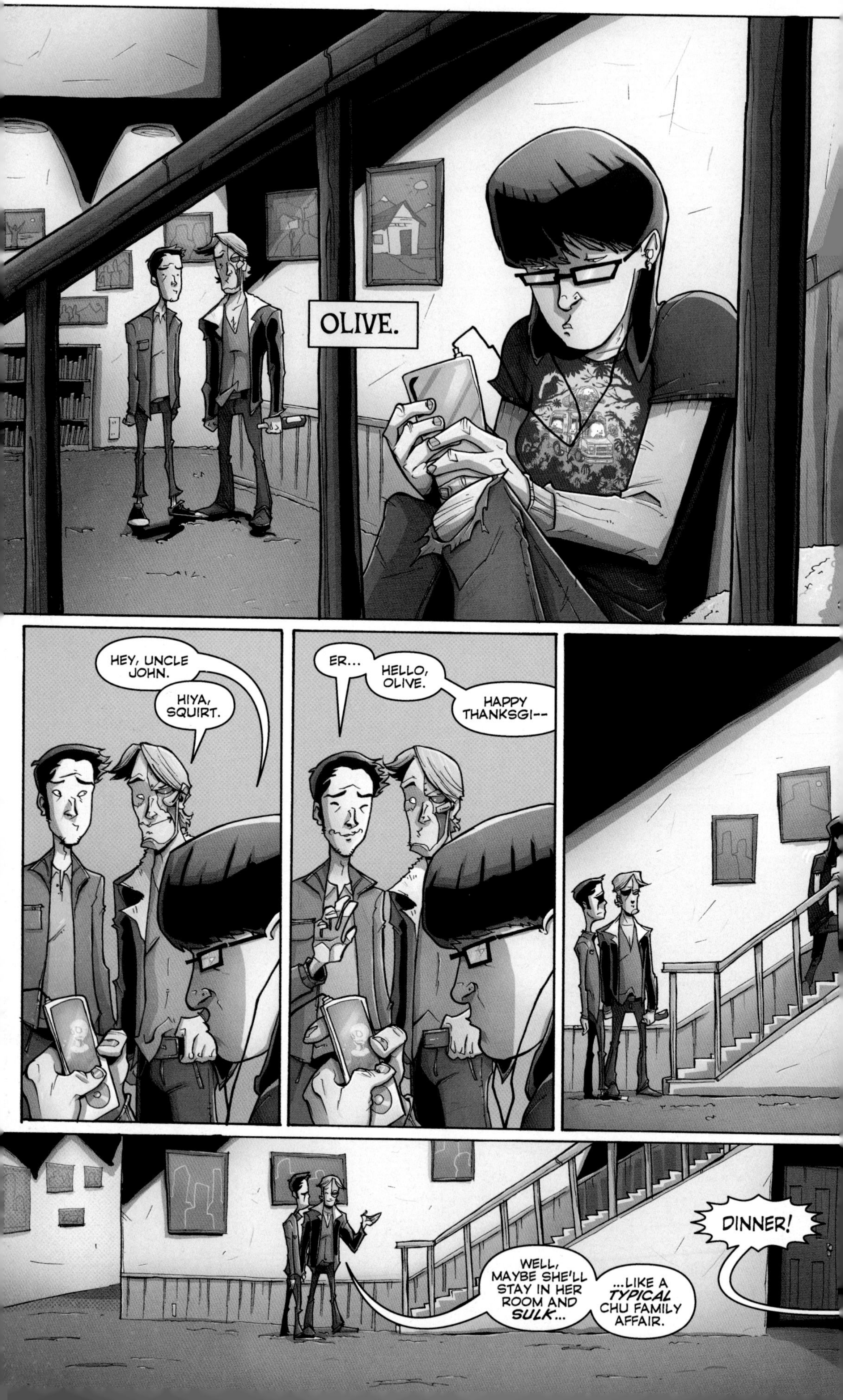
OLIVE.
HEY, UNCLE JOHN.
HIYA, SQUIRT.
ER...
HELLO, OLIVE.
HAPPY THANKSGI--
WELL, MAYBE SHE'LL STAY IN HER ROOM AND SULK...
...LIKE A TYPICAL CHU FAMILY AFFAIR.
DINNER!

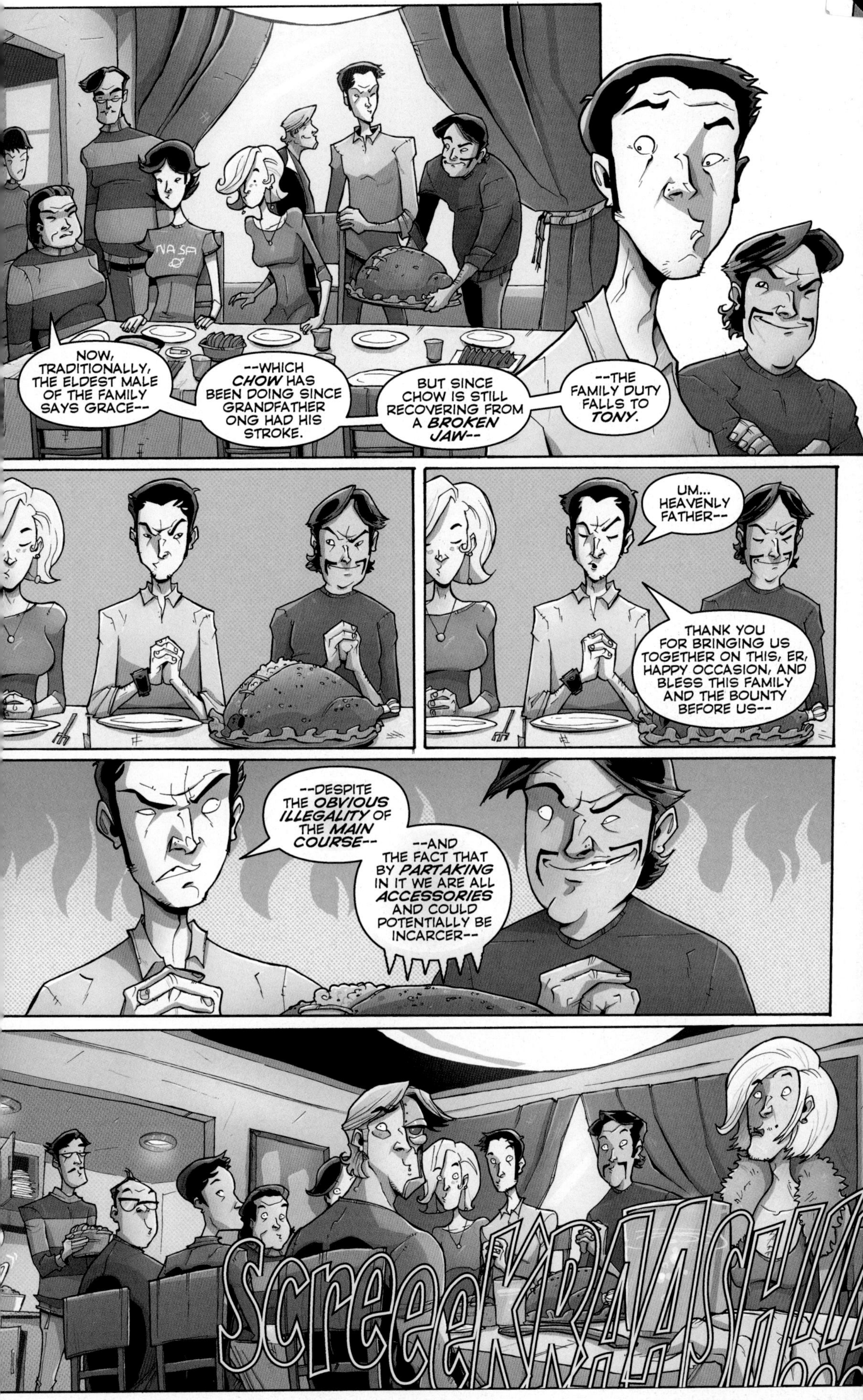
NOW, TRADITIONALLY, THE ELDEST MALE OF THE FAMILY SAYS GRACE--
--WHICH CHOW HAS BEEN DOING SINCE GRANDFATHER ONG HAD HIS STROKE.
BUT SINCE CHOW IS STILL RECOVERING FROM A BROKEN JAW--
--THE FAMILY DUTY FALLS TO TONY.
UM... HEAVENLY FATHER--
THANK YOU FOR BRINGING US TOGETHER ON THIS, ER, HAPPY OCCASION, AND BLESS THIS FAMILY AND THE BOUNTY BEFORE US--
--DESPITE THE OBVIOUS ILLEGALITY OF THE MAIN COURSE--
--AND THE FACT THAT BY PARTAKING IN IT WE ARE ALL ACCESSORIES AND COULD POTENTIALLY BE INCARCER--
NASA
SCREEEKRAASHH

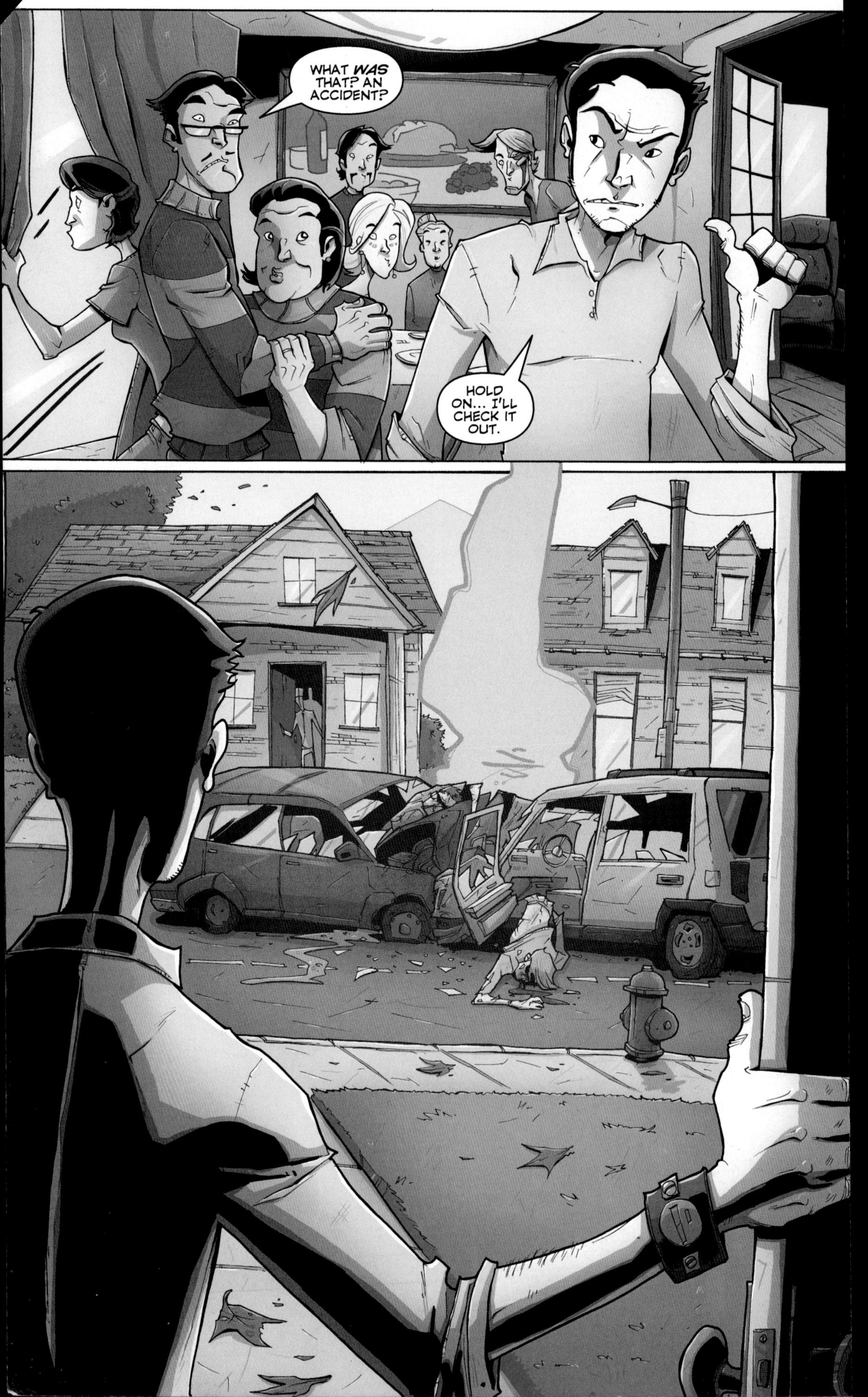
WHAT WAS THAT? AN ACCIDENT?
HOLD ON... I'LL CHECK IT OUT.

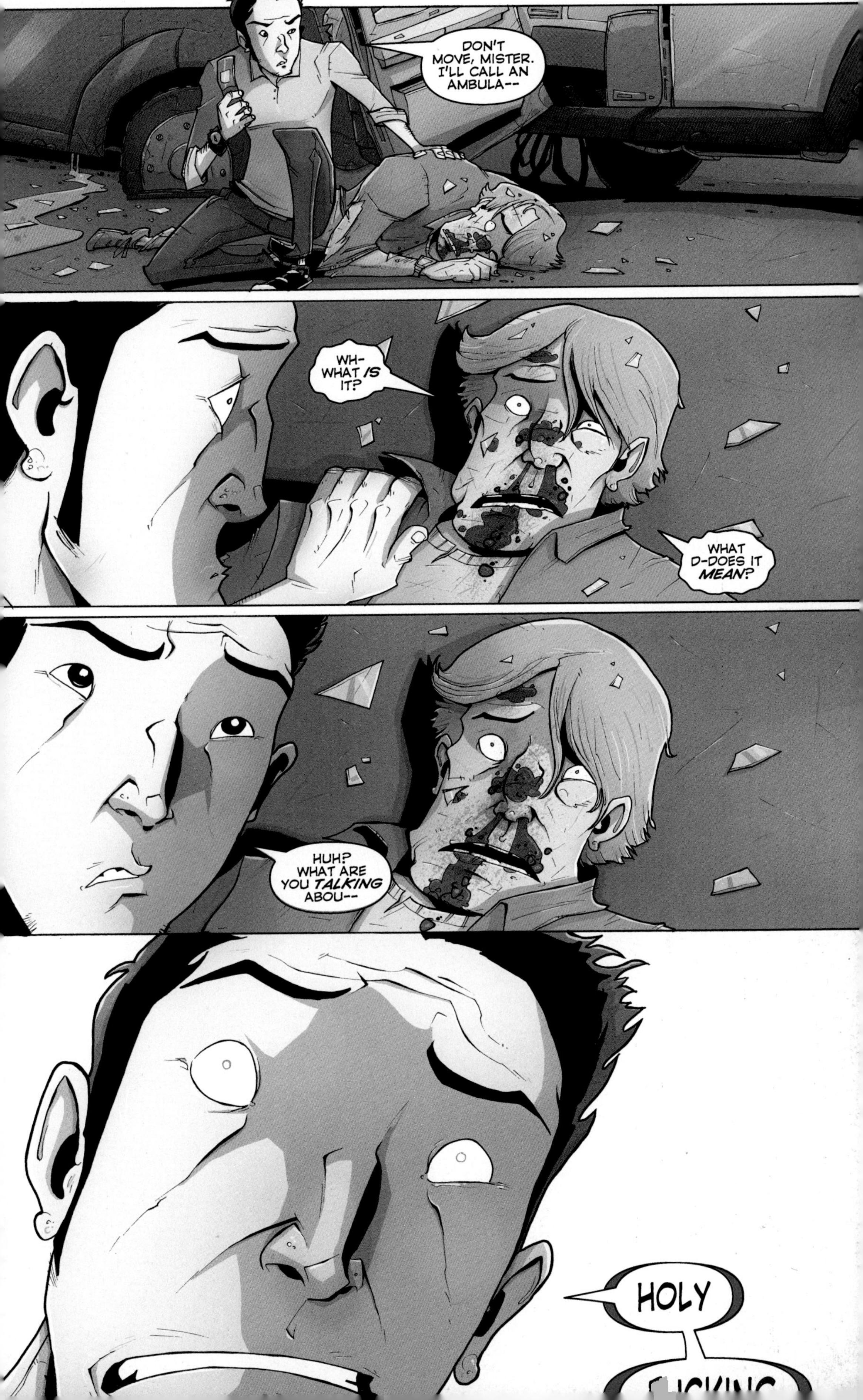
DON'T MOVE, MISTER. I'LL CALL AN AMBULA--
WH- WHAT IS IT?
WHAT D-DOES IT MEAN?
HUH? WHAT ARE YOU TALKING ABOU--
HOLY

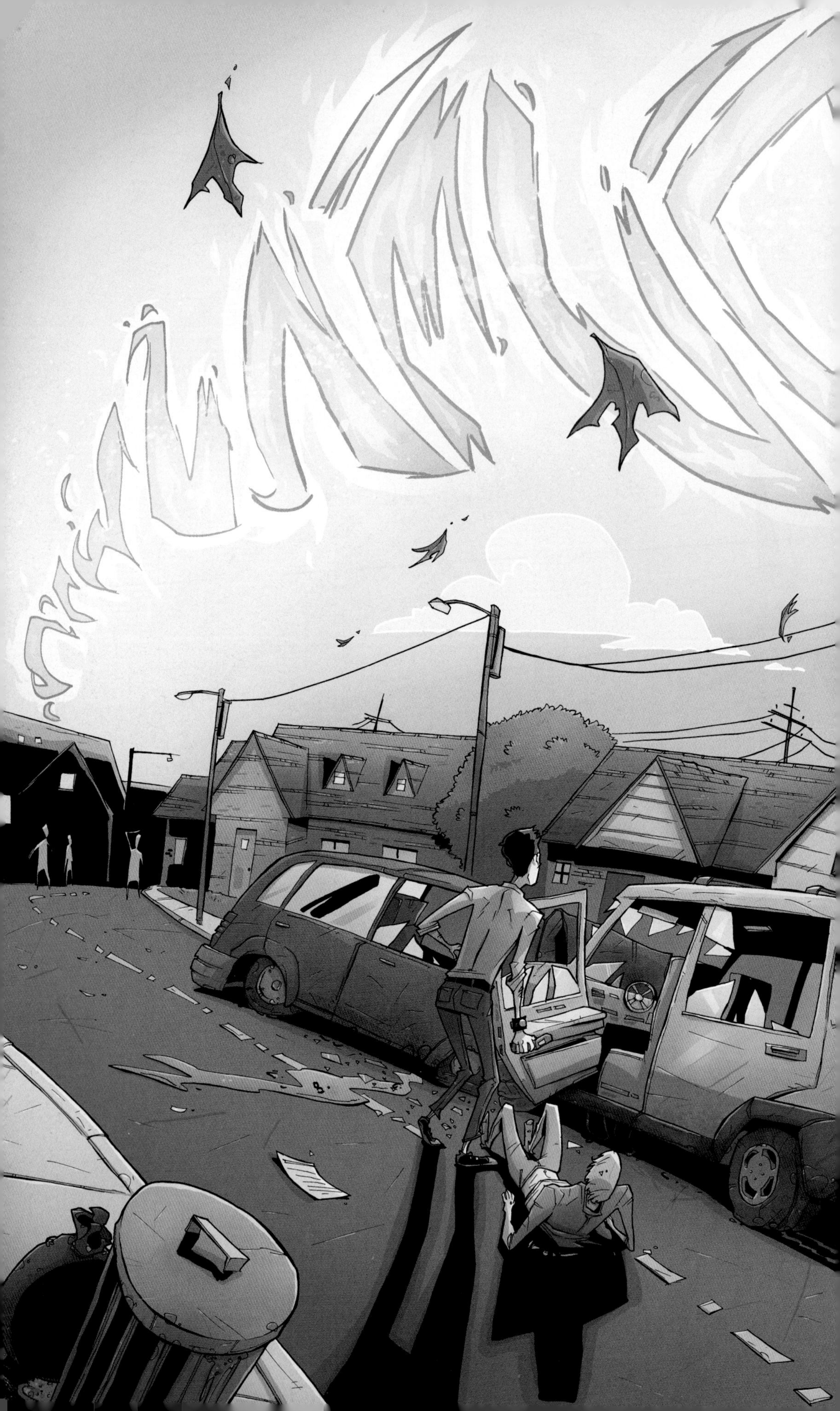

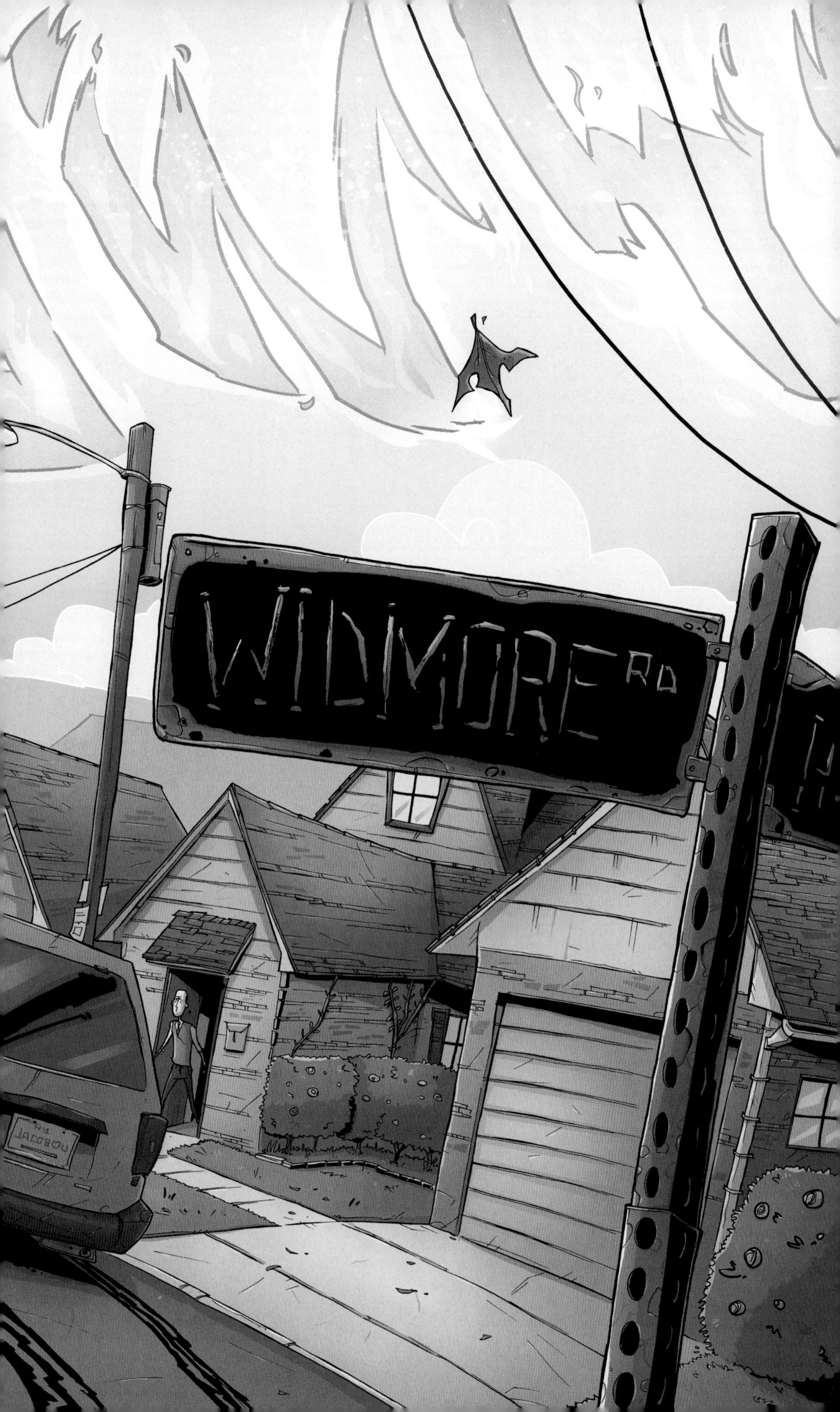
WIDMORE RD

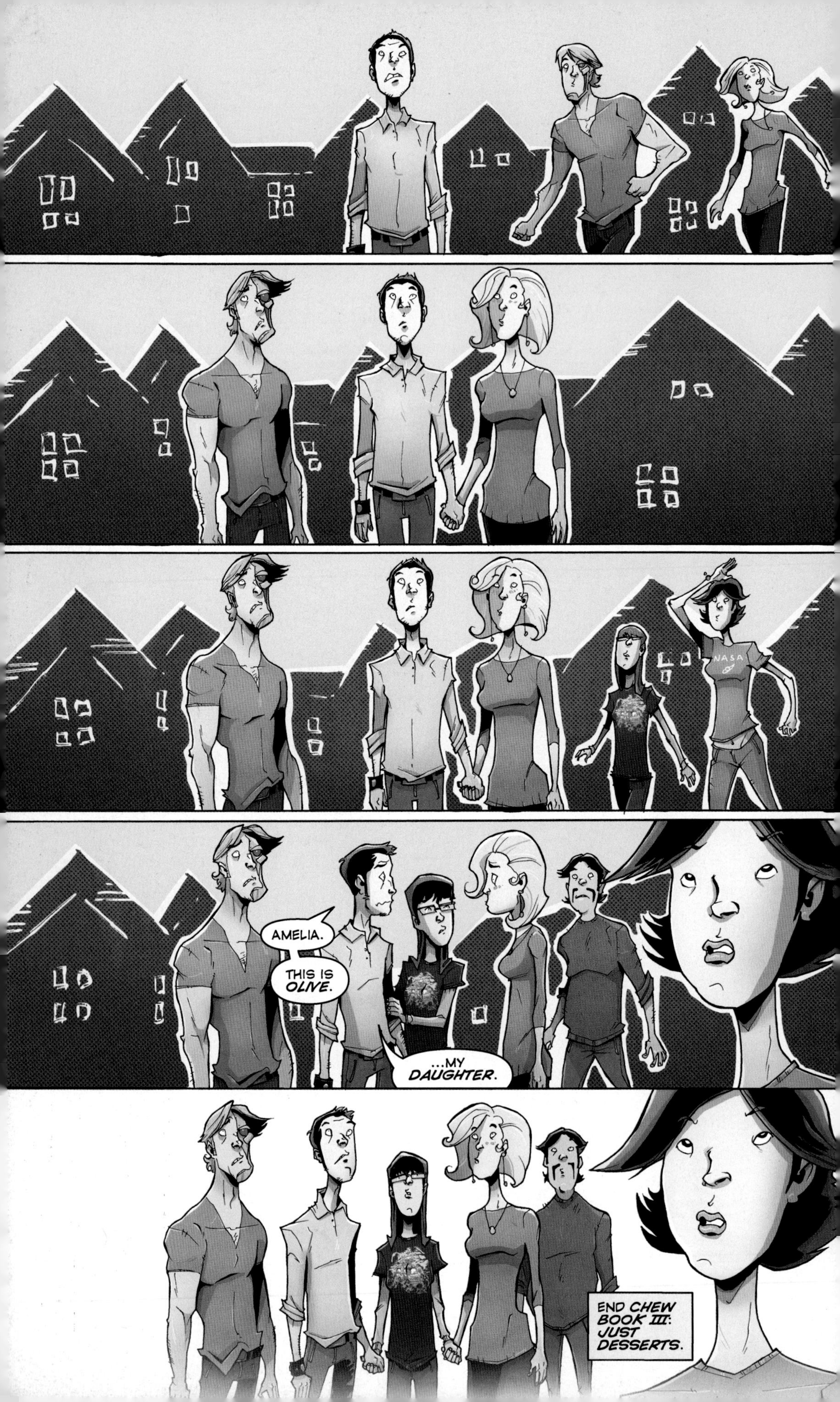

AMELIA.
THIS IS OLIVE.
...MY DAUGHTER.
END CHEW BOOK III: JUST DESSERTS.

Making the CHEW #15 Cover

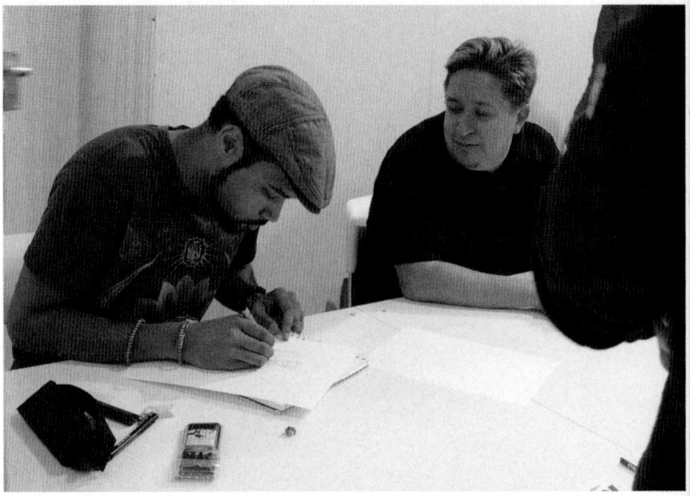

Since John and I began working on CHEW, we had set issue 15 as a milestone in our run. A milestone, because A) Issue 15 would be a quarter point of our planned 60-issue run, and B) If our weird little book could actually maintain a solid readership for that long, it would certainly be a shock and cause for celebration.

Of course, after readers began to respond positively, it became obvious that we'd get to do what we'd dreamed of from the start: A tri-fold poster cover of the entire CHEW cast, past, present and future. In Last Supper homage, of course. And in a weird bit of poetry, I got to design it in person with John at a comic con in Milan, home of Da Vinci's original masterpiece. Weird.

Overall, this piece is a love letter to readers for supporting us for fifteen issues. So fittingly, the image features all the major players of the series. Some you're met, some you haven't. Some are living, some aren't. But they're all significant. Even the dead bodies are callbacks to characters that have died in the series. Nothing went to waste.

Below's the original Milan sketch, and the complete image follows on the next few pages. Enjoy.

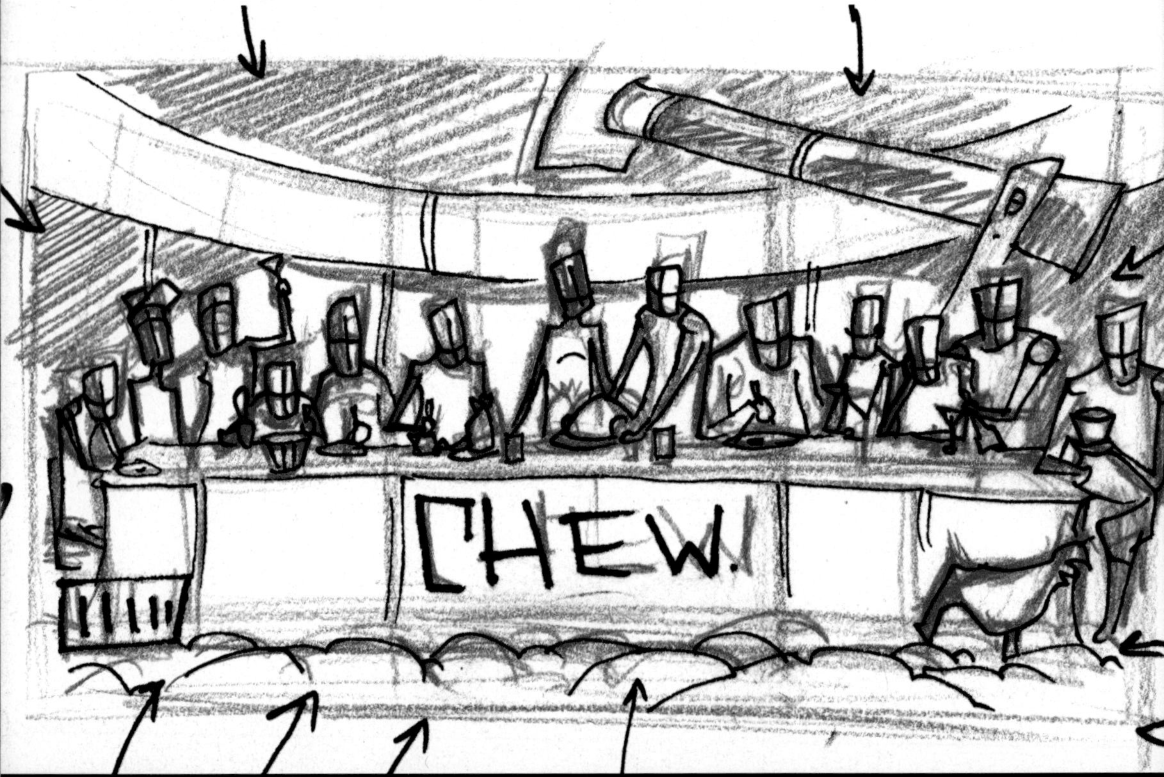
CHEW.

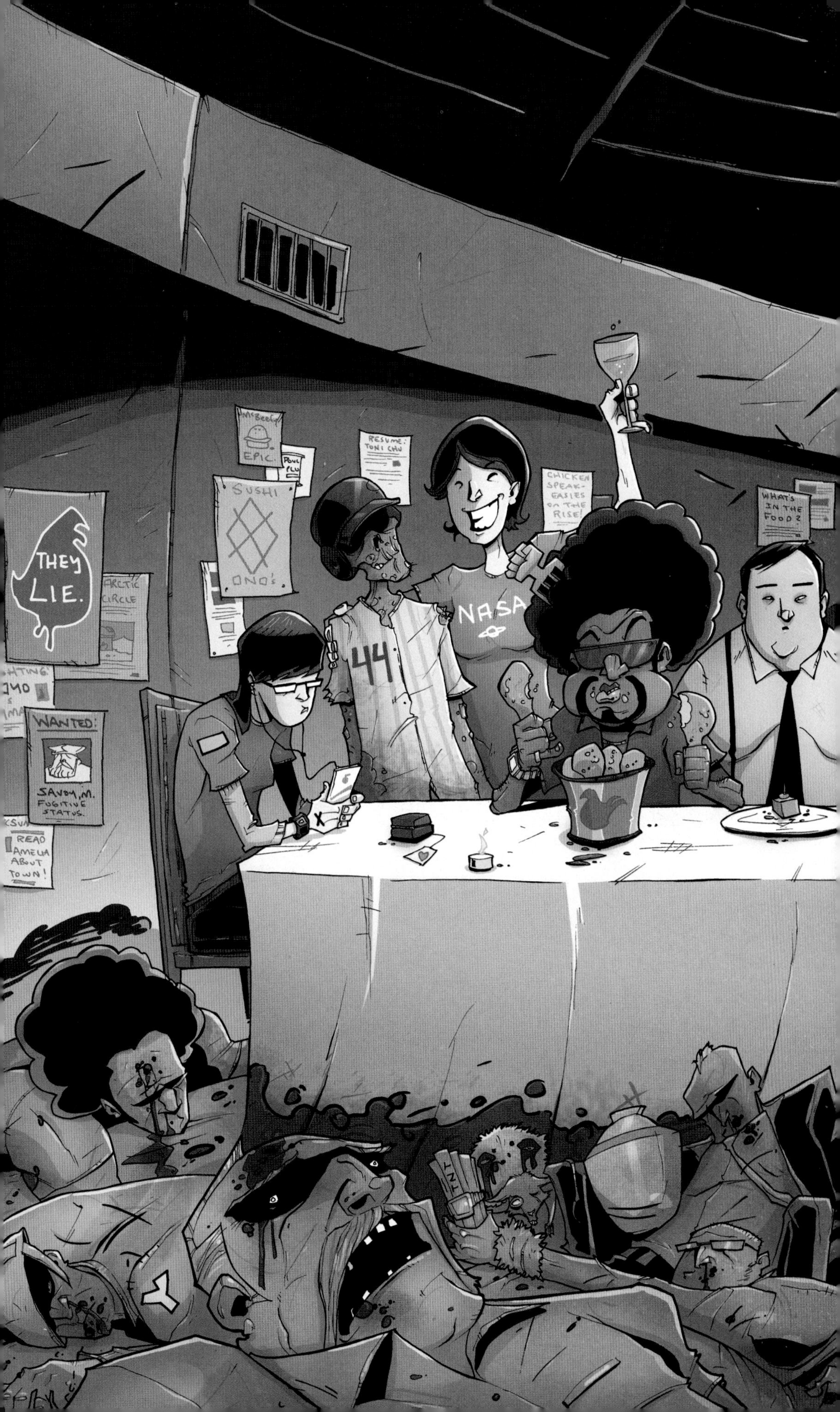
McBeefy
EPIC.
RESUME: TONI CHU
CHICKEN SPEAKEASIES ON THE RISE!
WHAT'S IN THE FOOD?
SUSHI
ONO's
THEY LIE.
ARCTIC CIRCLE
NASA
44
WANTED!
SAVOY, M.
FUGITIVE STATUS.
READ AMELIA ABOUT TOWN!
TNT

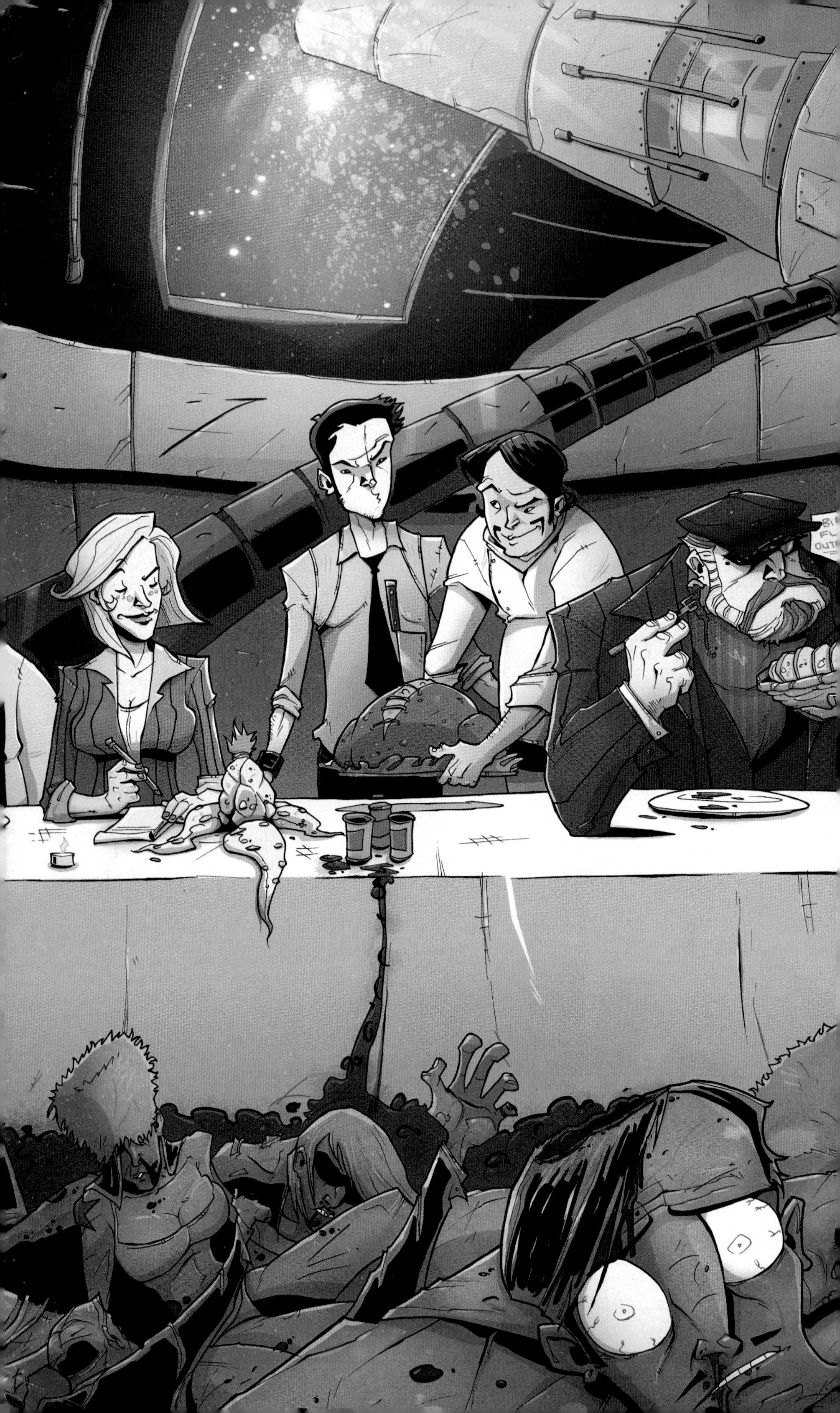

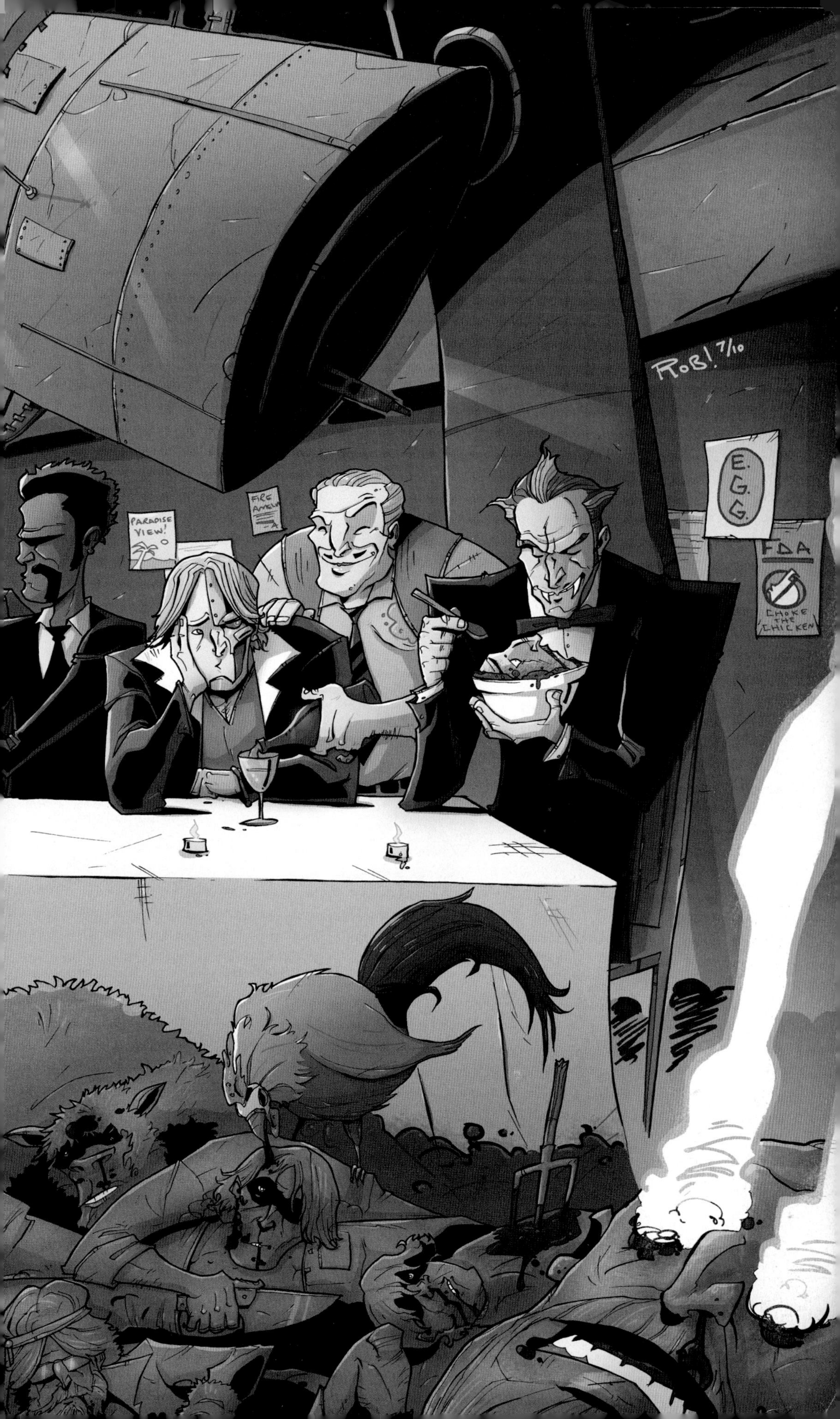

ROB! 7/10
PARADISE VIEW!
FIRE ANTHEM
E. G. G.
FDA
CHOKE THE CHICKEN

JOHN LAYMAN *Rocket scientist, genius, lover, international assassin, computer hacker, boy band falsetto and enthusiastic eater of expired yogurt, John Layman has three cats, Rufus, Ruby and The Smasher, and lives outside Phoenix, Arizona with a wife and young child.*

ROB GUILLORY *thinks that the greatest change in his life since the success of CHEW is that he is regularly profiled when depositing fat CHEW checks at his bank in Lafayette, LA. It's unclear whether he is profiled because of race, age, or the fact that John Layman sends the funds via Spongebob checks with Layman's serial killer handwriting on them.*
*Rob was also voted BEST NEW TALENT at the 2010 Harvey Awards. Crazy, eh? Visit **RobGuillory.com** for more.*

ChewComic.com
For Original CHEW Art, contact
ChewComicSales@gmail.com